Take My Husband, Please!

Take My Husband, Please!

Kimberly Jayne

Published by Word River Press 2015

ISBN 978-0-9892322-1-0

The characters and events portrayed in this book are fictitious. Any similarity to real persons, living or dead, is coincidental and not intended by the author.

Acknowledgements

So many darlings died so that this book could live, and so many people supported and showed love for me as I bled across the pages for so many years. Topping the list is my best friend Winter Desiree Prosapio. Love you, girl!

I had a lovely and amazing editor Blythe Jewell, and a great group of critiquers, brainstormers, and beta readers in my corner: Robin Allen, Julie Sucha Anderson, Andrea Eames, Jennifer Evans, Martha Gilmore, Patrice Kuechler, Eryn McCormick, Derek Pflaum, Anne Marie Turner, and Wendy Wheeler.

Thanks also to Marjorie Brody, Beth Carlson, Yvonne Cockrill, Sarah Foxworth, Michelle Grant, Sarah Hackley, Lacy Jemmott, Sherri Lindsey, Alexandra Marbach, Steve McCormick, Bee Pedersen, Christie Smith, and Debbie Winegarten. Finally, Delilah Devlin and Roses Colored Glasses, and my beloved Austin WriterGrrls who encourage me always to dare to suck.

With gratitude for their love and support and jokes at my expense, the beautiful loves of my life: Brittany, Aleta, Nicole, Tyson, and their families, and Mom and Dad. I love you all like crazy.

To Aunt Jeanne,
who fostered my inexhaustible love of writing
and who taught me the hard lesson that you
sometimes do get what you ask for.
Be thankful.

Take My Husband, Please!

Kimberly Jayne

Chapter 1

Mitch Houdini clung to Sophie's shoulders like the week's dry cleaning as she led him inside. Loud enough to scare off intruders, her strappy stilettos *click-clack-click-clacked* across the hardwoods and echoed off the walls, giving her foyer a deserted feel. She reached for the lights but thought better of it. In the dark, a few stubborn extra pounds and some baby-birthing stretch marks don't exist. Right?

Mitch kicked the door shut and twirled Sophie around, painting a wet trail of kisses along her neck that fueled her long-suppressed yearning to be touched and adored—worshipped even—by a man. *This man.* From the moment he'd whisked her off in his Lamborghini convertible for a happy hour that had lingered to midnight, Mitch had been a heat-seeking missile she could not deflect. Not that she wanted to after all those Mexican martinis.

She reached behind, dropped her keys on a wood console table cluttered with framed photos and a warming pot of orange blossom-scented wax, and discreetly flipped a family portrait on its face. After the date she'd had, prying eyes need not sabotage her mission.

"Sophie."

His voice vibrated the hair on her neck like plucked violin strings. He caressed her face in his hands and let his brazen tongue probe one ear, exploring every hill and cranny like he polished the chrome wheels of his cherished Lamborghini—cleaning and buffing and shining—and shooting chills right to her marrow. He quickly followed with an invitation for dueling tongues, and by then she figured there wasn't much that tongue of his couldn't do. Still, she had imagined he would taste more like Don Juan instead of Cuban cigars and Stolichnaya.

Mitch took a breath and shrugged out of his sports coat, revealing a wedge-shaped torso that strained against the fabric of his tailored shirt. She stood in the shadow of his six-four frame, the ceiling vents blasting cold air on her skin, while his hands ventured where no man had gone for nearly two years. He deftly thumbed her breasts through her little black dress and a pushup bra with its work cut out for it, igniting a white-hot desire between her legs. Every millimeter of her womanhood begged for the point of no return. Begged.

That's when he crushed himself against her.

Whoa. So the rumors were true. His manhood was the stuff of local legend, regaled in water cooler jokes about some hocus pocus that had to be kept under wraps—an industrial-length Mr. Slinky. Uncompressed, it could be dangerous. His massive hardness rolled against her bellybutton and his soft moans set her on fire.

Teasing him with a gentle bite on his lower lip, she drew him into the shadowy living room, around the sofa. He pulled her closer, his hands disappearing under her dress and searing his fingerprints into her bare skin. She felt her lacy panties shift and roll down until they stretched around her thighs. As his fingers explored the terrain between her legs, her breath caught and she could no longer wait.

She pushed him onto the sofa and pounced on top of him. But in less time than it took to say, *Wheeee!* Sophie felt herself flying backward. She landed on the coffee table with her feet in the air and her bottom winking at the ceiling.

"What the hell?" Mitch said, scrambling to his feet.

"What the hell?" came another man's voice.

"What the hell?" Sophie echoed, clapping her hands to turn on the lamp.

A man in a black T-shirt and sweats rolled off the sofa dazedly, as if he'd just woken up. His salt-and-pepper mullet spiked in all directions and he blinked furiously.

Sophie blinked furiously too. "Why the hell are you in my house?"

Mitch launched into a fighting stance with his fists up. "Who *is* this?"

"He's my— he's my—" She blew out an exasperated sigh. "Husband."

"Your husband?" Mitch's face turned the same shade as the Sultry Summer Spice lip color smudged around his bruised mouth.

"Ex-husband, actually."

"Not ex yet," the mullet-headed man said.

Sophie huffed and rolled her eyes, gesturing at each man by way of introduction. "Will Camden, Mitchell Houdini."

They made no move to shake hands, and a hot rash of

embarrassment spread across her skin. Will had never seen her with another man before. Had he heard her mouth kissing Mitch's? Her sighs escaping? Her primal need for fulfillment *screaming*?

The hot rash began to itch then, and she wiped her swollen lips. Her hair clip fell out and bounced noisily on the hardwoods, and that's when she noticed her push-up pads had dislodged themselves and wiggled up to her neck. Great. Now she had no boobs, an up-don't, and her dignity bunched around her ankles. It was official. She was a slut.

"I don't feel well." She held her stomach and wavered on her heels, reaching down to pull up her panties when the martinis went to her head, her eyes crossed, and the room swirled. Down she went like a felled redwood, face first.

Will extricated the panties from her heels and dangled them from his fingertips. "You wear a G-string now?"

Mitch hauled her up by the armpits. "Something you want to tell me?"

Sophie snatched back her panties and squeezed her eyes shut to quell the dizziness. "There's not much to tell. We've been separated for more than a year, and now we're getting divorced. The papers have been filed. Speaking of divorce, Will, did you forget you don't live here anymore?"

"I'm here because somebody had to pick up the kids from the slumber party. They're upstairs, sick."

"What? Both of them?"

"Too much sugar would be my guess. And omigod, the projectile barfing was epic. I'm talking some serious industrial-strength chum. First, one would blow and then the other. I think they were tag-teaming me. I divvied out the Pepto-Bismol, and at least *that* didn't come back up."

Mitch's mouth contorted through various incarnations of horror.

"Exactly," Will said. "Regurgitated strawberry shortcake is something you don't want to miss in your lifetime."

"Good god." Sophie dug her fingers into her forehead. A lifelong bachelor like Mitch Houdini had to be eased into the dark side of childrearing. Will could play tough, but he had his less-than-shining moments too; he was the king of squeamish stomachs. "You gave up a sympathy barf, didn't you?"

Will screwed up his face, not bothering to deny it. "Point is, I was here for the kids. I handled it. The kitchen, the staircase, even the big wet spot on your bed." Before she could ask, he waved it off. "They're fine now, I'm telling you. It's just that Keely had to see for herself that you weren't in there, and—"

Mitch backed into the foyer. "Look, I don't know who's

interrupting here, me or your—er, husband. So I should go and let you two work this out."

Dammit. This was her one night. She'd been crushing on this man for months; and after a handful of dates, they'd finally gotten past the hardest part, broken the slab of ice that had encased her libido for so long.

She thrust her palm flat toward him. "Please don't go. Will is leaving, aren't you? Because, at the risk of sounding like a broken record, you don't live here anymore."

"Ah, yes," Will said, his mouth an intractable slash. "Didn't mean to interrupt your..." finger quotes, "*big date*. Can't put a kink in Sophie's plans with the—" quotes again, "*big date*, now can we?"

"You know," Mitch said from the foyer, forming finger quotes of his own, "the *big date* is still here."

Will squinted at him. "Yeah, why is that, *Mitchell*?"

The way he said Mitchell was equivalent to verbal spitting. They both stood with eyes narrowed, chins high, and chests puffed out. A cockfight waiting to happen.

Mitch towered over Will by six inches with shoulders and arms to match. He extended a hand. "It's Mitch. Mitch Houdini. We're all adults here. Why don't we start over?"

Will grudgingly shook Mitch's hand, and each man's arm tensed in the protracted squeezing of Olympic wrestlers, jaws clenching and nostrils flaring. Mitch's biceps bulged through his dress shirt, and his face contorted with the effort. Will scrunched up his face like he might have been on the crapper.

Sophie planted herself between them and peeled their hands apart. "There we go," she said, as if breaking up two first graders. "There we go. All civil again. Isn't that better?"

Will pointed a wavering finger. "Houdini. Houdini Real Estate? *Where We Make the Home of Your Dreams Appear Like Magic*? Aren't you Sophie's boss?"

Sophie crossed her arms over her chest. "He's not my boss."

"I'm her sponsoring broker," Mitch said. "Sophie is her own boss."

The cuckoo lurched in and out of a tiny cubbyhole in the clock, crowing twelve times in a thick, gelatinous quiet, when Will turned a wary gaze on Sophie.

She opened the front door, tamping down the creeping swell of guilt. "We're past the judging phase, Will." The cool night air swirled around her bare legs, and she guided him with a scooping hand gesture toward the exit. "Thanks for getting the kids."

He got nose to nose with her. "Just one more thing."

She tapped her foot while he readied himself to say just one more thing. "Well?"

"Sophie," he said tenuously. Some apparent mental wrangling, a sidelong glance at Mitch, and then he muttered, "I'm staying in the studio for a while."

Sophie leaned closer. "What? The shed?"

"The studio, the shed, whatever. I'm staying in it for a while."

"Ohhellno, you're not."

"Ohhellyes, I am." He turned and headed straight for the back door.

She ran ahead and blocked the door with her body. "What's going on? You're not staying here unless I know why."

His voice dropped to a whisper. "I got... laid off."

"Laid off?" she shouted. "When?"

"Shhh." He peered over his shoulder. "Could we not yell it to the world?"

"You're a director of product development. You have *products* to develop."

He shook his head. "Whole division is gone. Three months ago. It makes business sense. They're reorganizing, and—"

"Are you kidding?" Sophie could feel her temper building explosively. "You waited till now to tell me? What about your condo?"

"Sold it. Buyers wanted in early. They're leasing it back from me till the closing, which is three or four weeks from this morning. So..."

"Will Camden! You seriously can't—"

She'd barely got the words out when he placed one hand behind her head and the other gently over her mouth. "Now, don't say something you'll regret. I know this seems like a good time to lay into me, but I just need the studio temporarily, till my money's freed up."

Her resolve to not speak wavered until he removed his hand. "There's no place to sleep down there. Junk's everywhere. You still haven't cleaned out all your stuff. The electricity isn't even connected. Not to mention the black widows and fat, flying, disgusting cockroaches."

"Come on, your cockroaches are not fat."

"It's got a padlock on it, and the door is all wonky and—"

"I *have* been here before, and I do have a key."

Sophie's lips pressed into a scowl, which was hard to maintain given that he was surely still mourning his father. It had only been a few months since Gus Camden passed. How could she be heartless and not help his grieving son? Still, a night in the shed for anyone, much less Will, was nonsensical. His eyes looked tired and red, and those broad shoulders she'd once leaned on with such unwavering trust now sagged. Had he lost weight?

She tilted her chin. "I want you out of my life, Will."

5

"Yeah? Well, I wouldn't take you back if you begged me."

"Good. Because I would *never* beg."

It was an exchange they'd volleyed back and forth repeatedly since he moved out and always resulted in a Camden Standoff, two ex-lovers, ex-confidants, ex-family, ex-everything glaring spitefully until somebody blinked.

Sophie raised a finger and opened the door. "One night. Do you understand? One night."

Will gave a withering last glance before he flipped on the porch light, crossed the deck, and descended three steps to the flagstone pavers that led to the erstwhile-music-studio-turned-dilapidated-shed at the far corner of an oversized yard. Head hanging, he looked back, affecting a weird, tight-lipped smile that did nothing to reassure her that he was all right.

But the massive oak trees cast opaque shadows across the yard; he tripped over Keely's pink Schwinn and landed on the chrome handlebars with dangling neon ribbons. His elbow thumped the rubber horn, and a clownish honk echoed through the air. He bounced up as if it had never happened and disappeared into the night with a slight limp.

Sophie shut the door, awash with questions. How bad were things that Will Camden would sleep in a bug-infested junk room?

The cuckoo's pendulum ticked off the seconds as she argued with herself about what to do. He was a grown man. Whose father had just died. Who'd just lost his job. Who'd recently been served divorce papers. And who had, not unimportantly, for the first time seen her with another man. Her stomach knotted.

"Where's he going?"

Sophie jumped, her hand flying to her chest. She'd forgotten she had a guest. "To our old studio, though I don't know what he's going to sleep on."

"Is that guy here all the time?"

"Hardly. His work is his whole life." She stared into the backyard and softened in the wake of Will's announcement. "At least it used to be."

"I get it, I do. But I don't feel quite right dating a married woman. I mean, I know you're getting a divorce, but maybe he's here again because he's not over you."

"That's not true, I'm sure of it." Her gaze fell to the floor, and she whispered the heart of the matter. "He's not in love with me."

"No? And what about you? Are you over him?"

She made certain her gaze didn't waver. "Of course."

"Really? Because none of my ex-girlfriends would ever let me step

6

foot back in the house once we called it quits. And you did let Will stay, right?"

"Out in the shed. Not sure I'd call that letting him stay." She scoffed to make light of it, but she could see Mitch wasn't buying it. "Look, you don't have kids, but maybe you can understand. Our mantra has always been *two parents*. Regardless of whatever else happens in our lives, Annabelle and Keely will always have two active and equal parents—though I've always been ninety percent more active and equal than Will."

He nodded, a gesture that filled the gaps while he seemed to think it through. "So I guess he's dating and all that too?"

She swallowed a hoot of laughter. "Um, yeah. He's actually, er, quite the ladies' man."

"A ladies' man, eh?" His crooked smile morphed into a cheesy attaboy grin that men give each other in solidarity, a tacit punching of their man cards. Add a Neanderthal grunt and a chest bump, and admit one to the club.

"Oh, yeah, yeah. He dates all the time. Casanova, they call him."

"Good to know. I guess if he's dating and you're getting a divorce, it's okay that we're dating." He took her hands in his. "We *are* dating, right? I really want to see you again."

She kissed him sweetly. "Yes, I'd like to see you again too. But..." With the thought of her two pukey angels upstairs, she sagged in the knowledge that the magic had come and gone without so much as an abracadabra, along with her chance to see Houdini's magic wand. What she'd felt earlier while in his embrace was no illusion. But Annabelle and Keely came first. "I need to take care of my girls now. Mommy duty calls."

Mitch's warm hands enveloped hers. "Of course, I understand."

"You do?" She walked him arm-in-arm to the front door. "Next time, I'll show you around the place. I've done a lot to the backyard. New flower beds, brick pavers, and I thought—you know," she shrugged, "a man like you would appreciate it."

She mentally gave herself a head slap. A man like him? A city man? A high-rise condo dweller? She might as well have said, *Come get a gander at my prize rutabagas, Opie.*

He picked his sports coat off the floor and leaned in for a peck on her cheek. "Next time. I hope you know how much I like you. I think a whole lot more fun is in our future."

A bud of awkward sentimentalism bloomed in her chest. "Er, fun sounds... fun." He smiled and took her face in his hands, laid a lingering kiss on her mouth. She added two points in the plus column for taking the abrupt end of their date so well, and another two points for not flinching when she said *Fun sounds fun.* "I'm sorry about how things turned out."

"Not to worry." He brushed his hand under her chin. "I'll see you Monday. After that, my plate will be a lot fuller. The Russian Princess demands a lot of my time, you know, and my travel schedule will be hectic."

And we are back to business. Will's work always took him away too. "I get it."

"What if you accompany me? After the morning meeting, if you don't have any appointments, we could all get lunch."

"Really?" Rumors abounded about Mitch's relationship with Rhuta Khorkina, the Russian Princess, but how true could they be if he was asking Sophie to join them? Besides, meeting an international celebrity was an opportunity she couldn't pass up. "I'd love that. If you're sure."

"Positive." He leaned in and deposited one last kiss on her mouth.

Sophie set the deadbolt as Mitch drove off in his Lambo, then padded again to the back of the house and peeked into the backyard. In the distance, a dim light sprayed through the shed's dusty transom window. Will must have found a flashlight. Now that was a pitiful thing. Twenty-four years of her life glowed through that transom, including a twenty-two-year marriage. After a year's separation and agreeing to end things for good, there he was again on her property. She almost felt sorry for him, out there in the equivalent of a junk drawer, and wondered if she ought to invite him inside.

But then his last, brutally uttered sentiment—the final straw that precipitated the divorce filing—replayed in her ears with razor-sharp precision: *I'm not in love with you anymore.* She blew a sigh into the windowpane. "Not after what you said."

She raised her chin, staring at the shed, imagining her ex sleeping with a creepy-crawly cast worthy of a horror flick. Served him right. She dismissed him then, relegating all concern for his welfare to tomorrow's to-do list. Then she hurried upstairs through a Pine-Sol haze.

Her pre-pubescent beauties snored softly in Keely's room, side by side under a neon pink-and-lime comforter. Brewsky, their gold cat with a fluffy white head, lay curled up and purring between them. Sophie brushed six-year-old Annabelle's dark curls from her forehead and felt for fever. She did the same to nine-year-old Keely, who stirred but didn't wake. Finding neither too warm, Sophie tucked the covers beneath their chins and kissed them goodnight.

In her own room down the hall, she clapped on the lamp, but her heart sank when she glimpsed her bare pillow-top mattress. No comforter, no sheets, no cozy snuggle spot in which to sink blissfully into slumber. Only a big wet spot where a darling daughter had searched for her mother and promptly barfed her disappointment.

She put on pajamas and tiptoed back to Keely's room where she slipped under the covers next to little Annabelle. She snuggled close and smelled the coconut-scented shampoo in her hair, and reached across her to rub Keely's smooth, lanky arm, quietly sending the message, *Mama's here. No matter what else happens, Mama will always be here.*

For hours, Sophie lay in the dark with her girls, reliving the evening: the dirty martinis, the fast car, the hot man touching her in places that hadn't been hot in far too long—and her soon-to-be-ex-husband tucked into the sofa cushions like last Super Bowl's beer nuts.

It would be hard facing either man in the light of day, given how things had turned out. Namely, Will interrupting her with Mitch, almost in the act. The *really, really, it's about damn time, boy, do I need that* act.

And then it dawned on her. *I was robbed.*

Chapter 2

Sophie awoke with her body jostling up and down like a raft in rough seas.

"Mommy," Annabelle said, bouncing on the bed. "Daddy's here."

Will? Here? Sophie bolted upright and struggled for her bearings. Five seconds later, the previous night's events skittered across the lining of her stomach. Will had seen her with another man—and lost his job.

Kee-rist almighty.

Annabelle leaped off the bed and ran out of the room. Keely, her fourth-grader, sat cross-legged on the foot of the bed wearing a plastic Mardi Gras mask complete with purple and blue head feathers, hand-painted black eyelashes, and large rhinestone teardrops. She stared at her mother through the gloomy white visage.

"Hey, baby," Sophie said sleepily. "Little early for a party, isn't it?"

Keely pointed to her mask, her lips moving behind the mouth hole. "Mommy, this is the face of sadness. Did you know Daddy slept in the shed last night? His back hurts now."

"It's temporary, sweetie."

"There's bugs out there."

Sophie slid from under the covers and traipsed across the hallway, through her bedroom, and into her bathroom. Upon re-emerging, Keely met her at the door. The mask sat atop her head, elastic string scrunching her tangled hair into a chaotic bouffant over one ear. On seeing her mother, she pulled the sad mask back into place.

"Spiders, Mommy. Scorpions and snakes."

Sophie yawned and brushed past her, sensing Keely on her heels down the staircase.

The strong smell of brewed coffee invited her to the kitchen. Will had made a pot. At least living alone had forced him to learn how to make it.

She stepped out onto the deck, watching her youngest daughter skip downhill, across brick pavers and grass to the far end of the yard, before slipping inside the shed. Sophie followed, preparing herself.

The mid-May morning was already hot, a prelude to summer, yet the air inside the studio-turned-shed felt cool. Two narrow transoms near the ceiling leaked sunlight. Fifteen years earlier, when she and Will had bought the property, they'd built this structure and finished out the walls, intending it to be a music studio. But things hadn't panned out. Will had instead switched abruptly to a demanding career in high tech, and the building was aptly relabeled "the shed." The same deterioration could have been said of his musical aspirations.

Will lay sideways in a wrinkled T-shirt and boxers, leaning on one elbow, atop a green sleeping bag he'd stretched across the built-in plywood workbench.

"Good morning," he said from behind the Saturday funnies.

Sophie took in the mess of a room. On the floor along one wall, a ten-speed was pressed into an upright position by a giant ice chest stuffed with faded orange life vests and an anchor that Will had saved from the sale of their old boat. Camping equipment was stored beneath the counter on the concrete floor. Fishing poles, tackle boxes, a pup tent, propane lanterns and a Coleman stove, a cardboard box of tins and utensils. Must have been a decade since any of it had seen a campground.

She drew in her arms. "This place is a disaster. Did you sleep out here? All night?"

Will sat up, folded the paper, and exchanged it for the cup of coffee perched on a box near his dangling legs. "Sleep is a rather strong word."

He slurped his coffee noisily. The whites surrounding his brown irises had turned a veiny scarlet, his scruffy tangle of hair spiked à la weather vane, and the salt-and-pepper sheen of a beard gave him that "Please deposit your spare change in my cup" look. Not quite the Casanova Sophie had described to Mitch.

"What's this?" Keely said, setting a small, wooden trunk onto a lopsided box.

Sophie and Will appraised the trunk and then each other.

"I imagine that's your daddy's old sheet music." Sophie flipped the rusty lever with her thumb and peeked inside at a stack of yellowed papers with Will's longhand scrawls and notes. The lyrics for "Sophie's Kiss" topped the pile. "Yet another reason to clean out this place. Don't you want to put these somewhere safe?"

Will shrugged. "What for? All in the past. Nothing in there I want to brag about."

"Once upon a time, you did."

"That's fairytale-speak for *Once upon a time, there was a one-hit wonder.* And we all know how that story ends."

Sophie spied the end of a guitar behind the ice chest, metal tuning knobs protruding like Frankenstein spikes from the top of its narrow neck. "You left your guitar out here?"

"Practice guitar. The decent ones are in the guest room."

Sophie looked down her nose. "*All* of them?"

"You didn't expect me to leave them in this mausoleum for exoskeletons, did you?"

"As if you ever play them anyway."

"Mommy." Sophie looked down as Annabelle tugged on her hand and pointed to webs suspended from the ceiling. "Spiders."

Not only spiders, but bug carcasses and a thick layer of dust—clinging to the webs and doorjambs and powdering the concrete floor.

Will sneezed three times and spilled hot coffee on his thigh. He jumped off the counter as if he could escape the burn, then sneezed three more times. Sophie caught the itch vicariously and followed with her own bout of sneezing. She ran outside and wiped her nose, tasting dust on her tongue while waiting for another urge to pass.

"Holy crap. That shed is not habitable."

Annabelle and Keely stood behind her, clinging to their father's arms and staring forlornly up at their mother. All they lacked was a picketer's sign that read *Free Willie.*

"I heard a death rattle, Mommy," Keely intoned behind her *sad* mask. "There's snakes out here too."

There was no winning this one. If her kids had to choose a parent to send into a nest of pythons, she'd be paralyzed and digesting in the dark right now.

But they were divorcing!

She couldn't believe what she was about to say. "All right. You can sleep in the guest room."

Annabelle jumped and clapped. Keely held tight to her father and tossed off her sad mask, bounced in place, á la pogo stick, and cheered.

"Hey." Sophie picked the mask off the ground. "The offer is for the weekend only, and it expires the *moment* I have to raise my voice."

Will nodded compliantly.

Sophie's chest tightened. Will looked so downtrodden, she fought a powerful urge to grab him and hug him and tell him things would be all right. But that would send the message that she still cared for him.

Which she didn't. Oh no. She had painstakingly shoveled a hole in the deepest, firmest ground of her psyche, dumped a ton of emotional dirt in with him, and staked it with the white flag of surrender.

Here lies Sophie and Will. Nevermore.

She turned back toward the house with a craving for a strong cup of coffee with a triple shot of Cuervo. Honestly, Will under the same roof with her again? That had *combat sport* all over it. She huffed her new mantra, *I don't care, I don't care*, and placed Keely's sad mask over her face. Surely, she could handle his proximity for one teensy weensy weekend.

She glanced over her shoulder to call the kids in for breakfast, just in time to see Will and Keely knuckle-bumping each other, their cheeks wide with triumphant grins; and she realized she should have buried him deeper.

Chapter 3

For the next few hours, Will deliberately made himself scarce. He had already moved his last few possessions out of the condo and into a storage unit the day before, and all that remained was cleaning up for the new owners.

Before sunset, he pulled his 1989 Jaguar XJ-S convertible, British racing green with barley leather interior and silver spoke wheels, into Sophie's garage. As the engine idled, the stench of rotten eggs enveloped him. If his mechanic was right, his V12 was running on only six cylinders and needed a new coil before the catalytic converter caught on fire. He turned off the engine and felt her shimmy into silence. His Jag was a major money pit, but he'd never give her up, not after the times they'd been through together.

A guy didn't give up on the good things, not if they could be fixed.

The black Escalade parked in the circular driveway gave him hope, its owner inside the house talking Sophie's ear off, he was sure. Maybe getting his ears singed by the sexy Tess Baker would take his mind off job layoffs and money woes and his wife with Houdini on the couch last night—a topic, no doubt, Sophie and Tess were submerged in right now.

His shoulders tensed as he reminded himself that Sophie was about to be officially single again, and with the exception of keeping the damn house instead of selling it, the preliminary divorce details were laid out the way they both wanted. Of course, soon enough the legal discovery process would uncover a couple things he hadn't yet worked up the courage to tell her, not the least of which was the news that he'd changed his mind about the house. Selling it would get him—and all of them—out of debt. When the time came to confess his financial sins, he'd have to hide the kitchen cutlery.

For now, he figured he'd keep his head high and cut back. But severance dwindled fast, and job prospecting had been disheartening. Still, Austin was the tech capital of the southwest, and his last twelve years in senior management for Waterloo Semiconductor had to count for something. Lots of guys went into consulting after a layoff, procuring a seed source to grow an entrepreneurial dream. After all these years, I.T. still didn't evoke a fire in him, but he couldn't rule it out. He wasn't in a position to rule out *anything*, including a teaching gig. Maybe it was time he put his doctorate to use, though the desire to teach had long ago come and gone. Meanwhile, might as well take advantage of the house he still owned and paid for, right?

He switched off his phone. No need to spark up The Fight, the one they'd had a million times, the whole basis for their divorce: too much work, not enough wife. He'd been available night and day for his teams before the layoff. Mattered little that there were no more teams. Felt weird being so out of touch. He pondered that and turned the phone back on, setting it to vibrate.

To save himself from fashion police brutality, he checked for a zipped fly, tucked-in shirttails, buckled belt, matching socks, and the absence of wet pit-moons. Then he popped the trunk and hauled out the ceiling fan he'd intended to install in his condo but never got around to doing. Instead, Keely's bedroom would be the beneficiary. And since he couldn't arrive empty handed for Annabelle, he'd picked up a new baby doll to replace the one she'd lost.

A man had to provide the important things, even if he had to rely on credit cards to do it.

He shut the front door quietly and inhaled the savory aroma of chicken dinner and some sort of sweet pastry that piqued his appetite. Sophie's music broadcasted through the stereo speakers, as usual. Music was a constant in this house, indoors and out. From where he stood, he could see to the back of the house, through the French doors that led to the deck where his daughters sat around a picnic table with construction paper and crayons.

Before making his big entrance, he deposited everything in the guest room just off the foyer. Hands free, he dropped onto the bed, his weary bones and the tense muscles of his back sinking into the cool white comforter. Thank god—and Sophie—he wouldn't have to sleep on that backbreaking worktable again.

With the drapes closed and the room cool and dark, he flirted with the idea of taking a nap, but his thoughts drifted to the many times he'd slept in this room before he and Sophie separated. The divorce was a long, torturous time coming.

He sat up and glanced around the room, at the antique headboard and dresser that once belonged to Sophie's grandmother and at his three old guitars and amps. If he thought storage wouldn't ruin them, he'd have stuffed them with his other furniture. He wasn't even sure why he kept them. Sophie was right; wasn't like he played them anymore. Back when he made a good living as a musician, a day without guitar picking would have been sacrilegious. Now, like family portraits, the instruments simply chronicled a part of his life and defined his *good old days*. This was not a place he wanted to hang his hat any longer.

His fists clenched when he returned to the shadowy entryway and noticed the turned-down family picture on the foyer table. *Speaking of sacrilege.* He set the picture upright, thinking he might steal it. Apparently, Sophie wouldn't miss it.

Reminded they were no longer a family, he thought about finding a cheap place to crash, starting tomorrow afternoon—or selling Sophie on the idea that having him around would be a good thing. Fat chance. He was stuck, unless a miracle occurred, like news that his financial-gamble-gone-south had been a big mistake and he instead *made* money. That, or his dad had left him a windfall. Unfortunately, his dad's lengthy bout with cancer had drained all the bank accounts. Fortunately, the US Marine Corps took care of the funeral.

Gunnery Sergeant Gus Camden's passing always seemed to sneak up on him. He leaned against the foyer wall and bit back tears. His dad had been a sturdy-as-steel marine who maintained a certain distance from everyone, including his only son. *Do what needs doing. Don't act like a girl. Where'd you hide your backbone today, son? Suck it up. Semper fi, dickhead.*

Will thought his old man might soften up once he retired, at age 50, but Gus rose religiously before sunup, did what needed doing, and maintained the corps lifestyle right through his 67th birthday. Right till the end. Which was why, early one morning in the hospital, he had caught Will so off guard.

"You know me," Gus had rasped through his breathing tube, his eyes yellowed and strained in the shadowy light. "I'm just an old devil dog. But I'll tell you this, nothing's more important than family. Nothing." His roughened hand had reached for Will's in a rare moment of affection. "You know what I'm talking about, son, don't you?"

Will had nodded, while the requisite "Yes, sir" had lodged in his throat, blockaded by a teary knot that could not be shed in front of the old man.

Then his father had dropped his hand and waved him off, adding in his more characteristic hard-edged bluster, "You gotta do something about it, son. Something real. Promise me you won't cheesedick your way through it."

"I don't know what you think I should do, Dad."

"You're a PhD. You gotta have some kind of idea how to fix a colossal SNAFU." Then Gus indicated the beat-up green guitar case standing in the corner of the room. "You gonna use that thing, or what?"

Will had shrugged. Gus was never a fan of his son's choice to have a music career, and when it all went to hell, Gus had reminded Will what a colossal SNAFU that was too.

"I didn't know if you'd want me to play—"

"You brought it, son, so play it."

Will pulled out his old acoustic and situated himself in the high-backed chair adjacent to his father's bed, one ankle propped on his knee. "Any requests?"

Gus's voice had labored to whisper, "Your mama's favorite."

As the sun rose behind the hospital building, Will quietly sang the lyrics to "Bye Bye Blackbird" and strummed and picked the song his mother had hummed until the day she died, almost thirty years earlier. Somewhere in the last stanza, Gunnery Sergeant Gus Camden slipped away. It seemed agonizingly poetic.

In the last few months, Will had replayed that scene in his mind so many times, he wasn't sure which words were his father's and which were his own. But the message hit home, loud and clear. The old man had late in life decided he valued family, when it was *too* late.

Sophie's cackling cuffed Will's ears from the kitchen. He stood up straight and sucked it up, like the old man had taught him. *Semper fi, dickhead.*

Standing in the foyer, he debated whether to seek refuge outside with his daughters or visit the kitchen where he assumed Sophie was entertaining Tess. A moment later, the music that was so loud inside faded. But since his daughters were up and dancing now, shimmying and shaking in princess dresses, he knew it still boomed outside. Their chins bobbed in and out, hands and arms darting at right angles, as they reveled in walking like an Egyptian to the Bangles tune. The beat and the melody batted his eardrums and flipped an internal switch. Details scuttled across his brain in ticker-tape fashion: "Walk Like an Egyptian," The Bangles, 1986, from their *Different Light* album.

Cataloguing songs was an ingrained process, a holdover from his days as a DJ, before his short-lived career on the Top Forty Hits list. More like a compulsion, after all these years. Song title, artist, year it hit the charts—always in that order. Sophie called it a quirk of platinum proportions; Will called it God's gift to the universe. Who else knew such divine things?

Of course, he called certain personal anatomy, specifically Little Will and the Heartbreakers, God's gift as well. Sophie never appreciated that either.

He heard more laughter from the kitchen and tiptoed closer, imagining Sophie and Tess jockeying around the granite island that Sophie insisted on when they built this house. Clanging bowls and pans announced that dinner was in progress. And the Big Girls were talking.

"Let me get this straight," Tess Baker said, in her upper-crust Dallas twang. "You almost had sex with Mitch, right on top of your husband?"

"Ex-husband," Sophie said.

"Not ex yet. Sister, you brought Mitch back to your house. You tempted fate."

"Did you forget that you *dared* me to bring him home?"

Will skulked along the wall with the sense that his attempts at being invisible were compromised due to his heavy breathing. The more he tried to be quiet, the more he perspired and wheezed. He considered that sneaking into the den and hiding behind the upright piano would give him a failsafe vantage point with crystal clear audio. With all the plants on top of it, he'd never be seen. Of course, there was that eavesdropping thing. Spying would be stooping low—an underhanded and despicable invasion of privacy.

But, if he didn't get caught, would it still be bad?

"It's not much of a dare when you're dying to do it," Tess said. "I don't know why you waited so long. You've been dating for over a month."

"I know, but what if it jeopardized my career? What if he thought I was easy?"

"What are you, thirteen? What if you are? Trust me, good girls might go to heaven, but bad girls go everywhere. You see an opportunity? You want an opportunity? You take an opportunity. Besides, you and Will are long done; it's time, Grasshopper."

Brewsky lay in repose on the sofa and got up to stretch as Will crawled past on hands and knees, which prompted the cat to hop on the floor and rub against Will's thigh. They'd never gotten along, even when Will lived there. Now the hairball wanted a love scratch?

At the piano, Will rose to a Neanderthal stoop, careful not to let his hips touch the exposed ivories. He peeked between two large wandering jews with yellowed leaves until a flurry of convulsing gnats caused him to jerk away.

Holy fumigation, Batman. On the other hand, *What great kitchen views from here.*

18

Sophie turned sizzling chicken breasts in a skillet. She had pulled her brown hair into a swishy ponytail and wore faded jeans and a white tank top. Except for Tess's auburn hair and freckles, the two could pass for sisters. Must have been a quiet Saturday in the world of real estate, he guessed. Tess was already in her jeans too.

"Will's a divine man," Tess drawled. She opened the oven door and peeked in at what smelled like cherry pie. "I don't care if his fashion sense is stuck in reverse or that he has a Clapper fetish. And a mullet. If he were my guy—"

"Oh, take him," Sophie said. "Take my husband. Please. Or I'll never be able to bring a man home for sex again. Maybe you'll even meet his standards. God knows I never did."

Will bristled. His expectations were high for Sophie—for her own good. She liked to moan about being a college dropout, but she couldn't drag her butt back to school, and instead preferred to wallow in the pity party she referred to as "standing in the shadow of his doctorate." Or his other favorite nugget when she compared her flailing career trajectory to his single hit song: "Only room enough in this family for one 'Sophie's Kiss.'"

In deference to her, he said often how she'd edged him out as a *two*-hit wonder when she produced Annabelle and Keely. But she never understood that he thought she had a PhD in common sense and drive. If only she'd stay focused on one goal instead of flitting around. She was a butterfly sticking her nose in every pretty flower.

Now that *bringing a man home for sex* crack... that kicked him in the 'nads.

Tess grabbed a pair of oven mitts and pulled out the pie. "Is he at least doing his fair share with the kids?"

"Same as usual. I provide the routines, he provides the means. For now."

"Well, that's something. The kids never have to worry about money with an executive engineer for a father. He's reliable, and he knows how to save a buck."

Sophie went tight-lipped—no doubt, out of embarrassment.

Only months ago, Will had swelled with pride—even bravado—at how well he'd provided. At how, with his investments, his early retirement was assured and the kids could go to the best universities instead of community college. In the aftermath of "Sophie's Kiss," when the royalties dried up and they could no longer afford a lavish lifestyle, he'd worked hard to climb back on solid financial footing. High tech saved them, until the layoffs. And the tanked investments. Nice to see Tess sticking up for him like the old days.

"Of course," Tess added, "being an executive engineer explains

19

why he's such a tight ass." She turned off the oven, shook her fingers, and licked traces of burgundy pie filling.

Sophie poured two glasses of red. "Yup, the free-wheeling, fun-loving stud of the eighties is long gone, that's for sure."

"How much fun we used to have," Tess said wistfully, "hanging out on the Drag, going to concerts, and being groupies?"

Sophie stirred something green and steaming in a pan, turned off the heat, and placed the lid back on it. "The things we used to wear. Oh, when I look at those old pictures."

Will's phone buzzed and vibrated against his waistband. *Bzzz, bzzz, bzzz.* He dropped to his haunches and fumbled to turn it off. Damn it! *Bzzz, bzzz, bzzz.* Desperate, he dropped it on the carpet and sat on it. *Bzzz, bzzz, bzzz.* All his guy parts absorbed the vibrations.

Omigod. I'm in a compromising position with my phone. If Sophie could see this.

When the buzzing quit, he pulled out his phone and realized he'd been taken out by his own motivational alert that said, "Generate more buzz for your business."

Maybe espionage wasn't such a good idea. Karma had a beat on him. He should go out and make a grand entrance so they'd know he was there. But then he heard Tess.

"You were too busy bonking Will's brains out."

Already they'd progressed to bonking?

"We used to be so much fun," Sophie said. "What happened to us?"

"Band guys got boring, we both got married, and STDs turned deadly."

Will unfurled to peer between the plants again, when Brewsky jumped to the top of the piano, tiptoed in serpentine fashion between the jews, and stuck his puckered butt in Will's face.

"Brewsky!" Sophie shouted. "Get down."

Will gave him a push before Sophie could storm over and do it herself and catch him lurking. The cat growled menacingly and leaped to the couch, stirring the air and the gnats so that Will snorted one up his nose. The thing must have been king size—and doing the backstroke in his nostril hairs. Its spastic gyrations made him want to sneeze—a certified kiss of death, if you didn't want to be caught spying on your wife.

He pinched his nose and realized his grave error: squished bug.

Sophie looked in Will's direction and he ducked, face to face with the piano keys. He tensed, held his breath, and listened to her soft-soled footsteps on the tile. Then he heard the fridge door close.

Close call, he thought, *and I still have a crime scene in my nose.* He had two choices: to blow or not to blow—and use his finger.

He examined his hands, the fingertips still thick and calloused from years of picking steel strings. As modern work implements go, a finger was comparatively large for insertion into such a small hole, and he'd end up pushing the bug higher. He thought of his toolbox, imagining something in the neighborhood of 3/8" or 1/4". Or some needle-nose pliers, ironically.

Brewsky observed, yellow eyes half-open, ringed tail twitching. A counterspy. Will jabbed a finger at him. *This is your fault.*

Resigned to the task, Will pulled his shirttail out of his shorts, enveloped his nose in the fabric and blew quietly—once, twice, a third time—and held up the results to the light streaming over the piano.

So that's a gnat cadaver—more muddy than bloody. Where are the rest of the legs?

His gag reflex kicked in, and if Sophie didn't hear that, she was deaf. Sweat beaded on his brow, and he clamped a hand over his mouth.

"It's the right thing," Sophie said to Tess. "At some point, you have to recognize that he's never going to change. You quit crying and do what's best for you and your kids."

The gag urge under control, Will rose to see Sophie cutting chicken breasts on kiddie plates. She forked a piece of chicken and chewed it up, just like she did his cgo. Next she would slice and dice his manhood and bisect his spousal performance like a coroner autopsying a dead man, scrutinizing piece by piece all the parts that made him whole.

"I had no idea," she bellyached, "when I married a musician with star potential—who used to say I rocked his world—that he would give it all up to become a twenty-four-seven Type A geek and abandon us."

And she delivers. Like it came right out of a holster.

Tess sneaked a morsel of chicken. "If I remember right, you wanted stability and babies and a gorgeous home. After 'Sophie's Kiss,' you got it."

"Yes, the bittersweet 'Sophie's Kiss.' Don't remind me."

"I'm just saying, you still had the lifestyle but not the income. What a blow to the guy's ego. No wonder he gave up music." Tess tilted her head with an empathetic smirk. "Kind of sad."

Sophie warned with an open-palms gesture. "The problem wasn't that he gave up on his music, Tess. The problem was that he gave up on *us.*"

"Yeah, I know. Sorry. I just miss you guys. You gave me hope. I thought you two, of all people, would last." Tess moved around the kitchen island to give Sophie a hug. "Good news is, unofficially at least, you're a free woman."

"Free and boring. I put myself to sleep thinking how much fun I'm not. I need adventure. Something that gets me jazzed to get out of bed in the morning, a passion for something incredible." She pressed her fingertips into her chest. "I want to feel sparks. I want to be loved and adored again. Is that so wrong?"

Will stared between the plant leaves at his wife. The old guilt shot through him, compounded by new guilt. How much guilt could one man shoulder, anyway? Till it put him in the ground, he guessed. He'd been a less-than-stellar husband, a musical has-been, and now an unemployed, broke-ass, soon-to-be-single father. What did he have to offer? No wonder she was anxious to get him out of her life.

"Honey," Tess said, "you just need to get laid." She pointed a peach-painted fingernail for emphasis. "Going without sex for two years makes you maudlin and crabby. I can't imagine how crabby Will is. Unless he's getting some."

"Please. The man is a machine. He eats, sleeps, and works. Trust me when I say, he never—*never*—has time for sex."

"So, he's not even dating?"

"I doubt it. It would make things a lot easier. Mitch would feel better about seeing me, that's for sure."

"After last night, I'm betting that if Will doesn't get another woman in his life soon, the odds of him catching you with your pants down again are pretty great."

Will nearly choked on his tongue. He swatted at more gnats and pinched his nose to keep them out. He was breathing through his mouth when a gnat flew in and landed on the back of his tongue. He gagged, grabbed his throat, and whimpered. If he could hock up the gnat before his stomach flip-flopped and he pulled a Annabelle all over the carpet, he could slither off without being noticed. *Wait.* He could do an open-mouthed sneeze and cough the gnat into something that muffled sound. *Sure, a snough.*

He turned in desperation toward the couch, where he saw two velvety maroon pillows with gold braiding, last year's handmade Christmas gifts from Sophie's grandmother. He lunged straight-legged over the armrest and thrust his face into a pillow as the *snough* burst out of him. The act was so forceful, it startled the cat, which leaped onto Will's head and sank needlepoint claws into his scalp. Will yelped as tiny daggers tore his flesh. His body jack-knifed and the toes of his shoes crashed onto the piano keys. A clunky cacophony of notes resonated off the walls and vibrated the fixtures. He rolled off the couch and scrambled to his feet with the cat still on his head, hissing and growling and spitting.

Will wrestled him off, but not before Brewsky ripped through a chunk of his ear.

Tess and Sophie peered around the piano as Brewsky went limp in Will's arms, pink tongue hanging out, eyes glazed and rolling back into his head. The back door opened and music from the outside speakers blared into the house. Kicky lyrics invaded his psyche from a song he once played to capacity crowds, "Should I Stay or Should I Go."

Keely and Annabelle raced in, squealing in delight, and clung to his legs, "Daddy!"

Will panicked and said the first thing that came to mind. "The Clash, 1982. A good year for them." And then he swallowed the gnat.

So much for snoughing. He gagged again, his eyes watering while his audience backed away in horror. "Karma," he choked out. "She's a mean mistress."

Chapter 4

His wife stared at him blankly, and Will's first thought was, "Hallelujah, I've left her speechless."

It helped to have an audience. Her face scrunched up, eyes scanning the green golf shorts riding high on his waist and the white ankle socks peeking above his old golf shoes, minus the cleats. After ten years, they were as worn in as shoes could get, just the way he liked them.

He ran his fingers through the fur ball in his arms and cleared his throat, wondering if torture by interrogation might be more pleasant than this silent critique of his fashion man-sense.

"Go wash your hands, girls," Sophie ordered the kids. "Dinner's ready."

Annabelle and Keely ran off to the bathroom while Sophie scowled a hole through him.

Tess gave him an awkward hug. "I'm so glad to see you, Will."

"Me too," he said, setting the cat on the floor. "It's been a long time." He felt his ear and took a look at his fingers—bloody from Brewsky's attack.

"Looks like you could use some first aid."

Tess led him to the kitchen sink, and he was grateful for the diversion.

"If memory serves," he said, "your birthday's this week. The big four-four?"

"You always remember." She ran water on a paper towel and dabbed at his ear. Then she clucked her tongue. "I notice you never seem to forget the number either."

"You'll always be a year younger than me. How could I forget?

Besides, you don't look like any forty-four-year-old *I* know."

He glanced at Sophie busying herself with dinner prep. Tess gave her a look too, then prodded Will onto a barstool and helped herself to the cupboards for another plate.

"Since you so rudely brought up my age, Will, let me say that my Fresh Factor has been compromised, and it's only getting worse. Last year I gave myself a nine. This year, a six. If I keep going this way, I'll pass my expiration date before I ever blow out a candle."

Will leaned back and checked her head to toe. "Tess, I'd give you a Fresh Factor of no less than twelve on your worst day."

"Boy, have I missed you."

The kids climbed on barstools adjacent to their father.

"Auntie Tess, what's my Fresh Factor?" Keely asked, brown eyes beaming.

"You?" Tess held Keely's face, the spitting image of Sophie, in her hands. "Oh, my gosh, on a scale of one to ten, you're a twenty."

Little Annabelle chirped, "Me too, Auntie Tess?"

"Of course. All the Camden girls have Fresh Factors of twenty. Mommy, too, even when she makes sour faces, like now. Don't you think?"

Keely craned her neck. "What do you think, Daddy? What's Mommy's Fresh Factor?"

Will perused Sophie in her form-fitting pink top. Pink always was her color, and he'd been a sucker for that figure from the moment they met—which was only maddening now.

"Your mother is... terminally fresh. No matter what she's wearing—if she's wearing anything at all. I'd give her a good..." *kick in the pants*, he wanted to say as he watched Sophie's defiance transform into a rosy flush. Again with the vision of her with Mitch. He tried not to grimace. "Ten, of course. I'd give your mommy a ten."

Sophie clutched silver tongs, divvying chicken breasts and green beans onto the kids' plates. Her brows knitted, and her jaw went askew as she slid her gaze toward him. After all these years, she had perfected the look. He'd eaten this particular specialty of hers before: stuffed annoyance, a dish best served frigid. That, or she pondered how to vice-grip his nuts in those tongs with so many witnesses.

Tess seemed to take in the awkwardness that filled the room. "I, for one, will never forget the night your mom and dad met. I was there, you know. I introduced them."

Keely brightened. "You did?"

"Oh yes. We were best friends even then. Freshmen in college. One night we went to see this band called the Wild Boys. We were all dancing, wall-to-wall bodies at the Punk Palace, slurping yummy little shooters. That's a milkshake for grown-ups."

"And flirting with every guy who moonwalked into the place," Will said, rising from his stool and making deliberate eye contact with Sophie. "That was when I first saw her. I was on stage, singing and playing guitar. Lead Wild Boy, you know."

"A copycat Duran Duran band," Sophie droned, as if that were a bad thing.

Tess looked back and forth at Annabelle and Keely, her excitement rising in the retelling. "We were in the audience when the crowd went crazy out of control. They kept pushing us forward—they were starting to trample us."

Keely covered her mouth. Annabelle's eyes ballooned.

Will helped himself to a steak knife from the drawer. "I saw them beginning to crush the most beautiful girl in the room—the one with the fuchsia spike job."

Tess whispered, hand to mouth. "I dared your mom to dye her hair wild colors and spike it up. She never could resist a dare."

"So the crowd pushed your mom and Tess into the stage," Will said.

"Which was four feet high," Tess added. "You know what that's like for shorties like your mom and me. Felt like a brick wall closed in on us."

"I was playing our most requested cover when the crowd squeezed in. Just as I got to the part that went, *Wild boys always SHI-I-I-INE*—" Will dropped the knife on the counter and strummed imaginary chords on an air guitar. "I got hopping mad and popped two strings. And then I pitched my guitar over the audience."

Annabelle and Keely's delighted gasps spurred him on. "It spiraled over a thousand hands and people jumped to catch it, which made room up front. But that's not the best part."

Sophie eyed him with her well-honed don't-go-there scowl.

"I bent down and reached into the crowd and pulled your mom up onto the stage."

Tess grinned. "And me too."

Will lunged for Sophie and grabbed her around the waist, pulling her toward him. She tried to push him away, but he laid her back quickly.

"I dipped your mom like Fred Astaire did to Ginger Rogers, just like this, and I kissed her smack on the mouth in front of everybody."

He bent toward her but stopped short of kissing her by mere millimeters. The kitchen went quiet in expectation of a first kiss that materialized only in memory.

And what a kiss it had been. Will could feel it even now. Though

Sophie had been surprised by it, she had completely relaxed in his arms. "You saved me," she'd said, staring up at him. He'd laughed and said over the deafening hoots and claps of the crowd, "It's a rule. If you save someone, they must marry you." He didn't know what made him say it, but when the words came out, they felt right. She didn't skip a beat. "When?" she'd said. Still in his arms, they'd kissed again. He knew then, she would change his life. Almost two years to the day later, they did marry, with Tess and Jake at their sides.

Twenty-two years after they said their I-dos, the woman looking back at him had a hardness in her eyes that the young Sophie did not. A twinge of guilt hit him when he remembered the big part he'd played in that.

Sophie smacked his chest to make him let go, and she pushed herself upright.

"The place went nuts," Tess said.

Will stared at Sophie, bypassing nearly twenty-five years of memories. "All to save the girl with the fuchsia spike job."

"And her friend," Tess said. "Can you imagine if your daddy hadn't jumped in to save us? Your mom and me would be flat as those chicken breasts."

Will puffed out his chest. "You see, Daddy was a hero even then."

Keely swooned. "So that's why you married him, Mommy? Cuz he saved you?"

Sophie's mouth pursed. "That's it, baby. Daddy was a real do-gooder back then."

"Actually, *all* the girls were after your old dad back in those days," Will said. In a long-dormant broadcaster's voice, he recited his old tagline: "You're listening to the Tunemeister on KFUN, 97.5 on your FM dial."

"Daddy!" Annabelle beamed. "You *were* gooder back then."

Tess pumped her fist in the air. "Oh yeah, your daddy was the *master* of music trivia."

"Six a.m. to 11 a.m. every weekday before doctoral studies." He made two fists and pointed both thumbs to his chest. "DJ Dynamo here."

Sophie rolled her eyes and tossed the dishtowel on the counter. "Will you be staying for dinner? Is there anything you want to tell me? Can I rent you a truck for that junk you have out in the shed? You could take it to the flea market and make yourself some extra cash since *you were just laid off.*"

The room went quiet with the abrupt announcement of his well-kept secret. Tess's gaze locked onto him as she absorbed the news with each wide-eyed blink.

"Or," Sophie said, "are you here to tell me you're leaving town? Like right now?"

Will exaggerated a laugh. "Thanks there, honey, but I'll be installing Keely's new fan tonight, and I've got a little something for Annabelle too." He did a dance shuffle with a cheesy grin. "I'll be here all weekend, folks."

Keely's eyes twinkled. "Oh, Daddy."

Annabelle squealed and grabbed his arm. "What did you bring me?"

Kids, Will thought. *The perfect leverage.* Sophie's brows knitted, her nostrils flared, and her upper lip curled, but the worst she could manage with an audience was an impotent tongue cluck. He knew what that meant though. The Tunemeister would pay for it later.

She turned her back then and disappeared into the hallway— probably heading upstairs to plot his demise in private.

"Sorry," Will said to Tess. "I hate when people witness our family feud."

"I like family food, Daddy," Annabelle said, green beans tumbling out of her mouth.

Tess shrugged and took a seat on the end stool. "So you got laid off. What are your plans now?" She cut into her chicken and took a bite.

Here it comes. The judgment and questions as the microscope zooms in tighter.

"Actually, this gives me the chance to explore starting up my own business. More importantly, I have more time to spend with my girls." He wrapped Keely's head in the crook of his elbow and rubbed her head playfully with his fist. "Snuggy!"

"How are you managing?" Tess asked. "I mean, since your dad..."

Will shrugged. *Where's your backbone, son?* "You know how it is. Even if you weren't all that close to your parents, you spent a lifetime trying to please them. I have no doubt Dad's looking down on me right now, saying, 'Way to cheesedick it, son.'"

Tess offered a sympathetic smile. Few people knew what to say to him about his Dad's death. Thankfully, she didn't toss out the *God has a better plan* adage. Tess knew him better than to throw out trite passages.

"I'm sure you miss him," she said. "And the job situation?"

"Oh yeah, we're fine. In good shape." He tried to sound both sincere and lackadaisical, extending his arms as he looked around. "Somebody's got to pay for all this. Till the divorce is final anyway. Besides, the job thing will be rectified real soon and, in the meantime, I'll be here for the kids. I'm betting Sophie needs me when the real estate thing falls apart. What career do you think will be next? By my count, she's had ten, if you include her stints as the Avon Lady and the Guilty Pleasures pimp." Twenty-four years of half-baked careers flipped through his mind, along with one marriage. "Sophie never sticks with anything."

"This is different. She doesn't *want* to need your help anymore."

Ouch. Will fluffed the hair on Annabelle's brown head, hoping his face hadn't betrayed him. At that moment he wished he still had that Pop Tart of a condo he'd lived in for the year he and Sophie were separated, just so he could disappear into it. "Well, I hope she does well."

Tess just looked at him. Not buying it.

"I do," he said. "It'll be good that she doesn't need me anymore."

Tess's silence said more than any words could, as if she knew he was hiding something. He rose from his barstool and pulled her aside by the elbow, whispering. "Okay, I'm a little freaked out, if you must know. I mean, unemployment is just a temporary inconvenience, but... Look, you know Sophie better than anybody."

"Yes," she said. "I do."

"So, you have to promise me you won't tell her what I'm about to tell you. I mean, I'll tell her later, but..."

"What is it?"

"Swear to me, Tess. You'll let me be the one to break the news."

"Omigod. Is it cancer?"

"What? No. I wish. I mean, of course, I don't wish. But I'd almost rather be sick than tell Sophie..." *Just do it. It will be like a pre-confession. A gauge for how Sophie will take it.*

He pulled Tess into the living room and braced himself for Part I. "I'm broke, Tess."

Tess cocked her head and hiked her eyebrows. "I think our girl might already get that."

And here goes Part II. "And we—er, *she* needs to sell the house."

"What? You can't sell the house out from under her. Didn't you guys agree to letting her keep it after the divorce is final?"

"Things have changed. I've lost everything, Tess. Everything."

"Holy shit. Everything? As in stocks, retirement?"

"And the kids' college funds."

Tess gasped and covered her mouth, and all he could see was her wide-eyed horror.

"Remember that investment that Sophie's grandfather was so gung-ho about?" he said. "That I said was too risky? Well, it was. Apparently I scared Grampy into pulling out his money—about the same time I invested my own, and a month later, the guy got indicted for fraud. Classic Ponzi scheme."

"Oh man." She rubbed his shoulder. "I'm so sorry, Will. I heard about that guy. He took a lot of very smart people, you know. You're not the only one."

"Do you think that will matter to Sophie?"

"Not one bit. Have you thought about moving to Siberia?"

"The Space Station wouldn't be far enough." He took a deep breath. "That money will be tied up for years before any legal settlement is reached, and even then, I stand to get back a fraction of what I invested."

Tess nodded, tight lipped, and he could tell her brain was parsing it all out.

"Help me, Tess. How do I tell Sophie? The way to dig out of this hole is to sell the house. Split the proceeds. Start over. I'm already two house payments behind. How do I break it to her?"

"From the Space Station."

"She's going to hate me, isn't she?"

"Yes."

Will groaned. "You could at least be more negative."

"Sorry, wish I could say something—"

"Don't say anything. Let me be the one. Just, if you could help me figure out a good way to do it..."

"Let me think on it. Meantime, being here for the kids is a good thing. Right?"

Will gave a look to his children, happily stuffing food into their mouths. Since the separation, they'd gotten used to veiled conversations.

"Yeah, okay. I'll figure it out, Tess. Really."

"Breaks my heart, you know. About you two."

Will hoped for a smart-assed comeback, but only one thought filled his head. "Breaks my heart too."

Tess hugged him and turned on some real estate cheeriness. "You're going to need me to help you find a new place."

Chapter 5

A dusky twilight swathed the patio deck where Tess and the kids chatted animatedly around a redwood picnic table. Sophie squinted to see them through the French doors, beyond the glare of her reflection, but the sounds of running water and dishes clanking in the sink drew her attention.

She moved toward him, fixated on his profile, and slowed under the cloak of nostalgia in the kitchen they had shared for so many years. "Are you on drugs? I mean, I was thinking, Will must be on drugs, because he *never* does dishes. Yet, here you are, *slaving* over the sink."

Will angled his shoulders to face her, a soapy plate in one hand and a sponge in the other. He seemed caught in deep thought and, Sophie was certain, a moment of unuttered sarcasm.

"You have to admit," she said, "you're out of your element."

"People change," he said, vigorously sponging and dunking the plate in the suds.

Not you. She stared into his profile, at the way his dark hair curled at the base of his neck, at that sweet spot she used to enjoy nuzzling when she curled up next to him on the sofa. On the other hand, it was quite like him to leave her wondering, expecting he might say something meaningful, only to crack a joke so he wouldn't have to reveal any feelings. *Feelings*, over the years, had turned into a four-letter word as he became more and more like his dad. He shied from deep discussions, preferring to tiptoe around the edges of the lake that was their relationship, seeing his reflection in the water but unable to dive in with her. If only he'd thrown her a lifeline once in awhile. Especially toward the end, she'd really needed it.

He sponged off two more plates and stacked them in the strainer.

"Just doing dishes, Sophie, not looking for verbal jousting."

If he wanted her to feel sorry for him, for his sorry financial state, it was working. And it was no small thing that he'd found her last night with Houdini. Despite their intention to divorce, she couldn't stave off the guilt. No matter the distance they'd wedged between each other, she didn't like the thought of hurting him.

"I'm sorry you saw me with Mitch last night. I mean, I'm sure you don't care, but—"

"Hey, sometimes you're the ax, and sometimes you're the chest."

She winced, and the sad set of his eyes added poignant emphasis that sucked the breath out of her. So many times, Will had been the ax to *her* chest.

He waved her off then. "Kidding. No worries, right?"

As always, his face piqued such emotional honesty she could hardy look at him without the twinge of loss. Their long separation had muffled much of that rawness, but how much longer before it went away?

She attempted to be stoic. "So, tell me, what's happened with you?"

"It's not complicated, Sophie. Company declared bankruptcy. Closed down my entire division in one massive bloodletting. You heard about it on the news. They just didn't make the management cuts till after the hoopla died down. That's why it never made your radar. Their budget for PR and damage control is pretty hefty, so no surprise there. I got a decent severance package, but you know how fast that disappears. I still have stock and my 401(k), though touching that is a last resort."

"And savings? The kids' college funds?"

"All under control."

"I hope you didn't gamble money in the markets, Will. You know how risky that is."

"Still watching my wallet?"

"You do have a tendency to be freer with our—*your* money than you should."

"Thankfully, you are no longer looking over my shoulder, nickel-and-diming me."

Emotion was backing up on her—the good, the bad, and the ugly. She straightened and squared her shoulders, tamping down the old urges to fight or take flight.

He paused mid-sponge. "Look, all you need to know is that we'll be *fine*."

"Fine," she echoed, in a whisper that unfurled her biggest insecurity: after the divorce, how would she, a single mom with two kids, be able to afford this house or another one with an even fatter mortgage? As a rookie realtor, her commissions were hardly making her rich. There was nothing fine about becoming a bag lady raising two soot-stained street urchins.

"I hear your imagination running wild, Sophie. Does no good to worry, and I don't need your stress on top of my own. Can't we be normal—as in, get along? We can do that, right?"

"Care to lay odds?"

He dropped the dish he'd been washing and braced on straight arms as he leaned over the dirty water. "Listen, I need my girls around me right now. Okay? I don't have any other family but you—I mean, these kids."

His admission did not come as a surprise, but the vulnerability in his voice—that did. She'd rarely seen him like this. Once, when he realized the big royalty checks for "Sophie's Kiss" were falling off, he'd confessed his panic at the thought of failing her; and he'd despised his father for predicting his music would be a dead-ender that would send them "straight to the poor house." Practically overnight, he'd abandoned music and given up his dream.

A second time at his father's funeral. As the preacher recited scripture, Will stood tortured and silent until the honor guard moved into position and fired so many rifle volleys, Sophie lost count. Each bullet had fractured the winter air and jolted her whole body. Through it all, Will's head drooped lower, his gaze locked on the casket suspended over a damp hole in the earth, his expression hardened into an aggrieved sculpture. Like now.

She bumped him out of the way with her hip. "Why don't you let me finish these?"

He bumped her back, harder, out of the way. "Obviously, neither of us wants to be under the same roof, but if you could let me stay till I figure out my next moves—"

"We agreed, Will. Just for the weekend."

"Or," he said brightly. "*Or...* you could let me stay until my condo closes."

"Which would be how long exactly?"

Running water masked a burst of mumbles.

"Excuse me?" she said, angling across his arms to turn off the water, twisting her neck to look up at him. "Did you just say four or five *weeks*? Oh, no. No, no, no."

"It's just temporary, and I'll be here for the kids. Isn't that what you always wanted? For me to be more present for the kids? Well, now you get your wish."

His goofy smile was infuriating. "Being present mattered a whole lot more when we were married. I don't know how we would manage that. I'm seeing Mitch now. I'm sorry, but tonight is all I can give you."

Will went back to scrubbing the pan, but each scrape sanded the fresh scab of their past until it ached, until Sophie felt compelled to apologize or offer some consolation.

"One of these days, Will, I'll earn enough to make the house payments, and then—"

Will laughed under his breath. "You've never made one house payment in your life."

"Well, things have changed. I've got a big deal coming up."

"Yeah, I saw your big deal last night. Think your boss saw it too."

A hot streak zipped up her spine. "You did not just say that."

Will scrubbed harder and glanced around, as if for little ears. "Oh, yeah. I did."

"Why now? You were never the jealous type before."

"I'm not jealous, Sophie. It's just—you two were on *top* of me. But, whatever. I don't care. See him, don't see him. Do what you want."

He pulled the skillet off the stove and jammed it into the water, charred chicken drippings and all. Water splashed and soaked his shirt, but he kept scouring a dull sheen into the pan; and it occurred to Sophie that her husband—soon-to-be-*ex*, man of few words and less inclination for chores—looked a lot like an adolescent boy.

She swallowed an all-too familiar mix of hope and fear, the same sobering cocktail that had waylaid her during their separation. "You don't see us getting back together, Will, do you?"

He looked hard into her. "Ridiculous. Of course not. You can never go back, right?"

He'd knocked her off-kilter, and all she could do was grapple for the many reasons they'd reached this point. She had done everything to get his attention—things well out of her comfort zone, and many a fight had ensued. Revealing how desperately she'd wanted things to work between them and pleading in the face of his single-minded dedication to his job had left her feeling needy, vulnerable, and weak. She'd pressed him to make things right, to help her fix their relationship, until one day he'd snapped and said words she would never forget—or forgive—and that had been the catalyst to file for divorce. And let him go. She stared at him now, reliving their last agonizing conversation, knowing without a doubt there was no going back.

"No. We can't go back. But you're acting like, I mean, is it because of Mitch? We're only dating. But you don't have to worry about the girls. He's a good guy—"

He dropped everything and stepped back, soapsuds sluicing down his arms. "The last thing I want to hear about is you and What's His Face."

He turned his back and walked away—an epic rerun of the past.

"Will, you have to move on and get out of my life."

Will spun and clicked his heels and thrust out a straight-armed salute. "*Das Fuhrer.*"

Annabelle and Keely stood in the open doorway to the back porch and giggled. They thrust out their arms stiffly in imitation of their father, shouting in harmony, "*Das Fuhrer.*"

At that moment, Sophie would gladly have sentenced him to death.

Will screwed up his face. "No, no, girls. Daddy was making a joke. It wasn't even a funny joke. Daddy is *really, really* sorry." He clapped his hands—the "on" switch to get not only the lamps to blink, but the girls to jump up and down. "How about we get Keely's fan up?"

Sophie watched her daughters skip behind their father and heard the stomping as they charged up the staircase. Her jaw muscles twitched as Tess tiptoed in and shut the door.

"*Das Fuhrer?*" Tess said. "Das fucked up. Why the World War II rerun?"

Sophie squeezed her eyes shut. "I swear, if I could just teach that man a lesson."

"What kind of lesson?"

"The kind he'll never forget."

"Oh, you mean the kind of lesson that proves what he lost when he lost you?"

Sophie stabbed a finger in the air. "That's the one."

"And how would you accomplish this *lesson*?"

"I don't know, Tess. The man makes me crazy. He's a mess. He doesn't even know where to start to get his life back together. He needs help."

"You mean like a shrink?"

"No. He needs, you know, to get out, and, I don't know, meet people."

"You want him to date? Like you?"

Sophie shrugged. "I don't know. He just needs to move on. Somebody needs to have a talk with him. He sure as hell won't listen to me—and why would he? I wing it every day."

"Aw, isn't that sweet? You're both virgins again."

"I'm serious. He wants me to let him stay here." Sophie opened the fridge, barely noticing the chills fanning across her arms, and pulled out two icy bottles. "Mitch won't date me if there's any chance Will and I could reconcile. Since there's not, I need Will out of my hair, and he needs to get a life instead of looking over my shoulder. We need a plan to get him, you know, *dating* so Mitch understands the divorce is really happening. Don't you think?"

"I so need my hearing checked. I thought you said *we*."

Sophie stuck each bottle into a pink koozie with puffy-printed words, "Doing kegels as we speak." She popped the tops and handed one to Tess. "You're my best friend, and you've known Will longer than I have. That makes you *ipso facto* obligated, doesn't it?"

"No, honey, that makes me *ipso facto* not going near it."

"But it was you who pushed me to go to Punk Palace to meet the guy *you* no longer wanted to date. This is your fault."

"You were perfect for each other. Can I help it if you screwed it up?"

Sophie shook her head. "We both screwed it up, and we're still screwing it up. We should at least be able to get along for the kids' sakes, right? Why can't we do that?"

"Because you're still mad at him?"

Sophie shook her head. "Is that horrible?"

"He hurt you pretty good, so maybe it's normal you'd still want to kill him. I still want to kill Jake, and it's been thirteen years."

"Sometimes I want to tear him up and throw his pieces to different parts of the planet." Sophie tripped through the mental minefield that depicted her last tumultuous years with Will. Was it any wonder she'd gotten resentful? She stared into the granite countertop, at the sheen of her ambiguous reflection. "I know, I know. I should let it go."

Tess was too quiet, staring gravely across the expanse.

"What?" Sophie said.

"I have to tell you something."

"Okay."

Tess pressed her palms out, placating. "This is between you and me, right?"

"Of course. What is it?"

Tess reddened as she squeezed her eyes and let the words tumble out so fast as to be unintelligible. "Will told me he wants to sell the house."

Sophie replayed the syllables in her mind until they made sense. "What?"

"I told him I wouldn't tell you. I lied. He should know I can't keep a secret, right? When have I *ever* kept a secret? This is *his* fault."

"But Will and I agreed we wouldn't sell the house."

"Shhh." Tess glanced toward the hallway and said *sotto voce*, "Listen, I've been thinking. Since you don't want to keep him—and you can't dismember him, even though that would apparently be fun for you—I think you should let him stay here."

Sophie cocked her head, Lassie-like.

"Sure, on the face, it sounds ridiculous, but he doesn't *want* to sell.

He just wants to get out of a jam; and he's kind of desperate, so you can understand his logic."

"Seriously, you're taking his side?"

Tess waved her hands ineffectually. "I told you his secret, didn't I? Thing is, if you allow him to stay here until he gets his shit together, you can guilt him into keeping the house. He'll see how the kids thrive here, and you too. He's an honorable man, Sophie. He couldn't live with throwing his kids out of the only home they've ever known. Plus, and this cannot be undervalued, he'll think it was his idea."

"Your logic and mine are miles apart. What about Mitch? Will would waste no time screwing that up for me. I'm telling you, Mitch won't date me if he thinks I still want Will—which I don't. But how can I prove that while Will is in my house?"

"Surely that's something we can handle. Let me put in a good word for you." Tess eyed a spot on the ceiling and lifted her arms like she was at church. "Oh, Big Guy Upstairs, Sophie needs a clear pathway to having sex with Mitch Houdini without Will mucking things up. Our girl is divinely horny. Send us a sign, Big Guy. We are wide open to your cosmic wisdom."

She paused for effect, until the doorbell chimed three times.

Sophie's eyes ballooned, and they clanked their condensation-beaded bottles in salute.

"Pinky-swear it," Tess said. "You won't let Will know I told you."

Sophie hooked her pinky around Tess's as she moved toward the hallway and saw the man standing beyond the sidelight under the spray of a pale front-porch bulb. "I pinky-swear it, if *you* pinky-swear you can help me keep my house. I can't lose it, Tess. I can't."

Chapter 6

Sophie hugged Jake Baker warmly, trying to get her arms around him without also embracing the cumbersome guitar case he carried.

Jake's wiry frame looked nearly the same as it had when Sophie and Tess first met him at a Punk Palace Wild Boys gig. Jake had been a guitarist—as accomplished with a six string as Will Camden, some said. Back then, he liked to sport the Duran Duran New Wave look. Now, a bluc Polo and long Bermuda shorts lent him the air of his college students. His handsome, angular face had fared well midway into his fourth decade, though longish hair and a scruffy goatee added that eccentric professorial quality thirty years in the making.

"It's been a long time," Sophie said.

"Five years, I bet." Jake handed her a weighty foil-wrapped gift in the shape of a wine bottle. "Place looks great, as always."

Tess's hug was more of a lurch in his direction. "Jacob," she said tightly.

"Hey, Tessie. You look good." His eyes lit up over a smile drenched in hope. "Your fresh factor is off the charts tonight."

"Don't start, Jake." Tess angled her jaw toward him to accept his lips on her cheek. "I see you brought your girlfriend."

Jake lifted the bulky guitar. "Thought Ursula might cheer Will up some."

"You thought his favorite guitar—that you cheated him out of—would cheer him up?"

Jake turned to Sophie. "I won it fair and square. You remember, don't you?"

"I do, though Will does not." Sophie wove her free arm around his elbow and led him inside. "He was three sheets to the wind, as I recall.

But since he hasn't picked up a guitar in a decade, I doubt even Ursula could get him to play anything tonight."

Jake's eyes roamed the foyer and up the empty staircase.

"Will's upstairs with the girls." Sophie exchanged a conspiratorial look with Tess, who wove her arm around his other elbow as they ferried him toward the back of the house.

Sandwiched between them, Jake's head swiveled to each woman. "Should I be worried? Is there a firing squad in my future?"

"Don't be ridiculous," Tess said. "We just want to chat."

"Okay," he said. "So I *should* be worried."

"Jacob," Tess said, "a firing squad is so... messy. Poison in a drink attracts far less attention." She raised her fresh bottle of beer to him. "Swig?"

He shook his head. "I'm good."

Sophie opened the patio doors and led him to the picnic table while Tess took the guitar and propped it against the wall beneath kitchen windows set high in the brickwork.

Jake slid onto the bench, facing the gently sloping backyard beyond the deck. "What are you two up to?" He had long ago exchanged his wire-rimmed glasses for Lasik surgery, and now his hazel eyes tick-tocked between the women who slid next to him in the light of three fat, flickering candles.

"Will's your best friend," Sophie said. "So, of course, you want what's best for him."

"Yeah," Tess said. "You'd do whatever you could to ensure his happiness, wouldn't you?"

Jake drew his arms to his chest and stood. "I just remembered I have to shave my back."

Sophie pulled him onto the bench. "He needs you, Jake. He can't stay here; it's too weird. We're done, so he needs to go home with you."

"Look, Will already knows I'd take him in, but my place is torn up with the remodel. As it is, I'm sleeping on a couch the size of a Kit Kat and pigging out on pizza every night. I love the guy, but two heterosexual men cannot share three crappy sofa cushions and come out alive."

"You see?" Tess said to Sophie. "You've got to let him stay here. I'm telling you, there's something perfect about this."

Sophie peered around Jake to glare at her friend. "There is nothing perfect about this except the grounds for murder. Even Jake thinks so."

"See, that's where you're wrong. Jake can keep Will occupied while he lives here." Tess looked at Jake. "Take him to bars, like the old days. You can introduce him to women, can't you? Surely you know women. You have a history of knowing women."

"Will knows women," Jake said. "Look, he won't do it. I've tried to get him to date for a year. Sorry, Sophie. When you guys separated, I thought he needed to get on with life."

"Of course you did," Tess said, "but if there's one thing I know about you, Jake Baker, it's that you give up too easy."

"Oh, now you're going back about thirteen years, right? I didn't give up. You threw me out. Maybe we ought to let Will find his own way."

"Spoken like the Jake I know, who only puts himself out when there's a payoff."

Jake tilted his head toward his ex-wife. "That's not true. It's just that, I don't know what the payoff would be for anybody here. Maybe I don't understand payoffs. Like I didn't know how great the payoff would be for paying better attention to my wife, or else I'd never have lost her."

Tess seemed to have no comeback. The way they were eye-locked, Sophie figured they were ten seconds from falling into each other's arms—except that she knew Tess better.

Sophie cleared her throat, breaking their trance. "Can we get back to Will? I feel bad throwing him out. Help me."

"Jake, just get him to date," Tess insisted. "Then Sophie can date Mitch without feeling guilty. That would work, right, Sophie?"

Jake turned back to Sophie with an illuminated light-bulb gape. "That's what this is about? You just don't want to feel guilty dating someone else while Will's here?"

Sophie felt herself shrinking. "Is that so wrong, Jake? We *are* getting divorced."

"You can't ask me to do that to my best bro. I can't blame him—"

"Nobody blames him, Jacob," Tess said. "We just want to make this situation work."

"Please," Sophie said. "At least get him out of the house. Get him motivated, maybe playing those guitars he's piling up in the guest room. Or better yet, talk him into selling them so he'll have some cash and I can boot him out again."

"Those old guitars aren't worth anything," Jake said. "They're not like Ursula."

"Ursula." Tess said the name like a redneck says *tree hugger.* "You always loved that guitar more than you ever loved me."

"Not true, Tessie. Ursula is not a guitar. She's a Strat that once belonged to Clapton."

"I rest my case," Tess said.

Sophie recalled the history of Ursula and how Will had purchased her back when "Sophie's Kiss" was topping the charts and cash was no object. "Will could not have been prouder of his prize possession," she said, "until he lost her to you in the bet over that damn song."

"'Venus,'" Jake said, as if that singular triumph stayed fired up on the launching pad of his memory. "Robbie van Leeuwen plagiarized that tune big time; but nobody ever called him on it, and he made a killing off that recording. And Will completely spaced it."

"He only spaced it," Tess said, "because he was drunk, and you and I were fighting—again—because you were so jealous. Of nothing." She eyed him sternly. "I see you getting your back up even now. It still bothers you that he dated me before you did. And before you start in, may I remind you, he and I had only a handful of dates, it didn't work, and then he met Sophie. End of story. That night you won Ursula, he got drunk to drown us out. And you took advantage."

Jake's bemused expression had devolved into something less friendly. "I think I remember it as well as you do, Tessie. That *was* the night you left me."

"You didn't deserve me."

They stared hard at one another, and Sophie was reluctant to interfere.

"Be that as it may," Jake said, "Will had no problem delivering Ursula into my very deserving hands."

Sophie turned her ear toward Jake. "Remind me again, what's Ursula worth?"

Tess shot her a vague warning that meant, *Let me handle this.* "You're a coward. You could get Will to date if you wanted to. How hard could it be? I could do it in my sleep."

"Then maybe you *should* do it," Jake said. "I'll bet you big time he won't do it."

"You're on. What would you give me if I could get him to date?"

"A second chance."

Tess feigned a groan, and Sophie observed their debate with the growing sense that Tess was orchestrating some quiet strategy, like she did working a big real estate deal.

Jake's words teased, but his expression did not. "You know you want it."

"Jake, Jake, Jake. We've already been down that road, and it was a deep, dark pit of demonic possession. You being the demon, me being the possession."

"That's my price, Tessie."

"Chicken shit," Tess said. "I'll do it myself."

Jake held his belly and laughed. "Like hell you say. Good luck with that."

"I'll find a way. You and Sophie have to work on your faith in me."

41

"Oh, I have faith, Tessie, that you'll fall flat on your face on this one."

"Oh really, Mr. Smarty Pants? Bet me."

"Bet you what?"

"Bet me the Strat."

Tess winked at Sophie. And Sophie, though she wasn't sure where all this was leading, felt in the presence of a true craftsman.

"You want me to bet Ursula?" Jake said. "No way."

"If you're so sure I can't get Will to date, what are you afraid of?"

"Nothing. I'm not afraid."

She held out her hand to shake his. "Then bet me."

"Why Ursula, when you know how much she means to me?"

"*Because* she means so much to you. It would prove she doesn't mean more than me."

"Okay, you get him to say he'll date, then I'll give you Ursula. But, if he tells you to go fly a kite, then *you* agree to date *me*."

"What?" Tess eyed him with consternation. "Jake."

"Those are the only stakes I wanna play with, Tessie."

Tess mulled it over—dragging out the suspense, Sophie guessed.

"Let's put a limit on that, shall we?" Tess said. "If Will says no way, then I agree to five dates with you. No more."

Jake grinned like he'd won a lap dance, and in that moment, Sophie elevated Tess's skill at getting what she wanted to the status of Donatello molding the bronze sculpture of David with one foot on the head of Goliath.

Then, with a straight face, Tess shook his hand.

Chapter 7

Will and his girls stood back and admired the newly organized Legos, coloring paraphernalia, and remnants of game pieces they'd separated into containers and stacked on the shelves in Keely's room. As a reward for all their hard work, he'd allowed them to pick out their favorite books before climbing into Keely's double-sized bed. He lay on top of the covers between them, reading aloud by lamplight, and wondered why he'd so rarely done this before. With their heads nestled on his shoulders, he read *Beauty and the Beast* and *Skippyjon Jones*—three times in a row—until the rasp of his voice caught up with his exhaustion.

Keely yawned and squeezed his arm. "I like when you're here, Daddy."

He turned and kissed the top of her head. "I like it too, baby."

"You're our dad," Annabelle's small voice said, as she snuggled closer. "So you won't never leave us."

"Of course, I won't. I'll always be here for you, no matter what."

In the quiet moments that followed, Will thought the girls had begun to drift off, until Keely sat up and leaned against him.

"Daddy, when did you stop loving mommy?"

His daughter's curiosity twisted Will's backbone into a sopping washrag. He pulled her against his chest and stroked her hair. "Oh, baby. I'll always love Mommy, just like I'll always love you. Even when I'm not with you, you're always in my thoughts." He lifted her up and looked into her eyes as his throat thickened. "You believe your daddy, right? Nothing is more important to me than you and your little sister."

Her round brown eyes pierced his heart, while his own eyes blinked damp reassurances. Why was he so damn sensitive lately?

Maybe because the girls were growing so fast. Now that he'd stopped racing through life like the paparazzi was on his tail, what he'd missed out on became so obvious, just as it had for his Dad. Annabelle had just turned six and Keely was about to turn ten. If only his dad were still alive to see them.

Keely snuggled closer and yawned. "G'night. Don't let the bedbugs bite."

"Sweet dreams, baby." He curled his arms around her, and when Keely's breathing indicated sleep like Annabelle's did, he rose and kissed them. For his final parental duty of the evening, he flipped on the Monster High nightlight and left the door ajar.

He had heard the commotion earlier, when Jake came in, but spending time with little people who didn't sit in judgment was preferable to big people who did. His financial straitjacket was constricting not only his bank accounts but his ego; and he could well imagine the inexhaustible questions that awaited him.

You sending out your resume? I know a dude in a suit and tie who knows a dude with a cousin who has a wife with an uncle whose high-tech wiz kid might have an opening—whaddaya say? You're not too good to flip patties at Cowabunga Burger, right?

Stepping into his big-boy shorts, he tiptoed downstairs, pausing on a creaky step to listen for Sophie. He felt like a belligerent teen, able to push all her buttons, break her rules, and tempted to do things on the sly she'd object to. No sign of her though.

Probably busy replacing the broken straws of her broom.

The kitchen still smelled of cherry pie. He snuck a slice, gulping it down while observing Tess and his best friend Jake through the window. The two sat on the same side of the redwood picnic table, chatting away like BFFs when the truth was just the opposite. They'd gotten married at the same time Sophie and Will did—literally, the same ceremony—but their marriage had only lasted nine years. Yet another interesting twist to the evening: Tess and Jake Baker, "together" after thirteen years. How lucky—or unlucky—was that little milestone?

His eyes scanned the porch and the darkness beyond for Sophie, but she was nowhere to be seen. To fortify himself, he grabbed a few beers from the fridge and headed outside. The night sky was as clear as ever but too warm for nine o'clock. He slid onto the bench across from Jake and Tess. A light breeze strafed his arms, forewarning another sweltering summer.

"Been a while since you two saw each other, huh?"

"Not long enough," Tess said, eying her ex-husband.

"Oh, I don't know," Jake said. "Maybe we should let bygones be bygones."

Tess looked down her nose at him. "You are so obvious."

Inside the house, the kitchen light flipped on. Will watched through the window as Sophie busied herself around the fridge and the microwave. With the sparks between Jake and Tess, it felt like old times. Except that time had removed the one thing he lived for—though he couldn't see it back then—the one true thing he'd come to believe was the reason he even existed: his connections. And not the business kind. Death and divorce were cruel teachers. Felt weird to be sitting there with all those old emotions running through him again.

The licks and riffs of Stevie Ray's bluesy "Pride and Joy" cut through the night air. Automatically, his brain pulled the album. *Rough Edges*, 1988. The chorus came around, and he leaned back, closed his eyes, and tilted his head toward the top frets of an imaginary guitar. He air-strummed the tune and, for an interlude, drifted back to the quiet balcony of their first apartment, the thick odor of summer rain in the air, Sophie dancing in cutoffs and a T-shirt, those tight thighs beckoning to Little Will and the Heartbreakers.

He palmed the remote that sat on the picnic table, pointed it at the window where the receiver shined a steady green light, and raised the volume. He squinted at the dusty speakers perched under the roof eaves, vibrating like his electric toothbrush with all that bass. Maybe he'd clean them for Sophie, if he felt generous.

The screen door creaked, and Sophie emerged from the house carting a tray of tortilla chips, a bowl of red salsa, and a crock of hot queso. In a surprise move, she sat on the bench right next to him. Ironic, he thought, considering the distance they'd shoved between them.

"Festivities starting without me, I see. Like the old days."

"Not quite like the old days," Will said, too aware of her proximity. "We're like the rest of the world now. Members of the Divorcee's Club. Who knew twenty-four years ago that things would turn out like this?"

Sophie balked. "Way to make it more awkward, Will."

"Hey," Jake said, "we have history between us, but we have a future too." He turned to his ex-wife. "Right, Tessie?"

Tess's look was a visual pushback. "No future for us, Jake."

"Tessie still thinks I cheated on her with one of my students," Jake said. He helped himself to a chip and dipped it in creamy yellow cheese that was already stiffening across the top as it cooled. "Never a student, Tessie." He leaned toward Will with an aside: "Despite how hot that girl was. You saw her. Party Marty? Beauty and brains that one. Aced American Lit without cracking a book. Heard she works for NASA now."

"How nice for you," Tess said, "knowing you conned a future

rocket scientist into space-docking with the Mars Rover."

"Ouch," Jake said. "Time has not inhibited your tongue, Tessie. I'm telling you, I didn't sleep with her. And it was only one slip anyway, when I was pretty sure you'd rather fillet me than sleep with me. Truth is, you spoiled me for all other women."

"Give it a rest, will you?"

"Hey," Jake said. "Remember when we went camping, before your kids were born, and we were sitting around the campfire eating that big fish Sophie caught? Blasting the boom box, and Sophie was bragging about how you knew every song on the radio?"

"I believe there was a wager involved," Tess said, "which Will won hands down."

"Damn straight," Jake said. "Sophie bet Will couldn't chronicle every song that played."

"He was a DJ," Tess said. "She knew he'd win. She was trying to make him feel better; she'd just shown him up, catching our dinner. Right, Sophie?"

"I knew he couldn't miss," Sophie said. "Not the Tunemeister."

Will slid his eyes toward her. "Assuaging my ego, were you?"

"Like always."

She pulled on her beer and he watched the way her throat worked as the liquid slid down.

"There was music in the air," Jake said, "and your husband knew everything there was to know about that. I'd be willing to bet he could do the same thing again."

"No doubt about it," Will said, with some bravado.

"Oh there's doubt," Sophie said. "You're out of touch now, Will. Stuck in a dark, dank hole when it comes to the new stuff."

She was egging him on, trying to get a rise. Two years ago, she'd have rubbed his shoulder and whispered in his ear, "You got this, baby." Even if he didn't. She'd since acquired an edge; now her tongue was a Ginsu blade, cutting him where she knew it would hurt most.

"You don't even know me anymore. How can you make such a blanket statement?"

Sophie scoffed as her eyes lit on each of them. "Okay, how have you changed?"

They stared at each other as he debated an answer. The only changes he could swear to involved his marriage, his job, his bank accounts, and his dad—all now dead. He wasn't sure how to verbalize any of those changes without shedding a tear and alerting his old man to send a lightning bolt from Heaven to strike him dead. He was grateful Jake intervened.

"Hey, man," Jake said. "Recognize this song?"

Will listened for a few beats, then tipped his head from side to side, cracking the neck joints like a prizefighter. "'Sugar in the Evening,' by Tiptoeing Two Lips." He'd recognized the obscure hit even before the words started. He rolled his shoulders, bobbed his head, and closed his eyes as his inner beat-master merged with the melody. What musician hadn't played those riffs before? He fought the urge to cackle fiendishly. "1988."

Jake pounded his fist on the table. "Outstanding. You still got it, man."

"You two had the world by the tail," Tess said.

Comparing the world he had then against the world he had now was a hard reminder that all he'd ever wanted was now history. "Things were a lot simpler then."

Sophie summed it all up with a dismissive quip. "Well, at least you knew all the great songs."

Jake didn't miss a beat, keeping the tempo light. "Still does. Solid gold doesn't tarnish, not in that bad boy's brain, does it?"

Indeed. Music was a million brilliant stars twinkling in his brain—one massive constellation that he knew as well as the feel of Sophie's lips. Nothing he didn't remember about those. That was the stuff he wished would dull and wither into a black hole. That, and the last conversation he had with her before she filed for divorce, the one that changed everything. She had begged him for some kind of emotional response about their relationship, other than a grunt. But he'd numbed himself to the arguments, and, if he were honest, to feeling like all he'd ever done was let her down. What he'd said that last day would be his crowning regret. The words had festered and eaten away at him, and now he deserved everything he got—which was apparently living with the guilt and no way to fix it. Nothing like burning the bridge to the Motherland so you can never go home again. Have another beer, Camden.

"What do you say, man?" Jake said, indicating the scuffed guitar case leaning against the bricks. "I brought Ursula. Want to play her?"

Too many bitter pills he'd swallowed this week. "Nah. I don't play anymore."

"How can you not play? Guy with your talent?"

"I just don't," Will said flatly.

Jake held up his hands. "Hey, whatever you say, man. I just thought—"

"What?" Will said, daring Jake to bring up the old lost bet, or the jealousy about Will dating Tess before Sophie.

Jake stared across the table, and Will knew he was contemplating if it was worth it.

"Nothing," Jake said. "It's nothing."

Tess and Jake exchanged a subtle look that Will couldn't identify. Something was brewing. They'd moved incrementally closer to one another.

That's trouble.

"So, Will," Jake said. "I know this lady in the UT library who just divorced her husband, and she's available."

"Seriously?" Will said. "A librarian?"

Jake waggled one eyebrow. "A sexy librarian."

"Please," Tess said. "How old is she, twelve?"

"Of course not," Jake said. "She's, I don't know, twenty-five, twenty-eight maybe?"

"No thanks, man," he said. "Way too young. Besides, it's been so long, I'd need a how-to manual."

Jake gave Tess an I-told-you-so look until her nostrils flared, and he refocused on Will. "You get back on the bike and pedal, buddy. Ask Sophie. She doesn't have a problem getting back on the bike."

"Why should she?" Tess said. "It's been more than a year."

Will gulped his beer as they all stared at him. "Yup. A whole year."

"Dude," Jake said. "If your wife can get back out there—"

"Ex-wife," Sophie corrected.

"My *wife*," Will said, "has a job. And a benefactor—said benefactor being me." He looked pointedly at her, and she turned away as if he'd affronted her dignity. "Plus a boss who's got the hots for her."

"He's not my boss," Sophie said curtly.

"Me?" Will said. "I've got other things on my plate. Like finding a job. Paying bills. Making up for lost time with my kids."

He felt Sophie's eyes on him, telegraphing a mighty loud "It's about time!" He mentally cringed, waiting for her to brandish the Ginsu. But she kept it sheathed, and he wondered if Tess and Jake had any clue. If they did, they'd surely scoff, "What did you expect? You were never around."

"But, it's not good to be alone too much," Tess said. "Why don't you date? Getting out and seeing women would be healthy. And you're free now, so you can spend time with any woman you want. Right, Sophie?"

Sophie jerked a shoulder. "Might as well. When it's done, it's done."

"And we are so done," Will said, delivering a scowl meant to look evil so she was sure to receive the full measure of his resolve. Or disdain. Or... What *did* he feel anyway?

"So," Jake said, "the guy you're seeing, Sophie. He's your boss?"

"*Not my boss.* My sponsoring broker. But what difference does it make?"

"No difference," Will said. "I think the men here think it's a little, shall we say, tawdry?"

Sophie contorted her whole face into an impressive "screw you."

"You need a jumpstart," Tess said. "What's it gonna take, Will? A lightning strike?"

"Nah," Will's gaze fixed on the splintering surface of the picnic table. "Lightning only strikes you once."

His memory—and his mouth—betrayed him with regularity now. Again, he'd skipped back in his head to the early years with Sophie, to days that had whizzed by in a blink, when he couldn't get enough of her and she couldn't get enough of him. He needed a muzzle.

Sophie's gaze met his then and rolled away on the crest of an annoyed sigh that reminded him they were long past reminiscing.

"What's your plan then?" Tess said. "You going to watch over Sophie's shoulder when she brings Houdini home?"

Will felt his backbone twist as he cycled through the ramifications of Houdini in his house. In his old bedroom. With Sophie. And then the sorest point of all, which he voiced loud as a fire alarm: "With the kids here?"

"She doesn't mean he'll stay overnight," Sophie said. "Calm down."

"Not yet maybe," Tess said. "But eventually."

Will let that sink in, though it didn't have far to go to mash his old private-property button. He stared right through his wife, waiting for her to dispute it.

"I suppose," Sophie said, fixating on some dark blur of trees beyond the patio lights. "I mean, eventually, he will. Maybe. I don't know. My life is officially off hold, and I can see whomever I want. And you should too. You're no longer tied to me, so maybe it's time to man up and hit the old meat market."

As if he ought to grow a pair? Jesus. "I get it, Sophie. You lead your life, I'll lead mine."

The air was dead weight around him, and if the abrupt quiet around the table was any indication, they all felt it too. Everyone took long swigs of their beers, and in the dearth of conversation, Jake finally spoke.

"You sending your resumes out, man? I know a dude who—"

"I'm not done," Tess said, shushing Jake with a wave of her hand. "What if I could make it worth your while, Will?"

Will groaned, much preferring a soul-squashing job-hunting inquisition instead of the ridiculous dating banter.

"Okay, Tessie," Jake said. "Who do you have in mind for my man? Some wart-nosed witch from the Dead Sea?"

At least Jake was on his side. "Thanks, but no thanks, Tess. Nothing would make dating again worthwhile for me. Maybe after my life settles down. Maybe then."

"What if I hooked you up with an old girlfriend?"

Sophie blurted, "What old girlfriend?"

"My old girlfriends never made a lasting impression, for good reason," Will said. "So, again, no thanks."

"What if she's, like, your dream babe?" Tess said. "What if she's the kind other men only dream of having?"

"Are you talking about *my* old girlfriends?" Will cast a doubtful glance toward Sophie, as if she could fill in the gaps of his memory. Nobody had been more his dream babe than her.

"Can't you think of anyone?" Tess screwed up her face. "Not only is she one-of-a-kind and gorgeous, she's worth a small fortune."

"Who the hell are you talking about?" Jake said.

"I'm just saying, she might have a lot of connections, and considering your financial situation, she could get you in front of some influential people. Get you back on your feet faster."

Will was stumped. Who from his past was wealthy? And gorgeous? And would consider dating him? And why was Tess being so cryptic? He stared at Sophie, then Jake, as if one of them would finally cast the punch line.

"If I could guarantee you'd have her in your arms once again," Tess said, "would you feel more like dating then?"

"For god's sake," Jake said, "tell the guy—and the rest of us—who you're talking about. Maybe *I* want to date her."

Tess shot him a glare. "It took you less than one hour to trade in a second chance with me for a total stranger."

"Hey, all's fair in love and war." He laughed and leaned still closer to her. "I'm kidding, Tessie. Put us out of our misery and tell us who the mystery woman is."

Tess blew out a big sigh, forewarning the end of her big tease, then got up and paced back and forth across the deck. "This is the deal, Will. You want to stay here at Sophie's, but she's got plans with Mitch. But if you're not able to ruin Sophie's mojo because maybe you're occupied— by say, *dating*—she'll feel better about letting you stay here. Right, Sophie?"

Sophie tilted her head, tightlipped, but Will knew that silence was screaming something unsavory, and Tess was not letting it sway her.

"So let me get this straight," Will said, watching Tess pace. "You want to hook me up with some old girlfriend so I'll stay out of Sophie's hair, just so she can date Houdini?"

"And so you can stay here till your escrow closes. That's what you want, right? Four to five weeks under her roof?"

"Well, yeah, but... that's all there is to it?"

Tess sat back down on the bench. "Not quite."

"Here it comes," Jake droned, rubbing one side of his face.

"Just go on, say, five blind dates over the next five weeks, like one a week, and then I'll hook you up with your old girlfriend."

Will busted out with a laugh, and even Sophie seemed surprised at Tess's proposition.

"I assume you're joking," he said, "but I'm going with a big fat *no*."

Tess gave Sophie a conspiratorial glower that was more of a shove, and Sophie stuttered into tag-team mode. He'd seen that move a time or two over the years.

"Tess is right," she said. "You staying here wouldn't be... *unbearable*, if I thought for sure it was temporary. You're forty-five years old. You need to get out. Date. It's not that hard."

"Yeah, you just need a little nudge," Tess said.

"You mean a wrecking ball?"

"Please," Sophie said, her tone tiptoeing on derision. "Back in the day, dating groupies was part of the gig, right? That's what radio personalities and musicians did, and I don't remember Will Camden having any problem with it."

Will couldn't help but think how quickly she'd turned on the sales pitch. Tess's influence? Or Houdini's? "Seriously. Blind dates? Five of them? And you don't think I should have a problem with that?"

"Why would you? Look, I know it's been a long time, so if you need help, I'm sure Jake can give you pointers. Or Tess. They could be like your personal *GQ*—which you should probably get a subscription to. Don't get me wrong. You're still a great-looking guy. You just need some, you know, tweaking. Time to enter the new millennium."

She studied his hair and his clothes with the superior air of experience, which set his molars on edge.

"Ah, you think I need to learn how to walk and talk like a new millennium man—versus dragging my knuckles on the ground— because you're such a dating aficionado?"

"You chicken, Will?" She flapped her elbows and clucked. "Bock bock, bock bock."

He felt like the unsuspecting gerbil dropped into a python pit. "Define *dates*."

"Meet and greet," Tess said. "You know, drinks and dancing, whatever floats your boat. Like when you and Sophie were dating."

"Come on, Will." Sophie craned her neck, eye to eye with him. "Where's your sense of adventure? What happened to the kick-ass guitar player who stayed out all night just because he could or played a set on stage with somebody else's band because everybody wanted you to jam with them? Everybody knew who you were; everybody thought you would go all the way in music. You haven't even picked up your guitar in, what, ten years?"

Great. She wanted a fight? He obliged, nose to nose with her.

"You might remember that royalties from 'Sophie's Kiss' were drying up fast—*and* you wanted kids. How was I supposed to support a family on the equivalent of a piggy bank? Did I think remotely that you'd want to live on a poor musician's tip jar? No. I quit music because I had to—and you wanted me to."

"You got scared." She poked her finger in his chest. "You lost your nerve. The Will I married, the all-night party guy, hung it all up for a safety net, and after years of playing it safe, you forgot how to have fun."

"Did you forget how safe *you've* been playing it? Just when you start to succeed at anything, you give up."

Sophie blinked. Her nostrils flared. Her lips twitched. But no words came out, and he knew she was holding back. The narrow space between them flickered with electricity while their audience acted like they were watching a movie.

"I don't have time for dating," he said.

"You know, I don't take your unemployment lightly," Sophie said, "but you do have some extra time on your hands. Good-looking women only. Right, Tess?"

"Of course. Look, I'm going to sweeten the pot for you. If you go out on five blind dates, I'll hand-deliver your old girlfriend." Tess paused a few beats. "Your old girlfriend, Ursula. Who's worth a whole lot of money."

Sophie sat up straighter. "Ursula?"

Jake practically shouted. "Ursula!"

The wheels turned full speed inside Will's head. Ursula, his pride and joy, before he lost her to Jake in that damn bet. Ursula, the rare Stratocaster worth a small fortune. Ursula, who could get him out of debt, with the right buyer. He saw where Tess was headed now.

"Uh-uh. No way," Jake said. "I'm not giving Ursula back. I won her fair and square. Didn't I, buddy?"

Tess waved a threatening finger in his face. "You just made me a deal, not thirty minutes ago, that if I could get Will to go on five dates while he's here at Sophie's, you would give *me* Ursula."

"Well, I sure as hell didn't think you'd use Ursula against me as a bargaining chip."

"Why not? *You* did. You offered Ursula right up when you thought there was no way I'd get Will to date. When you were sure he wouldn't do it, that I'd lose that bet and have to go on five dates with *you*, you thought Ursula was a fine bargaining chip."

Jake unfolded himself from the picnic bench and grabbed his guitar case from where it leaned against the wall. He hugged it to his chest, panic stricken. "Not fair, Tessie."

"All's fair in love and war, remember?" She leaned over the table and extended her hand to Will. "Now will you do it? For Ursula?"

Will felt a grin slide across his face. He couldn't help it. Getting Ursula back? Getting to stay in his old house with his kids? For five or six weeks? He squeezed Tess's hand. "Oh yeah. For Ursula, I'll date."

Jake slumped onto the bench with his back against the table edge, the unwieldy guitar snug in his embrace. "You tricked me, Tessie."

"Take heart, Jake," she said. "Maybe he'll screw it up royally and not get his five dates in. Maybe you'll get to keep Ursula after all."

"And you'll keep up your end of the deal? If he doesn't date five women, you'll date *me* five times?"

"Yes," she said. "Five whole times. But he'll do it. Won't you, Will?"

"Stampeding rhinos couldn't stop me." They both clinked beer bottles and took long swigs. He couldn't tell if Sophie was happy with this arrangement or not, but she was going along with it, so something in the Universe had righted itself.

"Who's picking the dates?" Jake said, raising his hand.

Tess spit her beer across the table. "Sure as hell won't be you. Goes against your interests for Will to win that Strat. If he goes on five blind dates, you lose Ursula. And if he doesn't go, you win five dates with *me*. Sorry, but to be fair, you have every incentive to sabotage this thing." She looked at her best friend. "Sophie will do it. That's the only way this works."

"What?" Sophie launched herself upright, eyes ballooning, arms flailing like the *Lost in Space* Robot: *Danger, Will Robinson.* "The whole point is to get him out of my hair."

Will's eyes traveled up her body to her face. "I feel so used."

"And when you send him on his dates," Tess said coolly, "he will be out of your hair."

"I'm not doing it. It would be too weird."

Tess and Jake shrugged in a collective *Sorry 'bout that.*

Sophie's eyes bulged. "Tess, this whole thing is your idea. You choose them."

"Hey, you planted the seeds. But that's precisely why I can't do it. I'm the final arbiter of who wins, so I'm Switzerland. Somebody has to choose Will's dates. It's either you or Jake the Saboteur, and we all know what his agenda is. It has to be you, Sophie."

"Now who's chicken?" Will said, flapping his arms. "Bock bock, bock bock."

Sophie delivered her most venomous sneer.

"Hey, you don't want to do it," Jake said, "I'm good with it. I'd rather keep Ursula."

"Sophie Camden does not turn down a dare," Tess said, "so I'm going to have to dare you on this one, girl."

"You're supposed to be my best friend," Sophie said. "This is so unfair."

Will spoke like the DJ he used to be, summoning his broadcaster's voice. "Yes, folks, Sophie accepted many dares in her impulsive, younger days. And this guy can describe a few in deliciously incriminating detail." Sophie rolled her eyes, which he took as permission to proceed. "Like the time we snuck into the country club and played tennis under a full moon, and I dared her to play with her clothes off."

"I remember that," Tess said. "Legend has it, it took all of five seconds for Sophie to go commando."

"She beat me three straight sets," Will said. "But in all fairness, I was distracted."

Sophie shook her head and squeezed her eyes. "Oh, for god's sake."

How fun to see his wife in the hot seat now. Brought a special warmth to the cockles of his—well, just to his cockles. "Me thinks you made a deal with the devil in your own camp. I don't know what you're up to Tess, but I kinda like it. My wife—"

"Counting down the days till that's no longer true," Sophie muttered, crossing her arms over her chest.

"My *wife* has to choose five blind *debacles* for me—let's call them what they are, shall we? And if I go on all five—which I will—I win back the Strat."

"Debacles they may be," Tess said. "But we agreed. They all have to be good-looking women. Right, Sophie? We don't want him suffering too much. They have to be pretty."

Will suspected Sophie's withering stare held some incarcerated rancor that was busy chiseling an escape route, but she was in it now. Stuck, like he was. No doubt she would fix him up with some real ball busters, pretty or not.

He wiped his forehead, ran a hand through his hair, and tried not to think about five women pawing and clawing at him. Better men than he had chewed off an arm trying to abscond from a scenario like this. On the other hand, maybe it would serve her right, seeing him with other women. Payback for him seeing her with Houdini. At the same time, he wondered what ulterior motive Tess had for this scheme.

Jake chuckled, apparently all in now, and gave Will a high-five. "I don't know whether to root for or against you, but I'm completely intrigued by how this may turn out."

For the moment, Will rode high on the crest of his potential Strat win. Winning and then selling that guitar would replenish the accounts sitting empty from that freakin' Ponzi scheme. If all went well, he'd be financially flush again before Sophie ever got wind of it. For the first time in months, he felt hopeful. *Damn* hopeful.

Sophie rubbed her temples, and Will handed her a fresh beer. "Kinda funny, isn't it? You're supposed to fix your husband up on five blind dates."

"Debacles," Sophie said, heaving a sigh. "Debacles."

Chapter 8

Sophie bounded down the staircase, pulling her red suit jacket over a floral print blouse. Monday mornings were hectic, but today she felt particularly scattered. And fatigued. She'd hardly slept two winks, so filled with nervous anticipation about what this day would bring; and then she forgot to shave her legs, necessitating the grannyhose she reserved for emergencies.

Will met her at the bottom of the staircase with two giant mugs of coffee and what was surely a manufactured smile. "Whoa, a power ensemble," he said, remarking on her suit. "Must be important stuff going on at Houdini Real Estate, huh?"

"Indeed," Sophie said, taking a mug. The heated ceramic filled her palm and the steamy aroma floated up to her nose. "What's this?"

"That would be coffee. With a shot of that cream stuff you like."

"I know what it is. *Why* is it? Why are you being so considerate?"

"Must there be some ulterior motive behind a cup of coffee?"

"Not for normal people."

"I'll take that as a compliment." His half-smile burrowed into one cheek, and he pointed to a small box on the foyer table. "You got a package from the Home Shopping Network. It was on the front porch."

Sophie rushed over. "Wow. I ordered this Thursday, and it's already here? I couldn't sleep, so at three a.m., between Benny Hill reruns, I watched the Russian Princess hawking her Kayfuyu Collection on HSN."

Will loomed behind her with a pocketknife. He nudged her aside, slit the taped folds, and opened the cardboard flaps for her. "Kay-fu-what?"

"Kayfuyu." She set her coffee on the table and dug through the packing peanuts. "Haven't you seen those commercials for Khorkina's Kayfuyu?"

Will shrugged.

"Really, Will? Ruta Khorkina? Former sixties model, like Twiggy? Russian Princess? None of that rings a bell? International jetsetter? Tabloid target?"

"Never heard of her."

"Of course you haven't. She's the one I'm meeting today with Mitch. She's his good friend." She hesitated to look at Will while dropping that last bit, and pulled out a jewelry box containing a platinum ring with a blue tanzanite stone. She slid it onto the ring finger, where her wedding band used to be, and admired it.

"Damn," Will said, "it's the size of a roof turbine."

"I love it. And what's this? A free gift?" She opened another small box containing a mauve-colored tube and read the packaging. "Kayfuyu Exotic Anti-Aging Handcream. Cool."

She twisted the cap off, took a whiff—sweet and earthy—and rubbed the velvety lotion all over her hands. *Perfect*, she thought, tossing her prizes into her briefcase. Now she'd have some things to talk about with the Russian Princess.

"Good morning, sleepyheads." Will was beaming at his kids, lugging their backpacks down the staircase like they were going to a funeral.

"Morning, Daddy."

"Happy Monday," he said, but the girls weren't having it.

Sophie was used to the kids' early morning grumpiness. Will was a different story. After his Friday night admission of money woes and Saturday night commitment to a dating scheme he might end up loathing her for, it seemed implausible that Will Camden would sport anything but a surly demeanor; yet Sophie could only describe him as chipper.

He looked physically intact. No obvious head injuries. Freshly shaven; longish mullet still glistening from his shower; toothy grin; and clean white T-shirt showcasing his larger-than-she-remembered biceps and flatter-than-she-remembered abs, tucked into non-holey jeans that sat low on his waist. Annoyingly attractive.

Wait. De-spiked golf shoes so soiled and scuffed his big toes were poking through. Nah, same old Will.

"I take it you slept well?" She took a hot gulp of coffee.

"Unfortunately, no."

"Did you get some good news?"

He gave a mouth shrug. "Not that I recall."

"Are you on drugs?"

"Nope."

"Then who are you, and what have you done with the father of my children?"

His wattage brightened. "Let's just say it's a beautiful day."

"Thank you, SpongeBob Squarepants. If I'd known you'd be this excited to take your children to school, I'd have recruited you long ago."

"I wish you had." Annabelle stopped on the bottom step, and he rustled her hair. "Got your shirt on backwards, Princess."

She fell into him. "Daddy, do we have to go to school today?"

"Sorry, pumpkin. Just a few more weeks and you're off for the whole summer."

Keely plopped down on the last stair beside her little sister and blew out a sigh. "I don't want summer to start. I won't see my friends till fifth grade."

Will pulled Annabelle's shirt over her shoulders, Tilt-a-Whirled her around, and helped her arms back inside the sleeves in four seconds flat. "Tell you what, we're going to be so busy having fun this summer, you won't even miss them."

"We are?"

Annabelle jumped and clapped. "Daddy, we're going to Shitterbun?"

"*Better* than Schlitterbahn."

"Better than Schlitterbahn?" Keely gushed. "We're going on a vacation? All of us?"

Will grinned like George Bailey after he got his wonderful life back. "It's a surprise. But I promise, this will be your best summer ever."

Keely turned to Annabelle, her former gloominess evaporated, and held out her hand. "Bet you five bucks we're going to Disney World."

Annabelle put a finger to her chin and announced in earnest, "I see your bet and I raise you to Vegas Baby."

Sophie and Will connected over their offspring. The family penchant for bet making was alive and well. "Las Vegas?" Sophie said. "What do you know about Las Vegas?"

"Mommy," Annabelle said. "Mrs. Palmer went to Vlos... Vlos Vegas, and she said it was spark-tackullar. She spinned a wheel and winned lotsa money and everybody was happy."

"Mrs. Palmer?" Will said. "Your kinder teacher?"

Annabelle nodded.

Keely's mouth twisted. "Everybody was happy till they got divorced. Cuz Mrs. Palmer got fat in Vegas."

"What do you mean, Keely?" Sophie said. "Mrs. Palmer is pregnant."

Will sniggered. "Guess not everything that happens in Vegas stays in Vegas."

Annabelle and Keely stared blankly at their parents. Will winked at Sophie. Again with the oddly happy grin as he knelt to Annabelle and swept her up in a bear hug.

"Nope, not Vlos Vegas, baby. Something even better. Daddy's got it in the works right now." He planted a big kiss on her cheek and set her down to knuckle-bump her big sister, gazing at both of them as if he'd never seen anything so delightful.

Who'd have guessed, Sophie thought, as the girls ran off. *Will Camden, back under my roof, being all attractive and interesting and daddy-like. Despicable.*

"What?" Will asked at Sophie's stare.

"You better not make any big purchases till you get your keister out from under my roof. And you'd better not be smoking the hooch either." She sniffed the air near his face, inhaling some sort of woodsy aftershave. "What are you wearing?"

"Offended, Sophie. I'm wearing a little something called Offended."

"So that means you *didn't* buy something you can't afford?"

"It means, I bought something before I got laid off, and now it's on hold till I'm gainfully employed again."

She looked down at her watch. "Which should be about what time?"

"About the time you get that giant stick out of your butt." Will looked at his watch too. "Shall we synchronize and see who gets their wish first? Oh wait, those are both *my* wishes."

Sophie clenched her body everywhere that was clenchable. "And to think, you will still be here when I get home."

He crossed his arms and leaned against the staircase rail, daring her. "Unless you can find someone adorable for me to pick up from the meat market."

"Ooooh," she said. "That's right. I almost forgot about your auto-emasculated disease. Maybe one day you'll be able to recover your dignity and find your own women to date. Meanwhile, I hope you enjoy the meat market I send you to. It's the one for hotdogs—like *you*, all lips and *ass*—"

"Mommy!" Annabelle shouted, running back to the foyer. "Did you say a bad word?"

Will's face was a smug caricature that took delight in watching her squirm into Mommy the Good Example Mode. His smile challenged her to get out of this one.

"No, baby. Soon as Daddy wins his bet and sells that guitar, he'll be all lips and assets."

Regular, decaf, hazelnut, amaretto. Sophie scanned the coffee carafes lining a serving table draped in crisp white linen, the usual fare for a Monday morning meeting in the Houdini conference room. She and Tess were first to arrive, but in minutes, they'd be mid-crowd.

Sophie had already maxed out on caffeine, but a croissant demanded accompaniment. She poured a creamy hazelnut swirl into her coffee and watched the shimmering black liquid fade to a velvety topaz. "What a weekend."

Tess tucked her auburn hair behind her ears, reached for the regular blend, and gave her friend a sideways glance. "Only you."

"Me? You're the one with the light-bulb moment. Using Ursula to bribe Will into dating was a stroke of genius. He's always wanted that guitar back. It's like lost treasure. I think he regrets losing that more than our marriage. I swear, I'll be so glad when that man is completely out of my hair. But really. Me, Tess? Choosing his dates? What were you thinking?"

"Please. *That* was the stroke of genius. You get to fix him up. And I do mean *fix* him."

"There's no fixing Will Camden. He's Humpty Dumpty after the fall. With a mullet."

Three coworkers filed into the room, bee-lining it for the coffee setups. Two were brand new to real estate, but even after being a member of the sales force for a year, Sophie still felt like the rookiest rookie of all. Maybe because this was her first real paying gig, after twenty years of volunteerism where the only requirement was to show up and do the best job she could, but then walk away when the event finished or she got bored—whichever came first.

"Think about it," Tess said, close enough to rub shoulders. "*Fix* him, as in teach him a lesson. You said you wanted to teach him a lesson, so this is your opportunity. You get to choose five women who can, you know, teach him stuff."

"That's just weird. I mean, we're talking about Will. My first true love."

She didn't want to imagine other women teaching him stuff. They had taught each other stuff when they were young. Intimacy with Will Camden had been her domain, until he'd shut her out.

"Relax," Tess said, prodding Sophie away from the gathering crowd. "The fixing I'm talking about is payback."

"Why? Because you would like to have given Jake payback? For cheating on you?"

"Believe me, he's had thirteen years of payback—ignoring that man is all it takes. But losing Ursula? That's the ultimate. We have to make sure Will goes on all five dates. Jake won't give her up otherwise."

Sophie chewed on a flaky chunk of croissant and washed it down. Walking alongside the length of the conference table, she couldn't deny the appeal. "Will has put me through the ringer, that's for sure."

"Exactly," Tess said. "That Strat is worth about three hundred grand. And you know what that means?"

Sophie stopped behind the chair where she'd parked her briefcase. She was too nervous to sit. Her eyes searched the clutch of sales staff. "I know. He won't make me sell the house."

Tess swiveled her chair around and eased into it. "Bingo. But to get Ursula, he has to go on those five dates so I can win my bet with Jake."

"Right, and then you'll give Ursula to Will."

"Yes. And since you have to fix him up, might as well fix him up good—with women he'll have nothing in common with. It'll be fun. Think of it as Sophie's Kiss-off."

Sophie wasn't sure it would be fun at all. It seemed the opposite of fun. Besides keeping her house, she just wanted to get naked with Mitch. That was the whole point. How did Will get to occupy a bigger space in her life again?

But then, as if the universe opened up and unfolded a brilliant pathway to wondrous wisdom, she saw it. There, in the palm of her hands, she held the supreme power of payback. For all the times Will had criticized her, for all the times he hadn't been there, and for the last thing he said that made a sham of their whole marriage, "I'm not in love with you anymore." All she had to do with her new power was wield it.

"You know what? You're absolutely right. Sophie's Kiss-off. I like it."

"Thought you might." Tess switched tacks. "You ready to meet the Russian Princess?"

With a deep inhale and long exhale meant to negate the coffee jitters that fueled her anxiety, Sophie mentally jumped the track from dating to deals and dropped into her chair. "No. I'm too keyed up."

"I don't know why. Ruta's not your client. She's Allison's, so don't sweat it."

In the year since acquiring her license, and with her best friend's mentoring, Sophie had transacted $850,000 in home sales. But splitting commissions to get her meager three percent wasn't exactly setting her world on fire. As the contracts got bigger, Mitch had taken notice and thrown her a sweet deal he didn't have time for. She had a feeling his generosity came by way of his growing attraction—he'd amped up the flirtations noticeably. After the deal's quick sale, he'd asked her to lunch. And then... sparks, which led to another lunch, stolen glances in hallways, and dallying for no good reason by the water cooler, which led to dinner and dancing and, finally, a daring foray on Sophie's couch—thwarted, thank you very much, by her ex. And now Mitch wanted her to hang out with him and one of his most influential friends, the queen of home-shopping networks.

"It's her nickname," Sophie said, keeping her voice down as people took their seats around the conference table. "I mean, when someone's called the Russian Princess by the whole world, it does put your own little life in somewhat harsh perspective. I feel like one of Will's old groupies again—out of my league. Like today I'll be exposed as a poseur—a mover and shaker by association only. Just the thought is giving me an equatorial hot flash."

"Celebrities are people too," Tess said drolly.

Sophie wiped her sweaty palms on a napkin. "It's not just that. I feel like I'm being lined up for a chat with the KGB. She's Mitch's friend, so I can't screw up. Thankfully, I'm not in the spotlight on this one. I'd implode."

Tess waved to a colleague across the room. "Think about something else, Sophie, like getting laid by Mitch. That'll loosen you up."

"The only reason you're encouraging me is so you'll know if the rumors are true."

Tess gave a palms up. "Wouldn't hurt to keep a tape measure in your purse, just in case."

"Not gonna happen."

Sophie's anticipation set her teeth on edge. Mitch was due any minute. She squirmed in her chair, the tailored fit of her red polyester-blend suit only exacerbating the discomfort. It felt tight across her shoulders and too snug around her hips. A zit played peek-a-boo on her forehead, PMS threatened her sanity, and her control tops twisted from her water-retaining belly all the way down to her toes. If pantyhose still had seams in the back, she'd look like a candy cane.

And now that she'd entered bitch mode, maybe she should have worn lower heels. Black ones instead of red. Gold earrings instead of red. Red, red, hussy red. Except for the pearls, she was all red, and it felt all wrong.

She looked at Tess. "Do I look like a fire hydrant?"

"I know some big dogs around here who like seeing you in scarlet."

Sophie's vision of men hiking their legs on her prompted a bout of giggles that siphoned some of the tension out of her. Maybe now was a good time to test herself.

She rose and moved toward the skyscraper's floor-to-ceiling windows and scanned the low-hanging clouds outside. Like she did every Monday morning, she took a deep breath, gathered some resolve, and willed herself toward them.

It wasn't like she could fall twelve stories from a window that never opened, but the thick glass that separated her from the panoramic cityscape and its dirty concrete foundation below provided no comfort. A fall at age ten from her grandmother's roof remained a visceral memory, and now, two feet from the windows, she relived the sensation of plummeting through the air. There'd been no lifeline to prevent the sudden impact of her tiny body into muddy earth, no protection from the awful thud that knocked the wind from her lungs. Soreness had radiated from every bone, muscle, and fiber when she'd crawled to her feet. Vertigo became her enemy after that, not to mention her lifelong vocation as a klutz.

"Just another foot to go," Tess muttered behind her.

Sophie jumped and screamed and grabbed her chest. "Tess!" She glanced about self-consciously, amid a stadium wave of muffled giggles. She backhanded Tess's shoulder, staggered toward her chair, and plopped into it. "Thank you so much for the jolt. Why didn't you just stick me with a cattle prod?"

"Sorry. Didn't mean to scare you. You did good though. At least a millimeter farther than last week. Next, you'll be making fish faces on the glass." Tess nodded toward the door. "Speaking of things that are scary..."

Twenty-nine-year-old blonde bombshell Allison Summers swished across the room in a hip print top and white slacks and sandals that depicted spring fashion more than business sense—a combination that worked well for her. Allison had shot out of college at full sprint and stumbled onto a streak of million-dollar deals. Appropriately impressed, Mitch took her under his wing and she never looked back.

Sophie had done her best to befriend Allison, but the effort lacked reciprocation. Allison forever looked the other way and any conversation they did manage was stilted, as if they both realized they didn't click and were too lazy to make something work that was so contrary to their natures. *Office pet*, Sophie thought. *And pet peeve.*

"You know," Tess said, "if you bought some boobs and showed them off like Mitch's protégé, you could increase your sales tenfold."

"You think?"

"Couldn't hurt."

Sophie hoisted an eyebrow and stared at breasts that belonged on a statue as Allison strode around the conference table in a calculated cantor. She had a tiny nose and a large mouth that pulled into a gleaming white, horsey grin.

"Nothing jiggles on her," Sophie said. "Not those boobs or those perfect thighs. She could squeeze a man's head between them, and he would die happy."

"The boobs or the thighs?"

"Look at the way she carries herself, like she's on top of the world."

"Whatever. I'd consider her for a date with Will, though."

"What?" Sophie pictured Allison's perfect thighs around Will. "No way."

"Way." Tess nudged her playfully. "I hear she's easy."

Sophie scrunched up her face. "Oh no. Not even. She is way too haughty and doesn't have near enough cellulite."

Contrary to her usual avoidance, Allison took a seat beside Sophie. Full pink lips pulled into a smile, á la Seabiscuit, as she loomed in close.

"Hey, Sophie. Heard you'll be joining us today when we give the Russian Princess the lake tour."

"I hope you don't mind. I'd love to see how you work this deal."

Allison's big round eyes narrowed on Sophie's. "Of course. Just remember, Ruta Khorkina is very important to Mitch, and to me, so I don't want anyone mucking it up."

Sophie's maternal instincts kicked in. She liked to imagine people she didn't like as somebody's child, to practice tolerance. "Of course. Really, I'm just along for the ride. I'm not trying to wrangle this deal away from you. Mitch asked me to come along."

Allison's gaze never wavered. "Apparently, he thinks you have some potential or he wouldn't have asked you to join us."

"I would hope so, but not for this deal with Ruta." Sophie held her right hand vertical. "I swear you have nothing to worry about."

Allison tossed her hair back. "That much I know."

And then the man himself appeared. Mitch Houdini gusted past the conference room windows like a northern jet stream, with his coat flapping and his tie swishing. The poster boy for expensive perfume ads, striking in his fitted gray suit and crisp blue shirt, silvery brown hair combed back with a touch of gel. He stopped inside the doorway and flashed a Hollywood smile.

Allison's cool hand grazed Sophie's. "Good to know we're on the same team. If you ever need my help, you know where I am."

Sophie turned to Tess after Allison had gone. "What was that all about?"

"That little display of sweetness? Allison marking her territory."

Allison met Mitch at the head of the room and gave him a hug, but his eyes had found Sophie's. His mouth curled up, he sidestepped Allison's embrace, and he headed toward Sophie.

"Uh-oh," Tess said.

Sophie brightened. "Jesus, he's sexy. Think he likes kids?"

"Only when the chef's out of red meat."

Sophie barely heard, unable to disengage from the sight of him.

"You're swooning, for god's sake."

Sophie elbowed Tess away and swiveled her chair outward.

Two male agents in gray suits beamed as they walked toward the coffee station. The goofy one with his hair slicked back like Fonzie winked, and from the corner of her eye, Sophie saw Tess give them a toodle-oo with her fingers.

"Martin's had his eye on you since you came on board," Tess whispered. "He's kind of cute."

"Please," Sophie said. "Is there a bigger nerd in this room?"

"Besides you?"

Mitch swaggered up and knelt between them. "Good morning, ladies." His feigned Texan drawl escaped through a dazzling display of teeth. "You're looking mighty pretty today."

Sophie felt flush with him so near to her thighs.

"Houdini," Tess groaned, "you are a disgrace to your Italian-Polish heritage and to rednecks everywhere."

He winked at Sophie. "And how are you?"

Damn, that man could make her heart sputter. Sophie only hoped no one else could read her body language. The last thing she wanted was to be the talk of the office or subjected to Mr. Slinky jokes. She tried not to look at his zipper.

"Ready for my coming-out party," she said.

"That's what I like to hear. Nice outfit. Fiery colors make your eyes pop—" his fists opened "—like starbursts."

Sophie mentally fanned herself. Maybe scarlet suited her after all.

"See you after the meeting, huh?" he said. "Looks like a capacity crowd."

With most every seat taken, Allison was forced into the only open chair, beside Sophie.

With a lingering last look, Mitch returned to the head of the table.

Sophie liked the way he moved when he opened his briefcase, the power in his hands, the strong cords of his neck under that starched collar—even the lilt in his voice as he greeted everyone. He was an expert at making people feel special, and this morning his likability quotient spiked through the ceiling.

Mitch Houdini sponsored over a hundred agents, but this morning he welcomed about thirty with the ping of a spoon on his water glass. He slid on his reading glasses and ran through the agenda: lead tracking systems, the newfangled copy machine that did everything but birth babies, the annual company party on Lake Travis, the upcoming frou-frou black-tie real estate gala benefiting Habitat for Humanity, and ways to curtail office politics and gossip, which drew quite the round of suspicious glares.

Sophie mulled Tess's remark about Allison marking her territory and decided a friendly overture might sand off any rough edges between them. And she had the perfect peacemaker.

Discreetly, she foraged through her briefcase and plucked out her new Kayfuyu hand cream. She leaned close to Allison and whispered. "I came across this fabulous hand cream from Ruta's Kayfuyu line. Want to try it?"

Allison leaned toward Sophie, her gaze dropping to the offering.

"Go ahead," Sophie said. "You'll love it. It's like velvet on your skin."

She uncapped the tube and squeezed. With a noisy sputter, a huge blob squirted onto the back of Allison's wrist.

Allison sniffed the musky floral deposit and smoothed it all over her hands and arms. "Mmmm. That *is* nice. Thanks."

"Sure." Sophie turned to Tess and flashed a look of triumph.

Minutes later, Allison began scratching her arm. As Mitch droned on, her scratching got worse, and before long her arms had pink swells that turned into angry red bumps.

"What the hell is in this stuff?" she said, her tone frantic.

"Just hand cream." Sophie took the tube and read off the ingredients. "I can't even pronounce these words." But she said these words just fine: "Oil of eel."

Allison shrieked and leaped out of her chair. "Eel! I'm allergic to eel!"

"What? Who's allergic to eel? I mean, how would you even know?"

"Sushi? Hello-o-o. I ate it one time and broke out in hives. Like I'm doing now."

The room went silent, and Sophie realized all eyes had diverted to Allison, bouncing in place and shaking her hands as if they were ablaze.

Sophie rose beside her and inspected the welts. Even Allison's neck and face were pimpling up like an acned high schooler. Who knew when the label said exotic it meant *eely* exotic. Allison's face looked on the verge of combusting.

Sophie remembered one of Keely's classmates who was allergic to peanuts and carried an emergency fix. "Do you have an epi-thing?"

"Sure," Allison snipped, "on the off-chance I'm going to roll myself in eels?"

Mitch called from the head of the table. "Ladies, did you want to share something?"

Tess said blandly, "Allison is allergic to eels."

66

"Eels?" Mitch said, rising in alarm. "How would you even know?"

"Sushi!" Allison shouted.

"You ate sushi?" he said, approaching them. "For breakfast?"

"No," Allison cried. "Sophie rubbed oil of eel on me."

"I didn't know," Sophie said squeamishly. "It's exotic."

Mitch wagged his eyebrows. "Kinky."

Allison slapped his chest, tears cascading down her cheeks. "This is horrible."

Everyone went still until Sophie suggested the emergency room. "I'll take you."

"Tess can take her," Mitch said. "Right, Tess?"

Sophie shook her head. "But this is my fault."

"You're coming with me to meet Ruta at the airport." He held up one hand, as if that were the exclamation point on the matter.

Allison whimpered, scratching her arms raw. "Seriously? You'd go without me?" Mitch shrugged and Allison flashed a hive-stricken glare at Sophie. "You did this on purpose."

"I didn't, I swear."

Mitch put some distance between them, his arms outstretched as if to keep her at bay. "You don't look so good, Allison. I don't want to sound uncaring, but there's nothing any of us can personally do about this, other than get you to emergency."

"I'll do it," Tess said, tugging Allison by the hand. "I want to try out my new camera."

Chapter 9

Mitch wrapped up the meeting with an announcement. "As you know, my dear friend Ruta Khorkina will be in town today. Allison Summers was going to spearhead the property tour of lakeside listings, but since she's on her way to the ER, Sophie will make the presentation."

Sophie almost choked. "What? But... but..."

All eyes turned to Sophie, glowing red as her suit in the spotlight. Did they think she'd sabotaged Allison on purpose? Did they expect her to stumble and let Houdini's esteemed big fish get away? Did they look at her and see a fire hydrant?

She felt pebbles of doubt lobbed at her polyester armor.

Mitch tucked his glasses into his briefcase and smacked his hands together. "Showtime, Sophie. You ready?"

"I feel so bad about Allison. Are you sure you want me doing this?"

"I have full confidence in you. Gertie's bringing Allison's listing file. You can get up to speed on the way to the airport."

Gertie Fishbein, the receptionist, stuck her rusty head of curls out from behind Mitch, thick glasses riding low on her wide nose. "Here's what I could find," she said, handing a thick file to Sophie. "By the way, Mr. and Mrs. Roberts are here. I told them you were in a meeting, but they insisted on waiting, so I put them in the small conference room and got them coffee."

"Thanks, Gertie," Sophie said. Then, to Mitch, "Give me a few minutes?"

"That guy Roberts always expects you to be available day or night. Thinks he's the king."

Sophie shadowed Mitch, stuffing the file into her briefcase as they walked out. "I didn't know you knew Henry Roberts."

"Not many multi-millionaires get by me. What's he buying?"

"He's interested in the Pecos listing."

Mitch scoffed. "The old guy lose some money in the stock market? Wait, let me guess, he's lost everything, and all he can afford is a cottage for eight hundred grand?"

Sophie stopped in the hallway near the small conference room. Behind the glass, Mr. Roberts thrummed his fingers on the table and fidgeted in his swivel chair. In the chair adjacent to him, Mrs. Roberts mirrored her husband's impatience.

"Eight hundred thousand dollars isn't beneath anybody," Sophie said. "They're buying the house for their daughter, as a wedding present. They're lovely people."

Mitch rubbed his face with a gaudy-ringed hand. "Ay, ay, ay. I've been trying to get the man's business for years, and in you waltz—a rookie—and snatch him up. I'm telling you, you were made for real estate."

"I can't take all the credit. I had help from Tess. But it's my first deal of this size, so I'm crazy excited." She started walking backward, toward the small conference room door. "We're supposed to look at the house on Wednesday, but let me see if something's changed, and then I'll be ready to meet your Russian Princess."

Mitch gave her a flirty smile. "You're going to be my date for the gala, right?"

She felt a flutter in her stomach. "Is that you asking me?"

"Is that you saying yes?"

"It's a month away," she said, burying the schoolgirl excitement. "I'll have to check my schedule."

She wheeled into the small conference room. "Mr. and Mrs. Roberts, I'm sorry you had to wait. I wish I'd known you were coming."

Mr. Roberts stood and shook her hand. His deep southern accent belied the razor-sharp mind that had poised him atop one of the most prominent high-tech firms in California, corporate branch in Austin. "Not to worry, dear. We knew it was a risk, but we wanted to have a look at that house before we headed back to Santa Barbara."

Mrs. Roberts sat in her chair like the prim southern belle she was and adjusted an ornate butterfly pin on the lapel of her rose suit. "We're leaving earlier than planned," she drawled. The woman had picked up right where her husband left off, which Sophie attributed to forty-some years of matrimony. They were in sync. "Tomorrow evening," Mrs. Roberts continued. "Can we see the house this morning?"

Sophie felt instantly torn. This was not at all good. "I'm sorry, I'm booked all day with another client who's in town just for the day." She pulled out her smart phone, perusing her calendar with the thought that no matter which client she chose, there would be unpleasant consequences. "What about tomorrow morning?"

Mr. Roberts deferred to his wife, who shook her head. "We're booked solid. What about tomorrow afternoon, say three o'clock?"

Sophie double-checked her appointments. "Three is perfect. Shall I meet you here at the office and we can ride over together?"

Mr. Roberts shook her hand again. "It's nice to work with you, Sophie. I feel like you're on our team. We know we can count on you."

"Thank you, that's kind of you to say. I'll do my best."

He chuckled and sandwiched his hands around hers. "Sweet girl. Isn't she Margaret?"

Margaret Roberts stood and pulled her husband's arm to leave. "Yes, Henry, she's a dear. Now, Sophie, our flight leaves at six-thirty p.m. We'll have just enough time for a walk-through."

Henry pulled Sophie with him as they wandered toward the lobby. "If the house is what we're hoping for, I'll write you a check."

"Checks are good." Sophie imagined the commission she was about to earn on this one, her biggest yet. It would go toward making her first house payment and, for the first time ever, she'd have money enough in the bank and wouldn't have to rely on Will.

"You're going to love the house," she told them. "I'm sure your daughter and her new husband are going to be pleasantly surprised by your generosity."

Mr. Roberts looked down his bulbous nose as they entered the Houdini foyer. "My dear, she expects it."

"Oh," she said with a nervous laugh. "Kids. You want to give them things you never had growing up, and hope you're not spoiling them by giving them too much."

The elevator opened and the couple got in. "We had everything, dear," Mrs. Roberts said. "So do our spoiled children. See you at three tomorrow."

Sophie stood with Mitch under the awning at Austin-Bergstrom International Airport's passenger pick-up, trying to channel a professional demeanor. According to her exhaustive research, which she committed to memory, the woman she was about to meet had descended from real Russian royalty. And that was just for starters.

Ruta Khorkina's talent for the runway was discovered in the late sixties when she was a pre-teen. Though Twiggy's fame overshadowed her modeling career, Ruta made millions as the "Russian Princess." She married a British royal and divorced him on their one-year anniversary, which set the tabloids on fire. The paparazzi blitzed the public with images of Ruta, topless on a yacht in the Riviera, bejeweled and besequined at posh nightclubs, and mugging with celebrities. Six weeks after the first marriage ended, she settled down with a little-known British actor, followed one month later by yet another divorce and another wedding in Madrid to a regular Jose that lasted eighteen months. Husband number four was Griffin Hayworth, a wealthy American with fingers in media, airlines, and resorts. During almost twenty years with him, she had developed her own lines of haute couture, jewelry, and accessories in two product lines called The Princess Collection and Kayfuyu.

And products containing exotic eel oil.

"What Ruta wants, Ruta gets," Mitch said. It was the line he'd repeated three times already in preparing Sophie for the meeting.

She paced in tight circles. "That's just making me more nervous."

Mitch rubbed her shoulder. "Relax. She's really down-to-earth. Just don't forget, a deal with Ruta could make your career. Or break it. But let's not get ahead of ourselves."

"Meetch Houdini." A six-foot amazon of a woman, who reminded Sophie of Ivana Trump in a form-fitting red silk suit, fell into Mitch's arms. He picked her up and twirled her in a bear hug, her black pumps a foot off the ground. Two pale, heaving breasts nearly overflowed from a white silk tank as she grinned and wriggled down his chest.

"Ruta," he said, in a sexy growl. "You are a breath of fresh air."

Sophie watched it all in slow motion, a wave of nerves undulating through her stomach. Maybe the rumors of their old affair were true. They were like long-separated lovers, a younger man, an older woman... with some nice work done.

Ruta was impossibly magnificent for her age: face velvety smooth with high cheekbones and pouty lips, an angular chin with no trace of middle-age jowls, and no neck wrinkles and shallow gullies from lost elasticity. With spun gold hair scooped up in a bun and the faint scent of lemons blossoming around her, Sophie gave her a fresh factor of ten, plus one. Ruta was striking and regal. And really tall.

Two skycaps pushing hand trucks off-loaded an entire pallet of suitcases, garment bags, and carry-ons into the limo's trunk. The woman had packed for more than a day trip. A strapping man in an expensive silk suit oversaw the transition. Sophie imagined the guy in the boxing ring. He shook Mitch's hand, eye to eye, both about six-four.

Ruta wagged her finger, counting off each piece. "Jimmy," she said to the man. "Make sure eez all there."

Jimmy did as asked. Ruta shouldered a large bag with a silky Asian print, and Mitch guided her toward the limousine.

"I want you to meet Sophie Camden, one of our brightest new agents."

Ruta extended a bony, freckled hand. She wore a classic wide-band ring with diamond-cut emeralds and diamonds in a floral pattern that overpowered her French-tipped manicure and sparkled like a Christmas-tree ornament.

"Sophie," Mitch said. "This is Ruta Khorkina."

Ruta's Russian accent was thick and sturdy, and her mouth moved as if her tongue wrestled with marbles. "Nice to meet you, darlingk."

The great and powerful Ruta Khorkina had spoken to Sophie the Amateur, and it was as intimidating as the bellowing Wizard of Oz. Sophie heard her own voice squeak, "Nice to meet you, Ms. Khorkina." Like a munchkin from the Lollipop Guild.

She shook Ruta's hand and smiled up at her, but the twinkle Ruta displayed for Mitch had paled. Sophie sensed the reason: two women, blood red suits. A power clash.

Mitch explained about Allison's mishap and indicated that Sophie would take over. Sophie plastered on a weak smile and groaned about her starring role in said mishap.

"Fine weet me," Ruta said with a shrug. "Someting about that girl. She tries too hard. You don't try too hard, all right?"

"Yes," Sophie said. "I mean no, I won't try hard. I mean, I *will* try, but, you know, definitely not hard."

She gave a self-conscious laugh, when Mitch stepped in. "So, are we ready?"

Jimmy, Ruta's bodyguard, possessed a demeanor sure to deflect anybody messing with his charge. He watched closely as the limo driver swung open the heavy door and motioned his passengers inside.

Ruta deferred to Sophie. "After you."

Sophie climbed in and eased onto the seat.

Ruta bent as if she were getting into the limo and tossed her giant bag onto the opposite seat. The bag had a narrow leather bottom and a huge opening with a button closure between the handles instead of a privacy flap, the kind you could fit a VW in. The emblem on the bag read *Kayfuyu!* Ruta folded herself like Origami and moved to the rear-facing seat across from Sophie. Her movements seemed awkward, and Sophie figured at six feet tall—a height no woman in her family had ever approached—Ruta must find it challenging to maneuver in such a confined space. But once situated, she gracefully crossed her tanned, endless legs and rifled through her bag, withdrew a shiny gold compact and applied bright red lipstick.

"Meetch," she called out. "I could use stiff drink."

"I've got just what you need," he answered, from the sidewalk. "Stocked up on the hard stuff for you."

"I love the hard stuff."

Sophie inspected her own legs, which fit her five-foot-two frame quite nicely—willing them to look as long and sexy as Ruta's. She crossed one leg over the other, thinking they may not have been as bronzed or spa-buffed—and maybe under her grannyhose a temperate grassland thrived on her thighs—but Mitch had gushed over them only Friday night. Those are some great gams, he'd said.

She wondered what Mitch thought now as he tripped over those great gams trying to negotiate a seat between them. Propelled forward, he came to an abrupt stop with his face in Ruta's lap.

Ruta threw her head back and laughed. "Yeah, baby, straight for the hard stuff."

He pulled himself up and adjusted his coat and tie, snickering with only a trace of embarrassment. "Sorry," he said, relocating Ruta's bag to the middle of the floor and settling into the seat.

When the limo left the airport, Mitch launched into consummate host mode, foraging for three highball glasses and a bottle of Stoli from a low-level cabinet.

"None for me," Sophie said, pressing a palm at him.

"Nonsense," Ruta said. "It is cocktail hour, no? I don't trust someone who doesn't drink with me. Where I come from, eez standard practice."

Sophie was unfamiliar with the standard practices of international celebrities, but she did know, *What Ruta wants, Ruta gets.*

Mitch cocked his head toward their guest. "So let it be written, so let it be done."

Cocktail parameters thus established, Sophie said, "Um, I guess maybe just one."

Mitch poured three fingers into each glass, and he and Ruta threw theirs back straight. To Sophie's he added generous splashes of cranberry juice. Nice he remembered her status as a liquor lightweight but, even diluted, the vodka burned its way down her throat. However, after the first three glasses, she hardly noticed.

Halfway through the 45-minute ride to the Lake Travis listing, Ruta nestled into the luxurious leather of the limo, one hand holding a highball and the other gripping her cell phone. She looked every bit the billionaire heiress of Khorkina-Hayworth Industries.

"Nonsense, Griffin," she spouted into the phone. "Eez business trip and you know eet."

Mitch talked on his cell phone too. He didn't even have to try to monopolize the auditory space in the car. It came naturally, all rolled up in his fast-paced, smooth-talking sales package. Sophie felt like she ought to be talking to somebody too, so she called Tess to check on Allison.

"That girl's as squirmy as a seal in a shark tank," Tess said. "Doctors shot her up with epinephrine, gave her oxygen, and hooked her up to an IV. With any luck, they'll knock her out before I do."

Sophie heard Allison screech in the background. "Tell Sophie, payback's a bi—"

The voices sounded muffled after that, with some apparent phone wrangling.

Tess said hurriedly, "Allison said to tell you she hopes you and Ruta are hitting it off, and she will pay you back with part of her commission for pinch hitting."

Allison yelped, more phone scuffling ensued, and the line went dead.

Sophie hiccupped and poured herself another half glass of vodka with a shot of cran, while admiring Ruta's carriage and demeanor, which transcended couture clothing and fine jewelry. The Russian Princess was the ultimate intimidator, comfortable in the knowledge of her station, self-assured, collected, and directed in a way that Sophie only aspired to be. Around Ruta's celebrity, she felt upgraded to first class, eligible for cutting to the front of the line, deserving of the hot hand towels divvied out by airline attendants with tongs. It was a nice feeling, first class. In fact, she felt pretty good all over. *Hiccup.*

Ruta continued to argue with her phone, her free hand waving emphatically. "Griffin, how I can conveence you what I do eez not your business anymore? I dee-vorce you." By way of explanation to Sophie, she circled a finger around her ear.

Like everyone else in the country, Sophie had seen Griffin Hayworth on the news. Ruta's fourth husband was a pasty, middle-aged white guy. An eccentric recluse. Sophie couldn't comprehend how he ever hooked up with the vibrant Russian Princess—and for twenty years.

Ruta sighed as she clicked off her phone, tossed it on the floor, and stomped it with the pointy toe of her stiletto. She followed with an obscene hand gesture.

"Men. Can't leeve with them, can't shoot them. What else can you do?"

Get them to date someone else, Sophie thought. And make them suffer.

Mitch's brows knitted above his long Roman nose, and he covertly bobbed his head toward Ruta, a hint that now was a good time to talk about the listings.

Sophie breathed deeply to shore up her confidence. "I'd like to talk to you about the properties, Ms. Khorkina." She pulled Allison's file and a brochure out of her briefcase. "The first one is in Lakeway, a seven-bedroom Spanish villa, right on Lake Travis with more amenities than you can imagine. The asking price is six million, but I think we can get it down to five-five, possibly five-one."

Ruta took the brochure and set it on the seat beside her without looking at it. "You are married, Sophie?"

Sophie sipped her drink. "Er, uh, no. Well, not anymore."

"Children?"

"Two daughters. Six and nine."

"Ah, nice leetle family."

Ruta looked at her gleaming platinum, gold, and diamond watch and then at Mitch with his cell stuck to one ear, shrugging that his conversation couldn't be helped.

Ruta continued. "You remind me of seester. Half seester. Tiny like you and my father. Not redwood like me. She has two children also. I have not seen her for many years, since she married a man who hates my guts." She grew quiet and gazed out the window.

Sophie waited to see if Ruta planned to divulge more, then downed the last of her drink and pointed to the brochure. "The Lakeway property sits up on a thirty-foot bluff, so views of the Hill Country and the lake are magnificent. I was there last week at sunset, on a property tour, and I can tell you—"

"You are sleeping with Meetch?"

Mitch's eyes cut toward Ruta. Sophie gulped her drink and hiccupped, covered her mouth with her fist. She had fantasized about straddling Mitch Houdini in this very limo, if she was honest, naked under an open moon roof—getting to know Mr. Slinky intimately while screaming out in a wildly cosmic orgasm. *Hiccup.*

She tried to sound professional and detached from the emotional yarn of her personal life. "No, not sleeping with him, but I am in the middle of a divorce."

Ruta's mouth curled to one side. She leaned forward in her seat with furtive gray eyes that took pleasure in secrets. "With Meetch around, most women wind up dee-vorce."

"No, no. That's not the way it is. I've been separated from my husband for a long time, so you see, it's way past time to get a dee-vorce."

"How your husband likes you doing beez-ness with Meetch?" Smile lines formed around Ruta's mouth but not the taut skin of her forehead. "Mine eez green as pea soup."

"Well, it's really not my husband's—" *hiccup* "—my ex-husband's beez—er, business."

"Come, come, darlingk. Meetch eez wolf. I cannot imagine a man with wife beautiful like you would be happy she rides around town with beeg-est playboy in Texas."

Mitch disconnected his call and tucked the cell phone into his pocket, settled back with one arm over the seat behind Ruta and one leg crossed over the other. His subtle smirk alerted Sophie to the fact that he was now paying close attention. And, strangely, the limo was leaning.

"As I said, I'm getting a divorce." *Hiccup.* "So, first off, what I do is not my ex-husband's beez—business. And third, I'm not just riding around town with Mitch. I mean, we're in a limousine, yes, but it's strictly a beez—*business* pros-position."

She laughed and tossed her head back as her eyes drew spirals on the ceiling. "Well, it's not a pros-position. I mean, it is, but not in the sex-shual sense."

"Word of advice, darlingk. I am married four times. I know tings. Watch out your husband doesn't go off the deep end."

Sophie tried again to straighten up, ignore Mitch's intense gaze. And stop laughing. *Hiccup.* "Will and I, we work at having a good, flendy—*friendally* relationship, because we have two kids who need us to be thivil—er, thiv— thiv— Agreeable. But I've got a plan to get him out of my hair, if you know what I mean. I'm fixing him up."

Ruta leaned forward. "How you *feex* him?"

And then Sophie realized she'd divulged too much—but who could blame her when her social gauge was soused?

"Fixing him up?" Mitch said. "I thought he was a Casanova."

Sophie flapped a dismissive hand. "Of course. Totally. I mean, *ppffftt.* He does his thing, and I do mine. He's dating all kinds of women. We just made a silly bet, that's all. And he lost."

Ruta cut her gaze toward Mitch and waved toward the near-empty bottle of liquid fire. Mitch started to fill Ruta's glass when she took the bottle and offered it to Sophie.

"More wodka, darlingk?" Before Sophie answered, Ruta poured a full glass—no cran to dilute it. "You are feexing your husband on dates?"

Sophie felt Mitch's eyes zero in on her, a reminder that Will being at her house was a sticking point. "He's, you know, almost my ex-husband."

"But he's definitely moving on?" Mitch persisted. "Not hoping to get back with you?"

"Of course not. I cann-nn-not wait until he's out of my house and out of my hair."

Ruta was still stuck on the "feexing up" aspect of things, and delighted by the idea, if her toothy grin was any indication. "Dear, you are picking new wife for your husband?"

Sophie hadn't thought of it in those terms. What if he did decide to remarry? Her kids would have a stepmom—someone to drive them all crazy, fighting over weekends and holidays and who knows what else. The prospective misery made Sophie's stomach turn, but before she could protest, she doubled over and tossed her wodka right into Ruta's bag.

Kayfuyu!

And that's when the lights went out in first class.

Chapter 10

The icy rag on her forehead shocked Sophie awake, forcing her thickened lids to scrape across her throbbing eyeballs. Her skull had that massive, rattling, rumbling, freight-train quality, and she groaned in attempt to sit up. The wet rag tumbled down her face and pajama top and landed in her lap, where it chilled her thighs and infused the pale cotton sheet covering her with a big Rorschach blotch.

In the blinding glare of the sun through her bedroom windows, she squinted at the cherubic faces of Annabelle and Keely, perched on either side of her and grinning as if she'd woken from a coma. On opposite sides of the bed, Tess and Will perused her with a tad less fascination.

Will gave his *Young Frankenstein* impression. "It's alive!"

Sophie moaned, her tongue fat and uncooperative. "I dreamed I was a volcano, spewing molten lava all over the mountainside. People were running for their lives and screaming."

"Mount St. Sophie." Will handed her a glass of water and three ibuprofens, then a large pan. "Barf bowl, if you get sick again."

On hands and knees, Annabelle and Keely inched toward their mother, four round eyes watching as she downed the pills and every last drop of water.

"Freud might say you're manifesting your deep, dark, very recent past," Tess drawled before taking the rag from Sophie's lap and disappearing into the bathroom.

"You know you barfed on your client," Will said, entwining his arms across his chest in an uncanny imitation of the principal who caught her in the lav dying her hair green. "Or rather, you barfed into her very expensive purse, and then you passed out cold. They brought you home around lunchtime, and you've been snoring ever since."

She glanced at the clock. Six-thirty? The memories whooshed back and Sophie grasped with agonizing clarity how appalled Ruta must have been. And Mitch.

"Please, tell me I didn't do that. I didn't even get to show Ruta the properties." Things could not have gone worse if she'd stripped to her birthday suit in the limo with Ruta watching. "Omigod, is that *all* I did? I only barfed?"

Tess held a fresh rag to Sophie's forehead. "Yes, Sophie. You *only* barfed on Mitch's biggest client. Other than that, Ms. Earhart, how did you enjoy the flight?"

"This can't be happening," Sophie said, devolving into tears and slumping into her pillow. If she could die right now, she'd be grateful. Since that wasn't likely, she blamed Will. "The kids barf, you barf, I barf. We all barf. We're a family of barfers."

Will air-braked her tirade with his palms. "Take it easy."

"You want a hairy dog, Mommy?" Annabelle asked.

"You mean hair of the dog," Tess said. "Mommy might like a little hair of the dog after the rough day she's had."

Sophie groaned and softened her tone for Annabelle. "No, baby. Mommy needs rest."

Brewsky jumped on the bed and padded gingerly between Sophie's legs, his glassy, gold gaze stuck on his mistress. Their decade-long love affair made her feel somehow less miserable—never mind that the measure of solace her boy cat bestowed was directly proportional to the tuna treats she lavished on him. He pushed his furry white head against her hand and insisted she rub both sides of his bony face in their standard pampering ritual.

"What is it, sweetie?" Sophie mewled. "You worried about me?"

Twelve pounds of warm gold tabby crouched between her breasts, his tail flicking, his eyes at half-mast, and his whole-body purr rumbling through her. Then he stiffened and stretched his neck, made gasping, gagging sounds, and horked up a three-inch hairball.

"Eeeww!" The girls screamed and scrambled off the bed.

Brewsky followed, much lighter on his feet.

Sophie gaped at the tepid gift on her chest, its accompanying bile bleeding into her pajama top. Will blanched and hunched forward, covering his mouth.

"Don't you dare," Sophie shouted.

Tess surveyed the scene. "You really are a family of barfers. Can I interest you in a little hair of the *cat*?"

Sophie held the rag to her forehead and curled into fetal position. Her eyes burned, and hangover hammers pounded her gray matter black and blue. Oh, to put herself out of her misery. With her stomach somersaulting, she verged on a crying jag and waved everyone out.

"That's it. Please, all of you, I want to be alone." For once, she was relieved Will was there to handle the kids.

"That's all right," Tess said. "I've got appointments. Call me when you're up to it."

Sophie grunted as Will tossed her a fresh T-shirt. The girls left wet kisses on her cheeks and he ushered them out, leaving Sophie to suffer in peace and quiet.

An hour later, the air conditioning wafted a comforting relief, but her head still hurt too much to allow more sleep. She hobbled to the bathroom, dragged herself into a hot shower, and slouched under the hard-hitting stream. Goosebumps exploded across her skin. When she'd massaged the shampoo into a foam farm on her head, she heard a knock on the door.

"Soph?"

Sophie tried to find her calm center as she spoke through a cloak of steam and suds. "What's so important that you're barging into my bathroom?"

"You have a visitor," Will said. "But you're right. He's not important. Want me to send him away?"

"Him who?"

"Him Houdini. Figured you wouldn't want to be caught dead without your paint job, so maybe I ought to handle him for you, tell him you'll see him at work or something."

Mitch? At her house? She looked a disaster. "Ask him to wait ten minutes and I'll be down." She slipped her hand through the open shower door and grabbed a towel off the rack, wondering which would be worse: Will handling Mitch, or looking Mitch in the eye after he'd seen everything she ate for breakfast, all pretty and pickled and packaged in a purse.

"You sure?"

When would that man ever leave her alone? "Yes!" Her head felt busted open from shouting. See what he made her do?

She dried off and dragged a comb through her wet hair and, on viewing her pale reflection, gave herself a Fresh Factor of three. Her eyes were as swollen as pufferfish. Maybe just a bit of mascara, she mused. Waterproof or soap-off? She still made mascara choices based on the odds she'd be brought to tears at some point during the day. Black smears were so unattractive. But she would waste no more tears on Will Camden. *Soap-off it is.*

She threw on a gauzy, yellow summer dress—never mind that it was too cool to start flouncing around in spaghetti straps.

Panties. She couldn't forget panties. Not after Friday night's peepshow. And sandals. Did she need sandals? She hadn't had a pedi in weeks, and she still hadn't shaved her legs.

She sank to the floor of her closet, surrounded by her personal warehouse of shoes, lined up on three five-foot-tall racks.

"Ten minutes my butt," Will said, peering into the closet. "You look a little vampirish. Bet you're dehydrated. Do you need help?"

Sophie peered up at him in the doorway and covered half of her face with a cool palm. "It's so deceptive when you look like a kind and normal person, but deep down, I know you're a sadist."

"Our daughters are entertaining your buddy Houdini. I get the feeling he'd much rather they were puppies so he could stick them in the backyard."

"Go away, will you? I'll be down in a sec."

After he left, Sophie rose slowly. She shuffled down the hallway and then the stairs and found Mitch in the living room he'd gotten to know Friday night. Before she made her presence known, she heard Mitch say, "So, I heard you're a regular Casanova."

"Casanova?" Will answered. "Says who?"

"Hitting the dating scene pretty hard? Guess when a marriage is over, it's over, huh?"

Sophie made her entrance before a street fight ensued. "Hey, Mitch. This is a surprise. Where's Ruta?"

Mitch sat in their tall-backed leather recliner. He still wore his business clothes, tie loosened at the collar. "She's getting situated at her hotel."

Annabelle and Keely balanced on the arms of the chair and gazed up at him curiously, bare toes tucked in the sides of the cushions.

Annabelle's look bordered on horror, as she pointed toward Mitch's face. "You have hair in your nose."

"Lemme see," Keely said.

They both searched two dark nostrils with the intense deliberation of brain surgeons.

"Girls," Sophie said. "I don't think Mr. Houdini needs your help for that."

Both girls jumped up and squeezed her possessively. "You feel better, Mommy?"

Mitch rose to greet her as well, his hard-soled shoes stepping on the girls' small, bare feet as he reached over them to kiss Sophie on the cheek.

Ear-piercing, open-mouthed yowls filled the air with dissonant harmony that sent spikes through Sophie's ears, straight into her temporal lobe. Will raced in from the kitchen and hauled his kids into his arms like grocery sacks.

Mitch recoiled from the melee. "I'm so sorry, Katie, Amy. I didn't mean—"

"It's Keely and Annabelle," Will said, in a tone Sophie translated as a death threat.

"Sorry." Mitch patted their heads. "Keely and Annabelle."

"This one's Annabelle and this one's Keely," Sophie corrected.

Mitch extricated his attention and took Sophie's hands. "I was so worried about you."

"The girls and I are making dinner," Will said with a hiss, not unlike Brewsky. "After which, I'll be helping Keely with her project for the Young Artisan's Festival."

"Oh, Daddy," Keely said. "Patty Martin is making the Great Wall of China with papier-mâché, and I was thinking we could go to the craft store and get the stuff for that."

Will blinked at his eldest daughter. "But we already decided on salt dough."

"Miss Marshall says papier-mâché is the most creative use of paper and glue ever."

"Miss Marshall has no sense of high-concept art," Will said. He turned to Sophie. "If you need us, we'll be in the kitchen." He clapped twice to turn on all of the living room lamps before he exited the room.

Sophie shook her head; his tactics were so obvious.

As Annabelle and Keely issued a collective glare at their hairy-nosed visitor, Sophie shot them a warning look. *Mind your manners.*

She turned back to Mitch. "I'm fine. Really I am, and unbelievably embarrassed about what happened today. Ruta must think I'm a lush."

"Nonsense." He squeezed her hands. "Some of her best friends are lushes. You did drool while you were passed out, but not to worry. We caught it all in a highball glass."

"Please tell me you're kidding. Did I—no, I can't bear to hear the gory details."

"Then you won't want to know Ruta's $4,000 purse is, how shall I say it—"

"Ruined? Wait, $4,000? What's it made with? Epidermis?"

Mitch led her to the sofa. "Not to worry. I think Ruta has a newfound respect for you. She'd rather you be a player, even if you're sloppy drunk, than a wallflower on the sidelines. She likes you a lot, so we decided to wait on seeing the properties till you've recovered."

"What about Allison?"

"Don't worry about Allison. She's on board with the split."

"The split? You mean, she agreed to sharing the deal with me?"

"In a manner of speaking. Just remember, it's what Ruta wants.

Allison will have to live with it. Anyway, Ruta's going to be here for the summer, so no rush on anything."

"The whole summer?"

"She likes to mix business with pleasure. This is the time of year she retreats to Austin. We're going to the lake tomorrow. You'll come, won't you?"

"Well, I don't know. Would I be intruding?"

His hands caressed her face. "Of course not."

Chills surfed up her back. He smelled good, like spicy testosterone.

He moved closer and brushed a warm kiss on her mouth. "I'll pick you up for breakfast. How does nine or nine-thirty sound?"

Nine-thirty, ten-thirty, any-thirty?

"Oh, no," she said. "I have a three o'clock with the Robertses. I guess I can't."

"Of course you can. I'll have you back on the dock by, say, two?"

Sophie couldn't miss this showing. It was her first big deal, and the Robertses were ready to buy. She focused on the potential commission she would soon need badly, since Will was unemployed. "How about one o'clock? I'll have to shower before my appointment."

"No worries." He kissed her hands. "See you tomorrow."

She watched wistfully through the glass panes of her front door as Mitch pressed a button on his keychain that made the Lamborghini's scissor doors open. He climbed in, fired up the engine, and waved as he drove out of her driveway into the sunset.

"Sophie."

She jumped at the sound of her name, her heart where her adenoids used to be. Will stood behind her with a spatula in his hand and an old apron around his torso that read, "D.A.D., Dads Against Diapers. It's not just a job, it's a doody."

"Will, you have to stop sneaking up on me."

"Just wondering why you've got your nose pressed against the window like a teenybopper." He turned and walked toward the kitchen.

Sophie followed. "Why again did I let you stay here instead of that bug–ridden hovel?"

"I'm fixing BLTs for me and Keely, and grilled cheese for Annabelle. When you get over the fact that I'm here in what used to be my house, you might want to let me fix you something too."

"No thanks."

She watched him lord over the griddle until her youngest took her hand, guided her to the dining table, and pulled out a chair. When Sophie sat down, Annabelle climbed into her lap, wrapped one tiny arm around Sophie's neck, and with the other rubbed her belly in circular motions.

"Feel better, Mommy?"

"Yes, thank you. You should be a doctor when you grow up."

Annabelle's expression turned grave. "You know how I puke."

Sophie kissed her on the forehead. "Maybe you'll grow out of it."

They both glanced at Will, the original sensitive stomach, the divvier of the family barfing gene, then looked back to each other and shrugged. "Or not."

Keely handed her mother a glass of ginger ale.

"Mmmm, very good," Sophie pulled Keely in to her. "You are both what I needed. Thank you, my lovelies."

Will stopped, mid-grilled-cheese flip. "You want a banana? You need potassium and magnesium. It'll help calm your stomach and relax your blood vessels."

"Sometimes your knowledge is insufferable. All right, a banana, please."

The house phone rang and Keely answered it. She looked at Sophie, who shook her head. *Absolutely no. No talky on the telly. Not tonight.* Her one call for the evening would be to Allison, a call of contrition, and that would be all she could handle.

Will took the phone from Keely's hands and spoke into the receiver.

"Sophie's indisposed right now," he said, sending Keely with a banana to her mother. "This is her husb—Oh, Casey, yes. Sure, I remember you." He made a face that meant he did not remember Casey. "Keely? I'm sure she's up for that."

He waved a cheesy spatula to get Sophie's attention, but she didn't want to think about Coach Casey and the Powder Puff League, not with jackhammers splitting her skull.

"She is?" he continued. "That's great news. Uh-huh. Takes after me? Well, I do work out." He topped this off with his Elvis impersonation. "Thank you, thank you very much."

Sophie swallowed the words, *What a dork.*

Casey and Sophie had worked together at Austin High eleven years earlier, when Sophie did a volunteer stint in the cafeteria while pregnant with Keely. Casey was a P.E. teacher then, and had since graduated to head coach. What was Casey, she of softball diamonds, smelly girls' locker rooms, and ear-splitting whistle blowing now telling the imbecilic Elvis impersonator?

"Of course," Will said. "I'll tell her. Absolutely." Extended pause. "Okay then. Bye-bye." Will hung up the phone and grinned like he'd won Publisher's Clearing House. "You made the summer softball team, Keely."

"Everybody makes the team, Daddy," Keely said. "I'm only nine, remember?"

"Oh. Well, you're now an official Jaguar. That was your coach." He looked at Sophie. "And there's your new team mom."

"What?" Sophie brandished her half-peeled banana. "I didn't commit to that."

"She said you signed up for it."

"I mentioned I would help if I could. I can't now."

"How was I supposed to know? You should have spoken to her yourself and explained your change of heart."

"You could have said I'd call her back."

"All you have to do is cut up oranges and stand on the sidelines. How hard could it be?"

"That's all I have to do? Easy for you to say, since you've never once done it." Sophie ticked off a litany of team mom duties till her head felt like a cheap balloon stretched to bursting.

"Look, I want to be there for Keely's softball, but a showing could come anytime. I can't drag Keely out of a game or leave the kids stranded on the ball field if it does. Making money for this family is my prime directive now." She tipped her head toward him. "You know that."

Keely sidled closer to her mother. "It's a serious job, Daddy."

Sophie stroked Keely's hair. "I'll call Casey and see what I can do, okay?"

"You don't need to call her," Will said. "You have a breakfast meeting with her at nine o'clock. Tomorrow."

Sophie shot out of her seat, accidentally knocking Annabelle off her lap. "What?"

"Take it easy. Casey said you set this meeting weeks ago."

Sophie vaguely recalled the conversation, but a meeting at nine would infringe on her nine-thirty pickup time with Mitch. A potential moneymaking deal was hanging in the balance with the Russian Princess, and no way could she miss that opportunity. She pinched the bridge of her nose, sensing Will's scrutiny. If he'd ever had to balance work, kids, and recreation—and dating—he might not be so smug. And then the ideas in her head suddenly balanced out perfectly.

Of course. Sophie's Kiss-off.

"You know, Keely, your father would make a *great* team dad. Since it's *so* easy and he has extra time on his hands, and he *did* say he wanted to spend more time with you guys."

Keely jumped up and down and twirled. "Oh yeah, Daddy. Would you?"

Will shook the spatula, dripping with yellow cheese, at her. "Whoa, whoa, whoa."

"Sure," Sophie said. "You could give them the guy's perspective. Who better to show those little angels how to take it when a wild pitch makes body contact, right?"

"Sophie—"

"You could teach them how to spit on the ground and say, 'Is that all you got?' And sportsmanship, like how not to pitch tantrums on home plate." She pointed at him, her arm jabbing the air emphatically, as if each idea was better than the last. "No throwing the bat at the coach. Yeah, the more I think about it, being team dad is right up your alley."

She waited for more protests, but he shut up, blocked by the idol-worshipping gazes of his daughters. His nostrils twitched as if great huffs of bullish steam shot from them.

"It's settled," Sophie said, with a sharp clap of her hands.

The girls shrieked as the lights went out.

Will clapped his hands to turn them back on. "Wait a minute."

"You meet her tomorrow morning in my place and announce that you'll be team dad. And guess what? Coach Casey is going to be your first date."

"What? No way. You're just going to spring me on her?"

"Relax. It's a coffee date. Time to work on getting Ursula back. Word of advice, though. Get there early and pick up a *GQ*." His expression turned stony. "See, girls, Daddy is a true man of his word. When he makes a deal, he follows through on it. That's how a real man rolls."

The girls ran to his side and full-body hugged him as he visibly shrank in his defeat. He was outnumbered and outwitted.

Score one for Sophie.

She sipped her ginger ale and peeled the last of her banana. "Don't you have something to say to me, Will? Oh yes, I think you do." She smirked triumphantly. "Thank you, thank you very much."

Chapter 11

Before light, Will stood in the guest bathroom, stripped to his skivs, and inspected his reflection from all sides. One thing for certain, he needed new underwear. What caused his briefs to get those suspicious little holes along his crack? Seemed symbolic of so many things biting him in the ass lately, not the least of which was this five-date fiasco with Sophie. Too many things to worry about without adding total strangers to the mix. At least he'd be one date closer to getting Ursula back and selling her for a nice profit.

He exhaled the tension as best he could, convincing himself that today's so-called date with Casey the Coach couldn't be all that bad. The woman had to be in tiptop shape chasing kids around all day. She did have a sexy voice, like Kathleen Turner in *Body Heat*, and she might be a nice diversion from the other crap going on in his life. After giving this considerable thought, he sucked in his gut and launched into various Mr. Universe poses. The Hulk made the most of his pumped pecs as he glared into the mirror, bottom teeth bared, neck muscles protruding like thick guy wires, throat grrr-ing.

He'd never been heavy into exercise—that is, until he could no longer avoid avoiding it. The taut, lean physique of his youth came as a byproduct of good genes, and he'd cultivated a lazy streak, along with a belly paunch, because of it. But last year, he'd hired a personal trainer for workouts three days a week. After the layoff forced everything into cutback mode, he gave up the trainer but maintained the workout schedule. He'd made significant gains, and Sophie seemed to think so too, the way she was always staring at his chest and his abs. He'd even sculpted a decent six-pack. But was it all for nada? She kept insisting he needed advice from *GQ*.

Whatever.

After shaving and throwing on some boxers without holes, he combed out his mullet and gave his reflection two thumbs up. Then he headed for the kitchen, brewed a pot of coffee, and started breakfast for the girls.

"Two mornings in a row of Mr. Domestic?" Sophie said with sleep in her voice as she shuffled past wearing shorty pajamas and rubber-soled slippers. She pulled a mug from the cabinet, then froze with her head cocked to one side. "Or maybe I'm still dreaming."

Will turned sizzling maple sausage links in a frying pan. The aroma made his stomach growl. "Making breakfast for my girls keeps my mind off ridiculous bets and set-ups with horny toads I don't even know, courtesy of my wife and my supposed friends."

"Ex-wife."

"Not for a few more weeks, baby."

Sophie exaggerated a sigh, peeked at his chest—as if he couldn't detect her not-so-covert interest—and poured coffee into her mug.

"Counting down the minutes," she said.

Will glanced at his watch, flexing all the muscles in his arm. "As am I. One hour till I'm dished up to your manless friend like a boneless pork chop."

"Boneless?"

"Severed from my dignity."

She leaned against the island, and he spotted the glint of amusement in her unglossed, pouty mouth. She fingered her chin, long-lashed brown eyes shuttering lazily as she visually devoured his physique. In the old days, they'd have sexed up every inch of that counter by now.

"It's coffee and bagels, Will. Try to enjoy yourself. You might actually like her."

"Look, you can call it a date, but I call it coercion."

"You're not having second thoughts, are you?"

"Does Satan have horns?"

"No one knows for sure, Will." She scrunched her nose. "But you are going, right? You can't back out now. You made a deal, and it's the right thing to do."

"That's debatable. I'm going; however, I'm not about to talk to Coach Casey like there's a chance in hell we'd ever do the mating mambo."

"I'm not asking you to bed her. Breakfast is a no-strings-attached event. It's like sticking your toe in the water—even less. It's a pool drive-by to see if you want to jump in for a swim."

"Fish outta water here, Soph. I flop around on shore because I don't *want* to swim. Truth be told, I forgot *how* to swim."

She cast a withering gaze. "You've been a floater for a long time, Will."

Will got to the Starbucks early and combed the copious magazine racks for so-called metrosexual magazines he'd otherwise never pick up. But how else would he figure it out? He plunked a *GQ* on the counter.

The coffee section swelled with the aroma of fresh roast. Behind the tall counters, baristas ground into liquid the energy of the gods. Will's mouth watered for a dose of dark, rich caffeine that his home coffeemaker never seemed to brew as well.

He stood in line behind a seven-foot Paul Bunyan wearing a red plaid shirt and holey jeans tucked haphazardly into mud-splattered boots. The guy had the face of an English bulldog, complete with whiskered jowls and big, droopy, bloodshot eyes. Smelled like he'd worked a full day in the heat, yet the sun had barely been up two hours.

"Three bear claws," Paul Bunyan said, in a voice that demanded reaction. He looked through the display case, screwing up his mouth and tapping his lips with grimy fingertips. "Make that four, and three jelly donuts. The peach ones. And two low-fat éclairs."

Will patted him on the back. "Hey, save room for dessert."

Paul Bunyan whirled around. His heavy brow folded over the bridge of his nose, his jaw muscles pulsed beneath the scruff, and his moustache twitched.

Bull, meet china shop.

He turned back to the counter clerk and threw down two crumpled twenties from his pockets. "Add a grande latte and two OJs." He cut his eyes to Will. "You got a problem?"

Will stepped back. "Easy there, big guy. Just being funny."

The burly giant let loose a steely stare that grabbed Will by the throat. "I don't do funny. And neither do you." He lumbered off, snaking between tables and bumping chairs.

Safely distanced, Will said, "I got two words for you, buddy: GQ."

His eyes surfed the coffee shop for his breakfast "date," whom he'd supposedly met before. He figured if she was that good looking, he'd have remembered. Sophie had described Casey as pretty, athletic, and blonde. "Watch for a woman about five-seven in gym shorts and sneakers, a clipboard in hand, and a silver whistle around her neck." Then she'd laughed quietly, as if a punch line were forthcoming.

Will expected the worst but made the best of it by treating himself to a tall mocha and a heated cheese Danish that was not on his high-protein, low-carb diet. As he waited for his order, he scoped out the coffee shop, which teemed with harried moms, post-kid drop-off; athletes before and after their workouts; a gaggle of high-school girls probably ditching first period; and business types dressed in dark suits. The same kind Will used to wear.

"Will Camden? Is that you?"

Will stood looking at a fortyish woman with an edgy, bleach-blonde cut, long and wispy at the neck and tufted at the top. Reminded him of a white-crested rooster. He'd seen that cut elsewhere, too, like his own mirror, which struck him as horrifying.

"In the flesh," he said.

"Thought so. I saw you at a softball game once." Coach Casey's voice was smoky, her northeastern accent unmistakable.

"Oh, yeah," he lied. "I remember."

Contrary to Sophie's description, she wore a gray skirt, a short-waist jacket, and a white, ruffled blouse that strained at the buttons between her ample breasts. Oversized pearly teeth and bright blue eyes shined in sharp contrast with her tan skin. He guessed her deepest stratum of skin was lily white, the melanin bronzed into textured rawhide from years of outdoor sports.

"Sophie just texted that you were meeting me instead of her today," Casey said. Her smile was more of a leer, and he wondered if Sophie had mentioned the date thing.

"Yeah, she—" *dumped you on me so she could go to the lake with Mr. Big Shot*, "had a conflicting appointment this morning."

She smiled like a barracuda and moved closer. "I was surprised you insisted on meeting me. Of course, I was flattered. And I have a confession. I used to sing 'Sophie's Kiss' in the shower. At the top of my lungs. Those were the glory days, huh?"

There weren't enough words for how much he hated people reminding him of the "glory days," implying that the rest of his days beyond music would be miserable and boring. Of course, that was kind of true lately.

"That was eons ago. I'm just here for, uh... " He cleared his throat, the words "coffee date" clogging his voice box. "Uh, I'm here for coffee and a chat about Keely's softball team. Maybe being team dad?"

"Excellent." Casey rubbed her stomach. "But food first, right? I'm starving. Why don't you find us a table, and I'll slide in after I swing a little something to eat."

"Okay." Will assessed her as she walked to the counter. All in all, the package was okay, except for the bird tufts. He felt the top of his head for comparison.

Two vacant easy chairs were positioned diagonally near the

windows. Will sank into one, sipped his mocha, and watched Casey fidget with the back of her skirt while waiting for her order. From across the room, those pearly whites gleamed back, and he imagined other activities that might be more productive, like tackling the old studio in the backyard—or taking a nap, because that's what the stress of unemployment made him want to do. Sleep, and forget.

Coach Casey returned with coffee and a breakfast taco. She fell sideways off one heel but didn't break stride and shook it off with a big-toothed grin. "Score! They gave me a grande when I ordered a tall. I'm lucky like that." She winked and looked him over. "Maybe we're both lucky."

She aimed her backside at the seat cattycorner to Will's and sank into it, lower than her knees. Her skirt hiked high on her thighs, just shy of revealing the color of her underwear, and her face flushed.

"I'm not used to this get-up," she said, setting her plate and coffee on the adjacent table. "But I have to be in court today. Divorce hearing. Sophie tell you?"

Will shook his head, his eyes darting to the swaying plumage at her crown.

Casey stood and tugged her skirt into place, huffing as if the exertion were taking a toll, and slipped out of her suit jacket. "I'm surprised. My husband owns a music studio in SoCo—which he's selling so he can move his carcass to L.A. without me. Maybe you should buy it. Then we won't have to declare bankruptcy, and I'll actually get something out of the divorce."

"Music studio? I wish. I'm not in a position to—"

"Yep, our divorce is big news around the school. Everyone knows he was bunting his production assistant, my hairdresser, and the school nurse. In my playbook, three strikes and—" She lunged sideways, threw out her elbow, and jabbed her thumb over her shoulder.

"He's... out?"

"Oh, yeah. But I hired a lawyer. She's coached me to throw plenty of heat when he's up there on the bench—exactly what I pay her for."

Will appreciated her sense of humor, though it added a weird, quirky aspect to her personality. And he felt for her, making light of real pain that her eyes could not disguise.

"Would you like to sit?" he said. "You seem flustered."

"This whole thing has knocked me out of the park, Will. Just like Husband Number One. Of course, that one was a switch hitter." She cocked her head sideways and shielded her mouth. "Liked the backdoor sliders, know what I mean? If only I'd known how much time he was spending in the bullpen."

He thought up something to say that wasn't sarcastic. "I can see the divorce has thrown you. Any chance for reconciliation?"

Her mouth stiffened and her eyes shimmered, and she seemed to be fighting the cry face. "He made a fool of me, Will. A man shouldn't steal a woman's pride like that, should he?" She swiped at wet eyes and stomped her feet. "I'm 'O' for two."

"Uh, you win some, you lose some?"

Her agonized expression went slack as she lowered herself into the chair, her rising hemline again leaving zilch to the imagination. She gazed glumly out the window.

"I can't tell you how embarrassing it is. I mean, sometimes I feel like my whole life is an embarrassment. Just once, I'd like to not be the one all red-faced."

"Look," he said, feeling inadequate to dispense advice—but what else could he do? "I know divorce is difficult. It's hard for me and Sophie, too."

"Can't be too difficult, if you wanted to meet me." Her head tilted again, and she squeezed his hand. "Nobody was bunting outside the marriage, were they?"

"No. No bunting. But I'd rather not talk about Sophie and me."

"Of course, of course. That's all in the past." She smiled expectantly.

Will checked his watch. "I don't have a lot of time, and it looks like you don't either, so why don't we talk about what you need for the team? Keely is excited to be a Jaguar, and I—" he swallowed the last vestiges of resistance, "I'll help wherever I can."

"Yes, unfortunately, I need to wind this up."

Casey launched into the team's needs—practices, provisions, schedules—and the way she was eyeing him, Will weighed the cons of being on the field or trapped in the dugout with her. He felt both sympathetic and perturbed. And it occurred to him that he'd often belittled Sophie for being so uninspired about the sports he loved. He hadn't meant to ridicule, but rather to get her more involved with the things he enjoyed, like donning a favorite team jersey, tolerating the weather at a live game, and scarfing stadium hotdogs; or whiling away a weekend afternoon with nonstop football, soccer, baseball, basketball, or golf on the tube. Amid Casey's flurry of baseballese, Sophie's passing interest seemed a godsend.

"Listen," Casey said, "I've been thinking. You're nice to offer, but this team is all little girls, so I'll have to get back to you. Some parents just prefer other moms."

"Hey," he said, "if you're sure."

"I'll call you. Maybe we can have drinks next week?"

A shot of terror rippled through his chest, and he stuttered incoherently.

"Hey, batter batter batter!" She laughed, poking fun at him. "We'll talk later. I really do have to run. Divorce court awaits."

They both bent forward, planting their feet and rousting enough momentum to drag themselves out of the deep chairs; but they rose at the same time, and Will's shoulder knocked Casey's hand, causing her to jerk and spill coffee all over her blouse.

"Oh geez, I'm sorry," he said, instinctively using his soiled napkins to sop the expanding brown splotches on her chest.

She dodged his hands. "Hey, hey!"

"Sorry, sorry. I didn't mean to—"

Casey examined her blouse. "Aw, hell. Be right back."

She hurried off, unsteady on her heels and pulling at her skirt with one hand while gripping her lucky grande with the other. She paused at the counter and spoke to the barista, handed off her cup, and then disappeared down the hall toward the ladies' room.

Will slumped into his chair and picked at the last half of his Danish, his appetite stomped by Casey's verbal cleats. He pitied her—maybe because she'd been betrayed or because she was now a victim of his dating debacle, too. Or maybe because of her festive mullet.

Once he could exit Starbucks, he'd have to call Jake to report mission accomplished. Such as it was. One date down—never to be repeated, thank you very much—four to go. Ursula, he reminded himself. Ursula was only four more debacles away.

He puffed his cheeks in exasperation, watching people come and go. Out that door lay freedom. He'd make a run for it if he thought he'd never see Casey again. But he would, at Keely's softball games.

Long minutes later, Casey emerged from the bathroom and picked up a fresh cup of coffee from the counter. She looked across the room at Will and tugged on her left ear, drew an invisible line across her chest, patted her right shoulder, and poked two fingers toward the cream and sugar counter.

That one operates in a league of her own.

When she turned, Will noticed her skirt—shoved into the back of her stark-white underwear—giant, cotton, old-lady undies that had to be visible from space. *Holy...* If he didn't do something, she'd be waving her fanny flag into the courtroom. Somebody would point it out, she'd die of humiliation and, of course, she'd know he saw it and did zippity-doo-da about it. His engineer's mind assembled a quick best practices scenario. It was insane, but if his plan worked, she'd never be the wiser. Then, exit stage left.

Yep, that could work.

He hurried behind her while she doctored her coffee, molding his front to the contours of her back—without touching—so nobody else could see his next move.

Casey noticed him over her shoulder. "Sorry about droning on. Didn't mean to go off about my ex screwing an entire roster. Nerves, I guess. Knowing you're available and all."

Sweat formed on Will's brow. "It's fine. Really."

She yakked on, stirring her coffee so furiously, a whirlpool formed in her cup. He figured she enjoyed him standing so close because she sure wasn't going anywhere.

So, he took a deep breath and went in.

Carefully, with one hand, he fingered the silky fabric of her granny panties and stretched them. With the other hand, he began tugging out the skirt.

Just then Paul Bunyan trudged by with his tray of jelly donut crumbs, gnarled napkins, and empty cups. His tray edged Casey.

"Hey," she said. "Watch it."

The mountain man snarled. "Watch it yourself, ya midget."

He jerked his hips into her, knocking her off her feet.

In classic domino fashion, Casey fell in to Will and he fell backward to the hard floor, striking his elbow and shoving his hand deeper into Casey's underwear. She screamed and then screamed some more, and the whole place turned to view the ruckus.

With her back flat-out on top of his front, Casey made her hands into a T. "Time out! Time out!"

"My watch is caught," he shouted, his hand cupping her bottom.

"Omigod." Sophie's voice soared above them in the pitch of a distressed peacock. "What the hell is going on? Omigod."

Will peered around Casey's bleached tussocks, trying to keep calm. "Oh, just, you know, getting to know Coach Casey. Like you said."

Sophie covered her gaping mouth.

Given the option of her seeing him in this position or falling on a rusty sword, he'd have already impaled himself. "Glad you could make it, Soph. Though it kind of makes my being here *pointless.*"

Casey tried to roll off Will's body, but her underwear was still stuck to his watch.

Will clenched his teeth. "And? You came here because?"

Sophie squinted as if she were in pain. "I wasn't sure that you... I mean, I thought you might not... Er, you seemed noncommittal and..."

Paul Bunyan pushed Sophie aside, grunted, and hauled Casey up by her arms. But Will's watch remained stuck, and while their separation dislodged Casey's wedgie, it also stripped all traces of the grannywear covering her crack.

Casey flailed until her stretched panties ripped and she plopped back down on the floor.

"Omigod, Will," Sophie said.

Will clambered to his feet. "Yes, Sophie. I think we've established that God has it out for me." He extended his freed hand stiffly to his so-called date. "Casey, let me—"

Casey cocked her arm and thrust her fist straight up, tagging him right in the bag. Sophie squealed and winced. Bunyan grinned.

Will doubled over, his eyes bulged, his teeth clenched, and his face writhed from maroon to purple. The satellite station drifted through the speakers, and the singer's wail matched his throbbing groin, note for note.

Don't touch me, you tease, I can't survive your heartless squeeze.

With one palm protecting his groin, he thrust a finger in Sophie's face. "Stained... L-l-ove." His pointing finger trembled and sweat trickled down his face. "1981." And once more with the emphatic finger: "Hard Cell. And that was a triple-fucking-play."

Only one thing left to do. He cradled what was left of his dignity in his hands and limped like hell outta there.

Chapter 12

The silver Lamborghini convertible squealed into the sharp curve from Highway 71 to Rural Road 620, headed for Lake Travis with its top down and the morning sun glinting off its spit-shined hood. Sophie leaned into a half-raised passenger window and clutched the oh-shit bar on the door, her hair thrashing her face. The idea that a practical ponytail could survive in this self-propelled wind tunnel had been wishful thinking.

Mitch yelled over the buzzing engine, blustering currents, and strains of "Beer, Bait, and Ammo" from the stereo.

"Feel that suspension? My baby glides around corners like a hovercraft on 'roids. Twelve cylinders make her purr like a kitten, but when 572 horsepower let loose, she growls like a tiger. Brute force in motion. Gives me a rush every time I get behind the wheel."

Oh, the wheel, Sophie mused. That little round thing resting between Mitch's fingertips like he was out for a Sunday drive on cruise control—in a quarter-million-dollar automobile better suited to the cliffs of Monte Carlo than the rolling hills of Lakeway. His baby went nowhere unnoticed. She cut a glance at him through sunglasses pinned to her brow, her lashes brushing the dark lenses every time she blinked.

Mitch was a study in contradictions. From the boardroom to a dais in front of five hundred real estate brokers, he exuded a degree of self-possession that Sophie had never before known: gray eyes alight with wisdom—and mischief—smile quick and easy as they sucked people into his aura and made them feel important, demeanor cool and collected under pressure. And then there was this adventurous side. His Hawaiian shirt flounced in the breeze, clumps of chest hair peeked over the V of his collar, and his eyebrows arched wickedly.

"When was the last time you got this kind of adrenaline spike? You were once a wildcat, am I right?"

"Put it this way," she shouted with the wind filling her mouth. "My inner wildcat may have been in hibernation, but she's wide awake now."

The last thing she wanted was to be a "once was" or the ex-wife of the guy who stuck his hands down Coach Casey's underwear. Sophie had just wanted to see her plan in action, feel the sweet revenge of Sophie's Kiss-off in person, to watch Will squirm at being set up with her quirky acquaintance. And then, as she raced to get home before Mitch arrived, she had to compartmentalize that little incident into a box labeled *We Must Never Speak of This*.

When Mitch shifted through six gears, Sophie squinted at the gauges. The needle edged past sixty, sixty-five, seventy. Then he hit the brakes for a red light and screeched to a short stop that felt like they'd been sucked back from a spurt through hyperspace.

Amid the acrid smell of burned rubber, Sophie stammered, "What's the rush?"

Mitch cocked his head. "You wimping out on me, Wildcat?"

"Who, me? God, no. I just... the wind, it's hard on my hair." She held out frizzed tendrils from her temples. "See?"

Mitch patted her thigh, his subtle smirk and the pressure of his hand an indicator that she wasn't fooling anybody, much less the head of Mr. Slinky, Inc. "You're adorable," he said.

The light turned green and Mitch pumped the accelerator. Hard, soft, hard, soft on the gas, causing Sophie's stomach to lurch. Boxed in by lesser, slow-poke autos made in America, he was forced into the acceleration of a snail on tranqs, a pace that tested his corruptible self-control. The muscles in his right leg twitched, on high alert for the split half-second when he could slam on the gas and explode out of this ordinary man's go-cart circuit.

"Look at that rust bucket," he complained at the oxidized red truck in front, spewing gray smoke and rumbling like it was missing important parts. He coughed and rolled his eyes bleakly toward Sophie. For more dramatic effect, he scrunched up his nose and fanned the air free of putrid vapors. "We've got to get around this guy before he asphyxiates us. Besides, you want to be back at the docks by two o'clock, don't you?"

"One o'clock. Of course, first I'd like to get to the docks in one piece."

"Relax. Safety is my number one priority. I've trained with the best for high-speed driving. I know maneuvers most people don't." He turned up the stereo, and in true New Yorker-turned-redneck style said, "Hey, watch 'iss."

Sophie got a bad feeling as he left more tread on the macadam and punched through a narrow space between the truck and a minivan. Her head bounced off the headrest, her body pressed into taut black leather.

"Zero to sixty in four seconds." He maneuvered into clear lanes that never stayed clear for long and picked up speed. Sixty-five, seventy. "Just cleaning out her pipes."

"You're about to clean out my pipes."

The speed both energized and mesmerized Sophie, and she couldn't help but giggle at the delicious insanity of her white-knuckled grip, the forceful wind surfing every plane of her body, and the adventure of doing something so contrary to her sensibilities. She hoped her guardian angel was awake, clearing the intersections and damming the inroads and otherwise making the world safe for a few breathtaking moments of joy riding.

They shot past the blur of black-and-white speed limit signs that read forty-five. At least, that's what she thought they said as she whizzed past a dizzying array of landscape: cars, buildings, hillsides, the water tower, and the local law getting into a cruiser at the Dunkin' Donut.

Sophie's heart tapped a river dance, and her mindless delight morphed into panic. "Cop!"

Mitch glanced at his mirrors and stomped on it. The cruiser darted onto the highway, its red and blue cherries spinning, claxons wailing. They fishtailed between cars and blazed through a red light that screamed "Stop!" almost as loud as Sophie.

"Hang on," Mitch said, seemingly in complete control of his faculties.

As they catapulted over the next hill, Sophie's howling echoed through the canyon.

Mitch slowed enough to make a sharp left and descended toward the lake on a narrow road flanked by gravel and brushy growths of cedar, mesquite, and prickly pear. Sophie winced as her head hit the window and her sunglasses flew into the breeze. The Lambo shot like a serpentine rollercoaster, up and down and sideways, catching air on two occasions while Sophie made the sign of the cross.

Through the gates of Hurst Harbor, the road dropped into a half-filled parking lot that sloped toward the water. Mitch parked on the high side under the shade of a swaying old oak, top heavy with spring growth. The car doors scissored open.

"Smell that fresh air? What a beautiful day." He got out and stretched. "What are you waiting for, Bonnie? We made a clean getaway."

Sophie's skin felt like dough molded across her cheekbones by a hurricane-force rolling pin. With her heart still dangling in her throat, she turned in her seat and slid a sunflower beach bag over her shoulder, set her sandaled feet on the pebbled pavement, and stood on shaky legs.

"Where's the bar?"

The marina harbored all manner of watercraft, from jet skis to double-decker houseboat-slash-party boats. A combination gift and bait shop resided across from a floating restaurant called Henry's Dockside. The faint fishy smell of lake water, mixed with inboard motor exhaust, filled Sophie with memories of her rebellious college years, when she and Tess spent their days worshipping the sun and their nights at beer-drenched parties.

She detoured past the Buoys room and slipped through the door that said Gulls. She gave herself the once-over in the full-length mirror. Hair like Medusa, complexion like death. White blouse, adorned with tasteful yellow daffodils, covering bikini top and belly pooch. Blinding white capris, wrinkled. Quick turnaround to the backside and—eek. Saggy bottom. Ankles a tad water retentive. Hardly the picture of a woman living life on the edge. Fresh factor: a big, fat four. However, her feet looked fabulous in strappy sandals with colored beads.

She splashed water on her face and did battle with recalcitrant tangles. By the time she'd cajoled her hair into a thick braid, tears stained her cheeks and her roots were sore. She took one last look in the mirror, in case she hadn't caught herself in the best light the first time around.

You again. The older, less vivacious version of me. Former neighborhood daredevil, original Girl Gone Wild, college dropout, the woman yet to accomplish anything, who still depends on a man to pay her mortgage. The disappointment, and now the fraud.

Suck it up, Sophie. You asked for this.

She tied her shirttails just below her swimsuit top so that her whole midriff showed, including her belly button. Surely she could hold in her stomach for four measly hours.

At the rear of the restaurant was a massive deck and outdoor dining area where patrons could sit above the lake as it sloshed two feet below. A row of ski boats rocked idly, tethered to the adjacent pier, while wedge-shaped, shirtless men and toned, saddlebag-less women in bikinis milled from boat to boat, preparing for a day of skiing and wakeboarding.

As she approached the table, she saw Mitch munching on chips and salsa under a red-and-green-striped umbrella. He had unbuttoned his Aloha shirt, which now flapped in the breeze, and she cautioned herself not to stare at his tanned rib cage and chocolate kiss areolas nestled in big, thick, sugar-cookie pectorals. Her mouth watered and her stomach growled, and she wondered how his skin would taste if her tongue were to run across it like a butter brush slathering warm breadsticks. Boy, she really needed to eat.

Mitch's khakis rode low enough to reveal a black underwear band and, to Sophie's infinite pleasure, his inny. A purely dark and erotic hole with such depth she could poke it with her finger and be sucked in, all the way to Heaven.

"I ordered you a Bloody Mary," he said.

He pointed at a tall glass of rust-colored liquid as she sat down. Seemed no life in the fast lane would be complete without vodka. After the Great Starbuck's Fiasco, that logic was making some sense.

She secured the celery stalk against the lip of the glass with one finger and tipped the glass to her mouth. The ice tinkled as she gulped. The liquid was frigid, spicy, and heavy on the Tabasco. She drank a third of it and wiped the icy residue from her lips.

Mitch signaled the waitress, who strolled over in a low-cut tank and denim mini. Her nametag said Stacey but her eyes said, *Yay, big tipper.*

"Another Bloody Mary, Mr. Houdini?"

"Thought you'd never ask—and your breakfast special. Sophie?"

Sophie skimmed the menu. "Eggs, bacon, and something sweet." She looked to the waitress for menu suggestions, but the girl was eyeballing Sophie's pooch. "Uh, well, maybe just eggs and bacon."

She watched as Mitch gulped the last of his drink, enjoying the way his throat worked when he swallowed and the soft wet look of his mouth as he licked off a trace of Bloody Mary. And then she felt his bare toes rubbing against her ankles, his mouth forming a lazy smile that set off little geysers of joy all through her.

Must stop gawking. Must play hard to get. Aloofness good. Drooling bad.

Out of nowhere, the earlier coffee shop scene crept back to her. Will had been copping a feel from their daughter's softball coach? How desperate was he?

Mitch's toes ascended beneath Sophie's capris, caressing her shinbone. A tingle jolted her, as Mitch's toes made the giant leap forward, all the way up to the inside of her thighs, striking up the machinery in her O factory.

Not that there's anything wrong with copping a feel now and then.

She swallowed the lump of nervous anticipation. Mitch was adept at hotwiring her engine under the table, stroking and striking her imagination and firing that baby up.

Thief! Oh, magnificent thief!

What was next, grand-theft orgasm? If she swished their chips and salsa to the floor, stripped and launched herself into splits on the table, would Mitch think she was easy?

Mitch's foot disappeared as he waved to someone crossing the deck.

Sophie turned to see Ruta Khorkina sashaying in the same regal manner she had once strolled onto the catwalk. Her silky blonde tresses fell around her shoulders, á la shampoo commercial, while her demeanor reflected an uncompromising zest that radiated from her infinitesimally small pores. Everyone watched her, always the Russian Princess. She wore white capris hip huggers and a white linen blouse with embroidered yellow roses, the front shirttails tied together to expose her long, flat midriff.

Sophie got a sinking feeling in the pit of her pooch that lulled the star-struck luster right out of her. *My god, I'm her evil, shorter twin.* Except that Ruta's "it" factor gave her a tony couture look and that just-showered spring freshness. Ruta was a vivacious garden of flowers in brilliant bloom. Sophie was a dwindling daffodil from the briar patch. A knock-off. Princess Squat Blossom from T.J. Maxx.

Ruta gushed. She held her arms out to Sophie, who rose as Ruta kissed her on both cheeks. "We are dressed same like yesterday. Except this eez from Kayfuyu Collection. You have good taste. Look, you have even shiny baubles on your sandals like me. We are *tweens*."

Mitch brightened as he kissed Ruta's cheeks and pulled out her chair. "I like twins."

Allison Summers strolled behind Ruta in a white fishnet cover-up that didn't cover up anything. Under the fishnet was a skimpy aqua bikini, and her skin glistened with coconut-scented lotion that gave her muscular arms and legs the afterglow of an exhaustive workout.

Sophie downed the last of her Bloody Mary, untied her blouse, and hid her midriff.

Considering her anaphylaxis the day before, Allison looked no worse for wear. Sophie had left several apologies via voicemail, but Allison hadn't returned any calls.

"I see you started without us," Allison said. Her huge lips moved across her blinding white dentin in horsy fashion, mouth set in a square jaw beneath a button nose.

"I have faith you'll catch up," Mitch said. "You brought my packages?"

"Of course," Allison said, taking the chair between Sophie and

Mitch. "Jimmy's delivering them to your boat as we speak."

"You look good," Sophie said to Allison. "I'm so sorry. I had no idea about exotic eels. Are you feeling back to normal?"

Allison spoke to Ruta. "What do you think about this place?"

"Eez beautiful here," Ruta said, admiring the vista of hills and trees and deep blue water. "What a great idea. I can't wait to see Meetch's new boat."

"Imagine if you lived around here," Sophie said. "You'd have this view every day."

Ruta's eyes scanned the horizon and the low hills that surrounded them, and Sophie scooted closer, anxious to be done with apology number two.

"I'm so sorry about yesterday," she whispered. "I hope your bag can be cleaned. I'd like to take care of it for you. I have the best dry cleaner—"

"Not to worry," Ruta said with a dismissive flick of her bony hand. "Plenty more where that came from. Besides, not first time."

"Somebody else threw up in your bag?"

"Oh, no dear. First time for *that*. I'm gonna be honest, I'm trying to forget about eet. I mean, not first time I have bag cleaned."

"Seriously?" Allison said. "You threw up in her bag?" The points of her eyebrows leached into her hairline and a French-tipped manicure shielded a gloating smirk. "You're a walking accident factory. You must have been so embarrassed."

"Surprisingly, not as much as now." A hot blush crept up Sophie's neck.

Mitch laid a quieting hand on Allison's arm, which made Sophie want to disappear rather than be subjected to his piteous stare. She held up her glass, summoned the self-assured girl she once knew, and eked out a fabulous grin that she hoped looked authentic.

"To memorable first impressions."

She tilted her head to drink the last dribbles of Bloody Mary, which instead became an avalanche of ice and celery. Frozen orbs bounced off the table and down her shirt, but two cubes got stuck in her throat. She stood up, choking. Her eyes watered and she doubled over, looking in desperation for help.

Ruta leaped out of her chair, elbows and knees akimbo as she assumed a straddle position behind Sophie. With her fists together, she pumped upward beneath Sophie's rib cage. Once, twice, three times, and out the ice cubes shot like high-velocity bullets.

Pop, pop! Right into Allison's forehead.

Allison sat up straight and palpated the pink splotches, unable to conceal her contempt.

Mitch burst into laughter. "Now that's an icebreaker."

Ruta snickered. "Perfect aim, darlingk. No offense, Allison dear."

Sophie laid a hand on Allison's arm. "Are you okay? I'm so sorry."

Allison pulled a compact mirror from her sun bag and surveyed the damage. Two asymmetrical lumps formed above her brows. "You could have put my eyes out. Another millimeter and I'd have wound up in the ER. *Again.*"

"You're fine," Mitch said. "Here, how many fingers am I holding up?" He held out three, and Allison batted them away. "See? She's fine. Ruta, you saved Sophie's life."

"I once give Heimlich to Bobby DeNiro. He choked on Russian bread at dinner party. Hard as rock, that stuff. But I tell you, the Heimlich just like sex. You don't forget."

Mitch outstretched his arms and praised the sky. "It's going to be one helluva day. Another Bloody Mary, Sophie?"

Allison growled. "Without the ice this time."

"Nonsense," Ruta said with a wry grin. "I pump eet out of her, she chokes again."

Her ribs felt sore, but if Allison didn't want her to have ice, then Sophie could think of nothing better. "Definitely," she said. "Lots of ice."

After a breakfast festooned with real estate chatter, they stopped at the marina gift shop that smelled mildly of sweaty patrons and strongly of fish bait. While Ruta made a phone call outside, Mitch and Allison picked out Neoprene beer koozies, and Sophie tried on a new pair of sunglasses. The lenses were darker than she liked, but the sun promised to burn bright today. She thought the huge red frames reduced her face to the size of a Kewpie doll, but the sparkling rhinestones might be too good to pass up. She was assessing them in a mirror the size of a credit card when a man's voice sent a surge of dread down her spine.

"Well, well, well," he said. "If it isn't Cupid Incarnate."

Sophie wheeled to see her ex on the other side of the sunglasses display.

"Looks like all you're missing is your crossbow and poison-tipped arrows." He moved around the rack and flipped the price tag dangling over her nose from the sunglasses. "Ouch. One-eighty? You that flush these days?"

From behind the dark lenses, Sophie glared up at him. She wanted to vent, but seeing his new change was a shock to her system. "Your hair."

"Yup," he said, brushing his hand over his head.

The close clip was a uniform inch all over and gelled to resemble petrified grass. "You look more like your dad now."

Genuine appreciation lit up his eyes. "I thought so too."

"Wait," she said, remembering where she was. "Did you follow me?"

"I don't think you get how hard I wished, after this morning, to never see you again. And I mean *never*. However, because of the two best and last things we ever did right together—and a little thing called my current financial straits—I am precluded from the nirvana of that reward until after I'm no longer alive to enjoy it."

Sophie scoped out her companions across the store and pulled him aside. "Why are you here then? Is it your mission in life to torture me?"

"Relax, Sophie. Unlike you, who snuck into Starbuck's to spy on me, I have a legitimate reason for being here."

"Like?"

"Coke." He held up an unopened can of Coke, the cold silver aluminum beading up from its introduction to the warm temperature of the shop. "You have a nice day now."

He walked to the cashier and laid a five on the counter, when Mitch Houdini noticed him. Sophie watched them shake hands, and she hurried over to monitor the situation in case Will had any ideas of sabotage; but by the time she reached them, Allison and Ruta had found him too.

"Sophie," Ruta said, eyes aglow with the discovery of a wondrous curiosity. "This eez your husband?"

Sophie's smile was anything but. "For the moment."

"Now it's a party," Allison said, sucking him up visually like he was a Bloody Mary. "What are you waiting for? Introduce us already."

Mitch patted Will's back. "Ladies, this is the famous Tunemeister and songwriter of 'Sophie's Kiss.' After we met the other night, I realized I used to listen to your DJ thing in the mornings, right after I moved here from New York. Ruta, the guy was incredible. Musical genius. Knows all the songs."

Will tipped his head toward Mitch as he eyed Sophie with a self-satisfied *See there?* "Yes, yes, I do."

The three of them huddled around him like he was a celebrity. *Great*, Sophie thought. *Now the pain in my ass is a party favor.*

She made formal introductions all around. As she finished, a paunchy, thirtyish guy in a blue Hurst Harbor T-shirt and khaki shorts entered the gift shop and lunged to shake Will's hand.

"Hey, man," the guy said. "Here's that info. Give me a call when you're ready to finalize the deal, huh? I'll hook you up."

Will took the proffered papers and folded them into his hip pocket. "We'll talk soon, Frank. Thanks, buddy."

Sophie refrained from asking, since her right to know was at an end, but Will looked like he wanted to tell her about it.

"You should come on boat weeth us," Ruta cooed, draping an arm over Will's shoulder.

"Yes," Allison said, coveting his other arm. "Right, Mitch?"

Sophie's heart flatlined as her gaze met Will's, transmitting the words *HELL NO* like a telepathic sledgehammer.

Mitch hesitated, caught between a pained smile and an all-out grimace.

Ruta squeezed her arm tighter around Will's. "Eez room on boat, no?" Her lush black eyelashes batted signals certain to have worked their magic on Mitch a few times before.

Allison straightened her back and nudged her boobs out enough to draw both men's focus. They exchanged looks that only men can appreciate, but Sophie understood the message loud and clear: *Hubba hubba.* Translation? *Whatever she wants.*

Great, Sophie thought. *Now the other pain in my ass is a party favor.*

"Of course, there's room," Allison said. "It's a bigass boat."

Sophie, wearing sunglasses too dark for indoors, mouthed to Mitch. "Not a good idea."

He pulled the sunglasses off her face and laid them on the counter next to his koozies. With a palm shrug, he mouthed to her, *What Ruta wants, Ruta gets.* To the others he said, "What the hell? Always room for more testosterone in a small space, right?"

"That only applies to locker rooms," Sophie said. "And like in locker rooms, there are things you do not want waved in your face."

Ruta pressed herself against Will. "We're going to have so much fun."

Sophie dug her fingers into her forehead. "This is a disaster in the making."

But her protests went unnoticed as Allison and Ruta buzzed around Will like he had nectar coming out of his pores.

"Excuse me, ladies." Gracefully, Will extricated himself and pulled Sophie aside. He bent close to her ear and spoke in a low, mollifying tone. "You don't mind, do you? The Princess might be a good connection for me."

The Princess? Something in the way he said it grated on her. But he might be right. She supposed, grudgingly, she could tolerate the father of her children for a few hours.

What could go wrong?

"Whatever," was the quickest encapsulation of her feelings—more an acceptance of defeat than permission.

Resigned to her day on the Titanic, she plucked a red baseball cap from the display and flipped it onto his head. "First foray into the sun with that short cut; better cover up." At his mirthful smirk, she regretted doling out the wifely advice.

He traded the cap for a canvas fishing hat poked through with hooks and lures. He plopped it onto his head, and the price tag dangled around his nose. "Old habits, huh?"

She surveyed his spectacular old-fogey look. "My thoughts exactly."

Chapter 13

The way to Mitch's boat slip took them through pass-coded gates along wide deck walkways. Trying to keep up with Mitch and Will without tripping on the planks or toppling into the harbor's murky water made Sophie feel vertiginous. Not to mention the distraction of Allison's bare gluteus maximus contracting with every step as she skipped along behind them.

Ruta kept stride with Sophie. "She has butt like bowling balls, no?"

"I think she's a bodybuilder in her spare time."

"Admit," Ruta said. "She is hoochie."

Ruta had been well Americanized. Sophie shrugged—her effort at being kind. "You have to hand it to her. Allison knew right out of high school that she wanted to do real estate. She's done exceptionally well in a short period of time. It's taken me twenty years and the equivalent of around-the-world-beer-tasting just to find something that holds my interest." She regretted divulging so much, but she couldn't take it back. Damage control: "Nothing I sampled made me happy until real estate. I love it."

Mitch stopped at the last slip on Row G. Jimmy, Ruta's bodyguard, was there, standing next to a sleek white ski boat with a thick blaze of blue and yellow from bow to stern.

Mitch jumped into the boat and spread his arms. "Ta-da. What do you think of my new toy? She's got a Corvette engine, 375 horsepower, and 390 foot-pounds of torque."

"Nice," Will said, stepping into the boat.

Sophie issued *oohs* and *aahs* from dockside, watching Will fondle the watercraft's lines and angles with his eyes. Probably nostalgic for the days he had his own boat and fished and camped on the Highland

Lakes—back when they used to be a fun couple.

Mitch pointed out the boat's amenities, like plush vinyl seats in the V shape of the bow and a cushy bench wrapped around the main compartment from behind the driver's seat to the rear sundeck and up the left gunwale. He lifted the sundeck to reveal the engine, then cranked the ignition so 375 horses could buck and whinny.

Arching over the driver's seat from both gunwales was a tower of aircraft-grade aluminum tubing, and dangling from the arch were four cylindrical speakers that piped out the Tex-Mex rock and blues of Los Lonely Boys. *Vamonos!*

Two wakeboards also hung from the tower, one in shades of purple and pink, the other a vibrant green with silvery swirls on the bottom. The purple and pink one said *Diva* and reminded Sophie of the high-top sneakers she'd crafted for her senior dance with fluorescent spray paint, black marker, and glitter. The green board had some sort of alien creature painted on it.

Mitch gleamed. "These little sweethearts are for Sophie and Ruta. Take your pick."

Will stood atop the sundeck and helped Ruta into the boat as she squealed. "I absolutely love eet!"

Sophie absolutely did *not* love eet. "I don't know how to wakeboard. I can't even get up on skis. Right Will?"

"Sophie prefers to ride in the boat and bounce around and look at the scenery," Will said. "Sometimes she gets in the water, but then she gets right out again as a matter of principle."

Sophie's eyes rolled, which she hoped sent a clear message.

He turned to the others then. "Kidding. Sophie could do it if she wanted to. She gives up on things too fast, that's all."

He offered her a hand, and she dismissed it, stepping into the boat without his assistance. But it was a bigger step than she realized, and she lost her balance on landing.

Mitch and Will both lunged to help her, but Mitch held on more firmly and pulled her to him with a reassuring smile.

"You'll have fun on the wakeboard. I'll teach you."

Sophie scrunched her nose at Will. *Take that.*

Ruta wasted no time choosing the *Diva*. "Eez such sweet gift. Don't you tink, Sophie?"

A wakeboard? Sweet? Puppies and kittens are sweet. Flowers for no special reason are sweet. Mitch's chocolate kiss areolas are sweet, presumably. Wakeboards are hard and smooth and demand stamina, not to mention they're slippery when wet. Normally, Sophie liked those qualities, but not when they stood between her and her pride. She watched the mental footage of herself skipping end over end across the water—a 120-pound rock with a floaty strapped to her feet. Every fiber quaked at the idea of busting her ass in front of the very four people on earth who could make her feel *more* inadequate.

Mitch tapped the green alien. "This one's yours, Sophie. She screams on the water."

The silver alien painted between the foot bindings with frizzed-out hair and demented yellow eyes looked a lot like Sophie's inner chicken. Will would never spend good money on something like this, a fact that would have irked her sixty seconds ago. Here Mitch had bought a fun gift, far removed from the mundane Clappers, Dust Busters, and Chia Pets of her past, and she had to force herself to appreciate it. Of course, it did brighten her spirits to see Allison the Callipygian waving her envy around on the dock, right along with her bare behind. Seemed she had not been favored by the Slinky God of Watercraft Offerings.

"How thoughtful to buy me such an *expensive gift*," Sophie said, peeking at Allison.

"Actually," Mitch said, "I bought them off of Allison, but she did charge me up the wazoo. Have a seat now, so we can get underway. Anywhere you like. Try the playpen."

Sophie glanced about. "Playpen?"

"Front of the boat."

Will shoved the boat away from the dock, and they all waved to Jimmy, who was given the day off. As Mitch began maneuvering out of the slip, Allison leaped aboard like a Lara Croft action figure and pulled off her pretend cover-up, all in one fluid movement. Her hard body sat in the seat adjacent to Mitch where she applied lotion to her arms and thighs, as comfortable in her nakedness as a cat in its own fur. In Ruta's terms, a *hoochie* cat.

Sophie balanced in the center of the boat, debating whether to join Ruta in the playpen or claim the wrap-around bench in the back, next to Will. Neither was appealing.

Ruta had already disrobed to her tankini and sat with her Pixie Stix legs as outstretched as they could be in a space the length of a matchbox. At her age—Sophie guessed upwards of sixty—her slender body was in great shape.

Sophie instantly wished it were too cold for swimsuits. She felt bloated and stuck in a physique not entirely her own, as if a distant relative had given her a loaner and the bitch wouldn't come pick the damn thing up, forcing Sophie to lug it all over the place. Her second overriding thought: half naked in the playpen, the perfect vantage point for a boat driver to see everything—the good, bad, and the fugly as she jiggled across the choppy water.

Lovely.

After carving ever so slowly through the no-wake zone, Mitch jammed the throttle and the boat roared to life, lurching toward deeper parts of the lake. "Brace yourselves, ladies."

The move dumped Sophie sideways onto Will's lap, her new shades picked off by her clumsy landing and the wind. She twisted herself into the seat beside him, groping for something—*anything*—to hold on to besides Will, whom she discovered had discreetly removed his shirt and now displayed enough hair on his chest to be mistaken for the Missing Link. He held onto his fisherman's hat with one hand, allowing his winged elbow to bop her in the head.

Once Mitch trimmed it back, he cut through the waves and landed with a thud that splashed shocking cold water onto the entire rear half of the boat. Sophie gasped and sputtered, and after another dozen dousings, she gave up, taking small comfort in the invention of waterproof mascara.

Wearing sopping clothes seemed pointless and unattractive, so she braved it and stripped to her swimsuit. Mitch was going to be indoctrinated to imperfection soon enough anyway, and she hoped he wasn't disappointed.

She stood, unzipped her capris, and let them drop just as the engine cut off and the boat slid to an abrupt halt, launching her into the bow with her ankles tangled in her pant legs. She tried to sit up, her thin blouse clinging to her breasts like oiled Saran Wrap and lake water dripping from her forehead, as she stared up at Ruta.

"So-o-o, *this* is the playpen."

"You remind me of seester," Ruta said. "Deed I mention?"

Allison peered over her sunglasses. "Having fun, Sophie?"

"Of course, she is," Mitch said, idling the boat into a large cove. "Allison, get out the life vests, will you? Ready, ladies?"

Sophie hauled herself up and stepped out of her capris, trying hard not to make eye contact with Will. She spoke in a hoarse whisper to Ruta. "You're going first, aren't you?"

"No, no, darlingk. You go."

"But this is your vacation. All that international jetsetting takes it out of you. You must be exhausted. You *deserve* to go first."

"Nice of you, dear, but I'm quite relaxed. You don't mind me to say, I want to see how eet's done first. After you."

Sophie swallowed a dry lump of dread. "Well then, if you're sure."

Allison simultaneously purred and hissed. "You blow any more smoke up her ass, Ruta might think you're terrified to get in the water."

"Eez okay," Ruta said. "I'm terrified too. You go. I see what you do wrong."

Allison hopped on the sundeck in her aqua strings, legs shoulder-width apart, hands on hips, blonde hair blowing in the breeze, glimmery lips sulking. A *Sports Illustrated* sexpot at a photo shoot. Her demeanor screamed, *Look at me!*

Sophie removed her blouse as well. Equally bikinified in a fluorescent orange number, her top resembled two highway safety cones (miniaturized, with discreet lift devices); and the bottoms had a heavy faux belt across the front, á la James Bond Girl (the one 007 gives his valet ticket to). Her demeanor screamed, *Warning. Inner Chicken Zone.*

Allison lolled her head back as she stroked her neck before gathering her hair and clipping it on top of her head, elbows akimbo, chest flared. "It's sizzling out here, isn't it? You don't mind if I go for a dip, do you?"

Mitch's mouth hung open. "Uh-uh."

Allison turned her bare butt to them and dove in. Gracefully. With the splash of a goldfish and nary a jiggle from her thighs. Sophie was amazed the woman could stay under for so long and wondered if maybe she'd drowned. But luck was not on her side today.

Allison emerged and floated on her back, heaving her breasts toward the sky. Finished languishing, she swam to the stern, hoisted herself on the platform, and squealed. "Woo. Now that's refreshing."

Will handed her a beach towel as water drained off her skin and her nipples protruded through the stretchy aqua fabric like clipped cigar tips. Mitch's pupils were fixed and dilated. He quit breathing and his lips parted like he wanted to say something. Sophie figured he was imagining a leisurely smoke on some Cubans.

"Bada-bing," he muttered. He took off his shirt and dropped his shorts, revealing a bikini Speedo and the conspicuous ridgeline of a gently draping Mr. Slinky.

Yikes. Sophie tried not to stare, but the man needed support. Wearing such a flimsy garment to contain his monstrous legacy was akin to Dolly Parton going braless in a gauzy tunic.

He rolled his shorts into a haphazard ball and stuffed them into a side compartment. One corner of his mouth nestled into his cheek, and his eyes brushed down her chest, bearing down on her mons pubis. He wasn't undressing her with his eyes; he was ravishing her.

He handed her his can of beer, and Sophie took a few sips, realizing only as the icy hops spilled across her tongue how thirsty she was. She handed the can back with a quickly uttered thanks, and Mitch's fingers brushed hers in a subtle caress that promised intimately more. Then he took a gulp from the can, his eyes watching her as he finished it off. The move felt suggestive, possessive, as if the sharing of a can where both their lips had been indicated a deeper level of familiarity that he wanted the world to see.

Or maybe just Will.

Will slumped lazily on the wide, white bench with his muscled arms outstretched, as if sunning himself were his only care. His geriatric fishing hat shaded his eyes and lent him the air of leisure, but his hands were not-so-tranquil fists. He opened and released them and scratched his face, then sat forward with his elbows on his thighs.

Sophie was determined he wasn't going to ruin her day; yet his presence created such awkwardness, she wanted to order him off the boat.

It seemed like a little bit of justice that, at that moment, he shot to his feet and dove into the water with his hat still on his head.

"Allison will drive the boat," Mitch announced. "I'll help Sophie on the wakeboard."

Allison handed Sophie a life jacket that looked like a red upper body cast with plastic buckles. Before Sophie could take it, Allison let go and the life jacket dropped to the floor.

"Oops." She pirouetted and sauntered to the back of the boat to work on the bindings.

Ruta stood up and stretched, calling Sophie toward her. "I be careful if I am you," she said in ominous tones. "That girl eez dangerous like alley cat. Always with claws out. Only one word for dat, and eet starts with H. You can take her, no?"

Mitch motioned for Sophie. "Let's get you harnessed in."

Sophie sucked in a deep breath. No backing out now. She trembled as he pulled her close, threaded her arms into her vest, and fastened the buckles tight.

Allison bounded past and plopped into the driver's seat. "You been working out, Sophie? Strength and endurance are key if you're going to wakeboard."

"That's what I was afraid of," Sophie said under her breath.

"We can't have you injuring yourself."

"I'll be right with her," Mitch said. "Take it easy when you pull her out of the water."

Sophie held her chin high and stepped on the gunwale, pulled the wedgie out of her crack, and dove in. Hitting the cold water, her sphincter squeezed to a pencil point. She shot to the surface, gasping, and saw Will climbing the ladder, his sodden hat squeezed in one fist.

Mitch's human cannonball sloshed the boat with his full weight in fish habitat. Allison and Ruta shrieked and recoiled, but the tsunami had already hit. Wearing a life preserver, he bobbed in the water and crawled toward Sophie.

"Let's have the board, Tunemeister," he called to Will. "You ready,

Sophie?"

"Uh-huh." Her hands shook, and it wasn't from the cold water.

Will tossed in the wakeboard, which surfed right into Mitch's hands.

"Don't worry," Mitch said. "I had these sized special for you. Come on, give me your foot. What do you think, are you goofy?"

"That's an understatement."

"Goofy means right-footed, in wakeboard speak. I bet you're goofy." He stuffed her feet into the boots and handed her the rope. "Tuck your knees up like you're sitting on the toilet and put the rope between your feet."

Sophie gripped the tow bar and pulled the wakeboard beneath her. The toilet-hugging position wasn't something she wanted to demonstrate in Mitch's presence, but since she was scared shitless, it seemed only right.

Mitch steadied himself behind her. "Relax your shoulders. There you go. As soon as the rope gets taut, you give Allison the thumbs up. It's going to feel like a lot of force on your arms. Just hang on." He moved closer behind her, and the timbre of his voice dropped. "I've been meaning to tell you how much I enjoyed last Friday night. Hope we can do it again soon." His breath swished her ear and his hand brushed her thighs.

Bada-bing.

Sophie tipped over and inhaled a quart of lake water. She coughed and righted herself, leaning back against Mitch as he nuzzled his chin in the nape of her neck. She was relieved to see Will heading to the front of the boat to hang with Ruta.

The boat cut through the waves, and the rope began to straighten. Water bubbled to the surface from the outboards when Mitch pulled her closer. She definitely did not want to see Will's face now.

"I'm out of town this weekend," Mitch said, nibbling her ear and sending goosebumps into places she didn't know she could get goosebumps. "But not till Saturday. I was hoping to get together this Friday night. If you don't have the kids, I mean."

"I do, but what about coming for dinner? They go to bed at nine, and after that..."

"Yes?" he said, close enough that Mr. Slinky knocked on her back door.

Holy Mother of Erotica. The cold water could not intimidate that one.

"After the kids go to bed?" He pulled her earlobe into his mouth and sucked on it. "You know you do amazing things to me, right?"

Huh? Kids? Amazing? Where am I?

She felt a tantalizing thrill way down south between her legs. "I'll get a sitter."

From the boat Allison shouted. "Say when!"

Sophie wasn't sure she heard right. "What?"

The boat powered up and heaved forward, and she felt a massive tugging on her arms. Her weight under the water dragged. Her thighs and calves flexed stiffly, ankles and knees strained. The board felt like brakes on her feet, preventing her from standing up and gliding. She didn't even want to think about the high-pressure jet wash on her butt. Water sprayed her face, and she feared drowning without ever going under. But the resistance was too much. The bar sprang from her hands.

She coughed up water and wiped her eyes.

Mitch swam toward her. "You have to *pull* yourself out of the water. Use your arms."

The boat circled around, slowing as it passed so the rope could drift near. Will moved toward the back to offer help, his eyes meeting Sophie's with a veil of concern. Mitch grabbed the bar and handed it to her while Allison maneuvered the boat into a forward position.

Boat exhaust buffeted her nose as Sophie signaled thumbs up. Again the boat yanked her forward, and she pulled herself upright, only to face-dive into the water. The wakeboard slipped beneath and popped up behind her so that the boat dragged her flat out. The constant push and pull between horsepower and water pried the board from her feet.

Mitch retrieved the wakeboard and laid on it as he swam toward her. He pounded between her shoulder blades, prompting water from her lungs. "Shrug it off. You got this."

Ruta leaned over the gunwale as the boat motored around. "Okay, Sophie?"

"She's fine," Mitch called out. "She's tough."

Allison shouted over the inboard. "Try letting go of the rope so you don't drown."

Sophie caught Will's glare at Allison, who simply flashed her brilliant white teeth.

Mitch was none too happy. "Easy on the throttle this time."

He doled out more words of encouragement, and Sophie took a deep breath, steeling herself for the challenge. Do or die, she decided, reaching for the tow bar.

She grappled for balance when a wave knocked her off kilter and the boat jerked before she was ready, dragging her as she struggled to pull herself upright. Out of the water, she braced for another header. When it didn't happen, her legs extended so she was almost vertical. As the boat sped up, her shoulders felt stretched, arms extended, hands gripping the bar, but she maneuvered the wakeboard under her and leaned back.

I'm up! She grinned stupidly, followed by a startled, *Now what?*

Hoots and cheers came from the boat as her board bounced over choppy waves, and she weaved through water that got choppier the farther she skied out of the cove.

The boat carved a wide, white-capped arc and, by then, Sophie's arms were exhausted and her thighs burned. As they circled around and closed in on Mitch in the water, choppy waves hit her straight on. She jounced hard and tripped up, swerving, flipping, and crashing into the water on her shoulders where her chin kissed the wakeboard. When she came up for air, her hair was plastered across her forehead, Donald Trump style, and the board had popped off her feet—along with her belted bikini bottoms.

She was still catching her breath and searching desperately for the bottoms when the boat coasted nearby.

Mitch swam over and gave her a knuckle bump. "I knew you could do it."

Ruta cheered, her fists pumping the air. Will issued two thumbs up and a genuine smile.

Allison rose higher on her knees in the driver's seat, allowing the boat to idle. "You looked like a major dork, but I guess you brought it home in the end."

"I'd like to come in," Sophie said, as the waves sloshed her in the water, "but I lost a little something when I fell back there."

Everybody zeroed in on what she might have lost. Unable to hide her white butt, they all laughed.

Great, she thought. *Now I'm the party favor.*

She curled into a modest ball. "Little privacy?"

They all turned away as she climbed out, except Will. He had an open towel waiting and wrapped it around her shivering body as the boat rocked. Instead of admonishing her nakedness, he looked into her eyes, securing the towel ends in his hands above her breasts.

A broad smile lit up his whole face. "You did it. That was awesome."

Under that wet fishing hat, she saw the face of the old Will. He, of all people, knew how many times she'd failed at getting up on skis in the past. He knew how much it meant. Her heart felt huge in a chest still beating wildly from the exertion, and she couldn't help unleashing a full-faced grin.

"I did, didn't I?"

Mitch got in the boat with water pouring off of him. "I knew you could do it."

He pulled Sophie into his arms and gave her a bear hug that lifted her feet off the ground. With her face buried in his chest and her arms pinned against her body beneath the towel, he leaned back and gave a loud *whoop* that sounded muffled in her water-filled ears.

When he set her back down, the waves from passing boats knocked her off balance. Mitch grabbed her as she fell into Will, at the same time Will caught her.

Mitch tried to tug her away. "Hey, why don't you ski next, buddy?" he said pulling Sophie under his arm.

Will pulled her back. "Nah, I'm good."

"I insist," Mitch said, jerking her toward him. "Everybody skis on the boat."

Will heaved her back. "After you. Let's see what you got."

Mitch's chin jutted and his chest expanded as he reclaimed Sophie against his chest. "Yeah? You wanna see what I got?"

"Hello-o-o," Sophie said. "Not a pinball here."

"Now *thees* eez entertainment," Ruta said, from the playpen.

Mitch released Sophie, then cuffed Will on the shoulder. "Girl's got some talent, eh?"

Will's whole body looked like one big muscle contraction in a forward posture that vibrated with adrenalin, and Sophie suspected his clamped mouth restrained a blast of cuss words and the need to act out some stabbiness. She'd never seen him so... so... *jealous?*

She secured the towel around her waist and quietly fumed. "What are you *doing*?"

His head turned fast, but his only response was a deep grumble that she guessed came straight from his fists.

"You should not have come," she said.

Their eyes locked until he blinked and looked away. He removed his hat and ran a hand through his new short crop before plopping onto the bench and staring sullenly at the distant shoreline. Satisfied he wasn't going to kill anyone, she left him and joined Ruta in the playpen.

"My turn," Allison announced. She lifted up the sundeck and traded Sophie's alien board for a deep blue mini surfboard with jagged yellow bolts and the words *Greased Lightning*. She tossed the board into the water and followed after it with a perfectly executed Esther Williams swan dive.

Sophie shivered from the wind on her wet skin and, despite Will and Mitch's pissing match, the exhilaration of her goofy-footed ride. But her pride of achievement went the way of the eight-track when Allison popped out of the water behind the boat, performing masterful tricks on her wakeboard.

Comparative perspective was such a buzz kill.

As the craft sped through the water, Allison traversed the lake with ease, gliding alongside the boat to give Mitch instructions and eyeballing Will like he was a chewy protein bar, with nuts. She did forward rolls and back flips, landing on her feet. Once she even landed with the rope wrapped around her body and the tow bar behind her back. On purpose.

"She was a champion skier in college," Mitch shouted from his driver's seat, over the roar of wind and motor. "Daredevil. Did a stint at Sea World San Antonio, skiing barefoot and balancing on people's shoulders. Phenomenal, isn't she?"

Sophie made a strangled sound.

Later, when Mitch cut the engine, Allison eased into the water and swam to the boat. "That was too fun," she said, hoisting herself out of the water. "Your turn, Will?"

Ruta leaned into Sophie's shoulder. "See what I say to you? She likes your husband."

Sophie shrugged, mentally distancing herself. "He's about to be my ex-husband, and then..." She listened to how the words sounded on her tongue. "She can have him."

"Oh?" Ruta said. "Then he really eez *available*?"

"Yes."

"You don't care who he sees now?"

"Of course not. Why should I?"

Ruta shrugged and indicated the activity at the back of the boat. "I didn't tink tings could get more interesting, but I was wrong."

Will had put on a life vest. Allison removed his hat and rubbed sunscreen on his face, into his clipped hairline. He buckled up the vest and thanked her—smiling dumbly, Sophie thought—and then he dove into the water behind Mitch.

Allison shoved a slalom ski toward Will, and both men readied themselves to be towed at the same time. Meanwhile, Allison idled the boat until the ropes had stretched tight. Mitch gave a thumbs up, and she pushed hard on the throttle, the front of the boat rising as the engine in the rear worked hard to tow two skiers.

"Hold on to your seats, girls. Playpen's gonna see some altitude."

When the bow rose high above the water, Sophie stared straight down at the rear of the boat, its motor churning a small canyon. She clutched the thin metal bar in the bow, surprised to feel Ruta clinging to her. With Ruta's weight, Sophie's fingers slipped off the bar and the two slid downhill, screaming, until they thudded into the base of the rear seat. They peeked over the platform at Mitch on his wakeboard and Will on his slalom ski. The boat leveled out, and Ruta stumbled back into the playpen, all knees and elbows.

As the watercraft carved deep ruts around the cove, Mitch cut across the waves on the left side of the boat's wake, while Will skied on the right side, glaring with steely determination.

"That's a lot of bravado for one lake," Sophie said, as she staggered back to the playpen. "Any bets on who'll be the last man standing?"

"I tink your handsome husband."

Even from far away, Will was an impressive sight, leaning back in the ski, thighs resisting the lake's turbulence, and biceps flexed with the grasp of the tow bar.

It had been seven years since Sophie had seen him ski. They'd gradually quit going to the lake after the kids were born and his work demanded more of his time and energy. As mad as she was at him now for ruining her day with Mitch, a trickle of joy welled in her throat to see him doing something he once loved with such passion.

Mitch Houdini was power and athleticism on the wakeboard, a dynamic force of nature. She imagined romance with him, great sex and adventure, and perhaps more. Of course, there was much she needed to learn about him, and she was ready to be schooled.

Houdini Phase II. Lesson One: Mr. Slinky.

The sun beat down on Sophie's shoulders and she pressed white spots into her skin. They'd been out on the water for, how long? She scrambled for her sun bag and pulled out her cell phone.

One-fifteen. *Oh no.*

She shouted to Allison. "How long to get back to the marina from here? I have a three o'clock that I won't make if I don't get back now."

Allison screwed up her face. "We'll be out here till sunset. You can't go back now."

"Mitch promised I'd be back at the docks by one."

Allison shook her head and indicated Ruta, sunning obliviously in the bow. "Ruta hasn't even had a chance to wakeboard yet. You should have cancelled your three o'clock."

"I couldn't. Stop the boat, Allison."

"Not a chance. We're not suffering for your poor planning."

Sophie dialed a number on her cell. The boat's motor and the wind were so loud, she couldn't hear a thing.

Thump, thump, thump. The boat hit a couple of waves straight on, and the bouncing jarred the phone from her hands, into the lake.

You've got to be kidding me.

She glanced back at Mitch and Will, gleefully hopping over the wakes in their quest to outdo each other.

"Sit down before you get thrown out," Allison shouted.

"Who's going to throw me, you? Turn this boat around now."

She grabbed the wheel and the two women fought for it, jerking the boat and jostling Ruta out of repose.

"Fine," Allison shouted, regaining control. "Hang on, Ruta."

The boat veered hard left and angled on its side. Sophie clutched the rail to keep from tumbling out, while Mitch and Will continued zigzagging through the water.

"You happy now?" Allison said.

"Happy is not quite the word." Sophie would be happy when Henry Roberts signed an offer on the Pecos house and handed her an earnest money check. As long as they were on their way back to the docks, that was enough for now.

After large waves from a cigarette boat came too fast; Will finally bobbled and spiraled into the drink. Mitch dropped into the water after, and Allison circled around to pick him up.

"I tink you never geeve out," Ruta called to him. "You have stamina of racehorse."

"It's one-thirty," Sophie said. "I'm going to be late for my appointment. I need to get back to the marina."

"One-thirty?" Mitch hauled himself onto the platform and ran a hand through his dripping wet hair as he scanned the terrain. "I'm sorry. I think from here it's at least forty-five minutes to the marina."

"But we're halfway there. Allison turned the boat around and..." Allison avoided their eyes, and it dawned on Sophie why. "You turned us in the wrong direction, didn't you?"

Allison shirked. "Turn around, you said. And to prevent you from killing us, I did."

"You made me think we were heading back to the marina."

"You thought what you wanted to."

"This is a disaster." Sophie's stomach curdled as she imagined the Roberts so angry they might fire her as their agent. "All I had to do was show up. The deal was ripe."

Mitch gave Allison a menacing look as he shrugged out of his life jacket. "Go pick up Will," he told her. "I'm sorry, Sophie. I really am. There may still be time, if we hurry."

"Fine, drop me off at the marina. I'll take a cab."

"No way. You'll take my car."

"Believe me, I should not be operating heavy machinery right now."

"I insist. I'll ride back to town with Ruta in the limo."

They picked up Will, who hardly got his life vest off before Mitch lay on the throttle. Sophie sat in the playpen as the boat flew across Lake Travis, worrying about losing her deal with the Robertses and stewing over her soon-to-be-ex-husband, sandwiched between Ruta and Allison on the backbench where their good time could not be contained. Over the course of the ride, Sophie's anger took on a nuclear mushroom-cloud quality, and on arriving at the marina, she gave curt goodbyes and hit the dock running.

Mitch accompanied her to the parking lot, while Will hurried behind with a lobster red torso and a pile of sun-bleached chest hair. As he split off, heading toward his Jag, he waved and shouted, "See you at home, Sophie."

That was purely for Mitch's benefit, she was certain. The man was incorrigible.

When they reached the Lamborghini, Mitch placed Sophie behind the driver's wheel and gave a fifty-cent tour of the console. She started it up, terrified and exhilarated to hit the gas. The engine roared to life, like a hive of bees under the hood—bees that slurped jet fuel for lunch.

He leaned through the window and planted a hard, wet kiss on her mouth.

Oh, that kiss.

She tried not to liquefy like a guppy in a blender before leaving him in a smattering of pavement pebbles. Her lips pulsed from the bruising of his mouth, her sex ached for the promise of fulfillment, and her whole body ignited from the power in her hands.

When she rolled past the stop sign, heading toward Mansfield Dam, she hit the gas. But she knew increasingly that she wouldn't make it in time, and there was nothing left to do but cuss to her heart's discontent.

She was coasting at sixty-five when a Lakeway cruiser's red lights flashed behind her.

Chapter 14

After filling the empty space in his stomach with Rosie's Tamales and stopping at Walgreens for a tub of aloe vera, Will drove home with one mission in mind: Egyptian pyramids. Keely needed her salt dough project transferred to the grade school arts center in preparation for Saturday's Third Annual Young Artisan's Festival.

The plan? Pick up the pyramids and deliver them to the school; pick up the kids from their afternoon care program; sink into an ice-cold bath before his fried skin melted off; and erase the mental images of Houdini in the lake with his wife.

Will traversed the hills around Lake Austin and hung a right where the road sloped past properties with lush, mature landscape. As their house came into view, he checked his watch. Four-twenty-five. It had been hours since he'd left Lake Travis, so he was surprised to see Houdini's Batmobile in the drive, powerful even without its engine running.

He stopped at the doorway wondering how to act. Like he didn't give a shit? Like he was damn happy to be rid of her? Like seeing Houdini touch her, hold her, kiss her didn't matter?

His knuckles brushed the face of the door, and he stepped into the foyer, listening. He checked the den (in case they were lusting on the couch again), checked the kitchen and the family room, and peered into the backyard. No signs of life other than Brewsky enthusiastically licking his privates on the lawn chair. Even had the lipstick out.

The cat stopped and eyed Will with his tongue clamped between his teeth as if to say, *You know you'd be doing this too, if you could.*

So, if they're not down here... what might be going on upstairs in his—er, *Sophie's* bedroom? At the foot of the staircase, he called up and listened to the tick-tock of the grandfather clock in the foyer. "Sophie?"

He tiptoed to the top of the stairs and skulked toward Sophie's bedroom door.

"Oh, So-o-phie-e-e!" He stomped the floor in dramatic fashion. "Here's old Will, traipsing through the house. Yep, picking up Egyptian pyramids for the festival." He stomped more in place. "Don't anybody be surprised."

He waited a few beats more, then huffed and moved on to Keely's room. The project sat atop her dresser on a two-foot by two-foot board, two massive pyramids surrounded by miniature plastic soldiers, hand-painted anew with Egyptian regalia. Painstaking work it had been, dipping those tiny brushes in and out of the colored paint pots and dabbing "clothes" over dull, green army gear. Keely had been a trooper, hand adorning more than thirty slaves; placing them strategically around one complete pyramid and one under construction. A labor-intense, creativity-sapping project now finished. Thank the pharaohs.

He balanced the project on his shoulder and carried it into the hall, his curiosity piqued as he neared Sophie's door. He leaned an ear against it. Not a peep.

"Sophie?" Carefully, he turned the knob, cringing in case she'd just forgotten to lock it and he was about to see them exposed in the throes.

Bed was made, coverlet smooth and neat. No signs of hot sex. No odd smells. But sounds came from the bathroom.

Dare he?

He pictured the walls inside that he had years ago painted teepee brown with the sponge daubing Sophie had suggested "for an antiqued effect." The paint had barely dried when she hung over the garden tub an enormous copper Kokopelli, the Ho-Chunk god of fertility, or some shit like that. She'd proclaimed the space her private sanctuary, and he'd given her hard time. Why wasn't it his space too? He'd done all the work, and why the hell would he want artwork of a guy with phalluses poking from his head? He regretted the fight he'd instigated, since he couldn't have cared less about a private sanctuary, but he never apologized.

He stood outside the bathroom door and rapped on it. Again he heard nothing, so he turned the knob, braced himself, and pushed the door.

Sophie glanced up from her submerged spot in the tub, a towel-turban wrapped around her head and thick bubbles encroaching on her neck. Water gushed from the tap. She startled and bolted upright.

"Dammit, Will. Stop sneaking around."

Her exposed torso was splotched with foam that concealed her self-described itty-bitty titties, and his memory captured her lower body beneath the big oval of bubbles. A big bowl of Rocky Road ice cream sat on the lip of the tub, and she held a glass of diet soda in her hand. Frothy prisms gusted with the scent of gardenias as the water jostled around her.

His eyes flitted in search of Houdini, but all he saw was Kokopelli, high on the wall, playing his flute and mocking Will through the silhouette of his big dickhead.

"Sneaking around?" Will wrestled the bulky pyramids through the door and set the tray on the counter between two sinks. "I called out, but you didn't answer. Thought maybe you were in here—uh, *dead*, or something."

"That's ridiculous." She turned off the water and stared at his head.

"What?"

"Just not used to you having no mullet."

He turned toward the mirror and examined his reflection. After the breakfast disaster with Coach Casey, he'd hit Shakeesha's Curl Up and Dye. The beauticians had gathered around him, clucking as the über-hefty one in silky purple Spandex snipped and clipped away his identity. He'd felt weak upon seeing the sad vestiges of his mullet swept into a dustpan.

"Me either." He shrugged and the fabric of his T-shirt scraped his burned skin. "Makes me feel naked."

"You have the kids?" she asked, sipping her soda.

"Not yet. Taking Keely's project to the school. Then."

Sophie had planted her feet on the end of the tub, and her fuchsia-painted toenails wiggled at the bubble line. She liked having her toes sucked, a memory that piqued some involuntary wood below his zipper.

"So, where's Houdini?" he said, self-distracting.

She leaned back, her sunburned shoulders a deep red contrast to the frothy white bubbles, and spooned chocolate ice cream into her mouth. "Why? You figure he was up here, ravaging me? When my children are supposed to be coming home?"

He stared into the tub, trying to pierce the bubbly fortress. Not time, distance, or anger could erase the slope of her back as he held her, the arc of her ass, the shape and feel of her thighs as his hands traced every curve; the soft roundness of her breasts and the planes of her abdomen; the yielding, velvety paradise that was her sex. Maybe her knees would part the sea of froth enough for him to see—

"You are a total Neanderthal. Ain't *nothing* for you between these legs, Will Camden."

Will jerked and refocused. "Ain't *nothing* there I *want*, Sophie

123

Camden."

But inside, the fissure ripped a little more. Those eyes of hers could penetrate his armor, shoot right to his core. He tried to erase the imprint of the kiss Houdini stole before she took off in his Lamborghini. He'd watched them from across the parking lot.

He slumped on the edge of the tub, his back to her, feeling the need to make a peace offering. "You were right. I shouldn't have gone on the boat with you guys."

"It wasn't your smartest move. Why were you even at the marina?"

"Personal business. What happened to your three o'clock appointment?"

She gazed into her mini-vat of confection and took a nonchalant bite, turning the spoon in her mouth, her sumptuous lips lingering on the stainless steel as she drew it out—totally oblivious about what that did to him.

"That didn't work out," she said, "but no biggie."

"You know, real estate isn't like your old volunteer jobs. You have to show up whether you want to or not."

Sophie's chin rose and her nose twitched, and he knew he'd said the wrong thing. "Why are you sitting? Why are you even in my bathroom?"

He stood and shook his head. "I have no idea."

"What I do isn't your business. You know that, right?"

"Is it my business how you got that bruise on your chin?"

She felt it with soapy fingers. "Must have been when I collided with the wakeboard."

"There's the bright spot in the day." He had to laugh in the face of her glare. "Take it easy. I meant you got up on the wakeboard. Used to be you gave up before you even got wet."

"Well, I had a good teacher this time. Think I found my new sport. Only wish I'd found it sooner."

He was filled to the gills now with her happy Houdini horseshit. "That's good. I'm happy for you. And I'm out of here."

"Wait, aren't you going to tell me how you screwed up your first date in twenty-four years?" The dimples deepened around her mouth. "How did you end up groping your daughter's softball coach? You should at least wait until your third date for a good grope. I think it's a rule."

"That's right. Laugh at my expense. The woman went to the bathroom and came out with her skirt stuffed into her granny panties. I was trying to save her from embarrassment."

"Seriously?"

"Not such a caveman after all, huh?"

She licked the spoon again. "Incredibly, she doesn't hold it against you. She wasn't even mad, once she calmed down. In fact, she wants to see you again."

"Not no, but *hell* no." As he moved to get the pyramids, he noticed a pink traffic ticket on the counter. *Figures.* "I see life in the fast lane is working out for you."

"Oh yeah," she said when he held it up. "That's for you."

He skimmed the ticket and felt his blood pressure rise. "I am not paying for this."

"Not the ticket—although it's only a warning. There's a card underneath it."

A business card lay where the citation had been. He picked it up and read the large scrawl across the front. *Spike Chingaso*, followed by a phone number.

"Why is this *my* little gift?"

"Because, William, Spike is not only a cop, she's a personal trainer."

"And?"

"And, I know you had to give up your personal trainer when money got tight. You have a mutual interest, and she wants to meet you. I told her you'd call for a Friday night date. You can meet her in a non-threatening environment—unlike the scary coffee shop."

He shared a fresh scowl. "I would never entertain a date with somebody named Spike."

"That's your problem, Will. You never entertain. Open your mind, spread your horizons, loosen up. Besides, she gets you closer to Ursula, remember? One down, four to go, and then Ursula comes home to you."

"That's all good, but... crap, I don't know why I let you guys talk me into this."

"Because you're broke?" Sophie licked ice cream off her lips. "Spike's a fiery Latina babe, and if you saw her, you wouldn't fight it. Trust me."

"Well, see that's just it, Sophie. I no longer trust you or my so-called friends."

"You're being melodramatic." Her legs sloshed the bubbles, and she set her bowl on the edge of the tub.

"What if I have plans Friday night?"

"That would be a first."

"And I suppose *you* have plans? You've got the kids this weekend." She looked away from him then. "Oh. You have plans with Mr. Money-Out-the-Wazoo, Mr. Buy-You-$180-Dollar Sunglasses. Mr. Let-You-Drive-His-Batmobile."

"You can stop now."

"Are you sure he's not trying to buy you?"

She sat up straighter in the tub, then seemed to remember she was naked and shrank beneath the bubbles. "You think I'm so into him because of his money?"

"So into him?" *Ouch.* "How old are you?"

She dipped her chin and peered up. "You don't get to judge me, Will."

"Me? Judge you? I'll let *you* judge how professional it was to let your feelings for this guy prevent you from meeting your clients. Real professional, Sophie."

"For your information," she said, blinking, looking away, "*that* was judging."

Shit, was she tearing up? He cursed and formed an apology that never left his tongue because of the she-devil eyes that met his.

"Get out." She batted the tears away, made a bucket with her hands, and sloshed warm, sudsy water all over him. Patches of bubbles hit the side of his head, fizzing and melting into his ear canal. "I said, get out. And take that judgment with you."

She sat up and cocked her arm back, her effervescent birthday suit parting so that her nipples played peek-a-boo with him. A loofa sponge glanced off his forehead.

"Ow. That does it. I'm out of here."

Her arm came out of the water again, this time with a sopping washrag that splatted against his chest. "Good. Stay the hell out of my life."

He caught the rag and fired it back. It smacked her face—a foot above his actual target, but a satisfying blow all the same. Suddenly she had nothing to say. He held up a quivering fist and hurried out, slamming the door behind him. He stopped then, trying to remember what he came there for.

"You forgot the pyramids!"

He barged back in and jabbed his finger at her. "*You* don't tell *me* what to do."

Her reply was the washrag in his face. "Call Spike. Friday night. I committed you."

"*You* ought to be committed." Water dripped down his shirt as he picked up the pyramids, jostling their heft right and left until he tugged them through the threshold.

She toasted him with a raised glass of soda. "To never, ever, *ever* taking you back."

He seethed through a contorted death-to-Sophie smile. "I wouldn't take *you* back, not if you begged me."

"You are still an ass."

"All part of my charm, baby."

"Omigod, if we weren't getting divorced, I would murder you."

"Ha. If we weren't getting divorced, I'd *let* you."

She tilted her chin defiantly. "Jerk."

"Slut."

"*Hhhh.*" She sat straight up. "Groper!"

Will's face bloated with fury. His fingers jabbed the air. "Groupie. Floozy. Diva." And with dramatic flair that required the stiffening of his whole body to execute, "*Succubus!*"

His eyes flickered to her sudsy chest again—not so sudsy anymore with the bubbles sloughing downward—and he couldn't help taking in every naked millimeter of her.

And he knew, in that moment, he was every bit the ass-jerk-groper caveman she thought he was.

Chapter 15

At four o'clock on Friday afternoon, Sophie hurried into the house lugging six bags of groceries for the dinner she planned to make for Mitch. She hauled the bags onto the kitchen counter and listened for her children. And Will. In the four days since their bathtub squabble, he'd commenced an intense campaign of avoidance, Sophie being the sole object of his efforts. On the occasions of closest proximity, they passed like commuter trains in opposite directions, sparks flying as they railed silently along.

The one bright spot was Will's apparent reinvention as a maid. Not that she wouldn't rather have him employed at the semiconductor plant, but coming home to spit-shiny floors, uncluttered and vacuumed living rooms, and a sparkling sink minus dirty dishes felt almost as amazing as great sex: intensely gratifying, euphoric, and so rare as to be obsolete.

She roamed the upstairs, calling out for Annabelle and Keely, and when she got no replies, she checked the backyard through Annabelle's window. Will must have been doing yard work. He stood in the grass beneath their ancient oak tree—which was actually two trees with fused trunks from the ground up. Each trunk was the diameter of a hundred-gallon water heater, and their combined massive canopy shaded a full third of the yard.

No sign of the kids, though, unless they were in the gazebo, where she couldn't see them from the second story. Probably hadn't even picked them up from after-school care yet. She hurried outside to get him moving. He had a date with Spike, and Sophie wasn't about to let him blow it off so he could hang around the house to ruin hers.

She'd felt quite smug ever since she talked herself out of a speeding ticket—with Mitch's help since apparently the hard-edged cop had expected her old friend Houdini to be at the wheel.

Will was going to be so surprised when he finally met her. Date Number Two promised to be a satisfying kiss-off. Sophie felt a wicked trickle of joy.

She squinted in the sunlight. No sign of the kids in the yard. Her shiny black pumps battered the wood decking in a percussive declaration of her arrival, until one narrow heel got wedged between the slats. In her forward momentum, she wrenched her foot out. She stepped out of the other pump and barefooted down the steps, across dirty brick pavers separated by loose gravel and grass tussocks.

"Isn't it time to get the kids? You still have a date tonight, right?"

Will continued tying a knot at the end of six feet of rope. She zoomed in on the back of his neck, pink with a film of sweat from the sun. He had been trapped in a *Quantum Leap* episode, circa 1987, with that mullet, and the new close-crop was nice. Brought out his eyes. Especially when he'd been trying to see what he could see while she was in the tub—a classic Will Camden move that, in their sex-craved, romance-fueled youth, was all part of his allure.

"Yes," he said. "Still have a debacle, and I already picked up the kids." He pointed up the tree.

Sophie's eyes scanned a rustic ladder of two-by-fours nailed into the trunk, leading to an elaborate fusion of wood beams and platforms nestled in the canopy.

"Hi, Mommy." Keely craned her neck over a wooden railing and grinned like Garfield. "Come up and see what Daddy did."

Sophie gasped at the sight of her eldest daughter's face, a gazillion feet overhead. Her nine-year-old stood in what looked like a giant crate—one of three, connected by steps and circling the tree trunks at different levels.

"You did not make my kids a tree house *that high up.*"

"Actually," Will said, "I made *our* kids a tree house. Didn't you ever see Swiss Family Robinson? It's every kid's dream."

"How could you build them a... a... *death trap* up there?"

"Mommy," Annabelle shouted, as she stuck her head between the railings. She looked even tinier, overwhelmed by the brown cascade of hair that fell around her face, and she dangled her Dora the Explorer doll with the oversized head. "Watch, Mommy. Dora can fly."

She let go of Dora's arm, and the doll plunged. Its hard, plastic body hit an exposed tree root and thwacked into two pieces, its head tumbling one direction, its body another.

Sophie's hands flew to her mouth as she supplanted the doll's untimely demise for a vision of her daughter's. "Oh. My. God. Girls, come down now!"

Will moved toward the makeshift ladder. "Relax, Sophie. It's a doll. I've reinforced all the braces and added extra siding so the kids can't fall out. We've already discussed the rules for the tree house, and they know they need to have an adult present at all times."

"Then it's a good thing I got here, isn't it?"

Will mimicked a laugh. "You kill me."

"Don't think that couldn't happen. Get my kids down."

The fear of her kids breaking their necks was unbearable. Her own fall from Grammy's rooftop felt like it happened yesterday. She recalled everything with perfect clarity. The dizzying logroll down a shingled pitch so rough it sanded the skin off her gangly knees, feet, and elbows. The susurrant gossip of brittle sycamore foliage, bearing witness to her slow-motion plummet. The wind slapping hair across her face, arms flailing, and dirt-smudged fingers grasping at air. The voiceless scream of terror and the clenching, tensing dread of the inevitable lung-collapsing impact of her body across an unyielding stratum of exposed roots, twigs, and rock. And the stunned, wide-eyed daze she couldn't shake while sunlight blinked through the canopy. Now she swallowed the dry knot in her throat. It could happen again.

Will climbed the ladder. "Come on up and see for yourself, Sophie. Just take one step at a time and hang on. It's easy."

Keely called to her. "Come on, Mommy. We have cookies."

"And juice," Annabelle added.

Sophie snarled. "You bribed them?"

"It's easy, Mommy," Keely shouted. "Daddy will help you."

Will climbed back down at the suggestion and held a hand out to Sophie. "Come on. Your kids want you to join them."

Sophie's eyes bore into his. "I can't, and you know it."

"Yes, you can. I'll help you."

"As you can see, I'm wearing a skirt."

"Go change then."

The girls tried coaxing her again. "Mommy, it's fun."

"You got up on the wakeboard, you can do this too."

Her new wakeboard bravado had disintegrated with the sudden resurrection of her acrophobia. Wakeboarding, she was on water. If she fell, the drop was a few feet into a liquid cradle. Up there in the tree house, the drop was fifteen feet to terra firma—case in point, Dora the *Exploder*.

Will's hand beckoned.

Up in the tree, Keely said, "I bet you ten gummy worms she won't do it."

"You're on," Annabelle replied.

Sophie heard them spit and clasp hands to seal the deal.

"Your own kids are betting against you," Will said. "This might be a good time to show them how a grown-up faces her fears and rises to a challenge."

Bastard had to be reasonable in front of the kids?

She had no time to change. If she was going to do this, it was now or never. She took a deep breath and slow, deliberate steps toward the tree, forcing her fear into stasis like she did on approaching the twelfth story windows in her office—and with just as much success. She reached out to grab the rung at shoulder level, her chest so tight the air felt squeezed out of her, and placed her bare foot on the bottom rung.

The girls hooted in delight.

Now she was in it. Why couldn't they scream tearfully, begging her to stay grounded and intact? With taut-muscled legs and grips, she climbed to the fourth rung where Will tiptoed in his sneakers. Fear rippled through her and, desperate for relief, she rounded her shoulders and eased into the safety of his broad chest.

"Don't hold your breath," he whispered, his breath tickling her neck. "I'm right here."

She stared into the tree bark, concentrating on inhales and exhales as Will repositioned himself. His body radiated heat, guarding her perimeter, feet straddling hers, arms parallel, and his abdomen steadying her backside. As she worked to calm her mind, memories flashed before her in annoying, vivid procession. Will naked. Sophie naked. Little Will and the Heartbreakers bumping against her, burrowing into her. In all the many places—indoors and outdoors—they dared to do it.

She pressed her eyes shut. "Dammit, what's wrong with you?"

"What?"

Shit. She'd said that out loud? "Not you. Me. And my stupid phobia."

She took another tentative step, bare feet finding narrow purchase on the rungs, her skirt inching up, sweat trickling from her armpits.

"There you go," Will said. "Keep your eyes on the girls."

Annabelle and Keely cajoled their mother upward.

Will stood a few rungs below and steadied her rise by applying gentle pressure to her behind.

She protested when his hand gripped one cheek. "You've got to be kidding."

"What," he said from below. "You think I *want* to grab your ass?"

"I'm sure you can think of a very recent groping incident with a certain coach we all know."

Will shimmied up behind her. "It was a groping *accident.*"

His hands grabbed beside hers, on the outside of the two-by-fours, and they rose up the rough bark together. His body spooned hers without touching, step for step.

And then the sound of leaves fluttering in the warm breeze disappeared. Her senses filled with the shape of his forearms as they flexed beside hers. Sweat glistened on his skin, his muscles contracting with each grip; and the scent of Will swirled through her nose with bittersweet nostalgia.

"Keep looking up." His voice so close evoked a shudder across her shoulders. "A few more feet and you can touch Keely's hand."

The top of his thigh nudged the bottom of hers, lifting her to the next step. In shorts, his exposed skin felt warm against her exposed hamstrings. Sitting essentially in his lap, her skirt hiking ever higher, she panicked. What was he—what was *she* doing? If only he'd quit breathing on her. If only her body wasn't so completely aware of his. If only she could quit remembering sex with him from behind.

"Stop," she said, elbowing him. "Stop. I don't need your help."

"Fine." He disengaged and dropped to the ground.

At which point Sophie made the fateful decision to look down. The grassy earth below seemed to undulate. Panic gripped her, and she froze.

"Wait," she said, panting and trembling, heart hammering against her ribcage.

"Oh, no. You got this. Look, girls. Mommy's doing it all on her own. Like a big girl."

Sophie couldn't move; her hands shook too much to let go. She peered down, despising him in her moment of need. "Will, please."

He squinted up at her with one hand to his ear. "I'm sorry, you say something?"

"I hate you."

"That's what I thought."

An unexpected voice rose up from ground level then. "Hey there, kids."

Mitch Houdini stood on the grass below her—the sweetest thing Sophie had seen all day. He said something about knocking and no one answering and then letting himself into her house, and then her joy descended into mortification. She was, after all, stuck in a tree and showing him her "big deal," as Will had recently put it.

A moment later, he was at her side. "Can I offer some assistance, Rapunzel?"

Sophie wanted to grab onto him, but she didn't dare unclench from the two-by-four. She nodded, and he wrapped one arm firmly around her waist.

"It's okay. I've got you. You can let go."

He was bigger than Will. Sturdier. She checked his hold on the rung below—a reliable grip. Trustworthy. And little by little, she loosened her death clutch enough for Mitch to budge her rung-by-rung to the ground—as if he'd been rescuing women his whole life and, not unimportantly, like she weighed no more than a Disney cartoon princess.

"Thank you so much," she said.

"My pleasure." He had the most heart-warming way about him.

Sophie adjusted her skirt and noticed Will staring—no, *glaring*. The muscles in his jaw convulsed, and she was certain a whole lot of indignation swirled inside that thick skull.

"You don't want to be late for your date with Spike," she said. "You better get going."

"You seeing Spike?" Mitch gave a thumbs up. "Awesome. She's a hottie hard body."

True to form where Mitch was concerned, Will's nostrils snapped like Chinese fans. "So, I have you to thank for this little set-up with Officer Spike?"

"Spike and me go way back, probably ten years," Mitch said. "She was my personal trainer and then she became a good friend." He leaned closer. "Not much intimidates that one. I can promise you, it'll be a *memorable* date."

"Good to know." Will's darkened gaze brushed Sophie and he called to his kids. "Girls, Daddy's got a hot date. The fun is officially over."

He turned and scaled the two-by-fours to guide Annabelle and Keely down. Sophie watched nervously, hands to her cheeks, as each girl descended to the ground unscathed.

"See?" he said to Sophie. "Monkeys. Sure-footed Camden monkeys, which should help you to *lighten up*." He bit out the last words as he passed.

"Girls," Sophie said, "you remember my friend, Mr. Houdini?"

Annabelle hit the brakes from a full sprint and shielded her eyes from the sun. "Hi, Mr. Hoodoody."

Keely turned up her nose and ran after her father, and the two disappeared inside the house. Annabelle trailed and slammed the door behind her.

"Sorry," Sophie said. "The kids aren't used to seeing other men in my life. My grandparents raised me after my parents died, and since I was an only child, Will and my grandfather are the only men the kids have ever really known. That's why I don't want them to see you and I as... well, as anything more than good friends. For now."

Mitch shrugged it off, sticking his hands into his pockets. "You can't blame them. I don't take it personally. Besides, a little girl's allegiance should be to her dad."

"They'll come around after they've seen more of you."

She shook off the irritation as they walked toward the house. "Did you ever want kids?"

"Me? I've been a bachelor for so long, I'm not sure family life will ever come my way. Maybe I was born to be alone. My parents weren't the best role models. They weren't around much. Dad was an international consultant and Mom was a very busy socialite, more in Europe than the States. But that's why I like you."

"Because I'm not a socialite?"

"You're social enough. I like that you're a real mom. You're here for your kids—and apparently your ex-husband, though I'd rather he were truly out of the picture."

She wondered just how deep his worry ran. "Won't be long."

His gaze softened. "And you're a kind soul. Makes you easy to be around. Makes it easier for me to be myself."

Score two points for the son of international socialites. "And I thought you were just a rascally playboy."

One corner of his mouth pulled into his cheek and he waggled a brow. "Maybe I am."

Where she had felt giddy around Mitch before—in a girlie, school-crush way—she now felt something more. Genuine affection? Or her nagging, lonely libido?

She liked so many things about him. That he appreciated her status as a mother first. That he wasn't only the playboy sales professional. That when he showed his vulnerable side, she saw the possibilities—no, *felt* the possibilities, like a deep-emotional massage. After the week she'd had with Will Camden, Mitch was a welcome change-up. He was uncomplicated and exciting, and she found him infinitely attractive when he opened up and invited her in.

But for the second time in less than an hour, she caught herself holding her breath, and the realization hit her: *fear*—the operative word for her whole life. What if she fell in love with Mitch Houdini and he dumped her? How fast and hard had she fallen for Will? And when it was over, how fast and hard was the landing? Falling was not something she took lightly.

She led the way into the house and distracted herself by unpacking groceries. Mitch leaned against the kitchen island and watched.

"Any word from Henry Roberts?" he asked.

Sophie would have given anything to *not* say, "He's not returning my calls." But no getting around it; Roberts was ignoring her. She emptied a plastic bag onto the counter: a head of leaf lettuce, two tomatoes, and celery stalks.

"The Roberts—is it Roberts or Robertses?" She shrugged it off. "They put a lot of weight in reliability—a lot of weight in *me*—and I should have made that appointment."

"I'm sorry, Sophie."

"And what's up with Ruta? I haven't seen her since the lake either. Is she avoiding me too?" She crumpled one empty bag and stuffed it into another.

"Of course not. She's been up to her Botoxed forehead in spa treatments. Sophie, Ruta's not in any hurry. You know that, right?"

"No, I thought she was anxious to get into a new place here."

"She is. Sort of. By the way, she got a call from her VP about a glitch in some merchandise she's marketing on HSN. She's off to New York in the morning, but she'll be back next week, ready for you to show those properties. Trust me, you're solid gold."

"Yeah? I must be rusty tin to Henry Roberts. I cut him, and now he needs a tetanus."

"You're taking this kind of hard. It wasn't your fault."

"You're sweet." She dropped a bag of rotini on the counter. "But yeah, it was my fault. I should never have gone to the lake with you guys. There wasn't enough time to do it all. I don't know how you do it. *All*, I mean."

"I don't. I pay people."

She hardly heard him. Her divorce loomed in her head, along with the anxiety that she wouldn't have enough in the bank to support herself and the kids without Will's spousal support. First Henry Roberts and now Ruta. Sophie *needed* the woman to be in a hurry to buy a property. Fear was turning viral in her gut.

"The Robertses wanted to do something meaningful for their daughter," she said, "and I had the chance to help. That house was their wedding gift."

Mitch stared at her, his incongruent happy face a sudden disconnect. For him, deals happened every day.

She tucked a bag of bagels in the breadbox and unloaded more vegetables. "You understand how important this deal is to me, right?"

"Of course. But it's not like the Roberts kids don't have more houses than they'll ever need in this lifetime. They're millionaires many times over, you know."

She brandished a cucumber. "That's not the point though, is it? I let them down. And now, not only don't I get the good feeling for helping them fulfill their plans for a wedding gift, I don't get paid. I'm tired of not getting paid. I volunteered for years, and I never paid my own bills. I *want* to pay bills."

"I gotta say, you're the first girl who ever said that to me. Lower your weapon, will ya?"

Will appeared behind him. "Kids are taking a shower, and I'm outta here."

Sophie dropped the cucumber and followed him into the foyer. "*That's* what you're wearing on your date with Spike?"

He stopped and surveyed himself. "Tattered T-shirt: check. Favorite running shorts, with a couple hits of Febreze: check. Brand new sneakers to replace the golf shoes you despise: check and double check."

"Where are you taking her, the flea market?"

"Let's rehash this, shall we? You said Officer Spike is a cop and a personal trainer, and, as it happens, I need a workout. *Perfect* match. You're very good at this, Sophie. Maybe matchmaking will be your *next* career."

"But it's Friday night. That's not a date."

"It is to me. I assume you will be so occupied here, you won't be tempted to spy on me this time." He turned her around and gently shoved her. "Back to *your* date now, huh? Oh, and based on your buddy's glowing commendation of Officer Spike? I wouldn't wait up for me."

Sophie fisted her hands. "I won't leave the light on."

She returned to the kitchen and unpacked the rest of her groceries in silence. She hoped Mitch might say something supportive to make her stop fuming about Will—who was exasperating beyond belief—but he just observed.

"You'd think the man wasn't interested in women. I mean, I picked a good one for him, and he's going to blow it by showing up as a homeless guy."

More protracted silence, until Mitch said, "You *are* done with him, right?"

"Completely. The man's a mess."

"Good. I'd hate to let myself fall for a woman who was in love with someone else."

Let himself... *fall for her?* Could he tell how fast her heart was beating?

"Will and I have been over since long before we separated. I do what I like now, and with whom. In less than thirty days it won't matter anyway. We'll be officially divorced."

Mitch looked like he needed more convincing.

"Honestly, why can't that man act like the ex-husband he was meant to be? I mean, what's so hard about just becoming a memory?

I'm happy to be one."

That got a smile out of him.

"If it's any consolation," he said, "Spike will have him eating out of her hands in short order, and you'll get your wish. You *will* just become a memory."

A shot of queasiness hit her stomach, and she blinked it away. "Believe me, getting Will out of my life would be a dream come true. But I don't think he's into women right now. Except for Ursula." She stopped herself from confiding the details of Will's money woes. It was enough she'd slipped and ranted about her own.

"Who's Ursula?"

"Oh, a guitar. His old guitar." She waved her hand dismissively. "It's a long story, but I think Ursula is the only woman he wants to play with right now."

"Or maybe you're right. Maybe he's not into women."

"Of course he's into women. He married *me*. I came with all the requisite female parts." *Though god knows, the last few years he never seemed to want me.*

"Lots of gays live a straight life for years before they come out of the closet."

Sophie imagined Will embracing some hunky underwear model and snickered. "Not Will."

"No? We'll see. If anybody can drag the truth out of a person, it's Spike. She has special, shall we say, interrogation talents."

"Okay, you have to tell me what that means."

Mitch held up a finger. "I got this." He pulled out his cell and selected a contact, then paced around the kitchen island with the device to his ear.

Sophie heard low-level murmurs from the tiny earpiece.

"Hey, Spike. Your old pal Houdini here. Long time, darlin'. Yeah, I know. I heard you're seeing Will Camden tonight." Extended pause. "That's cool. But I think he's maybe, shall we say, hiding in the closet."

He walked onto the back porch, and as the door closed behind him, Sophie heard him say, "Listen, if anybody could drag the truth out of him, it's you."

Chapter 16

Will stretched his quads by extending one leg behind him and pulling the heel of his Nike up to his butt. When the stiffness abated, he dropped his foot and repeated on his other leg. He warmed up near the footbridge that connected pedestrians and bicyclers from the north side of Lady Bird Lake to the south shore, waiting for Spike Chingaso, the cop-slash-personal trainer.

The pre-dusk shoreline seemed unusually active for a Friday, and the rush-hour traffic from MoPac above made him glad he had time off from the rat race to unwind.

Since Spike was a trainer during her off-duty hours, Will felt no need for the traditional trappings of a real date. It was enough that a sexy woman of authority, walking around with a badge and handcuffs, tripped his mental circuitry with vivid images of domination and lust. But other than the fantasy, he had no hope of sparking a meaningful relationship with Officer Spike. Still, he wouldn't rule out after-workout drinks, if she was game. If Sophie could do this dating thing, maybe he could too. But he'd do it his way.

As he stretched his calves, two well-built thirty-somethings huddled in animated conversation under a nearby scrub oak. The taller one, easily six-five, had just arrived. His oversized red lips reminded Will of wax candy, and with brushed blue shadow across his eyelids and pointy-arched eyebrows that seemed hand-drawn, Will couldn't stop staring. Judging by the shiny coat of red polish on the guy's well-manicured fingernails, he'd just come from the beauty parlor. A stretchy headband looped around his head, and a ponytail wagged from his crown.

Despite being bolstered with new insight after scouring his *GQ*,

Will had no idea what it all meant. The guy seemed less metrosexual and more something else entirely. His well-chiseled musculature was a mindboggling contrast, from his bloated chest and arms to his sculpted thighs and calves; but wearing slick blue short-shorts and white knee socks gave him the illusion of a walking American flag.

The short one had a lot going on with his hands, flipping his wrists and propping his fingertips on his chin. He looked the beefy guy up and down, his alto's voice belying his small stature. "All you're missing are sparklers, Murray."

The big man looked himself over. "It's all I had in my locker. Thought you were going to wait for me, and we were walking over here together. The stagehands were looking for you. They want your approval on the backdrops."

"Those people can't wipe their asses without my explicit directions."

"A little stressed, Arty?"

"I'm sure Spike will sweat it out of me."

What? *His* Spike? What were the odds that another Spike was supposed to be in this exact spot at this exact time? The last thing he wanted was a group session. Of course, that took even more pressure off of it being a date.

"Between you and me," Murray said, "I'll be glad when this production is over. I'm much better at giving direction than taking it, and being the star is too much pressure."

Arty laughed. "Still and always the diva. We won't have to pick you off the ground today, will we? How are your knees?"

"Skinned and sore. I haven't spent so much time on my knees since that Club*Men* vacation in Aruba. Did you catch my show last night? Wore that pink sequined number. The crowd went crazy."

Will took a deep breath, threw his backpack over his shoulder, and walked toward the twosome. "You guys working out with Spike?"

"Yup. There's our fearless leader now." The big man waved and called out as Spike crossed the footbridge over Lady Bird Lake. "Spi-i-ike!"

Spike wore sunglasses, black spandex shorts, and a tiny orange-and-yellow sports bra that revealed a bare midriff and rippled abs. She presented as the antithesis of her name, a gorgeous Latina with delicate facial features. Thirtyish. Curvy yet muscular and firm, silky black hair swept up in a ponytail. Exotic and mesmerizing. Using Sophie and Tess's vernacular, Spike's Fresh Factor was a solid ten.

"Hey, boys," she said, beginning a sideways stretch with her arms extended, elongating her sleek torso. And then she noticed Will and flashed movie-star straight teeth as they shook hands. "You must be

Will. Boys, Will is trying us on for size today."

Big Murray dug a business card out of a thin cloth wallet. "Whatever you need, man, and I'm available on quick notice."

Will shook Murray's huge hand and glanced at the proffered card: *Murray Moves It.*

"Don't you be rough on him," Arty said, fingering his chin. "He looks virginal."

Will tucked Murray's card into the back pocket of his shorts. "It's been awhile, but I assure you, I'm no virgin at this."

"Oooh, feisty too," Murray said, in singsong. "I like that, don't you, Artemis?"

"Don't start with me, Murray. Nobody ever called me Artemis but my whore-dog mother. I ever tell you how she died?"

"Gentlemen," Spike said. "If you're all good and warmed up, shall we proceed? We'll start with a run and then move into more exciting things to measure your fitness level, see how much stamina, coordination, and balance you have. Cool, Will?"

With her faint accent, Spike's melodious voice brushed across Will's synapses like Mexican birds of paradise in the breeze. "Cool," he said.

Once they began the run, he caught up to Spike, jogging in her stride across the footbridge. "I thought our, er, date, was a one-on-one session."

"Sorry, had to move my Saturday group to this evening. You don't mind, do you? I thought you'd fit right in with these guys."

Will thought about that for a few strides on gravel that tested the integrity of his ankles. "Wait. How do I fit in? I'm not a drag queen."

"My friends are actors, Will, and they're good at it. Murray has a starring role as Dorothy, the mathematical genius in *The Whiz of Oz*, and he's a leader in the LGBT community."

Spike was off-the-charts hot, and while he'd like to just say, *Yes, okay, whatever, your majesty*, he hadn't quite connected the dots to how he fit in. Maybe he'd throw in some humor. Girls liked that.

"I'm sure the guy's great in *The Whiz*, but I'm all male, baby. Seriously, 100 percent testosterone."

Spike kept her eyes on the trail. "But you're pretending to be straight, right?"

He felt like they were in two different conversations. "I am not pretending to be straight, because I *am* straight."

She shrugged. "If you say so."

"Why do you question it? My brain is twenty-four-hour girls gone wild. In fact, you should think of me as one gigantic Y chromosome."

She shrugged. "Maybe, but I heard you didn't like women."

Will blurted like a goosed soprano. "Say what?"

"You hiding something, Will? Maybe you need to come clean with your wife."

"Sophie? Are you saying she who knows me better than anybody told you I was gay?"

Spike smiled kindly and patted Will's shoulder. "Don't worry, you're still a man."

He felt his face balloon with blood, and he began to worry about what lay in store for him. Was this some kind of kinky sex group? He felt oddly vulnerable with Arty and Murray so close behind. His rectum squeezed tighter than a clenched fist with all the talk of his supposed gayness, and he slowed to let them go ahead. He had no problem with gay men or drag queens, or actors for that matter. Spike was twisting things.

He stopped on the trail and spoke to his compadres jogging past. "Look, I am not hiding secrets. I am open to everybody. All genders. I mean, for Pete's sake, I support everybody's right to be whoever they are."

"Methinks thou doth protest too much," Murray said as he and Artie ran by.

Will scrunched his brow and clamped his lips together so as not to appear like an over-protester. "I like girls," he mumbled to their backs.

The trail wrapped around a small inlet where people tossed crumbs to bread-fattened ducks, and the trees grew close together, swaying in the warming winds off the lake. Spike stopped at a fountain, her skin nearly dry while Will dripped from every orifice.

"What do you think?" she said. "Couple more miles?"

Will felt a sharp side-ache as he slurped from the fountain. "Did you say miles?"

Murray finished a long pull of liquid from a plastic bottle. "Oh, he's sweating like a pig, Spike. Let the poor baby rest."

"No rest," Spike said. "He's tough. Right, Will? Guy like you? You're just getting started, isn't that right?"

The way Spike eyed him, with one side of her mouth crimped and his manhood hanging in the balance, he got the feeling there was a correct answer, one that shouted to the world which way he swung. But he'd never been called a sissy and wondered how his identity had gotten so twisted up in his sexuality by total strangers.

"I can make it. How much farther?"

Spike was off again, following the trail around Zilker Park. By the time they'd crossed Barton Springs Road, his heart beat like a double-time metronome.

Spike detoured through a neighborhood and up a steep hill. Will lagged about twenty feet behind, and now with an incline that felt more like Kilimanjaro, throwing in the towel sounded tempting. He still had to make the trek back across Lady Bird to his car. He'd probably need a ride. In an ambulance.

In the gathering twilight, Spike veered left at the crest of the hill and jogged into a driveway. The Friday boys followed, panting raggedly. She turned and stood in the Wonder Woman posture, legs spread wide, fists on her hips as she watched him close the gap.

"Come on, Will. Get your patootie up here."

All Will's patootie wanted was a swimming pool crackling with ice.

He followed Spike into a huge backyard, shaded by towering oaks and littered with playground and industrial items. A small pond shimmered in the center of all the chaos. Spike flipped on outdoor Christmas lights that hung tree to tree, and Will saw more clearly that a covered patio adjoined the house, plain in its décor of picnic tables, a lumpy chaise, and a few folding deck chairs.

"Ever done an obstacle course, Will? It'll be fun, but it'll kick your ass."

Will dug through his backpack, found a water bottle, and emptied half the tepid contents over his head. "Did you just say *fun* and *kick your ass* in the same sentence?"

Spike fetched a towel from the stack on the picnic table and dabbed her skin. "Main thing is you'll know what you're made of when you get to the finish line. You game?"

A half-hearted peep came out, when his ego kicked in and bitch-slapped him. "Bring it."

Spike slunk whisper-close and sniffed his chest. "I smell fear, and a secret."

Will smiled, cheesy-like. "Actually, that's Right Guard."

"Ever raise the bar, Will? Push yourself to the limit? Done things you never dared before, just to say you did them?"

"Back in my stoner days. Look, I may not be the best jogger, but twirling on monkey bars is child's play and is in no way an indicator of which way I swing—sexually, I mean."

Spike tilted her head, and even though she was looking up at him, it felt like she was looking down. Her silent message was, *Aw, aren't you adorable?*

She wrapped a whistle around her neck and strode like a drill sergeant to the center of the obstacle course. "Who's first, boys? Murray, keep your knees up this time. How you gonna do burlesque with a bunch of bruises? People will think I beat you."

"No worries," the big man said. "I'm ready for this."

Murray lumbered toward the middle of the yard, to a plank buried in the ground, hand-painted with the word "Start." In front of him were ten tires, laid out flat and staggered so runners could step into each hole as they moved forward.

"Start the clock," the big man said.

Spike pushed buttons on her watch and raised her hand. "Ready... set... " She blew the whistle and pure shrill shot out of it.

Murray high-stepped through the tires and scaled the ten-foot fence. His long legs leaped over sandpits and water hazards, ponytail flying. He flung himself on the ground to belly-crawl beneath wooden beams and through hollowed thirty-five gallon drums; he lunged for dangling ropes and crawled up berms. He dropped from a perch high in the tree, bounced off a mini tramp, and landed gracefully on his feet. He crossed horizontal bars with rungs like a ladder and dove through an upright tractor tire, emerging in a forward roll and leaping one-footed onto a series of stiff cushions spread across the pond. He jumped to each, then out of the pond onto a wide plank that read, "AWESOME."

Finally, he fell to his knees, tube socks gathered at his ankles, and panted like he'd conquered the Iron Man with liquid leaking from every pore.

Spike snapped off the timer. "Three minutes, fifty-five seconds. A personal best."

Arty danced around, dousing Murray with pails of water. "Woo-hoo! You da queen. Woo-hoo."

Murray held his chest as the water fell around his shoulders, and he took a bow.

Spike patted his back and directed him toward the patio. "Go walk it off under the fan. Who's next?"

Will stepped toward the starting plank.

One side of Spike's mouth curled up. "You sure?"

He shrugged. "Piece o' cake."

"Okay then." She set her timer, raised her hand high, and blew the whistle.

After the plank came the tires. Spike waved him through with flourishing hands. "Pick it up! Come on, move it!"

Next came the ten-foot fence. Will grabbed the rope and hoisted himself up, walking horizontal like a spider, pulling the rope taut for leverage. Bone-dry rope fibers poked his smooth executive's hands. At the top, he balanced on his belly, then dragged his legs over and dropped deep into the sandpit.

His sneakers overflowed with sand as he leaped a water hazard; then crawled under the wooden beam. His knees scraped the hard earth and he ignored the smarting, but the log grating against his back was tougher to take. Air funneled through the new hole in his shirt and sweat stung a future scar.

He ran for the dangling rope, and midway over the second water hazard his hands slipped. He stomped into the pond, murky water splattering his legs.

The drag queens urged him on. "Go, Willie, go. You can do it."

Again, Spike yelled. "Pick your feet up, Straight Man. You're off the pace."

Will trudged up the berm. How quickly Spike's sex appeal had evaporated with the stridence of her edicts. Ahead lay a thirty-five gallon drum. When he was a kid, he'd rolled down the hill behind his house in one, roller-pinning Daisy Mayfield, the most popular girl in school, and arose so dizzy he barfed up his bologna and banana sandwich. Barfy was how he felt now.

"No pussies here, Will." Courtesy of Spike.

He crawled through the tunnel, his stiff, bony knees pressing into hard metal, dirt, and pebbles. Upright in the hot sun, he hurried toward the oak tree and pulled himself up the rope, knot to fraying knot. Halfway, he stopped, hanging on by sheer will, his palms bloody and slippery with sweat. His biceps quaked under the stress of sustained muscle contractions.

"Will!" Murray shouted. "You don't do this, you're not the man we think you are."

Will wanted to cry mama. A fraction less pride, and he'd be a bleating, castrated lamb. But the cheering audience and a whip-cracking Latina spurred him on. Failure was not an option. No sir, dying was preferable to the humiliation of his utter and complete lack of physical stamina, and apparent proof of Y chromosomes.

Fifteen feet straight up felt like fifty. His goal: a thick branch extending like a sailboat boom, perpendicular to the tree's massive trunk. He inched along the rough bark, abrading the underside of his thighs, and lost his balance. Shadows, leaves, and sunshine danced dizzily before his eyes as he flipped backward off the branch.

His feet hit the mini tramp, which launched him back up to the boom where he smacked his head. Grabbing at air, his fingers found a cluster of branches, which allowed him to play Tarzan over the horizontals. He let go and landed, straddling one of the bars. A rotisserie chicken, forked, right in the bum. With a grunt, his body stiffened and his eyes rolled back in his head. The plaintive moans from below told him he hadn't fainted, a fact that pained him as much as the mind-numbing throb between his legs.

Spike echoed in his ears. "No pussies."

"No dicks either," Arty cried. "Not anymore."

"Spike!" Murray boomed. "Don't be so hard on him. Willie, say uncle."

"Yeah, Willie," said Spike, the happy sadist. "Say uncle."

Nut by nut, Will unclenched and eased himself off the bar, hanging from the horizontals and seething through his teeth. His hands, like the rest of him, were awash in perspiration. He gripped tightly to keep from slipping and crossed over, one rung at a time. On the last one, he and his engorged scrotum dropped to the ground with a jarring thud that zipped up his legs and made him shudder.

The second thirty-five gallon drum dared him to bend over and take it like a man. No getting around it. He crouched down and crawled through it, every fiber, every bone, every nerve hypersensitive to movement, to touch, to anticipation of more self-inflicted, kick-ass fun.

"What's the matter, Will? Gutless?"

Spike's sarcasm only cauterized his ego. Did she think he would give up *now*? Was she trying to break him? *Never!*

Then it dawned on him that she really was trying break him. But why?

The upright tractor tire, archway to the finish line, awaited. He dove through the donut hole and rolled amid hopeful cheers. The last obstacle—the big pond—stretched wide as the Gulf before him, and he stepped on a floating cushion tethered to the muddy bottom. He wobbled like a Weeble but didn't tip over, then bobbled on one leg and helicoptered for balance. To prevent crashing headfirst into the turbid water, he lurched to the next floater, a sweat-drenched toad to a lily pad; then the next floater and the next, navigating all six and catapulting himself to the embankment.

With one foot on the finish line, an ear-shattering whistle in his ears, he tottered backward and forward, then back butt-first into two feet of liquid mud.

Murray and Arty plucked him out and wiped the guck and algae off his face.

Spike tossed him a towel. "Four minutes, forty-five seconds. Why don't you guys help him under the fans?"

Will felt the overpowering urge to puke, which he did. Then he hobbled to the covered patio and eased into the cushiony chaise as the sun disappeared from the horizon. His skinned knees and palms, the chafed undersides of his forearms, and the gash on his back stung.

"Spike is hard on newbies," Arty said, pulling up a deck chair. "Don't take it personal."

Will cupped his testicles. "Now why would I take being called gutless personal?"

Spike moved a small table in front of him and set a glass of ice water on it. She sat across from him on the bench. "You did okay for your first time. Really. I'm proud of you."

Suddenly, she was all *azúcar* and spice again. Sweet as a honey badger.

Will took no consolation in her chumminess. "You mean, I proved something today?"

"Do *you* think you proved something?"

"I think he did," Murray said. "No self-respecting queen would put his pecker through the wringer just to prove he was certifiably straight."

Arty agreed. "But a man who liked pussy would do it; especially for a good-looking pussy like Spike."

"He's got hetero written all over him," Murray said with authority.

Will's chest swelled and his heart sang gaily to the echoes of other penis bearers before him—those of the chick-loving persuasion. But after what Spike put him through, he would not be asking. *her* for a second debacle. Now, he wanted to figure out her angle.

Spike reached across the table for his hands, scrutinizing his dirty, skinned palms. "Come on. You need doctoring. I've got just what you need, in my office."

"Uh-oh," Arty and Murray said in tandem. "That's our cue." They picked up their backpacks, hopped into the Forerunner in the driveway and left.

"Feels kinda like I've been left to the wolves," Will said, following Spike up the stairs to the garage apartment. "Or wolf, as it were. Should I be afraid?"

"Only if you're a tasty mouse," she said, reaching the top landing. "Are you?"

"A mouse?"

"Tasty."

So the wicked witch had turned vexing vixen. How did a modern single guy respond to that? His Casanova's IQ had disintegrated to Teletubby status, but knowing Sophie was home with Houdini, he wanted to go all Transformer and shit.

"I bet you taste sweet and salty," Spike purred, closing in on his neck. "It's been some time since I've..." She licked his neck between words. "Eaten" *lick* "something" *lick* "tasty."

Will shivered. Her cryptic sound bites left him confused. He had to wonder if he might be served up as a tasty *last supper*. Her tight orange-and-yellow midriff reminded him of nature's big joke on prey; the deadliest were always the most attractive.

She pushed open the door and backed inside, pulling Will in by his T-shirt. "I'm so hungry, I could eat a python."

Will's legs quivered. He liked her unpredictability as much as he disliked it. Mostly, he didn't understand her mood swings. Sophie's mood swings consisted of things like wanting an elaborate date night one minute but popcorn and a DVD the next, followed by sex—the kind he liked. The kind he expected. At least, she did in the past. By comparison, Sophie was blessedly predictable. Spike? He would not take bets on what Spike liked, and he didn't know if that was a good thing or not.

The room was dark. Black drapes covered the windows, and a scented candle burned on a corner table. Something musky. A funky disco tune played through the speakers to his right. Automatically, he catalogued it: "Super Freak," Rick James, 1981.

He squinted as his eyes adjusted to the shadowy din. To his right was a queen-sized bed with a brass canopy draped in a ton of gauzy black fabric and the occasional braided gold tassel. Aside the bed was a freakishly large, purple, upholstered stiletto that one could sit on.

Next to that was— What *was* that? Some kind of steel-framed apparatus the size of a wardrobe box that reminded him of gymnastic equipment. Four heavy-duty chains hung from each corner of the top stabilizer bars and connected in the middle to a shiny black leather swing. Imagining the sort of competition that took place on *that* contraption made his face screw up.

The far wall contained a hanging assortment of feathery boas and other paraphernalia he couldn't make out. Seemed Officer Spike was a jack of all trades. His "uh-oh" tachometer spun wildly and quickly redlined.

"Not to worry, Will. I'm only going to give you some first aid."

A cheap dinette with skinny metal legs sat directly in front of him, and Spike pushed him into one of the chairs with a tall back.

"Relax," she said. "I'll make you feel better in no time."

Her voice floated around his eardrums like imported black silk, a resonance that portended all things soft and intimate and moist, and his body reminded him of that earlier run-in with a horizontal bar. No savage sexual soirees tonight.

"Can I show you something, Will? Something you must feel first, before you see it?"

That had nasty all over it. But before he could object or remind her of the delicate condition of his manhood, she wrapped a blindfold over his eyes. He flinched, and his hands jumped to the mask. She pushed them away.

"Easy, Will. You can trust me."

This from the ball buster. That she was an officer of the law and some sort of dungeon master intrigued him. Add a good long year of orgasms with Me, Myself, and I—and Sophie home with Hoodoody—

and he was willing to give Officer Spike enough room to prove it.

"This might sting a little," she said.

"Sting?"

He heard shuffling, clinking bottles, and the handling of other unidentifiables behind him. He presumed a table of miscellaneous first-aid supplies, since he smelled antiseptic. Then he sensed her presence, low in front of him. He was conscious of the hard feel of the floor beneath his sneakers, when she brushed something gauzy and wet against his knees—cleaning and tending his cuts and scrapes? Even his embattled ankles got the treatment as she wiped around them. This was getting weirder.

He sensed her movement again, felt the air on his skin as she lifted his T-shirt to examine the gash in his back. He flinched as she palpated the surrounding tissue. But she had a gentle touch, dabbing his cuts and scrapes with cold antiseptic.

"Uh-oh, this one is worse than I thought."

He reached behind to feel the scrape himself, when he felt something cold and hard on his wrists. A tiny latch clicked, and he realized she'd handcuffed him.

What the hell?

He tried to turn, just as he felt a roughened leather restraint placed around his neck. He pitched forward and choked himself. He tried to stand and found his ankles tied.

When had that happened?

"Hey, come on now." He tried to stand, but the chair wouldn't budge. Bolted to the floor? His stomach flip-flopped and his manly voice cracked. "Spike? Not feeling the kick-ass fun."

He listened to the flitting behind him, then in front. Drawers opened and closed, fabric rustled, hard heels clacked across the floor, giving the room a hollow sound. And then it was as if she'd disappeared. No sounds from her at all.

Meanwhile the funky music faded. Small clicks signaled disc changes. Something acoustic drifted from the speakers, altering the ambient mood in the air, though not the ambivalence in his gut. Plucked guitar strings flicked his subconscious, and he strained for clues as to where he'd heard the tune. His thoughts staggered between the arresting pull of the melody and the noiseless void that was Spike.

What the hell is she up to? Why is that song so familiar? How hard am I going to pay back Sophie for this? Those riffs—I know those riffs.

And then it struck him—that song. *Her* song, without the lyrics. It was different than he'd ever played it, with more texture, more staccato, more complexity. The sounds vibrated across his shoulders and filled his chest until his whole body absorbed them all the way in.

He'd never thought of playing "Sophie's Kiss" with a Latin rhythm, but it was genius.

For long moments, he was suspended on the chords he'd written by flashlight, out on the lake, camping with Sophie—on the heels of their lovemaking, when he'd been filled to bursting for the love of his life, when the words and the melody couldn't be contained. While she slept five feet away in their tent, he'd scribbled the words, toyed with the tones. It had all come together in less than an hour. The perfect anthem for his devotion. This new version, so pure and simple, collided with the past in his head.

Until a distinctive *whoosh* cut through the air, followed by a keen snap that hiked his senses to full alert. A whip.

He heard a door shut, a lock turn. Another cracking sound through the air forced his stomach into his windpipe.

Who the hell is this woman?

Her disembodied voice wrapped around his ears. "You like whipped cream, Will?"

He stuttered into blind space. "I-I think you should know, pain and me, we don't mix. How about taking this blindfold off?"

Snap! went the whip.

"Ah, but you proved how tough you are, Will. You're twenty-four-hour Y chromosomes, aren't you? We're free now to enjoy ourselves. I have something special in mind for you."

"Actually, I took a nasty fall on your horizontal bars, if you get my drift." He felt stupid, talking without seeing. His imagination ran rampant. "I thought you were just, you know, hungry. Maybe you've got some chips and dip?"

He heard the whip snap sharply—way too close—and he accidentally let out a scream that he regretted since its pitch was sure to cast doubt on his alleged assortment of Y chromosomes.

"Dear god. Hey now. Spike?" The words shot out of his mouth in rapid-fire procession. "Listen. Can't we talk? Seriously. I'm not into black-and-blue marks. I have an aversion to cowering and begging for mercy." *Snap! Snap!* "Which I would certainly entertain if you would just set me free."

The whip snapped yet again, whisper-close to his left cheek.

"You talk a lot of nonsense," she said. "I'll have to shut you up."

"Wait—"

Snap! The whip cracked next to his leg, the hairs stiffening in its wake.

And then Spike kissed him. Her lips were hot and wet and hard. He resisted as she jabbed her tongue in. Her hands massaged his pectorals and his clenched abdomen, and then his inner thighs as she whispered in his ear.

"I'm a bad girl, Will, and I want you in a bad, bad way. You want me, too, don't you? I can tell. Little Will's calling my name."

"No-no, that's Benedict Arnold, and he is *not* thinking straight—ironically."

Snap! The whip snapped close to his ear, and while it didn't sting, it had the potential. A message hit him from on high, his brain firing with stirrings of volcanic change, of earth moving outward from his inner core, of a more divine transformation than he'd ever experienced.

"Christ almighty, you were right. I'm gay. I totally prefer the company of men."

"Don't toy with me, Will. Let's slide your shorts off. I want to see your naked flesh."

He shook his head violently. "I swear, I lied before. I'm completely G.A.Y. Ga-ay."

It was quiet as a funeral home, Will his own sobbing mourner while Little Benedict Arnold keeled over in flaccid horror.

Spike ripped away his blindfold. He blinked to focus and found her in a black leather collar with sharp, one-inch silver barbs, thigh-high lace-up boots, and a bustier that converted her modest breasts into swelling cupolas. She swished the whip over her shoulder, perching it like a parrot as she moved closer, bent down, and looked into his eyes.

"There, there," she soothed. "See how easy that was?"

He gaped at her. "You *wanted* me to be gay?"

"Just getting to the truth, Will. Don't you feel better?"

Chapter 17

"Where is he, Mommy?" Keely asked, holding her mother's hand.

Sophie stood under the awning at J.J. Pinkerton Elementary and glanced beyond the distant chain link fence to the parking lot. She watched for Will's Jag while trying to keep abreast of the judging activities going on behind her at the Third Annual Young Artisan's Festival.

"Daddy'll be here soon."

Annabelle concurred, assuring her big sister with the superior knowledge instilled since birth (*You're just like your father*) that she knew more about his business than anyone. "Don't you 'member? He *said* he's coming late. He had an *appomen*, right, Mommy?"

"Yes. Daddy had an appointment."

"I remember," Keely said. "But the judges are almost done."

Annabelle could usually be found in Keely's shadow, trailing in her footsteps even as Keely protested, wearing the same Mary Janes, the same clips and bows, and repeating the same sentences. Yet she was no less obliged to make her sister's life unbearable when the opportunity arose. "I think they like Patty Martin's best."

Keely crossed her arms brusquely and rolled her eyes.

"Okay, Annabelle," Sophie said. "That's enough."

Making notes on closely held clipboards, the judges loitered around nine-year-old Patty Martin's papier-mâché exhibit of the Great Wall of China, three tables from Keely's, like it was the real thing. The Wall had been constructed of various conjoined and glued forms, painted in bright shades of red, blue, and yellow enamel. The resulting celebration of art, history, and culture was the Wall come-to-life as a Chinese dragon snaking across a five-foot platform of faux mountain ridges, grassy valleys, and desert plateaus.

Sophie was impressed, but she wondered if little Patty had put as much work into the project as her mother, the neighborhood gossip, effervescent head of the PTA, and editor of the school newsletter.

Keely moaned. "I told Daddy we should have used papier-mâché."

"Baby, the judges aren't finished looking. It's too soon to worry." Sophie rubbed Keely's head, careful not to catch her fingernails in the pigtails her eldest had earlier determined were *just perfect.* "You did an excellent job, but even if the judges don't recognize your pyramids as blue ribbon material, we all do. We're very proud of you."

Annabelle pointed at Will's Jaguar snaking through the parking lot. "There he is." She ran across the field to the chain-link fence and waved madly with both arms.

Keely covered half her face. "She is so embarrassing."

Sophie had to admit, "Kid comes by it naturally."

Minutes later, Will came into view wearing his gray silk suit and tie. Must have been an important *appomen*, Sophie thought, for him to dress up on a Saturday.

"Why is he walking that way?" Keely said. "He walks like Grampy."

Will hobbled across the pavement. His arms moved stiffly as he lifted his hands chest-high and laid them on top of the fence. Annabelle backed away as he hoisted himself above the fence and threw his legs over, his slacks catching on the exposed links across the top bar. His forward trajectory halted and his upper body pitched straight downward, causing his head and forearms to impact yellowed grass. A cloud of dust exploded around him as his suit jacket folded over his head, his shirt slid up to expose his bare back, and his pants remained fixed while his body slipped halfway out of them.

Keely ran to help her father while Sophie watched in horror. Apparently, she was not the only one to notice his absurd climb over a fence meant to keep people out, when only a hundred feet separated him from a gateway that would take him directly into the schoolyard. She shrank behind a pillar in the wake of laughter that rippled up and down the walkways. Adults and children pointed en masse.

Upended, Will thrashed and donkey-kicked to free himself. The one sign this did any good came from the increasing reveal of his underwear and the top of his crack. Then the quick-thinking Will Camden, while on his head, kicked the loafer off his trapped foot and unzipped his slacks. He wiggled out of them like a newborn butterfly from its chrysalis and clambered to his feet in a haboob of dust.

His metamorphosis complete, Will stood *sans* pants in dusty black dress socks, disheveled BVDs in stoplight red, dress shirt, coat, and tie. As if in the privacy of his bedroom, he plucked his pants from the fence and snapped the dirt out of them, slipped back in them and tucked in his shirt before zipping. To compound Sophie's shock, he gave a theatrical bow.

"Did you see that?" Little Patty Martin's mother, editor of the *Pinkerton PTA Press*, was flabbergasted. She megaphoned her mouth with her hands and shouted across the courtyard. "Sophie! Is that Will? Is that your husband?"

From across the field, Will saw Sophie in the crowd. He took a deep breath of courage, knowing she would have *questions*.

Hours earlier, he had been revived by the cacophonous blare of his alarm clock, shocked upright in a body that had overnight morphed into a dehydrated bag of muscles, bones, and tissue—thanks to the über-obstacle course at Spike's. It didn't help that his hands were shredded from scaling frayed, weathered ropes, and his back and knees were scraped like he'd been dragged spinning behind a racehorse across macadam.

To counteract his aching anatomy, he'd popped a couple of his dad's leftover Percocets before he left the house. Then he'd driven to a remote ranch in the Hill Country for a low-key meeting with his lawyer about his Ponzi case. The double-dose had done a fine job, carrying him through a three-hour meeting and instilling a superhero ego that made him think he could leap a four-foot fence in a single bound. It was upon arcing over the chain links that he'd discovered the fatal flaw in his strategy: jagged metal edges trump anesthetized Superman skills every time. Important thing was, he had arrived for his daughter's showing.

A couple of the men met him halfway across the schoolyard and accompanied him in. Jim Martin, the most henpecked man in Texas, thanks to his PTA-maven wife Suzie, shook his hand. "Man, you got some *huevos*. My old lady would be kicking my ass all the way home by now, and I'd never hear the end of it."

Vern Avery, the oldest living surfer and transplant from Oahu, slapped him hard on the back. "Dude, that was wicked." What little was left of Vern's pale white hair curled in all directions across his leathery head. "You rode her all the way down, man."

The unexpected praises did not assuage the contempt on Sophie's face as she slunk around the beam.

"I see you," Will said. "And so does everyone else."

She looked him up and down. "Thank god, you wore underwear. Think how much gossip you saved your daughters. But really, why didn't you just wear a thong?"

"Nice to see you've lightened up." She didn't scare him.

"Are you drunk?"

"Are you serious?"

Her lips twitched and she turned up her nose. "Don't go anywhere. I want to talk to you." She marched off in a jeans skirt, tank top, and high-heeled sandals, which looked pretty cute on her. Especially from behind. He had to wonder if noticing her outfit said something about his manhood.

That's it. No more GQs.

He glanced down at Annabelle and Keely, still holding his hands. Their dull gazes bore evidence that the Superman persona he'd cultivated since their births had been blown to Krypton, and a fumbling, real-life Clark Kent was all that remained.

"Daddy's a funny guy, isn't he?" The girls nodded mutely without the smiles he'd hoped for. "Okay. Has an artistic genius been chosen yet?"

"No, but they're almost done," Keely said bleakly. "They looked at our pyramids for a few minutes, and then they spent forever at Patty Martin's Great Wall of China."

"Patty Martin, huh?" Will patted Keely's head and noticed the faculty still hovering over the table that he presumed supported the Great Papier-Mâché Wall. He assessed Keely's project in comparison: miniature Egyptian workers frozen in movement, dragging colossal stones with ropes and carts and brute strength across the desert. He and Keely had drenched wet salt-dough forms with food coloring blended to a dung shade of brown. They'd used Popsicle sticks to carve asymmetrical stone shapes into the dough and pressed a rag into each for that five-thousand-year-old, limestone-and-mortar texture. Talk about brilliance.

"Not to worry, Keel," Will said. "You did an exceptional job, and nobody can take that away from you."

Her eyes teared up and he kissed the top of her head. Then he got a whiff of Chanel.

Sophie sidled next to him—astonishing, given their arctic relationship. "So, how'd your Number Two Date go with Officer Spike?"

Will could hardly recall the prior day's events without shriveling to a date nut inside, unlike Little Will's mutinous flag-waving effort as Spike massaged his thighs. He'd considered reporting her, but the risk of public recrimination and the entertainment value his wife and Houdini would find in these humiliating tidbits would be more than he could bear.

"That's what you want to talk to me about? Who are you, *The National Enquirer*? Your spy didn't report back?"

"No spies, Will. Just making sure you showed up."

Her mouth twisted into a self-satisfied smirk that seemed suspicious in its excess. "Annabelle, Keely, can I have a word in private with your mom?"

The girls complied, slumping into the metal foldout chairs behind Keely's exhibit.

Will urged Sophie forward by her elbow as he limped next to her. "I'm on to you, Sophie. Seems Spike had an alternate agenda last night. You told her I was gay?"

She had the decency to look offended. "Of course not. I *never* said you were gay."

"Then, why did she think I hadn't come out of the closet and was lying to you?"

Sophie shook her head and glanced around aimlessly, shrugging as if this question was the greatest unsolved mystery of life. "Ya got *me*. No idea."

He gave her a hard stare. "Look, just to clear the air of even an infinitesimal degree of doubt, I am not interested in men, nor have I ever been."

Her mouth was twitching to keep from laughing, but her eyes were practically guffawing. "So, I take it your date with Spike didn't live up to expectations?"

Her whole attitude implied she knew about things he wasn't fessing up to, and that was just annoying. Plus, her head was swiveling repeatedly as if she was looking for someone. A little more neck-craning, and she'd get a 360 out of it. His Percocetted brain made the leap to *The Exorcist*, and he recoiled in horror. Then he peered into her purse, just in case, for a big crucifix.

"I simply need to know when to select the third date," she said. "Jake called to see how close he was to losing his precious Ursula."

Will blinked to pull himself together and noticed people staring, witnesses to his swan dive. He held fast to the dream of submerging in a therapeutic Jacuzzi, mind-numbingly medicated. With junk food. He hadn't eaten all day, and the idea of eating food he usually avoided sounded like a gift he ought to give himself.

He stopped in front of the Bake Sale table and plunked down a five. "A dozen chocolate chips, please. And a coffee."

A young girl handed Will a paper bag of cookies, and Sophie intercepted it while he got his change. "You have no clue how to behave with a woman."

"You may be right—if by *woman* you mean nutcase. Otherwise, that is no reflection of my manhood. For your edification, Coach Casey was the equivalent of snorting a line of field chalk. And Officer Spike..." His upper lip curled as he remembered the blindfold, the sneaky way she'd handcuffed him, and the whip cracking in his ear, not to mention the anguish his family gems had endured. "Spike was a spicy habañero with a wicked kick that will haunt me long after the judge stamps our divorce decree."

Sophie fished a cookie out of the bag. "Guess she wasn't as special as Mitch said."

Will mulled a response as he harvested two more pain pills from his pocket and downed them with tepid gulps of caffeine. "Suffice to say, Officer Spike is not my type."

"Do you even have a type?"

"Used to. Back in our college days when your mantra was *Catch me if you can—or if you dare.* Back when you were fun. As I recall, you carved *Sophie loves Will* into the big oak tree at Southwest Texas after one of the biggest frat party gigs ever. *That's* my type."

Her look said, *Seriously?*

The pain pills were getting to him; he was feeling sorry for himself. And it was clear *Sophie did not love Will anymore.* Maybe if he saw *that* carved into a tree, he'd finally move on. Was that it? Had he not moved on as far as he'd thought? Why was Houdini like an annoying canker in his mouth that refused to go away?

"All you want to do is pawn me off on some other woman so you can go play hide the rabbit with Houdini's magic wand."

Sophie stopped mid-cookie chew.

"That's right. I heard all about his supposed world-class wanker, and saw it firsthand on the boat. Please, help yourself to the biggest dick in town. What do I care?" He enjoyed her oddly plastered scowl as people passed. After his disastrous encounter with Spike, somebody had to pay.

Sophie smashed the bag of cookies into his chest. "Just be ready for your next date."

"Nice." He grabbed the bag before it fell to the sidewalk. "Next time, how about a woman who doesn't have more testosterone than I do?"

A few minutes later, Keely's lower lip protruded and she crossed her arms petulantly. "I told you we should have used papier-mâché."

The kid was taking it hard. Will rubbed Keely's shoulders as cameras flashed, capturing Patty Martin's victory for the year's final issue of the *Pinkerton PTA Press.*

"Sorry, Keel," he said. "Who knew papier-mâché was making an artsy fartsy comeback in elementary academia?"

Sophie ventured the silver-lining-in-the-clouds bit. "Second place is an honor, sweetie. Think of everything you learned. Your next one will be even better."

Even Annabelle felt the effects of losing to paper and glue. "It sucks, Daddy, right?"

They stared at a massive blue ribbon with a cauliflower-sized sunburst that hung on the Great Wall's highest elevation so there would be no doubt who won first prize. The handwritten note pinned to the bottom of the ribbon read, "First Place for its architectural grandeur and historical significance."

"It sucks all right," Will said. "But it's not a reflection on you personally. You did a phenomenal job." Then, sotto voce to Sophie, "The kid got robbed."

The youngest judge approached and shook Keely's hand. Will sized her up. About his height, fresh out of college yet the embodiment of frumpiness in her plain white blouse, flowing skirt that hung just above her ankles, and hippie sandals. A mild-mannered girl-slash-woman of the earth. And filled with fresh-faced, unspoiled optimism that would soon be tormented out of her by the graduating sixth graders on exodus to middle school.

"Congratulations, Keely," the teacher gushed, her melodious voice infused with admiration. "What a wonderful exhibit. I'm so proud of you."

Keely flushed. "Thank you, Miss Marshall."

Clutching her clipboard, Miss Marshall shook Sophie's hand. "It was a tough decision. We were very torn between the Great Wall and Keely's Pyramids."

"The hard work paid off, I guess," Sophie said vapidly.

Will extended his hand. "I'm Keely's father. Will Camden."

"This is Edwina Marshall," Sophie said. "Keely's art teacher. I wanted to introduce you."

"Actually," Edwina said. "I know you, Mr. Camden—or, *of* you. My grandfather used to sit in on some of your gigs. Gerald Marshall? Steel guitar?"

"Gerry Marshall, man of steel and world famous artiste? He's your granddad?"

"Yes. If Gramps likes you, you must know your stuff."

"Well, it's been a long time since I played any gigs."

"Yes," Sophie said. "He got a more fun job working eighty hours a week in I.T."

Will ignored her. "So, Miss Marshall—"

"Please," Edwina said. "Call me Edwina."

"Edwina." Will paused and indicated Keely. "Tell me, what is it about the Egyptian pyramids you like best?"

"Oh, where do I start?"

While Edwina Marshall, art teacher and granddaughter to his old band buddy, prattled about the *sublime* color mixing and the *impressive texture of the salt-dough formations with unique, old world imprints* that gave the stones such *interesting vitality*, Will watched his family.

Keely beamed. Annabelle gazed at her big sister with renewed respect. Appreciation for Miss Marshall's kid savvy softened the lines on Sophie's forehead—and diverted the smirkfest—and Will momentarily blotted out his front-page swan dive. People smiled and said hello as they passed, and he felt like he belonged there. He missed this, being with his girls, being part of the family unit, being recognized as Sophie's husband. He hadn't appreciated that before; never quite made the connection.

Sophie was watching *him* now. The way he had watched her? Nah, something else percolated inside that brain. Something sinister.

"Edwina," Sophie said, "didn't I hear you were single?"

Edwina chortled. "Me? Oh, yeah, I haven't had a boyfriend in ages."

"Oh, sweetie, no." Sophie jutted her lower lip in exaggerated sympathy and patted the young woman's shoulder. "Gosh, that is so surprising; you're adorable. I mean, look at you. Right, Will? Young guys have no idea the catch you are. And pretty. So pretty."

She looked at him then, for validation of Edwina's wretchedness, and he hardly knew how to respond. He had not previously witnessed his wife's unpretentious nature transmogrify to that level of syrupy kindness. Ever.

But he was close enough now to see Edwina in ways he hadn't before, like through a fish eye—or maybe that was the Percocets. Her hair was pulled back in some sort of twisty thing. She had a milky complexion and wide, green eyes with black, garden-rake lashes, thick lips, and pale brown hair. Her demeanor was so unassuming as to hide the fact that she was indeed quite pretty.

Edwina shrugged. "I've been so busy with the school and my art, I don't have time for much else. But this summer, I plan to focus on an art show—my own, with my grandfather's help. I guess I need to come up for air once in a while and maybe date."

Sophie's eyes lit up as the magic "date" word invited free admittance. "I understand. You do need to get out. Attractive young thing like you. Will is looking to date, too."

"Uh, er—" So much for the retouched family portrait. Will mentally ducked for cover.

"Girls," Sophie said, "would you excuse us for a minute?"

"Again?" Annabelle whined, squeezing her head in dramatic fashion.

Keely dragged her little sister off. "They're talking grown-up stuff, Annabelle. Let's go look at the Leaning Tower of Pizza. They built it with real pepperoni and cheese."

"Ten minutes, girls, okay?" Sophie took Will and Edwina by the arms and began a promenade down the sidewalk that Will had only ever seen at weddings. "Actually, Edwina, now that Will's a single guy—you heard about that, right? Will's a bachelor, *and* he's available."

"Awkward," Will sang out one side of his mouth. Edwina had a naïve quality that reminded him of, what was it? Oh yeah, jailbait. Plus, she looked completely baffled.

Sophie swiped the air. "Oh, Will and me? We are so over. This guy is free as a bird, let me tell you. What kind of hobbies are you interested in? Will has so many hobbies, I bet you're interested in the same ones."

Oh, how the red flags were fluttering in her gassy breeze. Her happy divorcee shtick seemed designed to publicly cut off his nuts every time she opened her mouth.

Edwina blushed. "Well, I guess, I mean, what are you suggesting?"

Will went for damage control. "Actually, what my wife is suggesting—"

"*Ex*," Sophie said, with an overly reassuring smile. "*Ex*-wife, honey."

"What my soon-to-be-*ex*-wife is suggesting, Miss Marshall—"

"Edwina," Sophie said. "Edwina asked you to call her Edwina."

Will gritted his molars. "*Edwina*... is that you and I go out on a date." He looked pointedly at Sophie. "Did I say *that* right?"

Sophie snarled and Will paused in the absurdity of their tactics, the two of them ganging up on poor little art teacher Edwina like starving hyenas. Her innocence must surely be shaken to the core. On the plus side, he did have the advantage of seeing her first, ruling out the *blind* aspect, and—prize alert!—he saw no evidence of testosterone. Or, sadly, sex appeal. Still . . .

He sighed heavily, resigned to his fate. "So, Edwina, how about dinner?" He squared his tie and smoothed his dusty white dress shirt. No reason he couldn't look dignified in the wake of rejection.

Sophie nudged Edwina's shoulder. "Or goofy golf, huh? Now that's a load of fun."

Edwina looked back and forth between them and smiled. "I'm free Thursday."

Sophie's eyes flickered in surprise and Will's flickered in utter bewilderment.

"Okay then," he said. "Seven-thirty? Sullivan's?"

Edwina extricated a pen from her clipboard, turned Will's left hand, and wrote a phone number on his swollen palm in big loops and curves. "Still wearing your wedding ring?"

Will sniggered, as if to say *How'd that get there?* He slipped off the band, pocketed it, and displayed his bare hand, front and back. "There. Officially bachelorized."

"I'm looking forward to this," Edwina said with a sweet grin and arms hugging the clipboard to her chest.

Will smiled dumbly, feeling a momentary triumph—and a festering nausea—until he read the narrowing of Sophie's brown eyes and the crooked set of her jaw. What should have pleased her instead seemed to annoy her.

"Girls are waiting for us at the Tower of Pizza," she snipped, spinning Will around and pushing him away from Date Number Three. "He'll call you."

Chapter 18

"It's temporary, Gram," Sophie cautioned as she drove her Acura into the garage. "The escrow on his condo closes in a couple weeks, and he'll be gone. I don't want you to worry about taking over the guestroom. Will's fine in Annabelle's room, and I definitely don't want you trying to *fix* anything."

Eighty-five-year-old Eunice Gardner Wilkes sat in the adjacent bucket seat, looking small and gaunt in her coral pants and matching floral top. She had carefully ironed them for the plane ride from La Guardia and, on awaiting her luggage, complained they were now "just one big gosh darn wrinkle." She had applied a touch of makeup and pulled her thinning silver hair into a chignon at the base of her neck, from which the vapors of eucalyptus and mint emanated.

"Hey, it's cool," Grammy said, hugging her matching coral handbag at her side. "Whatever arrangement you and Will have worked out is fine. Far be it from us to interfere." She glanced back at her husband of sixty-five years. "Right, Hal?"

In the back seat, Grampy's big-knuckled, bony hands adjusted the settings on his hearing aid. "Did you say something, Eunice?"

Grammy doubled her volume as Sophie cut the engine. "I said, it's been a long day. Bet you're ready for a nap." Then aside to Sophie, "Bet he can't last an hour."

"Butter pecan in an hour?" Grampy shouted. "Count me in."

Grammy squinted at him over her shoulder. "We haven't even had lunch yet. Sophie, the man is always pushing the ice cream. As if my badonkadonk could stand getting any bigger, yo."

Sophie paused with her hand on the door lever. "I take it you picked up some street lingo from the kids you've been tutoring?"

"Sure did. Did you know *bone* is a verb?"

Will tapped Grammy's window and opened her door, a grin on his face as he tucked a thick stack of mail under his arm. "It's about time you got here." He helped her out and wrapped her shrunken frame in a welcoming embrace. "The kids are so excited to see you, they've been tearing around the house like puppy dogs with wet butts."

"So good to see you, William," Grammy said, craning her neck up at him. "I hear we're putting you out of the guestroom."

"Don't you worry about that. Annabelle's room suits me fine for as long as I'll be here, which I'm sure Sophie told you is just a few weeks."

Sophie watched as Will circled the back of the car to help her grandfather out.

"Too bad," Grampy said. His voice quavered as he unfolded himself, stood to his full hunched height, and accepted Will's welcome hug. "Can't complain about being surrounded by beautiful females, but life in the hen-pecked minority can get old."

"Tell me about it," Will said.

"Eunice hasn't stopped haranguing me yet about that Ponzi scheme I invested in. But how was I to know?" He waved her off before she could shush him. "Ah hell, we already made a small fortune, and if they want to come get it back, better bring the shovels, cuz we'll be smiling six feet under by the time it's all sorted out."

"Grampy?" Sophie said. "That guy they arrested in Dallas—you invested with him?"

"Don't be trippin', Boo," Grammy said. "Your inheritance is safe."

Grampy squeezed Will's shoulder for balance. "Good thing you didn't listen to me, son. If you'd taken my advice and invested, what a colossal blunder that would have been, eh?"

Will cleared his throat. "Yeah. Good thing I didn't listen."

The sight of her mail under Will's arm struck Sophie wrong. The mail was one domain he had no business touching since he was not a permanent resident. Yet he'd fetched it daily since his arrival, weeding out the junk and presenting her with a much thinner stack. Seemed her privacy had gone by the wayside in deference to his alter ego as a butler.

She stated the obvious with annoyance. "You got my mail again?"

"Doing you a favor," Will said. "Consider it just another way I'm earning my keep."

Sophie lugged Grammy's two small suitcases and gave him a warning glare. "Two more bags in the trunk, Mr. Belvedere. Would you mind?"

After dinner, Keely stuck a scoop of butter pecan ice cream into her mouth. "Mmmm, good, Daddy."

"You like that? That's your Grampy's favorite." Will carried his bowl to the dining room table, joining his kids and Grampy. He had intended to turn in early, after a nice hot shower, until the kids dragged him downstairs for a "nightcap with Grampy." In Grampy-speak, a nightcap meant *ice cream with a brandy chaser*.

"Whose turn is it?" Will pleated into a chair and scanned the game board. The third round of Sorry Sliders was in progress, and he had been consistently outgunned, even by Grampy's shaky hand. While Annabelle's undeveloped coordination ensured her pawns forever overshot the center bull's eye, Keely proved practice made perfect, bumping competitor pawns out of the target zone and grabbing all the points.

She giggled over and again. "Sorry!"

Sophie, who had disappeared with Grammy for a while, reappeared and leaned against the dining-room archway, behind her grandfather. She had slipped into pajamas that looked both comfy and provocative, from his point of view. The top had thin straps and a loose-fitting bodice. Her arms crossed beneath her breasts, elevating them into pleasant swells, and he was reminded of what lay beneath the fabric. His hands knew every curve, every dimple and notch, like a blind man knows Braille. But he liked her neck best because that was the spot *she* liked best. In his mind, he tasted the long slope of her throat, from her chin to the indentation at her clavicle. The more he remembered, the more agitated he felt.

Sophie's gaze followed his.

"What?" he said.

One eyebrow lifted. "Move along, Star Trooper."

She'd said it quietly, yet her eyes kept flitting to his chest too. For someone so intent on removing all traces of their former attraction, she seemed inordinately interested.

"What?" he said again, this time more insistent.

"Nothing," she replied, though clearly this nothing meant something.

He checked each face around the table for clues to the something he had missed, but everyone else was busy shoveling ice cream and shuffling game pawns. He could only surmise his workouts must be paying off. Sophie's apparent obsession with his physique made him feel like jumping on the middle of the table and launching into some superhero poses. Thanks to her admiring eyes, his ego had inflated to capacity. Made him wonder why women didn't appreciate their breasts being ogled as much as men.

"Are you going to just stand there?" he said. "Or do you want to play?"

Her focus shifted to his face, and she unlocked her arms. "I'm too stunned. I haven't seen you play a board game in, oh, a decade?" She headed toward the kitchen. "Eat up, girls. It's after nine-thirty, and you have school tomorrow."

"One more week, Grampy," Keely said, "and we get summer vacation. Daddy promised it would be our best summer ever."

"I heard," Grampy said, his dentures vigorously gnawing the buttery pecans in his ice cream. "You're graduating fourth grade, right?"

"And I'm grada-ju-ating kindee-garden," Annabelle said brightly.

Will kissed Annabelle's crown and walked his empty bowl to the sink. He ran water in it and turned again to survey his people: Sophie, tidying up the kitchen; the kids having fun with their game; Grampy a punching-game-bag happy to lose; and Grammy shuffling around in puffy pink house slippers and a floral Wal-Mart housecoat, content to help wherever needed. This simple night would soon be a memory, but every once in awhile a deep pang of regret whacked his gut.

"You should shave that off," Sophie said, breaking his contemplation.

Shave? He fingered his chin. He wasn't due for a shave till morning.

"You mean his chest hair?" Grammy said. "Yeah, all the kids are into manscaping. I personally appreciate a man with a hairy chest—it's what God gave 'em, after all. But then, I shaved my legs once upon a time, so what do I know?"

Sophie shrugged as she wiped down the counters. "Grammy does have her fingers on the pulse of American youth."

Will's ego sputtered like a popped balloon.

"Oh yes, dear," Grammy said. "I chaperoned freshmen on a field trip to Coney Island before Spring Break, and all the girls talked smack about the guys with chest fur. Girls can be brutal, for sure. By contrast, the smooth-skinned boys are considered *rawrrr*." She curled her fingers into claws and swiped the air.

Annabelle and Keely exchanged giggles and mimicked Grammy's claws.

"Thanks, Gram," Will said, "but I don't need to manscape."

Sophie tossed the sponge into the sink. "Don't waste your breath, Gram. Will's not into the *rawrr*; he's more attached to his monkey coat. What do monkeys say, girls?"

Annabelle and Keely launched into monkey poses and jungle calls.

Will gave Sophie a thankless stare. "You seriously think I should shave my chest?"

"At least your back."

"My back?" Will looked to Grampy for help.

"Don't ask me. I got no idea what the girls like until Eunice tells me."

One panoramic scan of Will's female audience was all it took. "Fine. I'll do it. But I'm going to need help. Which one of you is going to do the honors?"

He didn't wait for an answer and headed upstairs to find his can of Barbasol.

Sophie watched Will hurry off with the kids on his heels.

Grammy sidled next to her and extended her palm. "Pay the piper, girlfriend."

"Not so fast. I'll need to see it to believe it."

Grammy shrugged and waddled off. "Suit yourself, boo."

Ten minutes later, Annabelle came screeching into the kitchen.

"Mommy, Mommy! Grammy cut Daddy and he's *bleeeeeding*. Hurry!"

By the time Sophie reached the top of the stairs, Annabelle was frantic. She grabbed her mother's hand and dragged her into the master bathroom where Grammy was dabbing the upper left quadrant of Will's back with a bloodied hand towel.

"What happened?"

Grammy removed the towel to reveal the damage. "Man's got a lot of bumps. Who knew my hands weren't as steady as they used to be?"

Along with a half-inch gash on his shoulder blade, a large patch of Will's upper back was shaved while the rest was mottled with disintegrating white foam.

Sophie looked closer. "That's a lot of blood for such a little cut."

"Little?" Will said. "Feels like she took a machete to me. Sucker stings."

"The verdict is in." Grammy shoved the bloody towel at Sophie, along with a frothy razor sprouting curly brown and silver hairs. "I should never be allowed to wield anything sharper than a spoon at my age."

Will twisted to see his shoulder in the mirror. "Do I need stitches?"

"Hardly." Sophie set the tools of his near-destruction on the vanity and examined the evidence. "Looks like she shaved the state of Texas into your shoulder."

Grammy gazed up through her tri-focals. "Well, I'll be." She pointed to the cut, still seeping traces of blood. "Right there's the state capitol."

Will turned and strained to see it in the mirror.

"Mommy." Annabelle clutched Sophie's hips. "Can you fix Daddy?"

"Baby, that is a loaded question." Sophie pressed the adhesive ends of a large bandage onto his newly shaved skin. "Hold still, would you?"

Grammy gave a *tsk tsk* and turned to Sophie as they both stood back, crossed their arms, and perused Will's back as canvas.

"Shades of Rembrandt," Sophie said.

"More like Andy Warhol on acid. A man can't walk around like that."

"A man can wear a T-shirt."

Will craned his neck to better see his reflection. "Come on, you two. I look like a dog with mange. Help a guy out."

Grammy tapped the back of her bare wrist. "Holy smokes, look at the time. Annabelle, let's get you into bed and give Mommy the operating room, shall we?"

Alone with Will, Sophie assessed the situation. "She suckered me."

"Just clean me up, will ya? Then we'll be out of each other's hair, so to speak."

Sophie rinsed the razor blade and pushed Will around so that his back faced her. She peered around his arm, at the reflection of his shaved chest. She couldn't help but admire the whole package. The length of his striated torso. His small well of a bellybutton. The light sprigs of hair above his low-slung waistband. His flat, brown areolas and nipples—taut from the cool air-conditioning. All very, very... inconvenient.

"What do you think?" he said.

"Uh, better." *Centerfold better.* "You look more... evolved."

She steeled herself and applied more shaving cream, palpating and stretching the skin around his scapulae for a smooth razor surface. To prevent nicking, she moved in for a better view of the landscape and stroked the razor up and down, rinsing the foam and doing it again. Her hands smoothed his back, measuring his wedge shape and the slow in and out of his lungs. He'd always looked good, but their tortured relationship had eventually overshadowed her physical attraction to him. She'd found a new appreciation though. A lot of appreciation.

Disturbing, how much.

She wiped off the last traces of foam. "There. All clean and shiny."

He turned his back toward the mirror and looked over his shoulder at her handiwork. Facing her was his front side and all the spots he'd missed.

"Hold on," she said. "Let me finish you off."

Omigod. A raunchy line that implied sex. She grimaced up at him.

"That's, that's—"

He chuckled. "I know what you meant."

"Good," she said. "I mean, just because you *smell* good and—"

"You think I smell good?"

Did she really say that out loud? "Shhh," she told him, and herself.

She placed her palm on his bare shoulder to still him; took the razor and cleaned up the stray hairs he'd missed—slow motion-like, with great care around his areolas, along his breast bone, here and there down his abdomen; conscious of the rise and fall of his chest, the thumping of his heart beneath her steadying hand. Heat shimmered off his skin and burrowed beneath hers, flicking the emotional web of their past.

She'd worked hard to bury all memory of intimate moments like these. Now his nearness plowed the ashes, pierced the plating she'd wrapped around her grief so that she could move on. How fast her heart was racing; how hard the beating. Her abdomen had contracted and stayed that way since she'd walked in and saw him standing there half naked.

He looked so good. Smelled so good. *Felt...* so... damn... good. And— what's this? He'd grown hard beneath his pajama pants. A sigh of annoyance concealed the thrill piquing her psyche. He remembered her, as she remembered him—*everything* about him—not the least of which was the velvety feel of Little Will and the Heartbreakers in her hands, and how Will could so adeptly serenade her lady bits into a frenzy.

Her eyes traveled up his chest, past the muscled cords of his neck, and into the warm brown eyes she had once loved so fiercely. His eyes caressed hers, too. She wanted to touch him, run her hands across all of him as the old longing cascaded through her, and instinctively, she tilted her chin, looming closer, until her nose was inches from his chin. So, so sexy.

He clasped her wrist with the razor in it, his shadow blocking the light behind him, his gaze drifting to her mouth; and she imagined his warm, wet kiss on her lips. She could hear herself breathing as he lowered his head. Moving closer. Closer. Whispers away.

This is such a bad idea. She pressed her hands against his chest, their gazes locked together as the tug of war inside her raged. She took a deep breath then and stepped back.

"All done," she said, averting his eyes.

Will didn't speak for a few beats. "You sure?"

"You better get a cold shower. I mean, rinse off so you're not itchy."

She tossed the razor into the sink, fighting the mesmeric pull of him—of their comfortable old love. Just ghosts now. Anything they did would only fan the lie that they could ever go back again.

And she would not let that happen.

"So," she said. "See you downstairs?"

She glimpsed his face—just enough to see the flicker of disappointment—and slipped away, praying he wouldn't ask her to stay.

Chapter 19

Early Thursday morning, Sophie entered the lobby of her downtown high-rise. She shoved a folded *Business Journal* into her purse, reflecting on how jam-packed her schedule was, including an office tour for Grammy who shuffled at half-speed while clutching a frozen caramel macchiato, a coral handbag dangling from one arm.

Grammy's spry attention flickered like a light bulb in response to the sights, sounds, and smells of downtown. "Wowee," she said in a voice graveled by more than eight decades. "This is some fancy-schmancy skyscraper." She sucked down her iced coffee, screwed up her face, and shivered. "Oh, snap! I got a wicked brain freeze."

Sophie guided Grammy to the elevators and hit the *Up* button. A few feet away stood three workmen, two carrying toolboxes and one lugging a stack of storage boxes so tall, Sophie couldn't see anything but his shins.

"Dude," Grammy said. "Don't you believe in dollies?"

"Gram, please," Sophie said.

Grammy shrugged. "Just being sociable." The old woman's eyes darted and blinked, as if she were on the verge of blurting something that would test her granddaughter's patience. "William skipped out early this morning, didn't he?"

And there it was. *William.* "Did he? I hadn't noticed." The way Sophie's body had betrayed her the other night, staying far away from *William* seemed wise.

Grammy's bony, twisted index finger punched the *Up* button again, several times.

"It'll come, Gram."

Ten, nine, eight... Grammy had a ten-second-silence limit. *Four three, two...*

"I realize you've only been married for a camera-flash of time, Sophie Belle, but are you telling me Will has no redeeming qualities?"

Sophie cursed silently. "Gram, I was the only one in the relationship, and that's not sustainable or realistic for anybody. And then I became completely boring. I want a fulfilling life, so I've made meaningful changes. For once, I'm having a little fun and adventure."

"Yeah, you've been a real barrel of laughs so far." Grammy's dentures clicked. "Who quit paying attention to whom first?"

"I never quit paying attention. You've been married for sixty-five years, so I'm sure it seems crazy, but maybe the English teacher in you will understand. It was like, one day Will picked up this great book, and he got so absorbed in it that when I came into the room screaming and crying, he never even looked up."

Grammy snorted. "Must have been a real page-turner."

"And he read that book day after day after day, until I *quit* screaming and crying because he just didn't notice me. He didn't get it, Gram. And I stopped waiting for him to get it."

"But you can't deny, Sophie, the man loves those children."

"Of course, he does. Can we change the subject?"

"If he didn't love you, too, he wouldn't fight with you."

"Please. How else do you treat a person you don't want to be around?"

"I might consider arsenic. Saw that in a movie once." Grammy toggled the elevator button again, her bony free hand gripping her iced coffee. "I only have so much time left on Earth. I could croak before this elevator gets here."

Sophie had vowed not to discuss Will with her grandmother, but the dam had cracked. "For years I waited to hear more from him than, *Why can't you understand how important my work is? Why do I have to explain things over and over? Why can't you* [whatever, fill in the blanks] *by yourself? You're not over it yet?* And my favorite: *But I did what you said*—which was never more than lip service."

Grammy shrugged her bony shoulders. "He does have nice lips for a fella. Plus he's a crackerjack with all that computer stuff."

Sophie shifted on her heels. "I want someone who actually cares what I think, Gram. Someone who believes in me. Someone who's actually *in love* with me." She inhaled a lungful of strength that exhaled in muted anger. "You don't know how much Will had changed. He wasn't the same guy I fell in love with. He changed. And now I've changed."

The elevator doors slid open and Sophie stepped inside with Grammy hobbling behind her. The two workmen with toolboxes got on and Grammy held the *Door Open* button.

"You coming?" she called to the delivery guy with the tall stack of boxes.

"I don't think he's coming," Sophie said.

"Of course, he's coming. I'm holding the door. We don't have all day, buddy."

The man lumbered into the elevator, leaning back so that his upper body counterbalanced the unwieldy load. Pushed all the way in by a portly woman in a black business suit, the man bumped Sophie with the bottom box and backed his way into the corner.

"What floor?" Grammy asked him.

"Nineteen."

Before the doors closed, a small herd of men and women in dark business suits elbowed their way in. Sophie felt like she was in her coat closet. Grammy grew pensive, but Sophie's bliss was not to be savored. Grammy had been absorbing the world around her.

"I don't mean to rag on you, Sophie dear, but that outfit you're wearing? You can't get more boring than a black suit. You're pimping real estate, not tombstones. How are you going to find fun and adventure dressing like a stuffed-shirt executive?"

Four black-suited executives craned their necks toward her.

Grammy shrugged. "Why you gotta be hatin'? Just an observation. Right, William?" Her eyes cut toward the guy overloaded with boxes, immobile as a scarecrow.

Sophie glanced at the guy's worn shoes. Years ago, Will had skipped around in a scuffed old pair of sneakers like this guy's, until she had stashed them in the depths of a green lawn bag that Will later ferried over to Goodwill, never the wiser. Or so she'd thought.

She peered around the boxes. "What the hell? You're a delivery boy now?"

The elevator stopped at the eleventh floor, and Will's voice came muffled behind the boxes—his real voice, not the muffled falsetto she'd heard earlier. "I have business on the nineteenth floor. Helping John Dearborn set up his consultancy. Could be permanent."

"You are kidding me." Everyone in the elevator shifted uncomfortably. Sophie turned the volume down, but not the infuriation. "You cannot work in my building."

"I can and I am."

Two passengers exited and the elevator doors closed. The slight kick of re-ascent caught Sophie in the stomach. The elevator chimed and stopped again, its doors opening into an opulent lobby. The brass wall marquee boasted, Houdini Real Estate, *Where We Make the Home of Your Dreams Appear Like Magic.*

171

Grammy scuttled out. Sophie stormed off the elevator behind her, though she had not nearly exhausted the litany of profanities building inside her.

"Lucky for you," she said to the big box, "I'm the mature one."

Grammy blew Will a kiss. "Lucky for you, there's an audience."

With her fists balled up, Sophie watched the elevator doors close.

Grammy's mood seemed infused with a perverse delight as she lilted into the Houdini foyer. Her gaze bounced around the room at the rich décor. "Wow. Guess this place musta cost some dough. I see bling everywhere."

Gertie Fishbein walked from behind the reception desk wearing an ultra-mini brown leather skirt, white tights, and a caramel mohair sweater. Because of her top-heavy, barrel-shaped torso, the visual effect was that of a root beer Tootsie Pop. Her thick glasses sat low on her nose as she passed out mugs of hot coffee and chatted to Tess Baker—and Jake.

"There she is," Tess squealed. With arms outstretched, she bent and squeezed Grammy in a hug. "My gosh, were you always this tiny?"

"Elderly shrinkage, honey. But you, you're droppin' it like it's hot. You don't look a bit different from when I saw you last."

Tess turned her cheek. "Oh my, Grammy, that was years ago, when Annabelle was born. Did we leave our trifocals at home?"

Grammy shrugged. "They make me look old."

Jake held out his hand and bent over to accommodate her much smaller height. "Remember *me*, Grammy?"

Grammy peered up at him. "Sure. You're the guy Tess dumped. You're still around?"

Jake wagged his head. "Nice to see you too."

"You stole Will's Stratocaster, didn't you?"

"Grammy," Tess said. "Will lost that guitar to Jake in a bet."

"So you say," Grammy said, her lips stiffened.

"Well," Jake said, rubbing his hands. "I have a class to teach, so I'll be on my way. Call you later, Tessie."

Mitch approached from the hallway, and he flashed his famous welcome smile that made him such a hit with women everywhere. He swooped Grammy's hands in his.

"You must be Eunice. I'm Mitch Houdini. Sophie has told me so much about you."

"Heard about you, too." Grammy motioned to Sophie with a jerk of her head. "My granddaughter's gonna need another minute to pull herself together."

Sophie was poised near the elevators, absorbing Will's news and paying minimal attention to her companions. Jake kissed her on the cheek and punched the elevator button.

"Will has a job on the nineteenth floor," she said weakly. "Did you know that?"

Jake shrugged. "Man's got a job, Sophie. That's a good thing, isn't it?"

Sophie plopped onto the lobby sofa. "I'm never getting rid of him, am I?"

Tess sat beside her and passed her mug of coffee. "Here, say the Serenity Prayer and slam this. It's lukewarm, but I spiked it with Bailey's. We're celebrating something."

"Allison closed her three-mil Lady Bird Lake property today," Mitch said cheerfully. "Girl is pocketing a full six percent. That's worth a little breakfast party, isn't it?"

Sophie sank further into the cushions, slammed the coffee, and raised an empty mug to Gertie. "More please? Four shots of Bailey's, hold the coffee."

The elevator chimed and Jake kissed Tess's cheek, then got on when the doors opened. Meanwhile, Grammy surveyed Mitch intently.

"What are you, Eye-talian?"

"Eye-talian, yes." He pinched his fingers together near his face. "And a little Polish. But third-generation American."

She nodded approval with a sideways glint. "I can whip up some mean raviolis." She kissed her fingers and released them with a flourish. "You never tasted anything so good."

"Ravioli's are a personal favorite," he said.

"William's, too. You like fireworks?"

He looked confused.

"You and William both over for raviolis will be like Fourth of July."

"You're trouble. I can tell."

Sophie rose from the sofa to inject herself into Grammy's line of sight and, with one raised eyebrow, warned the old woman to play nice. She then turned her attention to Mitch.

"Sorry, I'm a little stressed today."

"Sure," he said, giving her a quick hug. "You want me to give Grammy the tour?"

"Would you?" Yet another reason to like Mitch Houdini. Not only was he sweet and considerate—unlike Will, who seemed determined to sabotage her—Mitch recognized when she needed space. "Gram, do you mind? Mitch is going to show you around."

"What do you think, I'm deaf? I heard you pawn me off. Lucky he's a looker. You're joining us, aren't you, Tess?"

"Of course. Someone has to protect you from Mitch. Lead on."

Sophie marched into a bathroom stall and wilted onto the toilet seat. She swigged her second cup of Bailey's and forced herself to meditate on a spot on the metal door to calm down. Will officed a few floors above her? What were the odds they'd run into each other after he moved out of her house, *all the damn time*?

Wait, was this not Thursday? Edwina Marshall Day? Surely, their date was still on. They'd probably have dinner and Will would be bored out of his gourd. She smiled at the idea of him stifling yawns, eyeing his watch every two minutes, and realizing what a complete moron he was for giving up his wife. Maybe he'd even shed a tear at the idea of spending the rest his life—deservedly—alone.

Sophie's Kiss-off strikes again. She was feeling better already.

By the time Sophie reached her office, Gertie was there with a large brown envelope.

"I think you've been waiting for this," she said. "Came last night after you left."

Sophie sat in her tufted-leather chair, leaning over her desk adrift in legalese. She had told her lawyer that for purposes of expediency and because he was under her roof, she would sign the divorce papers and hand-deliver them to Will. Now, as her stomach churned like sneakers in a cement grinder, she lost interest in reading the terms of their settlement. Especially visitation. It cut Will's time with Annabelle and Keely to every other weekend and Wednesday, plus alternating holidays. Seemed so confining and *unfamily*.

When he was never around and didn't seem all that interested in daddy-hood, a visitation schedule wasn't such a big deal; but now, she wasn't so sure. He had changed his priorities when it came to the kids. She had to give him props for that.

Tess poked her head through the doorway. "What a character. Grammy's making friends and enemies of the same people."

"That's my Gram. Salt and vinegar of the earth."

"You okay?"

"Fine." Sophie tucked the papers back in the envelope. "Busy day. Plus, I'm taking Gram to the middle school. She and Grampy are signing up to tutor kids on summer break. After New York inner-city kids, these Texas youngsters will be a breeze."

"I can't tell you how much street lingo I've learned in the last twenty minutes." She scanned the envelope in Sophie's hand. "Divorce papers?"

Sophie put her elbows on the desk and rubbed her temples. "Nobody but Will could inspire me to throw a temper tantrum on a crowded elevator."

"You need to get him off your mind. You seeing Mitch tonight? Or maybe I should ask if you've met Mr. Slinky yet."

Sophie cut her eyes to Tess. "Oh, we've met. Sort of. We always get interrupted."

"Well, in case you do encounter The Slink up close and personal, I have a surprise for you. Something that will come in real handy dandy."

"Handy dandy?" Before Sophie could guess what, a cackling commotion edged toward her office.

"Bada-bing." All of Mitch's punch lines lately ended with this emphatic expression. Normally, she thought it was funny but, today, not so much. He followed Grammy into Sophie's office and helped her into a chair.

"This youngster has more energy than a tiger cub," he said. "She's wearing me out."

"She does that." Sophie regarded her grandmother with deep love and affection tested by her Will-tainted stress level. "I've got a big day ahead. Shall we go pick up Grampy?"

Grammy's cheeks were rosy. "Give me a few minutes to rest my legs, will you?"

Mitch motioned Sophie into the hallway with a curling finger. She crossed the room and kissed Grammy's cheek, noticing also that Tess had circled her desk and buried something in her purse. Sophie guessed it must be something *handy dandy*.

"What's up?" she said.

"We're still on for dinner, right? It would do you good to get out and be with people who care about you. Including Ruta. She's expecting you to join us. And you know—"

"Yes, I know. What Ruta wants Ruta gets."

"You got it." He kissed her on the mouth. "See you tonight. We'll have fun, I promise."

Tess met Sophie in the hallway. "There you are. Grammy is texting."

"Texting? That woman has got to find friends her own age."

"I think it's adorable." Tess held Sophie's elbow and strolled with her down the corridor. "So, tell me the latest. Will's going on his dates, right?"

"I assume so." Sophie was exhausted thinking about Will.

"Enjoying Sophie's Kiss-off?"

She had to admit, choosing Will's dates was more fun than she'd imagined. "It's kind of delicious. I'm pretty sure dates one and two were calamities, so, small victories there. And he has a date tonight with a very sweet but dowdy young schoolmarm."

"And you thought *you* were boring. Well, good. I keep putting Jake off till the bet's over. Will *needs* to go on all those dates so I don't end up sorry I started this."

"Would that be so bad, Tess? You loved Jake once."

Tess stopped walking and squared herself toward her friend. "I think we both know, how much you love someone doesn't always matter, in the end."

Late in the afternoon, Sophie got off at the nineteenth floor with a thick goldenrod envelope under her arm. She wandered the halls until she saw the heavy wooden doors that read in gold letters: John Dearborn Consultants. Inside the Dearborn foyer, amid the smell of fresh paint and textured walls, she noticed the incomplete finish-out. Wiring hung from two of the overhead light fixtures and furniture sat in the lobby, covered by tarps. Of four small offices, only two had desks. A larger office had been furnished but lacked personal items.

Another office waited at the end of the hall. Sophie padded to it, stopping in the threshold. Will stared out the window at Lady Bird Lake, shifting on his legs, hands on his hips.

"I take it you missed me?"

She realized he could see her reflection in the glass. His tone came from the chip on his shoulder; he'd probably been fuming all day about the elevator scene, just as she had.

"If you're here to continue your tirade, I don't have the stamina for it right now."

"No. No tirade. I was just..." She clutched the envelope. "So, this is your new place?"

He turned and spread his arms. "Home sweet home."

She glanced around, noticed the gym bag leaning against his credenza, a racquetball handle sticking out of a zippered pocket. In the old days, before things went south, they played couples racquetball. A framed 8x10 picture of Keely and Annabelle sat on his credenza, next to another of the three of them at some park. No pictures of Sophie. She felt a pang of discontent; she was their mother, after all.

The longer she stood there, the more she second-guessed her mission. Her mental talons searched for small talk. "You the only one here? Where's Dearborn?"

His gaze brushed the amber envelope under her arm. "I'm actually glad you're here. I'd like to—I need to—I mean..." Something caught in his throat. A word. "Apologize."

Had she heard right? An apology from Will was rarer than steak tartar at a vegan spread.

"For not looking up from my *book* long enough to pay attention to you."

Ah, the marital analogy she'd given Grammy.

"You were right. I'm sorry. I was, as they say, blind."

"Uh, thanks. Two years too late, but okay." She paused, plumbing her brain for the reason she'd come. He'd shocked it out of her. "Anyway, I just, er, needed to know if you were still going out with Edwina Marshall tonight."

"Really. That's why you're here?"

She nodded mechanically, then remembered her mission—the papers under her arm. But he'd shaken her resolve. Had he done that on purpose? He knew how to defuse her when he suspected she might say something he wouldn't like or couldn't defend. Why else would she be there?

Well played, Camden. Well played.

"Let me guess," he said. "You need to know if I'm seeing the teacher because, one, you're perpetually nosy about things that no longer concern you; and two, you're still secretly in love with me. Did I nail it?"

Sophie gave a withering eye roll. "That would be Door Number Three, Bob. Look, you have a date, and since your first two went down in flames, I thought I could share some pointers that would, you know, *help.*"

Will sank into the leather chair behind a mahogany desk and propped his dog-eared sneakers on it, smiling disingenuously as his hands locked and cradled the back of his head, elbows akimbo. His face looked thinner. Had he whitened his teeth?

"What's so funny?" she said. "You can't expect a date to lead anywhere if you blow it right off the bat. It's like going zero to sixty with your parking brake on." He held the grin too long. Did he know she was stalling? Working up courage? "Whatever. Here's a suggestion. Try to find common ground."

"That's your brilliant matchmaking pointer?"

"It's not the only one. You could—"

"Force my date to marry me? Should I take my shotgun?"

"Keep an open mind."

He pointed to his head, teeth gleaming anew. "Like the Grand Canyon, babe."

"Remember, Edwina is very proper. No cussing."

He snorted. "You put us both to shame, sweetness."

So annoying. She paced, squeezing the envelope to her side, and ticked off on her fingers what she considered excellent pointers. "Edwina's young."

"You can say that again."

"So she might be giggly. Don't let that bother you."

He raised his arms and laced his fingers together behind his head. "A refreshing, youthful sense of humor would be a nice change."

"And no religion or politics. Because she's a schoolteacher doesn't mean she's a Democrat. No sense in offending her."

"Certainly, not on the first date."

"No eighties rock trivia. Stick to the new stuff. You might even enjoy it. Go with the flow, take her dancing. Women love that."

"That ain't happenin'. I got the music in me, but not the rhythm."

She jabbed her finger at him. "She's a woman. Don't underestimate her."

He bucked his chin toward her. "Learned that the hard way."

Biting her tongue was getting harder. "She has more upstairs than you might be willing to give her credit for. That said, innocence is optional. You never know what girls have up their sleeves these days."

"Or their skirts, as *you* well know."

Sophie let the reference to Mitch pass, but it reminded her: "Don't forget condoms."

She turned away, squeezing her eyes shut. *What am I saying?* She mentally stepped over the creepy inner conflict and pressed on. "Not the cheap ones. You don't want accidents."

"And you thought she was too proper."

"Just, you know, until you get to know her, don't divulge too much of yourself."

"After all that, you want me to be dishonest and keep secrets from my future wife?"

She made a bitter-beer face. "I just don't want you to turn her off right away."

"To think I thought you only came here to make my life miserable. Did you forget your dagger, because that would make things quicker, wouldn't it? Want to borrow my letter opener? I promise, it's rusty." He motioned toward the door. "Or, perhaps, I could show you out."

Sophie's stomach turned again. The envelope with their divorce papers chafed her armpit. She set it on the edge of his desk and slid it toward him. He stared at her, thrumming his fingers on the desktop, but made no move to retrieve it.

"Don't you want to know what it is?"

"I know what it is," he said. "Guess you brought your dagger after all."

Chapter 20

Will rang the bell of apartment 13G, staring at a turquoise panel door with a hand-painted Bavarian-type welcome sign hanging under the peephole. Inside lived Edwina Marshall, earth-mother art teacher, granddaughter to a steel guitarist-turned-world famous artist, and Debacle Number Three. Will vaguely remembered making the date with her since his painkillers had done such a superb job of blocking his normal "that ain't right" reaction. So she was an adult; he had an aversion to dating women outside his pop-cultural sphere. But now he was stuck.

He planned to make this a dinner-only affair, unless Edwina turned out to be fun. Maybe then he'd commit to putt-putt. If it turned out she was too boring even for him but nice enough that he couldn't bear to hurt her feelings, he'd pop for a movie where eye-dazzling, ear-splitting action scenes prohibited engaging in any kind of meaningful dialogue. If the date took a deep-sea dive, all bets were off and he was dumping Miss Fuddy-Duddy on her doorstep promptly after he paid the dinner check.

When Edwina opened her door, Will did a shuddering double-take. He saw himself in his head with Fred Flintstone sound effects.

"Hello, gorgeous," she said, giving him the once-over. "You're right on time. I like reliability in a man." She made a pathway with her arm. "Come in."

Will hardly recognized her. She wore a short black slip dress that hugged her body like static cling, and the bold, low-cut neckline accentuated her modest rack quite nicely. Her hair hung loosely across her shoulders, and she'd applied smoky make-up.

Did she feel comfortable in that? Or was it part of some wily scheme to entice him into performing stupid guy tricks that she would scold him for later? Coach Casey and Spike had left him gun-shy.

Edwina sashayed toward the living room in red spiked heels, earning an A+ on the legs, and the straps of her dress crisscrossed between her shoulder blades, which somehow drew his eyes toward a shapely bottom he wouldn't have guessed existed under her demure schoolyard get-up of last Saturday. He suddenly felt cheap for arriving empty handed. No flowers, no chocolates, no six-pack.

"Have a seat," she said. "But be careful of the recliner. It's a little finicky."

And old as the hills, from the looks of it. The leather was distressed at best. He decided instead on the loveseat, which separated the living room and the foyer.

"Can I get you some fresh sangria? It's homemade."

"I'm not a wine drinker, thanks." Thinking about a wine concoction laden with fruit and enough sugar to give him a cavity made him shiver, but when he remembered Sophie's advice about going with the flow, he reconsidered. "Actually, sangria sounds good."

"Awesome." She twirled into the kitchen with a cheery, "I'll be right back."

Two hand-painted lamps perched on the end tables, and a candle burned on the fireplace mantel, infusing the room with an aroma both sweet and pungent while an overhead fan creaked and spun frantically, like a tutu'd ballerina on crack. Dozens of framed black-and-white 11x17s leaned against the wall by the fireplace, waiting to be hung. But a smorgasbord of oil paintings already glammed up the walls, from surfer dudes on overcast sandy beaches to a toothless old woman on a cabin porch in the middle of nowhere. Shades of Michelangelo.

Like her famous grandfather, Edwina had an eye for capturing the essence of her subjects in eternal poignancy. Hers were the kind of paintings that hinted some hidden agenda behind her subject's eyes. He'd like to say he understood such things, but art was a riddle on the same plane as female hormones. Case in point, the schoolmarm turned femme fatale.

A stacked tower of silver-and-black stereo equipment lulled the air with love songs by Norah Jones. Will pegged the artist because Sophie listened to that CD sometimes. Combined with the stereo's ambient orange and cyan lights, the mood seemed set for romance.

A wormy chill slithered down his spine, and he thought of his daughters. If Annabelle and Keely dated a forty-five-year-old fart like him, he'd find it inherently creepy.

Dinner. That's all I'm doing. Just dinner.

He concentrated on Edwina's artwork. Most intriguing were the twin brass andirons flanking the fireplace screen. So heavy duty he couldn't imagine Edwina picking them up. From each andiron's base rose two feet of ornate shaft topped by a huge brass ball about five inches in diameter. Real brass balls. A lapping crimson tongue, like the Rolling Stones logo, had been painted on the face of each ball.

"Guess you're a fan of the Stones?"

Edwina returned with two long-stemmed glasses of blood-red sangria. "You like the tongues?"

"They're interesting. Why aren't they in the fireplace?"

She handed him a glass and sat down on the sofa, cattycorner to the loveseat, her knee touching his. "They're for Grandfather. He's the Stones fan. Besides, paint's still damp."

He made room for her legs and examined the wine glass, which had been drizzled with high-gloss green paint. He pressed a fingertip to the paint and found it dry, when he realized the glass itself was special.

"These handmade?"

"Yes, in Grandfather's workshop with special torches. He taught me how to make glasses and ashtrays and lamp shades, plus a bit of jewelry." She fingered the ruby pendant that hung from her long, silver-chain necklace. "Like this piece."

Will bent for a closer look, and she let the pendant fall between round breasts that reminded him of the Hostess Sno Balls his mom used to pack in his lunchbox, minus the coconut. "Very... er, artsy."

He diverted his attention back to the glass and inspected the sangria. Slices of lemon and orange floated between ice cubes, their flesh infused with crimson. "Looks rich." He held it to his nose and sniffed. "Brandy or cognac?"

"Brandy. Triple Sec, club soda, and, of course, red wine. Plus mango and strawberries." She leaned forward, *oh-so forward*. "And *passion* fruit."

Will took a thoughtful sip as his eyes flickered to where they were summoned. He wondered if Edwina had trouble hiding her alter ego from fellow teachers or the principal.

"Don't you love fruit?" Her satisfied smile revealed a gap between her front teeth that he hadn't noticed before. "It's so sensual. I like rolling a slice around in my mouth and tasting the tart and sweet on my tongue." The next part she whispered. "Before I swallow it."

Gulp. A cold burst of Sangria filled his throat, along with an orange chunk, and he grabbed at it, coaxing it down his esophagus. "Yup. Tart and sweet."

"I knew you'd like it." She threw her head back, downed the entire contents of her fancy glass, and wiped the sanguine stain from her lips with the back of her hand.

Caught in a surreal dream state, Will stared at her mouth.

"Hello, Will," came a voice from behind the sofa.

Will turned to see a double of Edwina breeze into the room. Except this one wore her hair bound in a clip at her crown. Her vibrant blue sheathe did not fit as snugly, but it cast the same mesmerizing effect.

"I see you've met my sister," she said.

"I have?" Will looked from one woman to the other.

"Jessica, you pretending to be me again?"

"Hey," Jessica-cum-Edwina said. "He bought it."

"I'm sorry." The real Edwina tipped her head to install silver hoop earrings as she sat beside her sister. "You can slap her on the hands, but that just makes her want to do it again."

"I left your sangria on the counter," Jessica informed her. "Will likes my glasses."

Will nodded, dumbfounded that they'd so easily fooled him. "Guess you're both artsy like your grandfather, huh?"

"Our grandfather has been fostering my artistic goals since I could hold a bottle," Edwina said. "I'd like to paint *you* sometime, Will."

"Me?"

"Does that surprise you? You've got great bone structure and a sort of dark, brooding sense about you. Perfect for what I have in mind."

"I'm the family photographer," Jessica said, indicating the black-and-whites stacked against the wall. "I'd like to take you on a photo shoot."

Will shifted in his seat, unsure that they weren't just playing with him.

"It would be fun. Right, Edwina?"

Edwina smiled the way he'd seen Keely smile at Annabelle when she felt the need to boost her sibling's ego. Loyal. Loving. Long-suffering.

"Yes, Jessica is a phenomenal talent. I wish she didn't get so bored with it. She's been experimenting with paint. Did you see the andirons? They're almost dry."

"Yes," Will said of the fat, red tongues. "So all the wall paintings are *your* handiwork?"

"Paintings are mine. Photos are Jessica's. She's promised to move them to storage this weekend. Right, little sister? I don't want to have to hurt you." Edwina smiled and disappeared into the kitchen.

Jessica dipped her head toward him, the fingers of one hand splayed. "Five minutes she slipped out of the womb ahead of me. You'd think it was five years. But Edwina's modest. She's following in Grandfather's footsteps. I only wish I had half her talent."

"I'm sure he's proud of you." Will wondered what Gramps would think of him dating one of his granddaughters. He'd given no thought to repercussions—until now.

Note to self: whatever happens, this date must end with Edwina recounting to Gramps that Will Camden's behavior was nothing less than chivalrous.

"Listen," Jessica said, "I just moved back to town, and it's been so long since I've been home... " She licked the sangria from her lips. "You don't mind if I tag along tonight, do you?"

One woman made him edgy enough. Two ensured that any gross errors of etiquette would be doubly noted and sent home in a report card to Sophie, and—

Wait! Wasn't he in possession of a two-fer? Didn't he just hit the jackpot? Every red-blooded man's dream? Edwina and Jessica would be twice the payback for Sophie, restitution for the fiascos of Coach Casey and Spurious Spike, and dessert for his bruised ego.

Did he mind? That was a trick question, right?

Note to self: You are one lucky bastard.

Will smiled lamely. "I hope you like steak."

Edwina returned with a full glass of sangria. "My sister is a serious carnivore, Will. I'm sure she'll be happy with whatever's on the menu tonight."

Jessica grinned and hiked one eyebrow. "I love a juicy, raw piece o' meat." Less of a statement and more of a growl.

Edwina squeezed next to Will, sandwiching him against the arm of the loveseat. "Mind your manners, Jess. Besides, he's *my* date."

Jessica sat back and crossed her legs. "Just explaining that my diet is low carb. Fresh protein is always welcome on the menu. The rarer the better."

Seeing them together, Will could pick out subtle differences. Edwina was softer, rounder, more accommodating. Her complexion hadn't seen the sun, and her nose was wider across the bridge. Jessica had a gap between her teeth, and her eyebrows were thinner with more of an arch. They were otherwise identical, but Will sensed more complex distinctions under the skin.

"When we were kids," Edwina said, "Jessica set records for the world's most finicky eater. Now she's got an appetite like a panther."

Jessica's dark-rimmed eyes narrowed, and she made a low-pitched guttural noise, like Brewsky gnawing on a dead bird he didn't want to share. Will imagined a trail of saliva dripping from her chin.

Somewhere, deep in his brain, right around where he stored his middle school memories, a dork meter kicked on. Fortunately, his high school libido stood sentry with a burning spliff, a pack of Trojans, and a

Joe Cool meter in overdrive. His teenage self officially copped an attitude: *Dorks 'R' Not Us. Not tonight. Tonight, you are one smooth operator.*

"Let's start the evening off with a toast," Edwina said.

Jessica raised her glass, her voice a silky purr. "Yes, to the wild animal in all of us."

Will watched the girls gulp their sangrias to the last drop, smiling. Like a dork.

"Honey, drink up." Jessica pushed his glass to his mouth and held it while he chugged.

"Thatta boy," Edwina cooed. "Now we're ready."

Sullivan's was in Austin's Warehouse District, a 1940s-style steakhouse that bragged on the caliber of its live jazz and high-end liquors. After a ten-minute wait, Will and his dates were seated at a four-top in the middle of the dining room.

He ordered escargot and a bottle of Pinot Noir, and nixed Jessica's request for onion rings. For the main meal, Edwina ordered broiled swordfish with mango salsa. Will eschewed his usual New York strip and, keeping with the evening's theme, went wild on broiled mahi-mahi and avocado-habañero pepper salsa. Jessica ordered broccoli with Hollandaise and steak tartare. With one bottle of pinot drained, she quickly ordered another, and Will wondered how much two twenty-six-year-olds could drink before they started slurring and running in tandem to the john.

He had acquired quite the buzz himself and recalled the days when drinking binges were the norm. So many gigs in smoky bars, and fans always bought him booze. An empty glass was just an SOS signal for a full one. What a lightweight he'd become—a thought that spurred him to order another bottle of wine. Heck, he could keep up with *a coupla girls.*

During dinner, the threesome was interrupted by one of Will's old I.T. buddies, Bob.

Bob sat at their table for a few minutes, sipping on a glass of whiskey and talking up Will's former high-level position at Waterloo. He relayed how the department had tanked in Will's absence and how management was always holding up Will Camden as the platinum standard for how things oughta be done.

"Makes you wonder why they sacked you," Bob said. "I think they regret it."

The whole report swelled Will's head, and when Bob left with a sly nod and a wink, Will scanned the dining room for anyone else he knew who might spread the word that he was out with twins. He almost wished Sophie had planted spies somewhere or that somehow they might make the ten-o'clock news.

Jessica then launched into tales of her adventures from New York to London with nefarious boyfriends. Edwina listened intently, basking in her sister's torrid escapades and offering only clipped anecdotes of her life as an unassuming academic. When, at one point, Edwina mentioned an upcoming art show, Jessica gobbled up the conversational flow. Edwina's accommodations only allowed Jessica to reveal more of her feral nature, but Will had to admit, both of them were pretty entertaining.

After Edwina excused herself for the restroom, not an easy feat given the sheer amount of ingested alcohol, Jessica leaned closer, one elbow on the table, chin cupped in her hand.

"You'd look ten years younger without those silver tips. I can fix that."

"Oh yeah? I've had the silver since I was twenty-five. I'm used to it."

Jessica fingered his hair while her toes tickled his shin. "So, Mr. I.T. wizard, what do you do for fun?"

Will swallowed a spicy bite of mahi mahi and wiped his mouth with a starched linen napkin. "My wife tells me I'm just a stodgy caveman." The pinot buzz had loosened his lips. "Think she's right?"

"I think maybe you're just bored. I can fix that, too." Jessica's sexy grin revealed a sprig of broccoli in the gap between her teeth. "Seriously."

"Sullivan's eez first place Meetch brings me when I come to Austin." Ruta relaxed in the limo with her Stoli and cran on the drive from the airport. "I always like eet. Especially now when I hate New York." She slid her gaze to Sophie. "Eez momentary, but I feel eet with passion. We can go to Sullivan's, too, no?"

Sophie had mentioned that Will and his date had reservations at Sullivan's, which had necessitated further detail about Tess and Jake and the bet for Will's old Stratocaster, and then the jokes at Will's expense started in earnest. Sophie didn't mind making fun of the whole Sophie's Kiss-off thing with Tess, but the rest of the world, she quickly discovered, were just trespassing on private territory—not that she hadn't invited them over. She just regretted it now.

Mitch had laughed nonstop; the whole thing seemed like an invitation to him. "What do you say, Sophie? Sullivan's for Ruta's favorite steak?"

There seemed no deterring those two, but with her curiosity maxed out about how miserably bored Will must be with his date, and despite her headache, Sophie relented. She had specifically chosen Edwina because the life of a plain, modest schoolteacher seemed more lackluster than her own—if that were possible. And she imagined, by comparison, she would look like a whirlwind of excitement and he would realize—too late, of course—that he didn't know what he had while he had it.

Now waiting for a table in Sullivan's bar, her headache seemed to expand with the discordant strikes of piano keys and sharp horn bursts from the jazz trio on a corner stage.

"Meetch doesn't like competition, you know," Ruta said into Sophie's ear. "He likes to *ween*. Doesn't matter if he's only man in the race."

Sophie gave Mitch a glance. On the barstool beside her, he bobbed his head happily to the music and chatted with the bartender.

"There *is no* competition. The bet we made was a means to an end. Everybody was supposed to win something. I won time to date Mitch without Will's interference, and it just works out that I get to heap some payback on Will for, you know—" Sophie struggled to encapsulate Will's shortcomings when she had plenty of her own. It was simpler to blame him and save the lengthy explanations. "Failing at our marriage."

Ruta gave a knowing stare, nodding long enough to verbalize a whole paragraph without uttering a sound. "So, they are here?"

"Probably in the dining room."

Mitch jumped to his feet and plucked Sophie off her stool. He twirled her around tall tables and barstools, guiding her fluidly around the room. Her steps mirrored his, and though she rode his feet a few times, she was surprised at her lack of self-consciousness about it. In his arms, she felt safe and cared for, desirable and daring. More than she had in years.

She thought, *I'm a cicada emerging from the ground after a long, deep sleep, ready to shed the past.*

And then she thought, *Ew. Cicada.*

But Mitch moved like Gene Kelly, unlike Will's White-Man Waddle. Sophie enjoyed their rhythmic romp, especially when Mitch pressed his body to hers and nuzzled her ear. Still wearing her boring black business suit, she wished she'd been able to go home and change before they picked up Ruta. She'd have thrown herself into something more provocative, more worthy of a sexy jaunt around the bar. And she'd have shaved the pubic hair on the tops of her legs so they didn't look like sidelocks, in case opportunity knocked.

"Wonder what takes so long for our table?" Ruta ventured, as Sophie scooted back onto the adjacent barstool.

Mitch huddled between his two dates and patted Ruta's arm. "Any minute. Have another Stoli and cran. We'll eat, we'll talk, we'll laugh. Bada-bing."

Jimmy loomed on the other side of Ruta, an ever-present accessory to all of Ruta's Kayfuyu ensembles. Sophie never doubted her bodyguard's preparedness. His eyes roved the crowd, checking people up and down and perfecting his no-nonsense, no-chitchat persona. Sophie hardly knew what his voice sounded like because he rarely spoke. People who recognized the Russian Princess often stared and pointed, something she was used to after years of being in the spotlight; but Jimmy made his commanding presence known and assured that his charge never encountered harassment. The occasional autograph was all Sophie had ever seen him allow and only after Ruta's subtle gestures gave the okay.

"When I buy lake house, I have party," Ruta said. "Call Martha to help decorate, no?"

"By all means," Mitch said, winking at Sophie. "Call Martha."

Ruta slapped his shoulder playfully. "You know who would be great at party? The *Cleentons*. Nice couple if you like Democrats. And that scamp Clooney." Her eyes rolled to half-mast toward Sophie. "You like George, no? Maybe you like to meet heem?"

Sophie brightened at all the namedropping, wondering if Ruta had real relationships to back it up. After all, who would know if the woman lied? She didn't put stock in tabloid news.

"Or, I could fix you with the Donald, but must wait now till he's tired of next wife."

Mitch wrapped his arms protectively around Sophie. "What are you saying? I'm doing my best to impress this woman. Stop sabotaging me."

The hostess came as soon as the drinks did, and she led them to a white, linen-draped table not far from Will's.

Sophie's nerves quadrupled. She squinted across the expanse trying to place the woman he was with because she looked nothing like Edwina Marshall.

But it *was* Edwina, and she'd had quite the makeover. Her little black cocktail dress fit her like a glove—or more precisely, a glove *liner*. Where was the rest of her ensemble? The girl tittered across the vast inch that separated her nose from Will's.

"That Will and his date?" Mitch asked.

Ruta followed Mitch's gaze. "Oh my. He eez quite sexy tonight."

Sophie wondered if he'd been that sexy in the last years she was married to him or if she'd just grown weary and immune to his charms—or if, with so many fights, he'd become unattractive in other ways. She found it hard to take her eyes off him now.

Mitch nudged her. "Go say hello or it'll be awkward, stealing glances and pretending they're not there."

"Looks like they need a room," Ruta said.

Sophie hesitated to jump into a fire, but Will's eyes found hers and she had no choice. She steeled herself, dreading his anger at spying on him, and strolled to his table. The closer she came the more she wished she'd changed into some dazzling cocktail outfit—anything to mitigate the matronly feeling that flourished with each stride. In the dim lighting of the restaurant, Edwina looked about sixteen.

"Hello, you two," she said on approaching. "I just popped by to say hello." And then she went completely blank. "Um, I'm so glad you could meet up tonight. Uh, Will never gets out much."

Will gazed up at her with glassy eyes. "We were just talking about that."

Another woman stopped behind him and set her hands on his shoulders. She massaged them and brushed her fingers casually up his neck.

Sophie had instant visions of garroting the woman. Her familiarity crossed the line, trespassed—

Wait. Edwina? Edwina's exact likeness sat beside Will—the woman wearing the black glove liner. And then it all became clear: twins. Fashionista Barbies.

No wonder Will looked so smug.

Edwina fondled Will's earlobe as she slid into her chair. As though he was her pet. "Nice to see you, Mrs. Camden. Kind of weird, but—"

Sophie indicated her table with Mitch and Ruta. "I'm here with friends."

The other young woman extended her hand. "I'm Jessica. You must be Will's *ex*."

The way she said ex, Sophie got the feeling she'd been referred to all night as the ex-slithering, ex-stinking, ex-stifling, ex-steaming sewer serpent of Will's sordid past.

"S-s-s-s-o-o," Sophie said, with a throaty laugh. "Twins."

"Yeah," Jessica said. "Our whole lives."

Sophie felt her jaws tighten. So, there was Artsy Fartsy Barbie and Little Be-otch Barbie—and their fuddy duddy slacker buddy, Ken.

"You'll have to excuse my sister," Edwina said. "She's been on a three-year vacation, and she's celebrating her return home with too much to drink. Will and I will take care of her, though. It was nice of you to stop by."

Sophie bit back a putrid green thunderbolt that might have stabbed both Barbies' dead. She smiled vaguely at her dismissal and returned to her table—but not before she overheard Jessica's catty quip, "No wonder you were bored, Will."

Sophie plopped into her chair and lunged for her Stoli and cran. Mid-guzzle, she was bumped hard from behind and spat most of it onto the white tablecloth and her blouse.

Ruta stood and jammed her hand across the table. "Hello again. You are having fun tonight, I can tell."

Will reached over Sophie to shake Ruta's hand. "You're looking lovely this evening."

Sophie's face burned as she mopped up the spatter. "Now you're Rico Suavé?"

Will bent close, his breathy laugh skimming her ear. "Thought we were clear on the spying thing. What are you doing here?"

"It's Ruta's favorite restaurant."

Ruta and Mitch had run their mouths nonstop ever since the airport, but suddenly they were wide-eyed little mutes. Jimmy, too, watched with heightened concern from his corner of the room but never made a move toward them. *Some bodyguard.*

"I see," Will said, though clearly he did not see. "Well, since you're in my proximity, I wanted to tell you the good news, just so we're on the same page."

She scrutinized his glossy gaze, inhaled his schnockered breath. "You're drunk."

"Close, but the night is young. See, tonight I have paid back my debt of a third date with Miss Edwina Marshall. I have also paid back my debt for a fourth date with Miss Jessica 'Hottie' Marshall. Be sure you tell Tess and Jake." He pointed to his table. "That would be two dates for the price of one, right over there."

"That's not our deal," Sophie said.

"It's our deal or I don't sign the papers."

Sophie felt a vein twitching in her forehead. He wasn't going to renege on the terms of their bet, and he sure as hell wasn't going to sabotage her divorce plans. "*I* get to *choose* the dates. Ask Tess." She indicated Jessica with her chin. "And I don't choose *her*."

Will held one finger in her face. "*Uno mas*, baby. One more."

Mitch popped to his feet, chin jutting and hands cocked stiffly at his sides like pistols. "Maybe you and I should go outside and have a little chat."

Crap. Sophie tugged on Mitch's wrist, hoping he understood it as a diplomatic "Back-off." He lowered to his chair like a sloth on Xanax, and she craned her chin toward Will.

189

"You can go back to your plastic Barbies now, *Kenny* boy. And don't think you're not just as stiff." She pitched her soaked napkin on the table and exited the dining room in a huff.

When Sophie bolted from the restaurant, Mitch's upper lip curled and he slammed his wadded-up napkin on the table with an impotent thwack before trailing behind her.

Will set his hands on his hips and laughed. That was kind of fun.

In the spirit of the evening, he felt like he should throw something, too. Instead, he exchanged business cards with the Russian Princess, who was then escorted out by her personal bouncer in Armani.

Feeling pretty good, Will took the long-and-winding road back to the twins. Not that there was a shorter route. Just seemed longer when one staggered.

Chapter 21

Will paid the check and requested the valet call them a cab so he could call it a night, but Jessica and Edwina would have none of that. Arm in arm, they coaxed him down the street to Polyester's, a retro nightclub Will had never been to, simply because he was no longer a nightclub kind of guy and because Sophie was right; he never got out much. In fact, the last place he wanted to be was a smoky bar.

But he was with twins.

He held hands with Edwina and Jessica, names soon abbreviated to Ed and Jess, and they dragged him under the strobe lights and a swirling disco ball where he was inundated with dance music from the seventies and eighties. He spent ten seconds whining that he wanted nothing to do with a dance floor, then let loose twerking and twisting, hunching and spinning all over the place with no semblance of dignity. He figured, if Sophie was so anxious to pawn him off, he might as well exceed her expectations. For once.

In his musical element, he sang along with every song. By the time Prince blared through the speakers, Will was improvising solos on his air guitar. His left hand floated up and down the invisible fret board while his right hand picked and tapped, strummed and shredded like the virtuoso he used to be, like he had longed to be in his youthful dreams, electrifying his audience as a rock star god. Back then, Sophie was his biggest fan. Back then he could do no wrong. Back then she only had eyes for him.

Ed and Jess—further abbreviated to E and J—took turns buying shots. Will had tasted Sex on the Beach, Buttery Nipples, and Mind Erasers before, but the Duck Farts and Alien Secretions were new to his palate. He reveled at being sandwiched between the twins' rhythmic sways and dirty dance thrusts, arms high over their heads or low and behind, bumping and rubbing his hips. The whole world whizzed by at a sweaty, breakneck speed.

For his finale, Will threw himself on the floor and wailed on his six-string, sizzling like a piece of bacon in a frying pan. This frenzied demonstration left the whole place crowing and chanting for more; and by the time they left, he felt possessed by the ghosts of rock shows past to mount a stage and pound out some old Wild Boys tunes.

But by then, he couldn't find his air guitar with both hands.

Sophie sat across from Ruta and Mitch at Truluck's, a restaurant several blocks from Sullivan's. With Ruta's bodyguard looking on from afar, Ruta signed two autographs until Jimmy stepped in and insisted on privacy. When they had finished their late dinner, the coterie watched out the window as three figures bopped arm in arm down the street. Will Camden—he who claimed to have no rhythm or desire for dancing—led the gyrations.

So much for fixing Will up with a nice, modest art teacher.

The ache deep in Sophie's chest clashed with the desire deep in her loins for the gorgeous man who sat beside her.

Mitch slurped his highball. "It's a law, Sophie. Men don't turn down twins."

"The Will I know is not the man out there. The Will I know likes his beer, but he doesn't get drunk. The Will I know isn't spontaneous. He doesn't even know how to *spell* fun."

"Of course he does: T.W.I.N.S."

Ruta donned a scowl. "Men gonna stick up for things men do, even they don't like each other. But you never know, Sophie; maybe one of the twins will be wife."

The thought of Edwina or Jessica becoming a stepmom to her kids was as appealing as Icy Hot on her crotch. Sophie shook her head, as if juddering Will out of her brain. "I give him five minutes before he's barfing up his guts. The man's got the stomach of an infant."

After the street stumblers disappeared, Sophie called home. She dialed the number and heard Grampy's voice.

"Hello? Hello? Hello?"

"Hi, Grampy. It's Sophie. How are the girls?"

"Hello?"

"Grampy?"

"Hello? Eunice it's a crank caller again. Somebody's heavy breathing into the phone."

Scuffling ensued and Grammy came on the line. "Turn on your

hearing aid, Hal."

"It's me, Gram."

"Kids are fine," Grammy crowed. "Fast asleep like haloed angels. Hal's been trying to rearrange your old shed out back, but the light bulb went out. You got any more?"

"No, but tell him Will is supposed to take care of the shed. I don't want Grampy hurting himself climbing over junk."

"Don't you worry, I'll keep an eye on him. Have fun. The 'hood is under control."

"Thanks, Gram—"

"Hello?" Grampy had picked up the phone from another room. "Hello?"

"Geez, Hal," Grammy said. "You already answered the phone and handed it over to me. Go to bed." The extension clicked as he hung up. "The man's memory sucks."

Grammy gave her blessing to "paint the town fun." Sophie hung up thinking two hours ought to be time enough to relax, forget about Will and his entourage, and maybe get to know Mr. Slinky on a first-name basis. It had been weeks since her first attempt.

Ruta picked up where they'd left off. "You know sooner or later, your husband will find someone, and you not gonna like her, I guarantee. But the girl gonna make heem happy, and that is what you want for heem, no?"

"Of course. That's why we're getting a divorce. So we can each move on."

"Good," Ruta said. "What about me? I am available. I can be Will's fifth date."

"I don't know if it's fourth or fifth yet. I need a ruling from Tess and Jake."

"Fourth, tenth, no matter. I can be next date."

Oh how things just got more complicated. "But, er, you're taller than he is."

"I am taller than most men, darlingk."

"She has big hair is all," Mitch teased, studying Ruta's high-swirling up-do. He flicked her ear with his fingers. "An exquisite, sexy look, I might add."

Sophie wasn't bothered by his casual flirtations with Ruta. It was an extension of their decades-old friendship and she didn't consider it a threat, but everyone was flirting tonight except her. And the idea of Will with the Russian Princess? He seemed destined to be surrounded by beautiful, alluring women; he was certainly having a lot more fun than she was. Irony in spades.

She contemplated Ruta as date material—or relationship even.

Ruta's freewheeling, jet-setting lifestyle assured that Will would stay out her hair—if not off the continent. Still...

"I didn't figure you'd be interested in a younger man," Sophie said, fishing, evading.

"Are you kidding? I love the young guys."

"You know he has kids. Are you saying you're mommy material?"

Ruta threw her head back in laughter. "Not least bit, dear. But I can be great date. Give him *international* perspective." She cocked one eyebrow. "I know tings."

Sophie hesitated to guess. "I'll think about it."

Ruta's lips pressed together thinly. "You tink I'm too old?"

"Of course not," Mitch said. "Nobody's a bigger party girl than Ruta."

Ruta's head snapped toward him with eyes that glowered, and she tapped her long red fingernails on the table. "That is all I am? Party girl?"

"Of course not. You're so sensitive lately. What's wrong? Is it the change?"

The smooth planes of Ruta's facelift revealed less than her words. "I like to go to my hotel. Take hot bubble bath. We meet early to look at properties, Sophie, and you will tell me how I can date your handsome husband."

"Well, that's a unique offer," Sophie said, with considerable clench in her jaw. "Sell a house and a husband at the same time. But what about Allison? You're technically her client."

"I don't care for dat girl." She appealed to Mitch. "That is done deal, no? I prefer Sophie show me the properties."

Mitch hooked a thumb toward Ruta, his delight overflowing on Sophie. "Like me, this woman knows what she wants. And that's you. Allison is out."

Sophie wasn't sure Allison would understand their logic, but no point arguing in the face of a much-needed commission. "Yes, I can meet you at eight-thirty in my office."

"Not *your* early," Ruta said. "My early. Ten o'clock. I have Mermaid of Sea treatment at nine, or Cactus Cooler terapy. Someting. I forget."

Twenty minutes later, Ruta and her bodyguard strolled toward the lobby of the Lake Austin Spa Resort. Sophie waved goodnight as the limo motored off.

"I thought she'd never leave," Mitch said. "Don't get me wrong, the Princess is a hoot, but I've wanted to get you alone all night. I know you're tired, but you look beautiful. I do love those sleepy bedroom eyes you've got going."

Sophie felt her chest expand as she settled into his arms. Maybe she wasn't *that* tired.

"What do you say to a few days at the coast?" he said. "Just you and me. I have a place in Rockport and a nice catamaran moored off my back deck. We could leave tomorrow night and come back Sunday."

"The coast?" *Sun, sand, surf, and sex?* She sat up, looking into eyes that tweaked her heart—and other parts. "I'd love that, if I can make arrangements for the kids."

He nuzzled her neck and pulled her earlobe into his mouth. His warm, wet tongue tickled, and his voice was husky. "Of course, we could get a head start on things."

With all that nuzzling, her body had already gotten a head start on things. But then she remembered: "I promised the kids I'd take them bowling tomorrow night."

Mitch's mouth grazed her throat. "Reschedule it. You can go bowling any time."

"Tempting," she said, as his mouth stoked the embers a lot further below. "I've been working so many long days lately, I wouldn't feel right."

He sat back, his disappointment obvious. "Okay. But soon, right?"

With her busy schedule and Mitch's frequent trips out of town, a lot of sexual tension could accumulate, especially with the volume of innuendo they bandied about in hallways and on phones. She sometimes felt flirted into a frustrated frenzy.

"Yes. Soon. Meantime, the kids would love it if you came bowling with us."

He mulled this over, seeming to say *yes* as he stared at her chest yet not uttering the word. "Bowling it is. But, I think you should make it up to me. Assuage my disappointment. Reveal something... personal."

Sophie gave a lazy smile and tossed her purse out of the way, laying back and inviting him to join her. He pressed his body eagerly against hers and slathered more kisses across her mouth and throat while working off her blouse. He paused to admire her, then slipped her bra cup beneath one nipple and lowered himself to suckle it.

Oh, yes. She heard herself moan at how wonderful it felt. Her body could not have been more dialed in for a good bout of S.E.X. if she'd just had a massage while watching porn. Press One for Wanton Lust, press Two for Titillation, press 0 to go straight to—*Yes, yes, yes!*

The expert machinations of his tongue had her gasping. A small, surprising nip, and she flinched and kicked her purse into the door. It upended and spilled its contents, namely her cell phone, personal items, and a cloth measuring tape that unfurled like a blowout party favor.

Tess's handy-dandy surprise.

Mitch turned to see what happened, and Sophie quickly pulled his face back to hers, wrapped a leg around his waist, and pulled him in to her. His hands slid under her skirt to caress her inner thighs, looming closer and closer to her—*hhhh!*—there, the hungry, lonely, wet space where her greed and need were one. *Omigod.*

"Want to go back to my place?" he whispered.

"No," she said raggedly. She'd fantasized about this, and it had been so long since she'd had an orgasm that wasn't self-inflicted, she was due. And why not? Two consenting adults, a safe, secluded place, and the will to be daring. Besides, after the other night with Will—

No, no, no. No Will. There's only Mitch.

"Here," she said. "Right here." She pushed him off and unhooked her bra, held it up and dropped it on the floor. "No arguments."

"You won't get one from me."

Sophie moved to the seat opposite him and slipped off her heels as her fingers found the intercom switch.

"Franklin," she said to the driver behind the black smoke window. "Cruise out to Spicewood, will you? And take your time."

She pressed a button that opened the moon roof. Under a star-filled sky, Sophie couldn't imagine anything more ideal. She removed her skirt and sat back in the seat, only slightly self-conscious in the shadowy light. Mitch's appreciation showed in his smile and the way his eyes followed her every move, caressed every millimeter of her nakedness.

"Your turn," she said, the frisson of naughtiness tweaking her sex.

His voice was thick. "But your fingers are so nimble."

Sophie daringly straddled his lap with one knee on each side of his hips, loosened his tie and buried her nose in the damp crook of his neck, left tender kisses on his throat and inhaled his spicy cologne and the trace of salty sweat.

Finally, she thought. She was so overdue for this.

She unbuttoned his shirt and ran her hands along his rock-hard chest, down his abs, and over the fabric of his slacks where Mr. Slinky strained against it.

"Think I'll need your help for this part."

She dismounted so Mitch could unpleat himself, but in the limo his head hit the ceiling at only half his height. He moved under the moon roof and widened his stance, positioning himself so that his upper body was above the roof. His voice filled with whipped air. "This is a first."

Sophie giggled. She couldn't say it was her first; she'd had sex with Will in several cars, but that had been many years ago. A limo, though—that was new.

With easier access, she unbuckled his belt, slid down his slacks and guided his feet out of them. On her knees she admired his chiseled physique and beefy legs, and she snorted at the argyle socks around his ankles. All that remained was his snakeskin-print underwear, inhabited, apparently, by a large squirrel stretching and pulsing against its silky cage.

She looked up his torso again, tenuously.

Mitch balanced himself on his forearms against the moon-roof frame, his cropped hair blowing as he scanned the nighttime Hill Country. Waiting, for her.

Inhaling gulps of brazenness, Sophie stuck her fingers beneath his elastic waistband and slid the underwear over his hips. That's when she was smacked in the face by an unapologetic superstructure. Mr. Slinky, he of humble, flaccid beginnings, had come to life swelled with his own magnificence. Add to that, hirsute testicles the size of meteors, and she wondered how this Goliath among mortals ever fit inside briefs without some scuffling and a takedown.

She stilled her nerves and steadied her backbone, gripped Mr. Slinky's girth and rubbed his full length. This was a job for two hands— and Tess's handy dandy surprise.

She extended one leg, toes poised to grab the purse handle. With a feeble foothold, she swept it toward her and snatched the tape measure, positioned herself closer to his hips to disguise her movements, and again peeked up his long torso. Mitch had closed his eyes, so she seized the opportunity to take measure of the man.

Holy torpedo.

The air flowing through the moon roof blew her hair around, and as Mitch looked down, she dropped the measuring tape. Quickly, she pulled Mr. Slinky closer, opened her mouth, and eased her lips around his tip—hesitantly, furtively, tasting, gauging, comparing.

So freakin' huge.

His wolfy smile as their eyes met was an all-systems-go signal.

She took a huge gulp of air, and then... *Looks like I'm going in.*

Her tongue tried to get out of the way as she took him deeper in her mouth, sucking and sliding him in and out, feeling the vibrations of his moans. She liked the idea of pleasing him and tried to take him still deeper, and that's when the limo hit a rut in the road and knocked her off balance. Which caused her mouth to slam shut. Teeth first.

The sound of Mitch Houdini's high-pitched howls filled the night sky for miles.

Will woke up. Unfortunately.

A noisy fan whirled overhead, pelting him with Category Five winds. He tried to open his eyes, but they burned as his lids stuttered across them. His body felt an intense bout of rigor mortis, though he couldn't believe death would feel this painful; and his mouth felt thick and dry, as if he'd eaten dirty cotton socks.

Where am I?

He panicked and sat up, his hands cradling his throbbing head, and peered at black shadowy squares on the walls and unfamiliar lumps in the night that he came to realize were oversized pieces of furniture. He was on Edwina's living room sofa. Naked.

As his eyes adjusted to the darkness, he spied thong panties draped over a lampshade, a black silk cocktail dress in a puddle on the floor, and stilettos littering the carpet. Another G-string clung to a rotating fan blade overhead.

He rubbed his face to quell the nausea and checked Little Will for signs of distress. His mind doled out vague snapshots of the evening. Edwina and Jessica, dancing in front of him and behind him, rolling on the sidewalk under the stars. They had swayed naked above him, his wrists trussed to bedposts, and... and... and all he came up with were sound bites that dragged in his ears like an old cassette player in need of new batteries. Did he get his *ménage à trois*? Had he been good in bed? What did the girls do to him that he could treasure for the rest of his ever-loving days? His blighted brain revealed nothing.

Somebody upstairs didn't like him—or conspired with his wife to simultaneously erase his memory *and* make him feel guilty. Oh, yes. She had that kind of insidious power.

Four thirty-five, according to the moon glow on his watch. He didn't dare turn on the lamp and risk waking the twins. He got to his feet, stomach lurching. *Please not again.* Funny how he had no trouble remembering hurling in the can after he'd staggered through Edwina's front door. His gut was a decrepit punching bag.

Clothes would be good. He trudged around the coffee table, looking for his underwear, and stubbed his toes hard on one of the fireplace andirons with Mick Jagger's fat red tongue painted on its brass ball. He hopped around the room on one foot, holding and rubbing his injured toes, cursing and cringing and cursing some more—and spying his underwear on a doorknob near the hallway.

He limped across the room, snatched his briefs, and opened the door out of reflexive curiosity. Inside, Jessica—or Edwina?—slumped naked over a vacuum cleaner. He squinted and heard her snoring, then closed the door.

In the foyer, he bent over to stick one foot through the underwear hole, followed by his other foot in the same hole, and toppled over.

Boom!

The last time his head made a dent like that in textured sheetrock, he was six and had misjudged the bouncy power of his bed.

Once he figured out the intricacies of his underwear, he located his socks and pants in a pile beside the old recliner. He heard rustling from somewhere, maybe the bedroom, and he picked up the pace, plopping into the recliner to put his shoes on.

The leather groaned as his weight sank into the cushion. As he put on his socks, the footrest popped out and the chair-back reclined. He lay staring at the ceiling for a few moments, listening for Edwina and Jessica in the dark, and then felt along the sides of the recliner for the lever. It was small, on the right side, and didn't want to budge. Sheer determination and brute force got the lever to flip. He heard a hard click and the chair buckled forward—all the way—snaring him like a pearl in a clam.

Doubled over with his head between his knees and his arms trapped, he couldn't reach the lever; and he couldn't physically last long in this position without a trip to the ER and a body cast—a predicament that exacerbated his massive hangover.

"Help," he whimpered. "Help."

After the seventh increasingly desperate *help*, he saw the spray of lamplight and heard Jessica's sleepy voice.

"Told you that recliner was finicky." She yawned and stretched, her joints cracking, then stooped in front of the recliner, peering into the space packed full of Will. "You okay?"

"Hard to tell," he choked out.

His gaze slipped from her brown-smudged eye makeup to her bare breasts and the hairy V about six inches below her belly button as she moved away. She flipped the lever and the chair flopped back into reclining position, squeaking and groaning. After a moment of collecting himself, he started to stand up when the recliner popped forward again and served him up like a tennis ball. He staggered into the fireplace and bounced off the bricks.

As he fell backward, his socks slipped on the marble hearth and he went down. Little Will and the Heartbreakers landed smack on the andiron, against Mick Jagger's fat, lapping red tongue. And he thought it exceptionally cruel that brass balls could make a grown man cry.

Chapter 22

Sophie ran through the forest in an ethereal fog, to the top of a steep, craggy hill with a serpent the size of a submarine on the heels of her red stilettos. At the crest, she glanced over her shoulder, right into its inky Cyclops eye. It flickered a long tongue across her body, and she recoiled, losing her balance and tripping and tumbling end-over-end down the other side of the hill. She rolled to a hard stop against a red-rock boulder where the serpent blocked her escape; and she cowered on her haunches while it lurched at her, spewing a gooey gunk from somewhere deep inside its undulating mass. She shielded herself, but it just kept coming and coming—endlessly, until she felt so suffocated, she screamed.

Sophie bolted upright, shuddering in the aftershocks of her nightmare. The front of her pajamas was splotched with lumpy beige stickiness from her décolleté to her bellybutton.

"Sorry, Mommy." Annabelle patted her mother's chest with the edge of the bed sheet. "I didn't mean to spill."

"I told you Cream of Wheat was a bad idea," Keely scolded. "I tried to catch her before she came up here, Mom. Grammy tried too, but she wouldn't listen."

Sophie felt obligated to speak, but her thick tongue needed coffee before agreeing to conversation, and in its stead she uttered bewildered gurgles and grunts.

Keely stared at the mess while Annabelle ran for a towel. "It looks like poople, Mom."

"Poople?"

"Grampy made potato soup with noodles yesterday, and he called it poople."

Classic Grampy. Sophie rubbed her temples.

"It does look like pooples, Mommy," Annabelle said, returning with a damp cloth.

Keely intercepted and handed it to their mother. "Are we still going bowling tonight?"

Sophie dabbed at the mess on her chest and tried to remember what day it was. Oh yeah, the morning after she'd chomped on Mitch's gigantic frankfurter. *Hot diggety.* She might as well have asked for mustard and relish. Her dental impressions would remain there for eternity, like a tattoo shouting *Sophie was here.* Her nightmare said it all.

"Um, yes," she managed. "I'll be home around four. We can go bowling and then to Hut's for cheeseburgers. How about that?"

Annabelle elbowed her big sister. "Told you. You owe me fifty cents. In quarters."

"Quarters," Keely said. "I need those for gumballs."

Annabelle tilted her chin, and Sophie saw Will's Mini-Me in her defiance. The Mini-Me jumped from the bed into a full gallop out of the room, bedheaded pigtails flying. "Too bad I know where your piggy bank is."

Keely squealed and tore after her.

Grampy sidestepped the kids in the doorway. His elderly reflexes seemed to twitch faster when the risk of getting knocked over loomed. "Those apples did not fall far from the tree." His voice sounded as frail as his ninety-year-old bones.

Sophie yawned. "No argument there, Gramps. So, poople soup?"

He ambled toward her with a small envelope in his hand, a grin spreading into his saggy cheeks. "Kids dug it."

Sophie dabbed again at her pajama top and tipped her face to receive his light peck. "How do you always greet the day with such a positive attitude?"

"You know how it is. Another day above ground is cause for celebration." He handed her the envelope before shuffling out. "Didn't want to let you get off before you saw this. I had to sign for it."

Sophie read the return address of the certified letter. Her mortgage company? She ripped it open and scanned the contents.

"What the hell?"

Sophie flew across the hallway. On their daughter's twin bed, Will lay supine and spread eagle beneath Annabelle's Hello Kitty comforter, visible only in relief beneath the pink-and-black overlay—Da Vinci's Vitruvian man, stinking of sweat and alcohol. One arm hung over the bed, curled fingers twitching. Snorting, gasping noises emanated from his face.

"Zzz-hhh-gkpk. Hhh-zzz-gkpk."

Sophie shook his shoulder. "Will, wake up."

He opened his lids fractionally, then resumed the cacophonous apnea. "Zzz-hhh-gkpk. Hhh-zzz-gkpk."

She shook him again. "Will."

"Huh?" His head rose two inches with a feeble grunt before falling into the pillow.

"William Camden. Wake. Up." She grabbed the puffy pink satin in both fists and jerked it off the bed, leaving him naked but for a pair of wrinkled red boxers.

He rolled into the fetal position and opened a swollen, bloodshot eye. "Don't tell me." His voice was hoarse from disuse. "I'm in the Ninth Circle of Hell."

Sophie did a double take. His signature salt-and-pepper mane was now jet black, and that, along with the memory of him cavorting arm in arm with the Marshall twins, had her seething all over again.

"Hung over are we? Not so easy to keep up with the children, is it?"

He groaned woefully. "Tis the she-wolf. Abandon all hope, ye who enter here."

"Really? I put a roof over your head, and this is how you repay me?"

"What are you talking about?"

She flung the envelope at him. "This is why you've been intercepting the mail? So I wouldn't find out?"

He blinked hard a couple times, as if moistening his eyeballs, and curled into a sitting position. The letter lay half-folded between his hairy ankles, and he took his time getting to it. That's when she noticed the smudges on his pink pillowcase.

Great. Black hair dye. That'll never come out. Her nostrils convulsed with the clenching of her jaws.

"Give me a minute to wake up, huh?"

"I'll give you ten seconds."

She clamped her mouth, blockading the tirade burning the tip of her tongue, watching his bare, broad shoulders hunch over the letter. *Nine, eight, seven...* She wondered absently at his biceps—bulging as if he'd just pumped a couple hundred pounds in the gym. *Six, five, four...* She panned down her front, to the tops of her bare thighs. Why was it so much easier for men to stay in shape? Even his calves said, "I just kicked ass on the 100-metre sprint."

Must not be distracted by muscles. Must not be distracted by nakedness.

She tapped her foot. A ten-year-old wouldn't have to skim more than the subject line, yet her PhD was staring like it was Sanskrit. "Well?"

Will blew out a weighty sigh, folded the letter along its creases, and shoved it back toward her. "Yes. I'm aware. I didn't tell you because I didn't want you to worry."

She blinked. "Why would I worry about our mortgage being three months behind? It's only our home. The only place our children have ever known. The place they're supposed to live until they leave for college. Our one secure investment—or it *used* to be. How did this happen?"

He bowed his head and ran one hand through his new black dye job. "Did it escape you that you just woke me up from a dead sleep to yell at me?"

Her voice bounced off the walls. "Who's yelling?"

"You know, to do this interrogation properly, you're gonna need jumper cables and a bowl of icy water for my nuts."

Heat shimmered off Sophie's skin like a July sun on West Texas asphalt. She reined herself in, clenching her fists to prevent acting out the mental movie clip of his sudden tragic end by strangulation. She envisioned the chalk outline of his body on the carpet.

Mrs. Camden. In the kid's room. With her bare hands.

"This isn't just about your layoff, is it, Will? Or your condo money being tied up in escrow?" His silence was maddening. "I'm not leaving until you tell me."

Fortunately, his instinct to shoulder guilt enough for everyone breached the cracks in his armor. She saw it in the yielding tilt of his head; the flattened, fidgeting lips; the mournful sigh; and the droopy brown eyes. The requisite white flags waving in surrender, she congratulated herself for a successful negotiation.

"It's not like I lied, Sophie. Soon as the escrow closes, the proceeds hit my pocket."

She shifted on her feet, attaching hope to every word. "Then what?"

"Then I pay the mortgage."

The telltale aversion of his eyes warned that something else was up, and it wasn't that she'd shocked him out of a dead sleep or a hangover in progress. She waited for more, but again he clammed up. Whatever. She could outlast him—stay put until the silence between them became so uncomfortable he'd be forced to break the tension and talk. She leaned back and crossed her arms through a thirty-second hush that couldn't have been more excruciating.

Finally, he slid his legs over the side of the bed, avoiding a direct eye connection. "Look, when I got laid off in February, I had a... *crisis of confidence.* I'd talked to Grampy at Christmas about his retirement and investments. The ones he was always bragging about. He made it sound so ironclad. His financial guru made him money hand over fist."

"What are you saying?"

"Gramps tripled his investment in less than a year. Did you know that? That's how he and Grammy took that extended trip to Europe last year. It's how they bought that fancy place by your great uncle in Montauk, how they could afford a new Mercedes. They're not even on Social Security. Did you know that?"

Sophie bit her lip. "Are you saying you took Grampy up on his suggestion to invest?"

Will covered his eyes with his fingertips and massaged his eyebrows into his forehead like he was molding clay.

She took that as a yes. "Jesus, Will."

"I was one of the last people to get into it. I didn't tell Grampy, so don't you tell him either. I don't want him to think it's because of him that we're in this position. That would kill him. I just wanted our kids to go to an Ivy League university if they wanted, instead of the local-yokel shit. I thought I could triple our savings, and—"

"Our savings? How much of our savings?"

His lips disappeared into a thin line, and he looked like he might implode. Instead, he crumpled the mortgage notice in his fist and fired it across the room. "Goddammit!"

Sophie flinched into high alert. Her even-keeled husband was not known for violent outbursts. His reaction unnerved her as much as the threat of foreclosure. Rooting her feet into the carpet, she watched him settle on the edge of the bed into a real-life statue of *The Thinker.*

"So, everything, Will? *Everything*? Our life savings? Our kids' college funds? When were you going to tell me about this?"

"I don't know. I guess I thought I might be able to pull something out of my ass before your attorneys found it."

Her eyes ballooned, and pure pissed-off adrenaline shot into her bloodstream. "For a PhD, that's pretty stupid."

"You know, smart people fall victim to Ponzi schemes all the time—case in point, your grandpa. In fact, *some* people confuse good fortune for intelligence, like your buddy Houdini, and bad luck for a lack of it."

"I've never doubted your intelligence. Yet we still have empty accounts."

"This is temporary." He fidgeted with his hands, rubbing them, fisting them; and then he swiveled toward her. "I'll get it all back."

"How?"

"My lawyers are working on it. There's a bunch of investors who've filed suit. I'm one of them. They say it looks promising."

"Promising." She hated that word. "Promising, as in, *I got laid off, but we'll be fine*? Promising, as in, *I love you*? Promising, as in, *'til death do us part*?"

"You're the one who filed for divorce."

"What choice did I have? How long can two people be separated? You weren't even trying, Will. And what you said to me—that last thing you said."

He squeezed his eyes shut as if he were squeezing the memory into oblivion—and her with it. *I'm not in love with you anymore.* The pain of that day was right there, standing between them like a hulking grizzly, bellowing soundlessly every time she had to deal with him.

"Sophie, sometimes people say things they don't mean."

"They don't say *that* unless they mean it. You made me feel like a fool."

His features hardened, and he stood and paced in a tight circle, naked but for those wrinkly boxers. He planted one hand on his hips and shook the other. "Why are we going all the way back there again? Talk about a fool. You've got me going on these ridiculous dates, as if I have the presence of mind to even think about other women, when the one I *have*—"

"*Had.*"

"Had! Is making a mockery of me. As if my life could get any more absurd."

"What, you're accusing *me* of making a mess of your life? *That* is absurd."

She glared at the foreclosure notice on the bed—the harbinger of doom delivered courtesy of the US Mail. Her mind lurched backward and forward, sifting for clues of a financial apocalypse she could so easily have missed, until it all ignited in a fiery red ball of "what the fuck" that left her lightheaded and achy.

The magnitude of his losses—*their* losses...

Accounts she'd entrusted to him for twenty-two years. *Emptied.*

Annabelle and Keely's college funds. *Gone.*

The money for their future. *History.*

Tears threatened to burst, and she knew it was a matter of time before she blubbered all over herself.

He moved toward her and laid his hands on her shoulders—something he'd not done in so very long. "Sophie—"

But she didn't want to be soothed; it would only make her cry. She shied away, catching a glimmer of hurt in his eyes that surprised her. A hurt that reached deep inside her to a place she'd boxed up long ago and marked *Fragile, Do Not Open.* That place from where, in the old days, when life got him down, she'd be the first to pull the love strings and soothe *him.*

He entreated with outstretched arms, and she turned away, steeling herself.

"I fucked up," she heard him say to her back. "But it went bad before I could prevent it. Like a tsunami, you don't have time to get out of the way."

Sophie closed her eyes and pinched the bridge of her nose. She sensed him hovering, felt his hands cup her shoulders and his breaths caress the back of her neck. This time, she didn't stop him. She swayed unsteadily, blinking back tears that would not be contained. Rain through a leaky ceiling. If she didn't get it together, she'd soon need a bucket. He was so close; so close he was almost holding her.

"And you are... so, so mad at me," he whispered. "So mad, I think you're going to blow your top. Like Krakatoa."

She heard the playfulness in his tone, trying to soothe her tears and tugging on ancient history where his attention was the gift that kept on giving, the fulfillment of their promise to love, honor, and cherish. And still mourning for those lost, precious days, she allowed him to cross the Great Divide that was her new promise to loathe, harangue, and chap his ass. But he'd barely set foot in his old stomping grounds when she remembered, *That's his modus operandi.*

She spun to face him. "Don't you make light of this, Will Camden."

He backed away, his gaze downcast, one palm shielding his face. He never could take seeing her cry. She braced for some semi-funny, kneejerk-discount of a comeback. And when his fingers kneaded the lines of his forehead, she imagined him assuaging his conscience into submission. But then the fault lines of his face shifted and his restrained outer mantle showed signs of crumbling. And she realized Will Camden was trying to keep it together.

"I'm not making light," he said in a voice struggling for less sharp peaks, more flatline. "It's... It's bad. I admit that. And I assure you, as much as you hate me right now... I hate myself far, far more."

A hard mass lodged in her throat, and she hugged herself. The threat of foreclosure was tough enough, but watching him suffer? Even if he deserved to suffer, even if she wanted to ignite a forest fire of suffering upon him, the fight that fueled her barbed tongue fizzled right out of her. Besides, what could either of them do right now to change things? Nothing.

Well, maybe one thing.

"You made a bet with Jake and Tess," she said coolly. "You're going to see it through. You're getting Ursula, and you're selling her because

I'm not letting you sell this house."

She knew her delivery pushed one of his oh-no-you-did-not buttons. Probably the blazing orange don't-back-me-into-a-corner button. But she couldn't unpush it.

He massaged his neck, eyed her sideways. "So, Tess told you?"

"Of course she told me. She's my best friend. And you cannot sell this house out from under me and the kids. I won't let you."

He nodded, stared at the carpet, then nodded some more. "I promise, Sophie, I'll fix this thing if it's the last thing I do." He held one hand over his heart. "I swear it."

She wanted to believe. Shit happened to good people, but the whole situation was exhausting—*he* was exhausting. Her faith in him had already been tested, and he had failed.

Will watched her storm off, then pause in the doorway. She looked over her shoulder, her eyes glistening as they met his—a punch to the gut if ever there was one. He waited expectantly as she turned a little more, hoping the Sophie who used to worship him would appear behind that furious façade and say *I get it, I forgive you,* and *I know you didn't mean to hurt us.* He so needed to see *that* Sophie, the one she buried.

The one *he* buried when he left her.

Come on, baby. I'm still here.

The space between her brows furrowed and unfurrowed, and her nostrils twitched with the effort of maintaining that precious self-control that boasted, "I got this," even when she didn't. She sniffed and smeared the tears across her cheeks, and still she stared at him, as if she wanted to say something but was too close to breaking down.

Come on, baby.

Finally, she floated one eyebrow and scowled. "Your hair looks lame."

An hour after Sophie had gone off to an appointment, Will stepped out of a hot shower, recovered from their argument only insofar as he felt relieved not to keep such a weighty secret from her. She was never going to forgive him, and he supposed he ought to get used to it.

He wiped the steamy fog from the mirror and stared at his reflection, at the number those Marshall twins had done on his salt-and-pepper. He ran a hand through the short black crop and laughed. Despite his bloodshot eyes and accompanying bags, they'd made him look ten years younger. That was something.

He shrugged off the Did-I-have-sex-or-didn't-I? conundrum as just one more thing that may or may not have happened during his wild night with a two-fer.

What he did remember was leaving Edwina's with the morning dusk and, once his head hit Annabelle's pillow, sleeping three fitful hours until Sophie shocked him awake with her unfortunate discovery. He figured he wouldn't be able to keep that secret for long, but he'd planned to bring it up when the time was right, not get blindsided by the postman. That she'd caught him off-guard and he'd been so unprepared as to make an ass of himself had the equal benefit of making him feel emasculated for not having the huevos to *just tell her already*—not that he blamed her for so deftly prying it out of him. She had a future with the CIA.

His head throbbing, he downed four ibuprofen and braved the octogenarians.

"I don't know what's going on," Grampy said, when Will entered the kitchen, "but that granddaughter of mine is madder than a hornet. Anything I can help with?"

"Sophie and I will work it out, Gramps," he said, not unkindly. "Nothing for you and Gram to worry about."

Grampy patted Will's back. "All right, son. If you say so."

Confrontation, confession, and further emasculation forestalled, Will hydrated with a quart of water and two banana chasers before leaving the house. He was certain the rest of his day had to get better, until he remembered that that just wasn't his kind of luck these days.

Chapter 23

By ten o'clock, Sophie and Ruta headed downtown, poring over listing information in a new Cadillac rental. Jimmy drove while Sophie navigated from the backseat. Keeping her mind off her own financial straits was a challenge while Ruta dished about a Mediterranean villa that she and former international model pals stayed in when she was slinking down catwalks. All Sophie could think was how to get this woman to buy a mansion fast, escalate the escrow, and deliver money to her meager bank account. That, and guilt for thinking it. Ruta had become her friend, even if the penultimate persnickety one.

The property tour was as brisk as Ruta was fickle. She'd breezed through four hillside properties in the best neighborhoods with Lake Austin views, going on about how wonderful the downtown homes were but then deeming them unsuitable for no particular reason other than the shrugged "Eez no good." Sophie ticked off items on Ruta's must-have list, but apparently something intangible was missing that Ruta could not define.

By the time they pulled up to the fifth property, Sophie began to wonder if Ruta was serious about buying. Jimmy parked the Caddy under a wide portico and opened the doors for his passengers. Ruta disembarked from the back seat and stood tall, glancing around as if the magnificence of this stone edifice with Grecian columns on these well-groomed grounds held but a passing interest. She beat Sophie to the front porch before Jimmy could secure the car doors.

"Eez beautiful," she said, in a blasé tone. "I like to get inside where it's cool."

The 10,000-square-foot, six-bedroom manor boasted waterfront views and the downtown skyline. Jimmy stood on the patio, gazing longingly into the crystal clear pool, while Sophie rattled off details about high-end, energy-efficient appliances, upgraded insulation, and the house-wide intercom system—until Ruta yawned.

"Sorry, dear. You know your stuff. I like the house, but honestly, I like to hear about last night. You and Meetch."

What was to tell? Sophie had jawed on the Johnson? Chipped some wood? Put a kink in the Slink? "We went for a drive and then he dropped me off at my place."

Ruta tilted her head. "Tell me truth, you two haven't—"

"Had sex?" Sophie felt uneasy just saying that out loud. Ruta seemed to feel more and more like she could talk to Sophie about anything and everything. "Not exactly."

"You might know, we once had fling. Eet didn't last. But I know how the man works. You don't mind me to say, he likes getting right to the beezness, so he must tink you are special. Makes it even more strange, I tink, you haven't slept together."

"He's supposed to go bowling with me and my girls tonight."

Ruta laughed heartily. "Bowlingk? You are serious?"

"What's wrong with bowling?"

"Nothing, dear. Eet's just, the Meetch I know eez not family man."

"Well, look at Warren Beatty, perpetual Hollywood slut, suddenly daddy of the decade to four kids. If Mr. You're So Vain can do it, anybody can. But, really, it's too early in our relationship—"

"I hope you're right. Speaking of men, you will arrange me to meet Will?"

Sophie tried not to sigh out loud. She'd been avoiding all thoughts of setting Will up with the Russian Princess. For one thing, a woman just didn't fix up her ex-husband with a friend. If Ruta and Will had sex, Ruta would undoubtedly broadcast it, and that would be bizarre. Besides, if any romantic relationship developed and went south, it could affect Sophie's business. See? Reasons enough right there. Ruta was not a good candidate. It wasn't personal; it was business.

"I'm not talking to Will right now," Sophie said.

Ruta's expression wilted. "We are friends, no? Friends do each other favors."

"What kind of favors are we talking about?"

Ruta tick-tocked her head. "I help you get what you want, you help me get what I want."

"What is it you think I want?"

"Your freedom, darlingk, and beeg commission." She raised her arms and let her eyes roam the mansion. "I buy house, you get beeg commission and financial freedom."

"What you're saying is that you are willing to *buy* a date with my husband?"

"Hmm, I see what you mean. Sounds so negative. Tink of eet as fair trade."

"For this house?"

Ruta looked around and gave her trademark shrug. "Not thees one. Eez no good."

Sophie stared blank-faced, concealing the anger that roiled in the pit of her stomach. Will wasn't an object. He was a man with real feelings—*her* man, once upon a time. She couldn't just pawn him off to the highest bidder, though after seeing him last night with the twins, that idea had teeth. Thankfully, not as much teeth as she'd shown Mr. Slinky.

No, she had morals. She had integrity. She had conspired with her best friends to get him to go on five blind dates, knowing that his own integrity would force him to keep his word and pay in full. It was official. Her scruples were pooples.

"Meetch like to see me here," Ruta said. "Downtown. Close to heem. I do like thees leetle house. Eez close to nightlife, and oh my lord, darlingk, the views. Stunning. But tell you the truth, eet doesn't excite me enough to buy. And I don't need thees much room myself, but I like seester to come, bring the kids. We can be family again."

"You don't want the party life, do you?" Sophie said, realizing as the words came out that whenever they'd talked about lake properties and lake parties or being close to downtown where the nightlife was most brisk, Ruta lost her party-girl glow.

"I'm getting older now." She noticed Jimmy turn toward her. "Older than last year."

"You want something quieter, don't you?" Sophie said. "Something beautiful, but less ostentatious. Something stylish but not stuffy."

The tightened lines in Ruta's forehead softened. Aging was an unpleasant issue for the Russian Princess, Sophie figured, considering her celebrated reputation as an international jetsetter. Must be doubly hard to get off such a public rollercoaster before the ride ended. It was so obvious now.

"You want less opulence and more charm. You want privacy for a family life where being the life of the party is the last thing you have to worry about."

Ruta bowed her head sheepishly. "You know these places?"

"Yes, ma'am. I do."

Ruta beamed and leaned close. "Don't tell Meetch. He tinks I am still thirty—when I go sunup to sundown burning the candle at my ass-end. But I get enough fast pace from the Beeg Apple. I like slower pace now. You understand?"

"I do, and I can find exactly what you're looking for. You might do well on a property in the Hill Country. Maybe the outskirts of Lake Travis. But we'll keep that between us for now."

"I knew I like you. I have seen enough. Jimmy, you have seen enough?"

Jimmy's husky frame never budged, but he swiveled his head and nodded with the bare glimmer of a smile.

"Good," Ruta said. "We are done here. I like to go to Burger King."

"Oka-ay," Sophie said, "do you not want to look anymore today?"

"Actually, I like to tink about tings over cheeseburger, then I decide."

"Is this about the favors?"

"We will see how tings turn out, no?"

"You would seriously buy a property just for a date with my husband?"

Ruta grinned slyly and reminded her, "Ex-husband, darlingk."

Shortly after one o'clock, Sophie pulled into her office garage. Her cell rang as she pulled into her parking space.

"Sophie," Jake said, from the other end of the line. "I just spoke to Tess."

"Yes?"

"Well, I hope you're okay with this. But we both agree."

"Okay. Agree on what?"

"The twins."

"What?" But she knew. Will had pleaded his case.

"We think they should count as two dates, not one."

Sophie's eyes rolled as she shut them and shook her head. Will's voice cackled in her head: "Tonight I have paid back my debt of a third date, and also a fourth date with Miss Jessica 'Hottie' Marshall. Two dates for the price of one."

Intolerable.

Part of her was all about counting them as two because then she'd have fewer dates left to fix him up with and he'd be that much closer to winning that priceless guitar. But the other part didn't want to let him have his way. There was still more Sophie's Kiss-off to do, and his date with twins made her inexplicably furious. In the end, though, she couldn't escape the overriding reason she needed to agree: Will winning Ursula meant money in their accounts to stave off a foreclosure.

"You still there?" Jake said. "Not like I want to lose Ursula to her original owner, but I think it's only fair. And, well, Tess agrees."

"Hey, it's fine. Really. Thanks for letting me know."

Sophie took the elevator to her office and felt the rush of cool air as she stepped into the Houdini Real Estate lobby. Gertie was accepting a delivery from Luigi's Deli at the front desk, and she stopped to hand Sophie a message.

Henry Roberts, the man she'd stood up while stuck out at Lake Travis attempting to wakeboard, had called looking for her. After only forty-seven phone calls, he'd returned one.

In her office, Sophie called Mr. Roberts and discussed his trip to Austin the following week where he would take that second look at the Pecos house. *Yes!*

She couldn't wait to share the good news with Mitch. She searched the offices until she found him in the conference room, concluding a meeting. She was so excited, she paced back and forth until his clients left and Mitch limped toward the lobby.

"Hey," Sophie said, following behind. "How are you doing?"

He didn't slow his gimpy pace. "Fine. You?"

"I thought maybe you might have gone to the doctor or—"

He waved her off. "No need. I'm fine."

Sophie caught up to him at Gertie's desk. "Did something happen to your leg?"

He turned without making eye contact. "Sorry. I'm way behind today."

"No sweat. I just worried about you, and we have a bowling date tonight and—"

He shook his head, flipping through Gertie's stack of manila folders. "I can't make it. Something's come up."

Or down. Namely, her chance for romance. Ruta's voice slid between her ears: *Meetch eez not family man.*

Gertie stood behind her desk and fished through stuffed Luigi's Deli bags. "Mr. Houdini, your lunch has arrived. We ordered in, Sophie, but there's plenty to go around." She pulled out a paper-wrapped item and read the writing scrawled across it. "Tube steak sandwich. How about that, Mr. Houdini?"

Sophie squelched a giggle and wondered if his mind had gone where hers had.

"No, thanks," he said tightly. "I'm not really hungry."

"No? How about Italian beef sausage? I can slice it in half; it's way too big for one person."

Mitch shook his head and grumbled something indecipherable.

"Sophie?" Gertie said, holding it up for inspection. "Sausage?"

"Thanks, but I already ate with Ruta. Burger King."

"Oh, did you have a Whopper? They're the best. Hey, Mr. Houdini, if you're not too hungry, how about a pickle?" She held up an uncut gherkin the size of a hothouse cucumber. "Wow, check it out. Seriously, who could get their mouth around this?"

"No, Gertie! Sophie, I'm sorry. I'm late for an appointment. I'll call you later."

Sophie and Gertie watched him hobble off, and it occurred to Sophie that he was being a big baby. After all, how could a little nip on his penis affect the way a man walked?

Of course, it did give credence to the Third Leg Theory.

Will figured he'd sweat the remaining alcohol out of his system before hitting the office. Fortunately, there wasn't another soul in his new gym except for the front desk attendant, so heavy into her chick lit she didn't even look up when he ran his membership card through the autoreader.

He warmed up on a mat in the yoga room, trying to get himself motivated. All the physical contortions made his nuggets ache. Three nut knockouts in as many weeks had to be some kind of record. He wondered if there was some way to fortify them against blunt force trauma without reverting to an athletic cup. This spawned a veritable inferno of brain activity wherein he devised a pair of lightweight underwear equipped with a full frontal airbag. On sudden impact, the bag would deploy. Benefits? One: protection, obviously. Two: medical attention; a fast-acting numbing agent would be dispatched to the gonads and shaft. Three: revenge; the offending knee, fist, or other object would be blasted with the sound of a foghorn and red paint that could not be removed even by turpentine. *Now that's an invention.*

He looked in the wall-to-wall mirrors at the reflection of the weight machines behind him and a lean woman who walked toward the lat pull-down apparatus. She was dressed in tight-fitting girlie workout clothes with her dark hair pulled back in a ponytail. He stopped what he was doing to watch her move the pin to the desired weight, grab the bar with both hands, and pull it down to chest level as she sat on the stool. Up and down, twelve reps.

Of all the gyms in all the towns in all the world, she walks into mine.

The threat of repeating their earlier argument loomed, but he vowed to avoid it at all costs. He slid into the pec-deck, bent over to reset the pin between the weights, and felt Sophie's eyes poking him in the back.

"Oh... my... god. This is *my* gym."

Will sat back in the seat and brought his elbows to shoulder height, forearms pressing into the pads. He squeezed his elbows together, causing his pecs to contract.

"For your information, this is my gym too." The weight felt heavier than usual, but he held his breath and grunted through another rep. "I pay to be here."

"It was my gym first." She pulled down her lat bar, resuming the reps.

He squeezed out another rep, but his system was compromised, his muscles sluggish. He couldn't hold the pads any longer and let his arms fly back with the natural swing of the overhead cams. The weights slammed with a loud clank that assaulted his ears and shook the walls.

"I'm not leaving," he said. "So you can get used to it, or *you* can leave."

She pulled the bar to her chest again and eased it up. "Can you *not* talk to me?" She gaped at his hair, driving home the point that she detested his new look.

He glared back and pretended to zip his lips. Then he relocated to the chest press behind Sophie, where he couldn't see her face. She moved to the shoulder press. For every rep she did on her apparatus, Will matched it on his. But he couldn't stop himself from fixating on her dewy skin, which enhanced her—Dare he think it?—raw sex appeal. The universe had it out for him.

She pressed three sets, wiped the equipment with a towel, and got on the elliptical machine. What did she think, that she was tougher than him? Ha. He had lived through three—no, *four*—debacles. Was she aware of the official count?

"Hey, Sophie." He held up four fingers with one hand and pointed to himself with the other, mouthing the word, *Four.* Then he counted off each finger, "Casey, Spike, Edwina, Jessica. Any way you look at it, that's four. So says Jake and Tess."

Sophie's eyes arced toward the ceiling, and for a moment they seemed stuck there, each lethargic blink like the Morse code of her disgust with him.

"Whatever," she said, stepping up her pace on the elliptical, relegating him to the land of the inconsequential, as if she had real work to do and couldn't be bothered.

That seemed like a challenge. No way could she outdo him. "I *spit* on your pissant effort," Will muttered, climbing onto the other elliptical.

When he cycled forward, Sophie cycled backward. When she cycled backward, Will cycled forward. After fifteen minutes of hitting it hard, they both sweated buckets but neither caved under pressure nor venomous glare.

Thirty minutes later, Will's rubbery legs stepped off the elliptical machine and he mounted one of six stationary bicycles positioned in a semi-circle. Meanwhile, Sophie's face filled up like a paint jar of burgundy blush. He figured, any minute, she would give up and head to the locker room. But she climbed on the bike cattycorner to his.

Their wheels spun faster as they pedaled in furious opposition. He was Lance Armstrong at the Tour de France and she was the Wicked Witch of the West. In his head, he heard her personal theme music: *Dum da-dum da-da dum. Dum da-dum da-da dum.*

After another grueling half hour, Will gasped like a coronary patient. His legs failed and he let the wheels spin to a natural stop, his feet limp in the pedals, muscles on fire.

Sophie stopped too, got off the bike, and pulled her cell phone out of her back pocket. She looked at the screen for a few seconds, squealed an exuberant "Yes!" and threw her hands up in the victory pose. In the next moment, she took two steps and collapsed to her knees.

His gut instinct was to leap to her aid, but his legs had turned to gummy snakes. His concern diminished when she clambered to her feet, shot him a vehement sneer, and limped into the women's locker room.

Ah-ha. She had overestimated her physical endurance against a god among mortal men. He mirrored her V for victory pose, eased off the bike, and crawled into the men's locker room.

After his shower, Will returned to his office and checked his voicemail. He had four new messages, so he grabbed a legal pad and started writing. One message was from Keely, one from Annabelle, one from his former boss at Waterloo, and one from women he never expected to hear from ever again.

"Sorry about my sister," Edwina said. "She means well. I had a great time with you. Are you loving being a brunette? Let's get together, okay? Just you and me. Jessica's not your type anyway. Oh, and Will? I'm working on a surprise for you. I can't wait for you to see it."

He had a surprise for her too. *Delete.*

Exhausted from her workout but sparkling clean after a long, hot shower, Sophie climbed into the back seat of Ruta's Caddy and gave Jimmy directions to a property out by Lake Travis. She had stayed on the phone for hours until she found something that might interest Ruta.

And she had made a decision about Will.

Once through the wide-swinging wrought iron gates, the Caddy meandered up a stone-paved tree-lined hillside, presenting magnificent lake views behind them and a driveway that circled an enormous teeming fountain ahead of them. A water feature had been on Ruta's list of must-haves, and she seemed delighted by this one—a massive statue of a naked Roman embracing an equally naked goddess, whose modest breasts heaved toward the sky with the help of her man's hand at her back. They both leaned against a large boulder while water fell over their heads, around their shoulders, and between their various gender parts before splashing into a ten-foot diameter pool. Jimmy was as spellbound as Ruta.

But Ruta beat Sophie to the front double entry doors and, once inside, took her time, lingering on the stunning circular staircase in the entry, the Juliet balconies, media room, library, massive wet bar, and an infinity-edged pool and cabana. She liked the dumbwaiter best, recalling her childhood in a European castle where she and her "*leetle seester*" hid from the nanny and used it like an elevator to sneak out after dark.

"What do you think?" Sophie asked, hopefully. "This one worth a date with my husband?"

Chapter 24

Will stood inside his old shed at the far end of the backyard, wondering if Sophie was happy that he'd steered clear of her for the last five days—not an easy feat under the same roof—but nothing he did made her happy.

He didn't even show his disappointment when she took the kids bowling and didn't invite him, though Keely and Annabelle had begged her to. Not that he expected to be included. It was just that when they left the house, he'd felt completely empty inside.

Just one more thing to suck up.

At her not-so-subtle requests, this afternoon he was clearing out his things from the shed, though her one caveat required it be done while she was not home. He had taken a certain satisfaction in making her wait, in reinforcing his belligerent statement that he'd get to it when he got to it. But even he wanted to get it over and done with now.

He flipped the light switch and found the bulb burned out, as Grampy had warned. Two narrow transoms, high in the cinderblock walls, leaked in late afternoon sun, but it was still pretty dark inside—not dark enough, though, to disguise that he was looking at a bunch of junk. With his escrow set to close next week, Tess was bugging him to preview houses. He needed room for the kids and enough space to store whatever he wanted to bring along, but did he want to take any of this?

Rakes, hoes, an edger, and a leaf blower hung from clamps screwed into the blocks, and two bags of potting soil were heaped onto a grimy fourteen-foot plywood counter that stretched from the east wall to the west. The same counter he'd flipped and flopped on the first night he'd moved back. Precariously stacked Halloween and Christmas boxes perched atop an ancient lawnmower still covered with dead grass from years past. Sophie's old ten-speed leaned against one wall, steadied by an oversized ice chest stuffed with life vests. Camping equipment had been shoved under the counter near a tangle of fishing poles and tackle boxes, an anchor, propane lanterns, and a Coleman stove.

His eyes caught on photos of Sophie tacked to an old bulletin board. String bikinis suited her well. She had liked dragging him on his slalom ski around the lake, and she enjoyed kicking back in a lawn chair and poking sticks skinned of leaves and twigs into a crackling campfire, their ends impaling a blue-blazed and charred marshmallow. He remembered her savoring each morsel like an exotic delicacy and feeding him every other one off her stick. Their kisses were gooey afterward, but it didn't stop them.

Further buried were the vestiges of dreams that once dominated his every waking thought: an old practice guitar, amps, microphones, headphones, crinkled sheet music, picks, and capos. Stuck between the guitar's frets and strings was a dusty Kodak envelope. Inside were shots of his band and his main groupie smiling her tremendous pride as he shredded and crooned his way through sets. He wondered if, when he let his dream of music die, he let his biggest fan die too, neglected like this shed and everything in it. How did one repair that kind of betrayal?

He knew he would toss everything in here. That was the way he did things. Ironic, considering how many times he'd accused Sophie of giving up on things too fast, moving toward something greener on the other side.

Grampy appeared in the doorway. He had started out on Will's heels, but his arduous gait slowed him considerably. Sometimes the old man used a cane, but not today.

"Biggest shed I ever saw," he said, his voice doddering. His dentures didn't fit as well as they used to, the uppers and lowers clicking and shifting across shriveling gums as he spoke. "Place has a lot of potential."

"Back when we first built it, it was going to be a music studio. Remember?"

Grampy pointed to his hearing aid, pulled the command box out of his shirt pocket, and adjusted the controls. "Sorry, too much background noise with this contraption. I don't use it unless I have to." He shuffled across the concrete. "I'd make this a secret hideaway, if it was mine. A place where I could sit and read. 'Course, large print for these old eyes."

Will patted Grampy on his hunched shoulder. "Or you could get the audio versions."

"Nah, even with the hearing aid, I can't keep up. When Eunice talks, she gets to going so fast, it's like trying to read the stock market ticker. After awhile, I just nod my head." He laughed and hacked up something from deep in his lungs.

Will squelched a gag. "Is that why your marriage has lasted so long?"

"I follow orders, son. She points left, I go left. She shakes her head, I go to my room. She says kiss her ass, I pucker up." He cleared his throat and patted the hearing aid box in his pocket. "That, or I turn down the volume. Accidentally, of course."

Over the years, Will had watched the fire in the old man cruelly tamped out with the ticking clock. From their conversations, he knew Grampy was tormented by his mortality. But at least he had his wife. Grammy would be there for him until he exhaled his last breath.

Will looked toward the house as a gust of wind kicked up dirt and leaves. He worried Sophie might come home before he escaped upstairs to his room, yet half expected to see her there, content to repot her plants, spray off the deck with the hose, or dance with their daughters like he'd seen her do so many times. Back then, he'd complained that she should be doing more important things. He had no idea now what could be more important. It was the little things he would miss now, more than anything.

Maybe he didn't have the stamina for cleaning the shed after all. "Think I'll save this project for another day, Gramps."

"Good idea, son. Bad thunderstorm's headed our way."

Will winked at him. "That's why I want to get upstairs, before she arrives."

The thin tendrils of Grampy's comb-over blew straight up in the gathering breezes and revealed his shiny, freckled pate. "She's working late tonight, so you can relax and have some of Eunice's raviolis."

"I'd like that." He patted the elder man's shoulder and walked gingerly beside him toward the house. "You understand, Grampy? It's hard between Sophie and me right now."

Grampy's sallow eyes teared up. "Sorry. Don't know why I'm so emotional about it."

"I know just how you feel. How about we go fishing next week?"

"You sure? I don't want to be a burden, son."

Will looked at the old man pointedly. "You listen to me. You are never a burden."

A slow smile filled Grampy's droopy-skinned face. "Count me in then. One thing though, can we hit Mickey D's? Gives me gas, but Eunice won't be around to complain."

"Hey, if they can't catch us, they can't stop us, right?"

Despite her age and arthritis, Grammy was a whirlwind in the kitchen, pure energy and clarity of purpose. Will tried to help but felt more like he was in the way. Still, she always found some small thing for him to do, like rounding up a potholder or a spice or fetching bowls from a shelf high in the cupboards.

"I don't mind telling you," she said, sprinkling Parmesan on garlic bread. "Sophie is stubborn as a mule when she makes up her mind about something."

"That's true," Grampy said, watching his wife work.

Eunice shrugged. "It's only because you set the standard so high in the beginning."

Will preferred ravioli to Grammy's insights, but he practiced patience. "Are you saying I spoiled Sophie?"

"I'm saying you stopped spoiling her." She paused and looked him in the eye. "Did you do that on purpose?"

Grampy fired off a series of staccato farts. *Bbbbb-wwpp, bbbb-wwpp,* like the howitzers he manned in WWII. All eyes turned, noses crinkled.

"Sorry," he said. "I got a hairpin trigger these days."

Grammy's upper lip curled. "I'm just glad he's shooting blanks."

Palms up, Grampy shrugged. "Some blanks, some loaded. It's always a surprise." He finished with a squeaker that hung in the air.

Grammy called to the girls then. "Annabelle, Keely! Supper's ready."

Will was never so happy for a few good farts. He was sure Grammy had been on a mission to needle him about his divorce before Grampy's intestinal crop-dusting sidetracked her. Now her liver-spotted hands shook as she scooped ravioli onto her husband's plate.

She slapped Will's hands when he tried to help her load the girls' plates. "Sit down. I've got your plate right here. Oh, Hal, you're not going to dribble your whole meal, are you?"

"I need to go lock up the shed," Grampy said, setting down his fork. "I promised Sophie."

Will patted his arm. "I'll take care of it after dinner, Gramps. You relax and eat."

Reluctantly, Grampy complied and everyone dug in.

Keely finished chewing a ravioli. "Are you and Mommy ever going to make up?"

The room was quiet enough to hear Grampy poof an S.B.D. Will could think of nothing more difficult than explaining broken relationships to a nine-year-old. "Well, Daddy's trying to make her happy. I'm doing what she wants, so she ought to be happy any minute now."

Annabelle said, "Because of Hoodoody?"

Will took joy from the mangling of Houdini's name. "Do you like Mr. Hoodoody?"

Annabelle and Keely looked at each other and shook their heads.

"I don't blame you. Who has a name like Hoodoody?"

Annabelle giggled and covered her mouth.

Keely showed no trace of amusement. "If you don't like him, I won't like him either."

While that made him ecstatic, he held his tongue. "I think you should decide on your own if you like the man, sweetie. But, there's no law that says you have to."

Keely thought about that. "Maybe when he learns my name."

Despite her grumbling, Will could tell Grammy was worn out so he insisted on handling the cleanup. He and the kids piled dishes into the dishwasher and reserved a covered plate for Sophie. With the sun down, Will directed the girls upstairs for their baths. He helped Annabelle get situated in the tub and washed her hair. Since she'd be a fifth grader in the fall, Keely preferred the privacy of a solo shower.

By nine o'clock, Grampy had gone to bed. Grammy settled on the family room sofa with a basket of colored yarns and the beginnings of an afghan. When Will's eyes met hers, she called him over with a "Wha's up, foo?"

Between Grammy's Ebonics and the fact Sophie was bound to return before he could escape to Annabelle's room, Will felt a sense of urgency. He kissed Grammy's forehead.

"Homegirl, I'm off to bed."

"Fo' shiggidy, my weeble. That's a good one, isn't it?"

"I don't even know what it means."

She wrapped yarn around shiny maroon knitting needles and made complicated loopty-loops with arthritic fingers while looking over her glasses. "Means *for sure, my friend.* Just practicing. I have a tutoring session on Monday with some sophomores in detention." She patted the spot beside her. "Sit down, dear. I was wondering what you thought of Sophie's new man."

"Hoodoody?" He couldn't hide the glee in bastardizing the guy's name. "You know, I don't have anything to say on that subject."

"That's crappappella, William. If you have an opinion on Sophie's new lover, you should be able to say it."

Bam! Grammy sinks one. *Sophie's new lover.* Didn't help that an eighty-five-year-old was hitting him in the face with it. "Probably better if I don't. What does Grampy think?"

"Grampy hasn't met him. He will Sunday at the barbecue." She paused then. "Oh, you didn't know about that? Sophie's having a get-together. I'm surprised she didn't mention it." Grammy prodded him with her knitting needle. "So this Houdini fella..."

"I don't trust him."

Grammy's eyes were piercing, her lips protruding stiffly amid the clicking sound of knitting needles. "Since getting this new job, she's stepped far out of her comfort zone, hasn't she? Gained some confidence and independence that she didn't have while she was with you."

Will stared at her, feeling like he was in the boxing ring with Sugar Ray Grammy.

She patted his thigh. "Time to speak frankly, dear. Mind if I get all up in yo' bizznezz?"

Sophie stared at the earnest money check, her hands fluttering with excitement. Even though the signed contract lay on the desk in front of her, she couldn't escape the lingering fear that she still had time to screw things up. Mr. and Mrs. Roberts had come back to town specifically to see the Pecos house and, after the walk-through, made a fair offer. Sophie had practically done a Herkie when the owners accepted.

Tess was with the Robertses in the small conference room across the hallway, slathering her Dallas charm all over them before they caught their plane back to Santa Barbara. She had coached Sophie on how to get the Robertses back on track, and now she was spit-shining her diplomatic efforts to a hard, gleaming finish that couldn't be cracked. Sophie had excused herself to make copies and wipe the cheesy grin off her face.

She stood in her office now, hunting for an envelope for the contract copies and reveling in her accomplishment. She had money. Or she would, when the deal closed in a few weeks, give or take. With the inspection already done and Henry Roberts being a cash buyer with the means to pull strings, the escrow would go faster than usual.

She located the envelope, along with her professional demeanor, and returned to the conference room with the copies. It felt good to send Mr. and Mrs. Roberts back to California, all smiles about consummating a great deal for their daughter and their new son-in-law. Despite the unfortunate missed appointment after the lake fiasco, Sophie had earned her commission. Very soon, she would be able to make a house payment or two and get her mortgage back on track.

Take that, Will Camden.

Then there was Ruta. The Russian Princess was returning today after spending a few days in Belize, considering whether she wanted to make an offer on the Lake Travis property. The waiting was a killer for Sophie—exhausting on every level while her bills remained unpaid and her mortgage hung in the balance. But today was a biggie. Today, she deserved to celebrate, except that it was already nine o'clock.

Sophie and Tess gathered their things and waited in the lobby. The elevator chimed, the doors opened, and Sophie came face to face with Allison Summers and Mitch Houdini.

Mitch had kept his distance since their night in the limo, so Sophie reluctantly took the hint, gave him some space, and adopted some nonchalance about the whole thing. However, the effort only fueled her feeling like a spurned teenager. Not having his attention, and not even talking about it, hurt her heart. Not to mention, it left a gigantic question mark in her head. Didn't adults talk about such things as penis biting?

Mitch and Allison got off the elevator, and Mitch caught Sophie by the arm as she passed. "Hey there," he said. "I was hoping to see you. You on your way home?"

"Yes," she said, backing onto the elevator. "But guess what."

The next thing she knew, while probing for more details about the Roberts deal, Mitch had prodded her out of the elevator. Bubbling over about the deal made it easy to disguise the jitters rippling through her just by being near him. She could hardly breathe while he held her arm, keeping her close—*so close.*

The elevator alarm clanged as Tess held the doors open. "You coming, Sophie?"

Sophie squeezed her eyes for some mental clarity. She needed to get home to relieve Grammy—and Will, if his sorry ass was still hanging around. He had played Daddy Dearest for two nights in a row, and while she was grateful, she still hadn't gotten used to him being around so much. Mitch looked longingly into her eyes, like he used to. And that was all it took.

"No," she said, flashing Tess a giddy smile. "You go ahead."

Tess returned a "whatever" smirk and disappeared behind the elevator doors.

Allison offered Sophie her congratulations but seemed otherwise bored by the news. "Are we still going to dinner, Mitch? I'm starving."

"Of course," Mitch replied. "Sophie, I'm so happy for you. I knew you had this one. You were made for real estate."

Allison continued to wait, tapping her toe and staring a hole through Sophie.

"Come to dinner with us," Mitch said. "We're going to The Rooftop for a few drinks and appetizers, and then we can all meet up as planned with Ruta."

"The Rooftop?" Sophie backed up, still unrecovered from the tree-house incident.

"Easy there," Mitch said. "The Rooftop, the bar upstairs? We're not jumping off, we're just gathering and, you know, hobnobbing. It'll be fun."

"Yeah," Allison said with a weak effort at cheeriness. "Hobnobbing. In a bar. With a floor and a retaining wall and everything."

Mitch's head pivoted to his protégé. "Can you give us a few?"

Allison stared, then disappeared down the hallway.

"Swear to god, she's like a kid sometimes."

"Juvenile," Sophie said, "delinquent."

Mitch gave a relenting sigh. "They don't come with more sales savvy than Allison. She could get your Grammy to buy a kilo of pot from a street gang—she's that good."

"That actually wouldn't be that hard. If Grammy thought it would help the kids, she'd be all up in some dealer's business, spearheading the deal herself."

"Listen, I don't know why you and Allison don't get along, but I wish you would. You're the only one I know who doesn't think Allison is the shit."

"Oh, but I do," Sophie said, a smile tugging at her mouth. "Think she's a shit."

Mitch pulled her to his chest and nuzzled her ear. "You know what I mean. I'll talk to her. Meantime, come to dinner with me. I miss you."

"Miss me? You've hardly spoken to me since—since the, uh..."

"Since the incident. I know." He looked sheepish but undeterred. "I was embarrassed. I'm sorry. Let me make it up to you. We can pick up where we left off, right?"

She looked into his eyes, remembering the Chomp Heard Around the World. "Well, maybe not exactly where we left off."

Chapter 25

Sophie drove her Acura into the cul-de-sac, the day's events tumbling in endless procession through her mind. She was exhausted juggling work, clients, grandparents, kids, Will, and a sex life—or lack thereof. Sleep sounded dreamy. She was halfway surprised to see Will's Jag in the driveway, figuring he might be out with the twins letting them *ménage* his *trois*. She had Date Number Five in mind now, and she wasn't sure how he would feel about it.

She found Grammy knitting in the family room and gave her a kiss on the forehead. "Hey, Gram. Everything okay?"

"Fine," Grammy answered absently, deep into counting off knits and purls. "Kids are sound asleep." She looked up and examined her granddaughter. "You're pooped, I can tell."

"Very. In a good way, though." Sophie glanced into the dining room and the edge of the kitchen. "Where's Gramps and that almost-ex-husband of mine?"

"Your grandfather's in bed. I don't know about William. Maybe upstairs."

Sophie took the stairs two at a time and hurried down the second-story hallway, clapping on lights. She peered through the darkness in Keely's room and found both girls sleeping soundly. Will wasn't in Annabelle's room or anywhere else upstairs.

Downstairs, she peeked into the darkened guestroom, where Grampy lay under the covers. Across the room, she saw shafts of light around the edges of the closed bathroom door. She ambled through the darkness, around the guest bed, to knock on the door.

"Will?" she whispered.

Grammy answered. "It's me, dear. Getting ready for bed."

Grampy stirred and snorted. "Eunice?"

"No, Grampy, it's me." Sophie stubbed her shoe on the foot of the bed. "Ow. Sorry, sorry. Go back to sleep."

Grampy rolled over. "Hurry, Eunice. I woke up with a woody. Hurry before it goes away."

"Christ a-mighty, Hal!" Grammy shouted from the bathroom. "Talk yourself out of it."

"Hurry, Eunice. I don't know how much longer I can keep 'er steady."

Sophie shot out of the bedroom and closed the door behind her, wishing she could have left the mental movie reel of her grandparents having sex there, too. Grampy and Grammy doing what Sophie had been dying to do with no luck was demoralizing.

The porch light drew Sophie to the backyard. She stood on the deck, squinting into the night as the wind blew her hair around. Storms had drifted in and out all evening, and it smelled like rain. She called Will's name, and when he didn't answer, she descended the steps and walked through the yard. The porch light was little help so far away, but she could see a shadowy figure slumped in a chair in the gazebo.

She stepped into the small structure and plopped into a wicker chair, feeling twigs and dirt on the flower-print cushions beneath her thighs. "What are you doing?"

He held a bottle of Corona to his mouth and took a long pull, then grabbed an unopened bottle from the six-pack in an adjacent chair, popped the top, and handed it off. It was icy cold in her palm, so she figured he couldn't have been out there long.

"Can I ask why you haven't returned the divorce papers with your John Hancock?" she said. "I agreed to all the terms, including expanded visitation and any Ponzi settlement—if and when you ever get our money back."

"Touché. But I do commend you for seeing past the legal subterfuge and allowing me the chance to fix things like I promised."

"Soon as you sign, my lawyer can walk the papers to the courthouse, and then it's done."

"If I promise to get you those papers by the weekend, can we agree to a truce?"

Truce? Contrary to the benign implication, Sophie distrusted what the terms might be. But ten minutes of truce and she could go back in the house, flop on her bed, and not wake up 'til the pops and whistles of morning cartoons bombarded her ears. "I guess so."

Will clanked his bottle against hers. "To truce, and nothing but the truce."

She pulled on her bottle, the cold liquid giving her a chilly shudder, and squinted through the dim light at his clothes. He wore Dockers instead of his usual faded jeans, and in place of his classic holey T-shirt was a collared pullover in some new-agey fabric with a sheen. Instead of old golf shoes stripped of cleats, he wore loafers—the kind he used to scoff at. It was as if a fashion guru had helped him navigate the alien burgoo of men's fashions.

"So, my Santa Barbara clients came back," she said. "They made an offer."

"The ones you missed by being at the lake?"

She paused, remembering their truce. "Yes."

"Sorry. My only point of reference."

"Anyway, the offer was accepted. They bought the house for their daughter as a wedding gift. It's a split commission, but it will be a good one."

"I have good memories of our wedding. Our *white* wedding. The flowers, the ribbons hanging from the trees, the priest, and that big arbor I stood under waiting for you. Even that crazy Jack Frost job you did on your hair."

Sophie had strolled between benches peopled in white, under a patch of grand oaks on a green bank of the Guadalupe River. Now she heard Billy Idol's rebellious wedding march in her head, the heartfelt vows, and naïve I-dos till death do us part. She was cursed with those memories, never to forget them and never to relive them. And now what could she do but squelch them beneath the weight of recent history? *I'm not in love with you anymore.* And divorce. And Mitch.

"You were white, too—as a ghost, I recall."

"Just nerves." He smiled in a way that was both warming and discomfiting. "I'm glad we did it our way. You looked so beautiful."

She fidgeted at the compliment. "Well, we were young and defiant."

"You want those days back, don't you? Oh, not us, of course, but the adventure of us. That's what you're looking for to fill some void in your life?"

One hasty comment and a fight could erupt. "Truth or truce?"

"Roll the dice, shall we?"

"We did a lot of things that didn't make sense then," she said. "But we were happy. And it felt like an adventure to me. We didn't have a big plan for how we would do things, but we were *us*. Sophie and Will. Facing the world together, meeting life head on, and that's all that mattered. And then, things changed."

He swigged his beer, gazing into the darkness in thought. But his silence felt vacuous, allowing their history to linger in the air like the smell of rain and newly mowed grass and all the time they spent in this gazebo while the kids were asleep.

Wasted nostalgia now. "Why don't we drink up," she said, "and you can go to your room and I'll go to mine."

He popped the top off another bottle. "Can I tell you something?"

Sophie sighed.

"Truce, remember?" He sat forward, elbows on his knees, head hanging and beer bottle dangling from clasped hands. "Remember on the elevator, when you told Grammy I didn't fight it when you threw me out? You were right. I didn't. But only because it was a relief to not fight anymore. It wasn't because I didn't love you enough to stay. I did."

"But you said—"

"I know what I said. I don't know why I said it. I mean, I guess maybe I... I was just numb." He paused, his brow furrowing, his gaze meeting hers in the hazy darkness. "But I know what I said was unforgivable."

She didn't know how to feel, or whether she even gave a shit anymore. She didn't want to give a shit. She'd worked hard at putting shit behind her, and she was successful at that until the second she got around him. He was a power switch to her past, and the connection seemed always in the ON position.

"I just knew it would be better for the kids if we got some distance from each other. I didn't want to take that away from them. Or you. Because, what you told Grammy? About me changing? You're right. After the craziness with 'Sophie's Kiss'—all that money and the celebrity—I went nuts. And then, well, I don't have to tell you what a failure I felt like being a one-hit wonder. I just, I guess I numbed out about everything. But I didn't mean to. I especially didn't mean to numb out about you."

Sophie felt her resolve to be cold-hearted weakening. After her win with the Robertses, she needed a victory lap, not a trip down Eulogy Lane. She shook her head. "Will—"

"After the kids came, I thought if I didn't produce *X* amount of dollars, it meant we were in another downward spiral. I remember one time after we got married, eating a can of Ranch Style beans for dinner and sharing a beer because that's all we had. Bet you do too."

One of their low points while he studied for his doctorate. "Ancient history, Will."

"But I didn't want to go back to that. My whole mindset from the day we met was that if I didn't keep you living a certain lifestyle, you'd be so disappointed, you'd leave me."

"You thought I was that shallow?"

"No. *I* was that shallow. I kept thinking how great it would be if the girls could go to the best universities, if I could pay off this house and the cars and neither of us would have to worry about layoffs or getting behind on bills, and if for once we could take vacations again— separate, of course—or, I don't know, if anything happened to me, my family would be okay, and if you all were set for life, I'd never..."

She heard him inhale, as if for courage. "Never what?"

"Well, if you were set for life, I'd never be able to let you down again."

Sophie felt a stabbing in her heart and mixed emotions wrapping around her backbone, culminating in an achy bulge in her throat.

"I know I let business get in the way of us, and the kids," he continued, talking fast, as if he feared she'd cut him off. "You relied on me, and I wasn't there for you. I didn't support you, emotionally, and I didn't appreciate the smart, intelligent woman you were—and *are*. I'm sorry for that. I thought you'd maybe like to know that I'm proud of you. And I know I should have said all this a long time ago."

She sat there fighting tears. It was too much.

"If I'd known you'd be speechless, I definitely would have said this a long time ago." He chuckled and took another hit of beer. "I just thought, if I got all that out, maybe we could have a permanent truce, for the kids' sake. I promise, when I leave next week, I won't even balk if you change the locks."

Sophie let her eyes wander the landscape as she pulled herself together. The canopies of the old oaks swayed in the breeze, their leaves fluttering with a shushing applause. Though she couldn't see much in the dark, she knew the flowerbeds were blooming. She'd planned to dig up more of the ground around the gazebo and plant anew. She loved this place.

"We've been here fifteen years," she said, wiping her face dry. "This is the only place our kids have ever known. We have good memories here. We shouldn't spoil it. I agree, we should keep our truce. For the kids."

A long silence passed between them until it became uncomfortable again.

"You've got deals in the pipeline, right?" Will said. "Russian Princess have her eye on some property?"

Sophie breathed a flood of damp night air and let the tension flow out, now that they'd quit talking so seriously of love and truths, regrets and apologies.

"I don't know about Ruta," she said, thinking maybe more Whoppers would help make up her mind—probably Will's whopper. "She's not an easy one to read."

"No? Maybe you'd have better luck reading *The Russian Catastrophe* by Hubitchya Khokov. Or its close cousin, *The Cat's*

Revenge by Claude Balls."

Ah, their old game of Famous Books Never Read, played whenever boredom set in.

"Or my favorite," Sophie said. "*Chastity Rules* by Stella Veerjen."

"*New York Times* Bestseller. How about *Echoes of the Grand Canyon* by Bea Gapusi?"

Sophie giggled and coughed into her hand as beer went down the wrong pipe. "A classic, just like *Hilarity Between the Sheets* by Tess Tickles."

"Reminds me of that pamphlet I once read, *Caulking Made Easy* by Phil McKrevis."

Will tossed out a few more, until his store of jokes was depleted—about sixty seconds. "What a crude pair we are."

An easiness passed between them then.

"So," she said, "when are you moving your things out of the shed?"

He shrugged. "Depends on you."

"Me? If I haven't missed anything in there by now, it's not worth keeping."

"You don't mean that. Lots of memorabilia in there, Sophie."

"I thought we'd already moved anything valuable inside."

"Most of it, but still plenty in the shed. I'll show you."

Sophie eased out of her chair and followed Will to the outbuilding. He opened the heavy door, and she leaned inside, flipping the light switch several times.

"Bulb's out," she said.

"Flashlight's over there somewhere. Be careful of your step."

Sophie tripped over a bag of charcoal briquettes and fell forward into Will's backside, spilling beer down his pants. "Sorry. There's just so much crap."

"Har, har." He turned to help her up. "You just wet my pants. Here, hang on to me. I was out here earlier, and I vaguely remember where Grampy moved things. My underwear is soaked. Do you have *any* idea what it's like to walk with beer in your crack?"

Sophie hooked her fingers through his belt loops. "Take it up with Phil McKrevis."

"I'm not kidding. This is weird. It's infiltrating other places."

She pushed him forward. "Please don't tell me what other places."

"Uh-oh. Lawnmower. Detour."

"This isn't a good idea." She was close enough to be spooning him upright. "We should wait until daylight."

"You're not wussing out on me, are you? Adventurous girl like you?"

"Shut up." She could barely make out his arms moving through the darkness.

He stopped again. "Hang on. More to the left."

Sophie followed, and flinched when the door slammed shut.

"Just the wind," Will said. "You're very jumpy."

A pale band of light from the back porch filtered through the high, dust-caked transoms, casting fluttery shadows on the walls. Sophie shuffled on the concrete, kicking Will's heels.

"There. Got it." He fumbled with the flashlight switch and shined a dusky circle of light on the ceiling. "Damn. How old are these batteries?"

"Pretty old. What do you say we get out of here? I can see this stuff tomorrow."

He shined the light on the door, and she shuffled across the room with him on her heels this time, dodging storage paraphernalia. Sophie turned the doorknob and pushed the door, but it wouldn't open. She repeated the same motions, pushing hard and kicking it, to no avail.

"It's stuck," she said. "Wait a minute. It's locked. From the outside!"

Chapter 26

Will nudged Sophie aside and threw himself into the door. The full force of his body slammed against two inches of solid wood, and the sound reverberated dully through the shed. It was locked all right. He rubbed his shoulder as they both stood there, trying to figure out the problem when it dawned on them.

"Grampy," they said in unison.

Sophie threw her hands in the air. "He's put on the padlock."

She could imagine the door on the outside, its hinged fastener slipped over the U-bar on the door. If Grampy had secured it with the padlock, only a key could free them. She pounded on the door, but Will quickly overtook her efforts.

"Grampy! Help! Grampy!"

They paused, listening to the wind against the shed, then started in again, pounding and yelling, jiggling an ancient knob that was already loose but nevertheless useless.

Will set his hand on his hips. "You know he doesn't have his hearing aid in, right?"

"It's not his fault. He didn't know we were in here. He's old and fragile. And I'm going to kill him the minute we get out of here."

"Okay, let's think rationally about this. Do you have your cell phone?"

"No," she said. "You?"

"Nope."

"Damn it."

Sophie grabbed the flashlight from his hands and nearly dropped it. Felt like ten pounds of batteries inside—dying batteries. She hefted the long black tube and shined it around the room. Stacked holiday

233

boxes covered the wall under the east window and, under the west, the ice chest sat near her tarnished old ten-speed. Where the wall met the ceiling was a narrow transom with a single pane; dust particles hovered in the pastel beam of porch light that sifted through it. Sophie wasted no time scaling the boxes, steadying herself with one hand on the window block.

"It's too grimy," she said peering through tiny clearings. "I can't see anything."

Will appeared beside her, balancing precariously. "We could break it, but I'm not sure I could push you through. You're not skinny enough."

"Please... step away from the fat girl."

Will jumped to the concrete and wiped his hands on his pants. "A two-by-four isn't skinny enough, Sophie."

Sophie began to climb down when the boxes swayed and collapsed beneath her feet. She screamed as she tumbled, and the flashlight spiraled from her grip. She landed upside down in the pike position with her head buried in the ice chest amid orange life vests, her skirt folded inside out and bunched at her waist, and her self-respect somewhere between the moon and her anus.

She pulled herself upright and gazed around dazedly. A beam of light shined at the ceiling from deep inside a half-open box.

"Will?" She smoothed her skirt and strained through the shadowy chaos until she heard a moan. "Are you all right?" She retrieved the flashlight, sank to her knees and shined the light on a gash in his hairline. "Oh, man. Did the flashlight hit you?"

Will slumped on a buckled box, blood drizzling down his forehead. "That was no flashlight. That was an anvil."

"We don't have an anvil."

He winced as she picked through his hair to assess the wound, and she recoiled when she saw it up close. Ugh. She scanned the room for rags, but everything looked grimy.

"You'll live. But I'm going to need your shirt."

"Okay. Is this you trying to get me naked?"

"Let's have it." She helped him tug the shirt out of his pants and pulled it roughly over his head.

Will crossed his arms over his chest. "Jeez, is this you trying to kill me?"

"Shush."

She handed him the flashlight and daubed the gathered edges of his shirt on the gash; then held it against his head to stem the bleeding while scanning his bare chest. The column of hair that ran from his belly button to below his waistband caught her attention, and she couldn't help peeking.

Oh my. That is so... inconvenient.

Their eyes met in the semi-darkness. Had he caught her admiring? "What's with the shiny shirt?" she said. "Doesn't seem like your style."

"I dunno. Met some new friends at your buddy Spike's place, and they've been sort of my secret shoppers. Apparently, they thought I dressed like I was still in the eighties, too."

"Friends of Spike?"

"Yes. Drag queens. And no, that doesn't mean I'm gay. Just better dressed. Even got a manicure. Check it out." He held out his hands, fingernails trimmed and buffed.

She examined his hands, then smirked. He was shaking, and she wasn't sure if it was from the scrape on his head or something else, but she held her smart-ass remarks in check.

He took the flashlight from her and rubbed the roughened business end smeared with blood. "Looks like somebody sanded this thing. Hmpf. Just old, I guess." He squinted up at her. "Unless, of course, someone had the forethought to sandblast the edges into razor-sharp teeth and planned to kill me all along. But you *failed* in your attempt."

"Try not to speak, Will." She pressed the edge of his shirt into his forehead again, while the bulk of it dangled in front of his face.

"I can't bleed, I can't speak, and I sure as hell can't see. What's left for me?"

"Hold still." She patted the wound, diverting her focus to first aid instead of his naked chest. And sex. The sweaty hot sex of yesteryear. *Christ.* So much for focus. She grabbed his hand and shoved it on his head to secure the makeshift rag. "Here, *you* hold this."

She stood up and heaved the fallen boxes back into place, her shoes crunching on gritty concrete. "Another fine mess you've gotten me into, Will Camden."

"What are the odds Grampy would come looking for you in the middle of the night and think, 'Hmm, Sophie and Will must be locked in the shed so I must find the key'?"

"Zippity do-da."

"So we either hack our way out of here with... I don't know what, or hope they come looking for us in the morning."

"What? Stay in here all night? With you?"

"Remember our truce," he said. "What choice do we have?"

"Start looking for an ax."

"There aren't any axes, Sophie. No crowbars to pry the door open, no sledgehammers to break down walls, no windows large enough to crawl through. We're stuck."

Sophie paced anxiously, noting that the flashlight beam was already fading.

Will pointed to the hefty bags of potting soil under the plywood counter. He cleared a space on top of the counter and hoisted them up, then turned them upright to form a seatback. He patted the clearing. "Hop up. It's stable; I slept here the first night. It's better than nothing."

Sophie hefted herself onto the counter while Will rummaged through the camping equipment and came out with a large wrench, matches, and a propane lantern. He glanced toward the transoms.

"We're going to need a little air," he said. "Cover your eyes."

Sophie peeked through her fingers while Will scaled the ten-speed and smashed a hole in the window with the wrench. Glass bits scattered and fresh air seeped in. He lit the lantern and hung it on a bicycle hook from the ceiling, its light casting soft, flat shadows around the room.

"Light won't last long," Will said. "There's a bit of old propane in there."

"It's safe, isn't it?"

"We'll be fine. My guess is Grampy will be out early in the morning to futz around in here. And if not, in fifty years they'll find our decayed corpses."

Sophie gave him a look that reeked *Not funny.*

"Just lightening the mood."

She listened to the lantern's soft whir and rain pelting the roof.

Will's voice cut through the stillness. "Like old times. Camping out."

"Hardly." Then Sophie saw small shadows with distinctive tails. "Scorpions!"

Will jumped on the ice chest as two brown creepy crawlies scuttled across the concrete.

"What are you doing?" Sophie shouted. "Kill them!"

"What? They look like they're just passing through."

Sophie tossed a life vest at him, and he flinched, losing his balance and landing clumsily on one shoe—and a three-inch-long scorpion, stomping it flat. She recoiled as Will examined the mess underfoot, its buddy darting into spaces between the boxes.

"We've invaded their territory," he said. "The one that escaped has gone to get his brothers. They'll be back for revenge."

Sophie re-enacted her *Not funny* look.

"Relax. They like storage rooms and they're active at night. Flashlight probably brought them out." He cleared off the other half of the plywood counter beside her, leaving five feet of soiled but open space. He pushed himself against the wall and stretched out his legs.

Sophie hugged her knees. Her eyes wandered the dusty space, alert for stingers attached to scuttlers. "How long did you say the lantern would last?"

"Hard to tell. You worried about scorpions?"

"Aren't you?"

He craned his neck and rattled his fingers, emitting a long moan with a low-grade Halloween creep factor. "Watch out, Sophie. It's Invasion of the Body *Snackers*."

Again she gave her *Not funny* look.

His grin said he thought he was hilarious. "Think about something else, Soph."

Sophie thought about the kids and her grandparents and Mitch and the fact she was stuck in a shed with her soon-to-be-ex. Of all the halfway predictable scenarios for her boring weeknight, this one had not come to mind. Strangely, their tenuous truce brought a sense of relief. Was it time to bring up his last date?

"You never said how your date went with the twins. Obviously, they have mad hairdressing skills, but was there anything—"

"You know, providing an oral report was not part of the bet."

"Just wondering. Are you seeing her, er—*them*—again? And what about Spike?"

"Let's take it from the top, shall we?" He screwed up his mouth and counted off on his fingers. "Psycho number one—otherwise known as Coach Casey—is a no hitter. Psycho number two, Officer Spike, likes it a little too rough. Edwina is too Jekyll and Hyde for my tastes, and her sister Jessica is too... Jessica. But I will say this, they have each taught me a lesson."

"Like?"

"Sorry, that's it for the oral report."

Sophie fidgeted in the tractor beam of his gaze. She'd have jumped down on the floor to put distance between them if a scorpion wasn't on the loose. Instead, she scanned the shadowy cobwebs on the ceiling. "Just thought, since you were on a roll tonight, you might tell me something real about, you know, dating."

"Okay. Here's real for you. They helped me put a value on what I no longer have. What about you? How's it going with Big Dick? Mr. Adventure the guy for you?"

Sophie had high hopes. "I don't know yet."

"What about kids? Does he have any? Or more to the point, does he like them? Yours are not too keen on him. I know he's all shiny and new, but..."

She didn't need his critique of her boyfriend—was that what Mitch was? "Look, I don't want to discuss Mitch with you. So save it, please."

"Save that sweet mouth for me." He sang the words from the song he wrote long ago just for her. "Come on and save that sweet mouth for me. Baby, please—"

She shushed him with her palm and turned away. "Don't say it."

He skipped past the sore spot: *I'll beg you, beg you, down on my knees.* Words that once held the weight of his passion for her; words that later became a sweet inside joke; words that now cut and mocked because they'd both used them against each other.

I wouldn't take you back... not even if you begged.

"Cuz I can't take just one sip. You're the honey I crave on my lips."

She didn't want to soften, but his voice caressed her synapses like muscle memory, arousing the woman she used to be. Long before he'd turned his professions of love into moneymaking lyrics, they were his gifts to her. He'd held her hands, asked her to stay.

A heavy quiet filled the space between them, and Sophie felt her breathing quicken as little thrills sparkled through her like fireflies in the twilight. Like the old days. Caught in some mesmerizing Will spell. She blinked free and remembered who they were now.

"Haven't heard you sing in forever."

Will pushed off the counter and tossed boxes until he found his dirty old beginner's guitar that he let kids use when he gave lessons to supplement their income while he finished his doctorate. He hopped back on the counter and tightened the strings, thrumming and listening and twisting the tuners. His fingers moved across the frets, and he picked some chords like only weeks had passed since he'd played anything.

"Still got the touch," she said. "Guess it's like riding a bike, huh?"

He strummed a few more licks. "The sounds that resonate in my head, the feelings some melodies evoke..." He cut his eyes to her and let them linger. "Some things you never forget."

When he strummed a tune that made her think of an old gig, she couldn't help joining him in the nostalgia. "Not that I want to get all cozy or anything—"

"Can't have that."

"But I'll never forget the time you sang a golden oldie on stage to a bunch of punk rockers. It was my favorite. Remember? Some dive down on the Drag."

He smiled, their old synchronicity intact; he needed nothing more than that cryptic description. "Audience thought I was drunk."

"I thought so, too, at first." She started to put her hand on his arm, but stopped. "You were playing the Duran Duran set, and next thing I knew, you were serenading me."

He didn't look at her but kept picking the strings. "Thought it suited us." He played around with the chords and began to sing "A Groovy Kind of Love."

He didn't miss a note, his voice still as affecting as ever, reminding her that he'd given up the dream to pull them out of financial ruin once the royalties fell off—to save their family. She never liked admitting that; never wanted to hear him say "Because of you," or to hear herself say "Because of me." It didn't matter now anyway.

She shifted uncomfortably, sat cross-legged and watched the way his mouth moved, like it used to but with subtle indicators that he was midway through his fourth decade. Gone was the thick mullet of the eighties, and now his hair had thinned. His mouth and eyes had earned laugh lines that suited him. His hands seemed larger, more worn in. She had always liked the way her hands fit inside his. How intimate the clasping of two hands could be. How when he left her, she helped herself go to sleep by holding her own hand.

He finished playing the song and laughed. "Pretty rusty."

"No. Surprisingly *not* rusty."

"Well, the song worked back then. I believe I made it to third base that night."

Sophie smirked in spite of herself.

"Oh yeah, I did. You jumped me like a starving jackal on a fresh carcass."

"Please. I hardly remember that night."

"You don't remember us driving to Zilker and sitting on the picnic table, me with my guitar in my lap, like now, and you moving in real close..." He leaned toward her, slower than slow, half smiling, half whispering. "Like this."

She didn't move as his mouth brushed hers. She couldn't. She watched his eyes close languidly, and sparks crackled all through her. His lips were warm, soft, wet. Foreign yet familiar. Scary, yet delicious. He paused, his mouth a millimeter away, his eyes softly locked on hers, his breaths against her face.

He's waiting for me to make the next move. If I do, will I regret it?

If I don't, will I regret it more?

So much water pooled under the broken bridge that had sustained her for so long, but resenting him was exhausting. She didn't want to resent him anymore. She just wanted to feel good. She kissed him back, gently, trying him out, feeling her way. And somehow her mind objected to thinking about what it all meant.

He kissed her neck and she pushed his guitar aside. It clattered across the boxes before landing sideways on the concrete with a reverberating thud. He unbuttoned her blouse, his tongue probing her mouth, while he worked the blouse off her shoulders and pulled her bra straps with it. Feeling more urgency, she popped the front clasp of her bra and freed her breasts. Then he lowered himself to kiss her nipples and struck a nerve—all the nerves left untouched by a man for so long, untouched by *him*.

Did he feel her tremors? She'd been waiting so long, wanting and needing. And who, besides the two of them, would ever know?

He pulled her forward, unzipped her skirt, and tugged it off. She sat up and unzipped his pants, said hello to her old friend who responded easily, emboldened by her touch to three times his resting size. His shaft was hot as she enveloped him, caressed his length. How happy Little Will was to see her. She fondled the Heartbreakers, too, and felt the machinations of her feminine parts—dubbed long ago as *The Groupies*—click into gear.

Then again, the sight of Big Will, the smell of his skin, the feel of his naked body next to hers made her feel like she had returned to a comfortable old sofa with cushions that cradled her, allowed her to get in touch with herself, freed her mind of the world's noise so she could concentrate on only three things: sex, sex, and sex. Despite all else between them, she'd always trusted herself with Will. She could let go with him, experience the elusive O with him. And oh, how she longed for the O.

Will pushed her to lay back and hovered above her, kissing her deeply, rubbing himself against her, their legs entwined.

The plywood was hard, rough, and splintered. Sharp needlepoints dug into her back. "Sleeping bags," she whispered.

"What? Who? Don't stop. Are we stopping?" Will made eye contact, then jumped off, tore through boxes, and came out with two musty sleeping bags rolled up tight as taquitos.

"Hurry," she said.

Before I change my mind and lose steam—before I remember...

He pushed aside the potting soil and unfurled both sleeping bags to make a cushy pallet on the plywood.

The counter wobbled as Sophie shifted her naked body to accommodate them. "Will it hold? I don't want to crash in the middle of—"

"It'll hold."

"Are you just saying that?"

"No."

"Do you think—"

He shut her up with a penetrating kiss that took her mind off everything but the sensations his body had awakened inside her. His hands caressed the inside of her thighs, and he pushed himself lower until she felt the warmth of his breaths and the slick pressure of his tongue. His fingers languished across her abdomen, then brushed her hardened nipples while his mouth worked expertly, tasting her, titillating and wetting her, coaxing her toward bliss so long missed. Carried on mounting waves of pleasure, she didn't want him to stop— ever! And when she finally slipped over the edge, gasping in intense, heart-stopping eruptions that left her limp and incredulous, she was embarrassed at how ardently her body had come and how unreservedly she had cried out.

After a few moments of recovery, she peered down and found him staring, admiring. He kissed his way back up her torso and her ticklish sides, her breasts, chest, and neck, leaving wet goosebumps that made her shiver and giggle. He suspended himself above her then, looking down at her face so lovingly, it frightened her.

She couldn't keep seeing that look and so kissed his mouth, bruising him, spreading her legs, tugging his hips, pulling him down, letting him know how badly she wanted to feel him inside her.

He worked his way in and filled her up. She'd been afraid it would hurt after so long, but the discomfort was mild, and in moments her only thoughts were of his deep thrusts and the friction—*oh, the friction!*

Already primed, her pleasure crescendoed and peaked with a second orgasm that burst from deep within her core in prolonged, powerful waves. Will's eyes shut, and he drove faster and deeper still, until finally he stiffened into an impassioned groan and his whole body shuddered.

After long moments, he relaxed onto her, his sweat-soaked skin melding with hers. He breathed hard and his spent body weighed more by the second, but Sophie felt gratified they'd both found so much pleasure in each other. One. Last. Time.

When he pushed himself up, Sophie couldn't bear the space. She wrapped her arms around him and pulled him back down, rubbed his back and kissed his shoulders and his face tenderly. With gratitude. Hot tears seeped from her eyes, burning trails across her temples, into her hair. She fought to keep the emotion from bubbling up, to escape his notice, to bear them in silence. If he realized it, he didn't say.

When it became so quiet, all she could hear were his inhales and exhales commingling with her own, he rolled off and spooned her from the side—so close she could feel his chest rising and falling against her elbow. He draped his arm across her stomach and caressed her hips, and she snuggled closer still. For the old days. For her first love.

"Will?" she said, her voice sounding small.

"Mm-hmm?"

It didn't matter now, but she had to ask. "Did you just... grow bored with me?"

He sat up on one elbow and looked at her. "No. It was me, Sophie. It wasn't you. I grew bored with myself. Maybe I blamed you for that. But..." He brushed the hair back from her forehead. "You were never boring."

He lowered his mouth and kissed her again, tenderly, deeply, until he surprised her by rolling her over on top. She straddled him and laughed, expelling all what-ifs and if-onlys from her mind. There was only now, only Will and Sophie.

Three hours, six positions, and four orgasms later, she disallowed all regret for what they had done, for what she had encouraged, and the consequences to come.

Chapter 27

The morning sun shone through the broken transoms and caused Will to squint. He felt sweaty and stiff, and his hips were sore from sleeping in one place too long. His stomach grumbled and he yawned. Then he rubbed his sore, scabbing forehead. And remembered.

Oh, man. It hadn't been a dream?

He propped himself up, marveling that Sophie was still curled up beside him in the sleeping bags they'd spread across the counter. Her light snoring piqued some small happiness in him, and he pressed a tender kiss into her hair.

Movement at the foot of the bag got his attention then, and he rubbed his eyes to clear the morning blur. More movement, and he realized: *scorpion.*

He kicked frantically inside the sleeping bag, popping the scorpion in the air and watching it spin end over end toward him. He bobbed to avoid it, and the scorpion landed on Sophie's head. He screamed and she bolted upright, just as Will smacked her head.

"Ow."

"Is it gone? Turn around. Let me see."

"Is what gone?"

He pulled her toward him to scan for their attacker. "Scorpion."

Sophie stared at him blank-eyed, then shrieked and tried to jump off the counter, her legs trapped inside the sleeping bag. Entangled, they fell together off the counter but somehow worked their way free. Sophie shook her head in a frenzy and high-stepped it like she was doing the "Maniac."

"Stop, stop," Will said. "I think it's gone. Turn."

She wheeled as Will checked her naked body, an instant turn-on so distracting that when a long shaft of light spread into the shed, along with a mournful creak, he hardly noticed. Then somebody cleared her throat, and it wasn't Sophie.

Beyond boxes and storage items, Grammy stood in the doorway wearing pin curls and a tangerine housecoat. Grampy loomed behind her in a short plaid robe, black dress socks on his rail-thin white legs, and the worn leather slippers he wore everywhere, including the market.

"Least somebody around here knows how to make a booty call," Grampy said.

"Hush, Hal," Grammy said. "You kids okay?"

Will turned his naked posterior to the old folks, hiding his morning wood and gathering Sophie close to shield her nudity. "Somebody locked us in here last night."

"Wasn't me," Grampy said.

Sophie peered around Will's arm. "Then who the hell was it?"

Grammy blinked. "No need to use the caps-locked voice, Sophie."

"Grammy!"

Grammy adopted a gangsta-girl pose. "Dude, why you gotta be all up in my grill?"

"I'm sure it was an accident," Grampy said. "Just chill and come up to the house. Little ones are up. Come on, Eunice." He pulled his wife by the arm and shut the door behind them.

"Don't lock it!" Sophie and Will shouted.

Sophie found her clothes and shook them vigorously. "I can't believe her. She knows better. She knows we're—"

What she left unsaid filled Will's head with questions. How would this all play out? Awesome or awful? Had anything changed? Did she regret it? Did he?

Sophie didn't wait for Will. "I'll go on up so nothing looks weird."

"Yeah," he said, smoothing his hair. "Nothing about us divorcees in the shed all night, naked, looks weird."

Sophie hurried, sure the smell of sex permeated her skin and *screamed* what they'd been up to. As soon as she walked into the kitchen, Grammy and Grampy's stares groped her for sensitive information. They whispered and sniggered as if they'd witnessed a high crime.

Check her out; she's been having orgasms all night. Will's goofy smile says it all.

Sophie halfway expected Grammy to pop off with some new street lingo: *Dude, you be stickin' it to that ho? You look* all *twisted out.*

The kids hadn't come downstairs yet, so Sophie excused herself to shower. She didn't invite Will to join her. It would be too obvious they'd had sex. Too bizarre. She stood under the hot spray and soaped him away, but the memories wouldn't wash away so easily. What had she been thinking?

That he was great in bed, that's what. He was never sad in the sack; it's just that last night he was so much better than she remembered. The results said it all. Four orgasms. But why now? They were so over. Yet, he was still with her. The sweetness of his kisses; the soothing vibrato of his voice; his heady, familiar scent; and his genuine tenderness. The unselfish, shameless giving of pleasure so that she could be satisfied. If only...

If only she hadn't been so damned horny. The whole thing was a breach of her agreement with herself, a 180 on her plans to move on. It was untimely, implausible, and foolish. After all, failure is doing the same thing over and over again and expecting a different result, right? Or was that insanity?

She stared vacantly at the drain as water pounded her shoulders, flowed around her breasts, and trickled down her thighs. In the afterglow, the tension had fallen away. Her body felt cleansed, purified, freed. Was that it? Sex with Will had been like a wellness check at the doctor's? Diagnosis: sex starved. Treatment: immersion therapy—orgasms. Four of them, missy. If only she could prescribe herself a regular dose. Sex, as needed, by mouth whenever possible. Refills: unlimited. Watch for painful side effects.

Surely Will realized it was a fluke. She was an addict, seduced by the lure of her old drug of choice—sucked in and overcome by the power of what they once shared, weakened by proximity and unexpected apologies and nostalgic music and, dammit, the need to be satisfied. Too bad, so sad, she could not allow it again.

The hickory smell of bacon made her stomach growl. She threw on shorts and a tank top and combed out her hair, wondering if Will had escaped her grandparents.

Outside her bedroom, Keely and Annabelle, still in pajamas on their first day of summer, toted their father's beat-up old Martin guitar in its black leather case. Keely carried the heavy end and backed down the stairs while Grampy directed traffic.

"Take it slow," he said. "Annabelle, don't push now."

Sophie blew out a sigh. "He's not playing guitar *now*, is he?"

"I want him to," Grampy said. "Might be the only chance I get before we go home."

"But you've got the whole summer ahead of you."

He motioned for the kids to keep going. "Sophie, don't blow this opportunity."

"Grampy, it's not what you think."

"Better question is what do *you* think it is?"

"Off limits."

He looked down his nose at her, the same way he had when she was a skinny kid, and she felt backed into a corner, pressured to make everyone happy.

She softened her tone. "Whatever it is, Grampy, it's between me and Will."

His frail, thin lips pouted. "Don't ruin it for me. It's my dying wish that you and Will work things out."

She rubbed gentle apologies into his shoulder. "Grampy, we *are* working things out, in our own way. And you're not dying." She kissed the sagging skin of his mottled jowls, and he dismissed her with a curt wave.

In the kitchen, Will huddled next to Grammy over the stove. He wore his old apron that somehow always seemed to be around. Beneath it, he was shirtless, which did nothing to help Sophie forget what they had done. He diced and chopped jalapenos, tomatoes, and onions on her cutting board. Crisp bacon curled up on paper towels and pancakes browned on the griddle. Sophie smelled coffee and wondered if he'd done that too.

"There you are," he said. "Hungry?"

Grammy peered through her trifocals. "Gotta love a man who knows his way around the kitchen. Especially one who knows Tex-Mex. Will's teaching me how to make migas."

Sophie wended between them for a cup of coffee. It should have been a simple maneuver but was more like zigzagging between orange highway cones. Will traded places with Grammy, who was asking how big to snap the corn tortillas and when to throw them in the skillet with the shredded cheese. Quite chummy, the two of them.

"I'd like to speak to you, Gram," Sophie said.

"We're right in the thick of things, dear. Maybe after breakfast." The old woman turned her back and snapped more tortillas for the scrambled egg-and-cheese mixture.

Will's scuffed old Martin was nestled in its red, fur-lined case, and the kids hovered over it plucking strings. Their dark bedhead hair hung around their faces, and they brushed strands aside to stay in the very serious groove of thumb-strumming.

"Careful with the guitar," Sophie and Will said at the same time.

Will laughed as his eyes met hers, and she knew he attached their old synchronicity to it, a soul-mate kind of thinking that had faded years ago, along with their relationship.

"We're eating on the patio," he said. "Perfect weather."

Sophie stood near the sink staring out the window to where patio table settings were already in place. Curious how breakfast had transpired so fast. She couldn't help letting her eyes find the gazebo and then the shed, and a shadowy sense of dread crawled across her shoulders. Like scorpions.

Grampy shuffled into the kitchen behind her. She felt his watchful eyes shift between surveilling her and flipping through the pages of Grammy's book, open on the counter. *Don't Bust a Cap: Easy Parlayin' with the Homies.*

Will inched closer and whispered against her neck. "You smell good."

Goosebumps pebbled her back and cascaded down her arms. He hadn't showered. His smell was subtle, musky, and an erotic reminder of his body's rejuvenating power. The thought of him naked, touching her in the glow of the lantern, sent a flutter through her pelvis and—

No. He was just physical therapy. A medicinal salve. A tryst of fate!

The hair on Will's arms grazed Sophie's and she tried not to respond. Now that she'd come back down to earth, her mission was clear: ensure Will harbored no illusions. But she had to be careful. A blatant rejection could incite the sort of epic clash families talked about for decades, not to mention Grammy and Grampy's certain mutiny.

"Girls?" she said, herding them out back. "Let's get ready to eat."

Shortly after, plates were piled high and they all squeezed around the patio table. Will sat next to Sophie, but Keely wriggled a spot between them. Annabelle sat between her great grandparents and debated song choices for her dad to play on his guitar.

"I want the *Frozen* song," Keely said. "Let it go, Daddy!"

"I'm going to request 'You Are My Sunshine,'" Grampy said.

Annabelle squealed, "Little Mermaid, Little Mermaid."

"That reminds me, Eunice," Grampy said. "Will is taking me fishing next week."

Grammy stretched her waddled neck and straightened in her chair. "You're too damned old to go fishing. What if you fall overboard? What if you keel over in the heat?"

Grampy leaned over Annabelle and got nose to nose with his wife. "What if I catch a big-ass fish and bring it home for supper?"

"We'll fish from the shoreline," Will said. "We'll be in the shade with plenty of ice water, and all the facilities like bathrooms and such are nearby."

Sophie looked at Will tetchily. "Since when do you take off a new job to go fishing?"

Will wagged his fork. "Since I make my own hours. Sometimes life teaches you hard lessons, and when you finally get it, you do the things that make you happiest."

"Makes sense to me," Grampy said.

Sophie sipped her orange juice and shoveled in migas. Her medicinal high had worn off. *Now* he cuts back his hours? *Now?* His gaze lingered, as if in wait for approval and praise, and she suspected her goal of getting him out of the house had been compromised.

As they finished eating, Sophie circled the table in cleanup mode. She hoped Will would forget about playing his guitar, but she was alone in that sentiment. While she loved hearing him play, it only prolonged the inevitable. Where was he, anyway? She didn't want to look for him and make it obvious.

Keely and Annabelle stared beyond her and giggled, and Sophie suspected their father lurked behind her, egging them on. She tried to pay no attention.

"What are you going to save her from this time?" Keely said, referring to Will's rescue of Sophie from a stampeding crowd the night they first met.

"Dishes," Will said.

Suddenly, and despite the fact that she juggled a stack of dirty plates in her hands, Sophie felt herself dipped backward. Will's face zoomed in close, and before he replayed their infamous kiss, uneaten migas dropped onto her face.

Will pulled her upright, beaming. "Oh, sorry, sorry."

"You know, apologies mean more when you're not laughing."

Amid her offspring's giggles, Sophie huffed into the house and cleaned herself off with a dishtowel, then stood over the sink watching out the window. Will reclined in a lounger, still in his apron and jeans, playing the simple tunes his audience requested and making up lyrics where he could cleverly slip their names into the mix. Even Grammy and Grampy were spellbound.

The son of a bitch.

When she couldn't stand being left out a minute longer, Sophie joined them. Keely cuddled next to her as she lay on the chaise listening to songs and eschewing thoughts of what could have been. She had Mitch now, and a small pang flit through her chest when she realized how much she missed him.

Grampy went inside to make a pit stop and came out with the house phone. "For you, Sophie. Think it's that Houdini fella."

She moved Keely aside and sat up to take the phone, feeling Will's eyes on her. He pretended not to listen, but Sophie knew him too well.

"On my way to Houston," Mitch said. "But I wanted you to know that I'm thinking about you. In fact, I think about you all the time."

Sophie smiled, tamping down the guilt of four incomparable orgasms. "I was just thinking about you, too."

Will began a new song. "Sing it with me now, *Little red caboose, choo choo choo, little red caboose, choo choo choo.*"

Sophie covered her free ear with a hand, but she couldn't hear what Mitch said next. "Sorry, say again?"

"I said, you're still having your barbecue on Sunday, right?"

"Oh yes." She rose from the chaise and descended into the yard for privacy.

"I'll be there. Who's manning the barbecue?"

Sophie glanced back at her family. Will's eyes blazed a hole through her chest, and he sang louder. "*Running down the tracks, choo choo choo, smokestack on his back, choo choo choo.*"

"Geez," Mitch said. "What is that god-awful noise?"

"Um, that would be a clown entertaining the kids."

"Man, I wish I'd had a mom like you. Listen, I don't have a lot of time. I just wanted to hear your voice. I'll call you tonight."

Will banged on his guitar even louder, inciting an all-family sing-along to "Kumbaya" with Grammy and Grampy standing arm in arm and rocking side to side. Dogs howled all over the neighborhood.

Sophie terminated her call and slipped into the house to finish up the kitchen. As she'd half dreaded, half hoped, Will followed her inside. But a few seconds of silence summoned a new level of awkwardness and weakened her resolve.

Will refilled his coffee cup. "So, do we need to talk about things?"

"Yeah. We do." She avoided looking at him and wiped the counters she'd already wiped twice. "I've arranged for your fifth date. We're having a company party on Lake Travis, one of those party barges. Next week. It'll be fun. And don't worry, Mitch will be out of town so... no Mitch, no weirdness. You can meet us at the dock and your last date will be on the party barge." When she glanced up, his face had turned purple. "Will, last night was... ex-sex, I think they call it. That's all."

"Ex-sex. You mean you used me?"

"Of course not."

"I am such a glutton for punishment. I thought—"

The back door opened and Annabelle ran inside. "Daddy, come on."

Keely dragged Will's guitar behind her. "Daddy, Grampy wants you to come back."

Sophie glanced out the window at Grammy and Grampy who, it seemed, had sent in their scouts to salvage the sing-along and the tenuous goodwill breakfast they had brokered. With Will's fury fixed on her, Sophie regained her mommy wits, along with a sad longing she thought she'd gotten rid of with her commitment to divorce.

"We'll talk later," she said. "Go sing songs, play your guitar. Do what you do best."

Keely pushed his guitar at him. "Here, Daddy."

Will took the guitar by the neck and shoved it at Sophie. "No. I gave this all up long ago—for you. Remember?"

He ripped off the apron and headed for the front door. Sophie lagged behind to watch him through the window as he got into his Jag and drove off.

She sighed, her head in a daze. How fast it had all gone south.

She turned to go upstairs but had to stop short. Keely, Annabelle, Grammy, and Grampy stood before her with arms crossed over their chests and faces bearing seditious pirate scowls.

Chapter 28

After storming out of Sophie's house, Will had checked into a downtown motel and parked himself on a king-sized bed in boxers and a T-shirt, thanks to MasterCard. Now, days later, he watched Tiger Woods drive 342 yards off the tenth tee, teenage vampires in a dreary place called Forks threaten to take down a hot meal without benefit of fangs, and a Sumatran python digest a grown man; yet even after a channel-flipping marathon that left his eyes swollen, Will's mind surfed elsewhere.

He'd had off-the-charts sex with a woman who, despite his conviction to get her out of his system, still held his heart in the palm of her hand. And oh those hands, that tongue, that body—what magic she worked.

For his part, her pleasure had been his sole pursuit. How mindboggling the contrast of their one night to the last few years of pushing their lives apart and erecting walls. Yet, she was resolute in her edict that the divorce should proceed as scheduled. So he was forced to just suck it up and go on his merry fucking way, right?

It wasn't his weekend, but he wondered if the kids could get him out of his funk. He'd phoned that morning to invite them to a day at the park, expecting Sophie to answer and wondering how icy her reception would be.

Grammy had answered instead. "They're all at the market, buying party supplies for the barbecue. You coming?"

Ah, the Sunday afternoon party to which the hostess had conveniently not invited him. That pretty much said it all. Besides, no doubt Hoodoody would be there, and god forbid Big Dick and Little Will should be in the same place at the same time. Maybe his Average

Joe couldn't hold a candle to Mitch's reputed pocket monster, but he had indisputable proof now, via his multi-orgasmic wife, that it was how one used his equipment that counted. Now his archenemy gathered at the gates of his old home for a good, old-fashioned grilling. Priceless. Speculating what else the guy wanted charred Will's ego to a sooty pulp.

"Thanks, Gram," Will said tightly. "Think I'm coming down with a stomach virus. Could you have the girls call when things settle down?"

"Of course. Can I bring you something? Soup and crackers?"

"Nah, thanks. No appetite here."

He disconnected and groaned as Phil Mickelson sliced a shot into the trees.

Hours later, Tess called his cell, a chorus of voices and laughter in the background. That she chose to call him from Sophie's barbecue seemed designed to unnerve him.

The noise and wind whipped through Tess's mouthpiece. "Hang on a sec," she said, apparently moving some place quieter. "Sorry. How's it going?"

"Catching up on work." He shuffled the papers on his cheap coffee table, remembering his lie to Grammy. "Stomach virus. Throwing up and all that."

"Hope it's nothing serious. Listen, where are you?"

"Motel in SoCo. Just for a couple days."

"Grammy mentioned you'd be cleaning out the shed soon, and that reminded me about your escrow closing. We're still looking at new places to hang your hat, right?"

As a matter of fact, he couldn't wait to put the past behind. Thinking about how Sophie wanted to throw out all his stuff along with their marriage was like pouring gasoline on a fire that already burned white-hot. It had been culminating to this point for years, yet the idea felt newly branded on his ego.

Of course, none of these feelings had anything to do with the fact that he was sitting alone in a fleabag motel while his old friend Tess, his children, and his grandparents—they *felt* like his—and the woman he'd made scorching love to days before were gathered in the sunshine having a great time without him.

His voice filled with contempt. "I'll be out of town. Maybe next week."

"Thursday?" Tess said louder, as if raising her volume would help her hear better.

"I'll call you."

"Okay. And, Will? You remember I'm your friend too, right?"

He would never presume Tess would supplant her twenty-five-year alliance with Sophie for him. Much as he adored Tess, anything he confided would go straight to Sophie's ears.

"See you Thursday," he said, and disconnected.

He got off the couch and paced the narrow spaces around the bed, on the verge of a meteoric crash. This whole thing was bullshit. He pitched his phone into the wall so hard it blasted a hole in the sheetrock. He regretted the outburst for all of three seconds. Then he tossed every pillow across the room and hurled the divorce papers into the air and watched them separate and flutter noisily to the floor.

Fucking divorce.

He upended his hard-sided suitcase and gave it a swift kick before realizing he was barefoot—and then his whole body stiffened and he wailed as the pain shot through him. Limping around, he tore bedspreads and sheets off the mattress and flung them into a table lamp that toppled with a clatter, along with the 5x7 of Annabelle and Keely that he always traveled with. He hurried to rescue it, hoping it hadn't broken, but the sweet smiles of his little princesses shined from behind shattered glass.

He heard himself gasping through tears and felt ridiculous when his father's voice rose from the dead. "Don't cheesedick your way through it, son."

Too late. He'd cheesedicked his way through everything. And it dawned that no matter how many things he destroyed, nothing would ease his rage and frustration—*his grief.* So much grief. Son of a bitch, just like his father, he'd realized the value of his wife—*his life*—after she was already gone. Only one thing would make him feel better. Wiping his memory clean. He had to let it go. All of it. All of *her.*

He squatted and rummaged through the papers he'd launched like confetti and found a white business card with a rainbow logo. He picked up the motel phone and dialed the number.

"Hey, Murray. You busy today? Mind if I bump up our appointment? No, not the suit fittings; the other deal. Yeah, yeah. Today's better. No, I don't care what you're wearing." He waited while Murray talked it over with Arty. "Fine. One hour."

Sophie was thankful Tess had arrived early to help with party prep or she'd have run out of time long before her guests arrived. First on the scene was Gertie Fishbein with an apple pie and her husband, followed by a dozen brokers and their significant others bearing chips and dips and beer. The guests milled around the backyard investigating the gazebo and the new tree house while Sophie and Tess set out jumbo batches of potato and macaroni salads.

Sophie transferred plastic plates and cutlery off a pantry shelf and onto a tray, trying to keep her voice nonchalant. "Was that Will on the phone?"

Tess tucked her cell into her purse. "Looks like you got your wish. The man's cutting his ties and moving on."

Annabelle and Keely raced full-bore through the house, their excitement turning into a sort of hyper-kid mania. "Girls, settle down!" Sophie's shoulders tensed, and her neck felt like an iron bar as they continued to ignore her. "Am I invisible? Girls!"

She blew a strand of hair from her face and balanced the tray. "Can you get the back door, Tess?"

"Good thing, I guess, that the whole mess is finally about over."

Sophie proceeded through the threshold as Tess held the door. "Grab the basket of napkins, too, will you? Girls, can you get the ice chest out of the garage?"

Tess followed outside and set the napkins on the table. "You're happy about it, right?"

Kee-rist almighty. Sophie inhaled the smoky scent of grilled chicken on the barbecue and a deep swath of too-warm summer air, and shut her tired eyes. Like this day, memories of her sexual marathon with Will would not end soon enough. She'd wanted to confide in Tess, but after she'd ranted nonstop about Will being the bane of her existence, how could she justify doing the unthinkable?

"Yes, Tess. Of course, I'm happy. Don't I *look* happy?" She plastered a toothy grin on her face and felt ridiculous. "Sorry. I'm so frazzled. I must be coming down with something. Stomach virus maybe."

"Mm-hmm, looks like that's going around."

The doorbell rang and Sophie yelled for someone to answer it.

She was ferrying a bowl of fruit salad outside when Mitch caught up with her, his arms full of pretty gift bags and a bouquet of spring flowers in a vase. Not the least of his surprises was Allison, who stuck close enough to be his date. Allison's outfit consisted of white short-shorts and an ultra low-cut, form-fitting blouse with a lacy built-in bra that pushed up trophy breasts voluminous enough to set a couple beers on.

Sophie adopted her best poker face. "Welcome to our home."

"Look, Mommy," Annabelle gushed. "Hoodoody got us birthday presents."

"It's not your birthday, sweetie."

Mitch set the flowers on the picnic table and kissed Sophie's cheek. "No, but it's Sunday at Sophie's, and I'm happy to be here." He handed a bright red gift bag and helium balloons to each of her daughters. "Here you go, Annabelle. This one's for you, Keely."

"Wow," Sophie said, less because of his grand gestures than the fact that he remembered their names and matched them to the right kid.

"Go big or go home is how I roll," he said with an easy laugh.

While Keely and Annabelle sat on the deck stairs to open their gifts, Mitch presented Sophie a red six-inch-long box and squeezed her arm gently. "For you."

"You didn't need to buy me anything."

"Yes, I did. And I wanted to."

"Mommy," Keely said, spinning as she read the packaging. "Fashionista Barbie."

Annabelle looked at her package with less enthusiasm. "S-s-s-kipper?" She compared her girl-next-door doll to Keely's fashion plate and tossed her doll into the dirt.

Sophie opened her box and pulled out a platinum tennis bracelet with diamonds and rubies. "Oh, Mitch. This is too much. I couldn't—"

"Of course you can." Mitch's eyes crinkled at the corners. He removed the bracelet from the box and clasped it around her wrist. "A beautiful woman needs beautiful jewelry."

The exquisite platinum shined and the gems sparkled. Part of her wanted to give it back and take things slower. Or was it the lingering guilt that made her feel unworthy?

"Keep it," Grammy said blandly, moseying past with a tray of hors d'oeuvres. "A home girl can never have enough bling."

Sophie yielded with a kiss to his cheek and admired her bracelet as it glistened in the sunlight.

"Ruta should be here any minute," Tess said. "Where's the Stolichnaya?"

"I set two bottles on your kitchen counter," Allison said, descending into the yard. "Let me know if I can help."

Sophie called after her. "Actually, I could use some help with this table cloth."

Allison returned to the deck with a stiff slash across her face that served as a smile. "Of course you could."

Sophie spread red gingham plastic over the table and smoothed out the air bubbles. "If you'll help me tack it down, that would be great."

Allison followed Sophie's lead, pushing tacks through the gingham into the wood, until suddenly, she screamed and shook her fingers. "Omigod." She squeezed blood out of her middle finger. "Omigod!"

Tess returned with the vodka and moved in for a closer look. "Yeah, that looks bad. You need to go to the ER? We had so much fun last time, I'd be happy to take you."

Sophie shot Tess a recriminating smirk. "In the kitchen, there's a first-aid box. Upper cabinet left of the fridge."

Allison stuck her finger in her mouth and sucked on it while retreating into the house. Minutes later, she came back outside, shoving the door open so hard it bounced off the side of the house.

Grammy had followed behind her carting a dish of sweet and spicy baked beans fresh from the oven. Sidestepping the door, the old woman nearly fell. Mitch appeared out of nowhere, grabbed the dish by the potholders, and ferried it to the table for her.

"Holy bejeebus," Grammy said. "I almost did a face plant. You're like some kind of super hero, aren't you?"

"Just good timing," Mitch said, winking at Sophie.

"Gram, you should have told me," Sophie said. "I'd have brought that out. You've done enough. Go rest your feet."

Tess gave the tiny woman a hug. "I marvel at you, Grammy. You put me to shame with your energy."

Allison sidled beside Mitch and tugged on his arm. "Let's go see the tree house."

Mitch ignored her. "Can I help with something else, Sophie?"

"She's got it under control," Allison said. "Right, Soph?"

Soph? So congenial.

Grampy was in charge of grilling, but his task had been subverted by inquisitive party guests in need of a personalized tour of the grounds. He seemed so entertained by the act of entertaining that Sophie couldn't pull him away, and Mitch volunteered to take over.

"On it," he said. "Allison, feel free. I'll catch up."

Allison tromped alone into the yard, and Sophie couldn't deny the satisfaction in that.

"Trouble follows that one wherever she goes," Grammy muttered. "Doesn't she know you've got your eye on Houdini?"

"She knows."

"And you invited this girl to your party?"

"Not exactly. She's Mitch's protégé and always seems to turn up."

A shriek came from inside the house and Ruta Khorkina emerged on the deck waving her arms. "Hello, everybody. I am fashionably late, no?" She greeted Sophie with cheeky air kisses. "Sorry so late, darlingk. I had wonderful massage and fell asleep. Imagine, they let me stay there, snoring like rhinoceros. I am so happy to see you. Will eez here today?"

"No, but I told him about the lake party next week. I'm sure he'll be there."

She stopped herself from admitting how ultimately *unsure* she was about that as her guests gathered around Ruta and became the entourage she was accustomed to in New York but lacked in Austin.

When Mitch had finished grilling, everyone gathered plates and dug in. Mitch served up Ruta's favorite Stoli and cranberry juice and the two regaled the crowd with stories of their party days, sprinkling in a surplus of celebrity names.

Sophie sat in a lounger with a full plate on her lap, listening to the chatter and grateful to take the load off. She had begun to think this harried day had finally improved when the gravelly grinding of engine gears sounded from the cul-de-sac in front of her house. At first she dismissed it, until the sound got louder and more obnoxious.

Grampy was down by the shed, waving like an air traffic controller. Sophie called out to him when an enormous white panel truck hurtled through the backyard. Its big tire treads tore up the lawn as it groaned past the gazebo, veered toward the shed, and circled toward the house before stopping and backing up.

Fearing he'd be run over, Sophie got to her feet and sprinted toward him. She pulled up when she realized the truck had stopped and he was not in danger.

A man exited the truck and strode between the churned-up tire tracks to her grandfather's side. Before Sophie saw his face, she recognized the faded green Duran Duran T-shirt, holey jeans, and Rangers ball cap.

The Wild Boy had arrived. And by the look on his face, he was hungry like the wolf.

Chapter 29

If Murray hadn't stuck his business card into Will's backpack that day at Spike's, Will would never have known that in addition to his alter ego as an actor-slash-drag queen, Murray also made money shopping for folks with no fashion sense and moving people across town. Luckily, his moving services were available on short notice; but seeing how the truck had torn up the backyard, Will figured the secret shopper gig was more the guy's true calling.

And now he could see the real error in his thinking. The way Sophie was storming toward him, Will braced for the ultimate lambaste.

"What the hell's going on?"

"What's it look like? I'm clearing out the shed."

"Today? You had to do this *today*?"

Will walked around the truck gauging the distance between the ramp and the shed, then pounded on the side panel for Murray to back the truck closer. "Ho," he yelled over the engine. Moments later, the diesel gasped and died.

He turned to Sophie. "What's the problem? You said the sooner I got my things out, the better."

"Has it escaped your notice I'm having a party? Don't you think we should have talked first?" She suddenly seemed to catch sight of her grandfather, loosening the shed's padlock. "Grampy, don't tell me you're part of this."

Grampy shrugged. "Man's gotta do..."

Sophie looked over her shoulder at her guests who'd followed en masse to check out the commotion. "Omigod."

Will walked toward them and shook their hands. "Hello. Nice to meet you. Hello. Will Camden, Sophie's soon-to-be-ex-husband. Lovely day for a barbecue. Hello."

"Will," Sophie said.

"Sorry to shake things up," he said, ignoring her. "We'll be out of here soon. See, everything in that shed there, that's all Sophie's past. It's all the history that Sophie and I shared, and let me tell you, she is dying to get rid of it. You understand, it's important to Sophie."

He eyed her straight on, challenging, refusing to blink.

She looked nearly apoplectic. "Can I *please* have a word with you?"

"William," Grammy said sharply.

Will spied the tiny woman among the onlookers. Chin high, scowl punishing. He averted his gaze, preferring her orthopedic loafers to the shaming net she'd cast.

"Sorry, Gram. This is something I have to do."

"That's whack." Grammy waved her arms at the crowd. "Let's leave these beefcakes to their business, shall we?"

Murray hopped out of the truck dressed in an Early Larry Bird ensemble straight out of Boston Gardens and sashayed primly to the back of the truck to open its doors. Arty emerged from the other side of the truck, along with another of their theater friends, Daniel, who wore old army boots and a pink chiffon babydoll dress, and whose guise was complete with boobs, bracelets, and a scruffy beard. Arty topped that with a snug-fitting, stark-white, sequined jumpsuit; white platform boots; and a matching purse. Heavy foundation gave his complexion a cream-cheese frosting look.

Murray gave them the universal sign to keep their mouths zipped and clapped his hands so loud it was like a shotgun start. "Let's get after it. Three hours till rehearsal."

Arty clucked his tongue and swatted his hand through the air. "That's a nice-looking high horse you're on today, Murray."

Will helped Murray drag the steel ramp from its berth under the truck, pointed to the shed, and gave the big man instructions. "Everything that's not nailed down."

Mitch nudged Sophie's arm. "These guys are unbelievable."

Just the sound of that guy's voice stoked Will's *fed-up* bonfire with a flaming *fuck-you* log. His hands rolled into fists. "What did you say?"

"Daddy!" Keely wound her way between adults with a Barbie in one hand and Annabelle in tow. "Daddy!"

Annabelle looked up the giant beanstalk that was Murray and came to an abrupt stop, her eyes doubling in size.

Will muzzled his bad attitude and knelt to Annabelle's level. He took her little hands in his and steadied himself. "That's my friend Murray. He's helping Daddy clean out the shed. There's lots of heavy stuff we'll be carrying out, and I don't want you girls in the way and getting hurt, so be good and go on up to the house."

Annabelle held up Skipper. "Look what Hoodoody gave me. Keely got Fashist Barbie."

Keely hid the Barbie behind her back and snuggled against Sophie's leg.

Annabelle pointed. "Hoodoody gave Mommy some jewry."

The sight of diamonds and rubies encircling Sophie's wrist might as well have been lighter fluid, and Will's internal temperature spiked.

"Apparently, you *can* buy my wife," he said.

"Girls," Sophie said, her voice shaking. "Please. Up to the house. Everybody, please go back and finish your lunch. I'm so sorry for the interruption. Gram, the kids?"

Grammy and Grampy whisked the kids away and most of the crowd followed. But a dark-faced Mitch Houdini remained and moved toward Will.

"Obviously, " he said, "you're not welcome here."

Sophie tried to intervene. "Mitch, please. I'll handle this."

But Will had already absorbed Houdini's threatening tone. Who was this guy, trying to kick him off his own property? Trying to protect Sophie from him? The kill switch flipped on, and he lunged for Mitch.

Mitch tried to fight back but took a stiff one to the jaw and went down. Will dove on him and they wrestled until Will felt himself yanked upright, the swishing skirt of a babydoll dress brushing one thigh.

Murray and Daniel held both of his arms, and Will didn't know where to look first, at Houdini or the guy in army boots and pink chiffon.

"All right, guys," Daniel said sternly. "Let's take things down a notch."

But Mitch had found a weak spot. He leaped to his feet and jammed a fast, hard fist into Will's unprotected gut.

Sophie screamed as Will doubled over and coughed like he was going to barf.

Arty screamed too, one hand splayed across his besequined chest. "You people are uncivilized!"

Murray and Daniel pulled Will upright again, and glowered.

"That was a low blow, asshole," Murray said.

Mitch danced like a prizefighter, his lower lip bleeding, his fists at the ready. "Oh yeah? Come on, Queenie."

With an invitation like that, Murray and Daniel dropped Will to the ground and pressed forward like Romans on the battlefield, picking up Arty along the way.

Murray's brows pinched and his nostrils flared with the ferocity of a brown bear. "You say Queenie like it's a bad thing."

Arty marched with his chin high and his chest puffed out. "Honey, you don't look like you have enough testosterone to take all three of us."

Daniel's right fist ground a warning into his left palm. "Shall we find out?"

The remaining crowd seemed reluctant to tangle with three pissed-off queens, and Mitch took his army of one back a step. "You've already ruined Sophie's party. Why make things worse?" With a shrug, he blew off his adversaries. "You coming, Sophie?"

"In a minute." She glared at Will with that shame-on-you face she had perfected.

Tess swept closer to him with a vaguely concealed smirk. "Glad to see you've recovered from your stomach virus enough to cause a riot. Not still throwing up, I hope."

Will wiped the sweat and blood off his face and dusted his backside. "Let's just say I'm purging myself of everything."

Two other women remained, staring at Will like he was King crab on a platter. The tall one was Sophie's client, Ruta Khorkina. The other he remembered from the lake, the pro wakeboarder. He gave them a menacing look, and they exited the combat zone as well. Audience dispatched, Will hurried into the shed.

Sophie followed. "You must be so proud of yourself."

Will gave his guys directions, and they began carting things out at a lively pace. The ice chest, the fishing and camping gear, the boating equipment, the old ten-speed, all of it. Murray and Daniel did the heavy lifting and Arty took the job of pointing.

"Are you listening to me, Will?" Sophie stayed on his heels. "We need to talk. I'm not going to let you brush me off."

Will paused and shrugged, squinting at her. "I see your mouth moving and a lot of words are coming out, but…"

Yeah. She did not like that one, and he wasn't going to hang around to get the earful he was certain she had planned for him. He picked up his rusty toolbox and carted it out, up the truck ramp where he dropped it on the grimy plywood floor.

When he started back down, Sophie blocked his path. He never would have guessed her face could turn that particular shade of burgundy, but he'd be damned if he'd wimp out and apologize. Being an A-hole was all part of his charm now.

She gripped his arm and pulled him to the far side of the shed where they couldn't be seen. "We *are* talking about the other night."

He wiped his brow with his sleeve. "We already did that. Breakfast, the morning after, remember? You introduced me to a new term. Ex-sex."

"You're emotional, and it's affecting your judgment."

He scoffed derisively. "Thinking quite clearly for a change. You were right. We screwed each other's brains out, and though I noticed you enjoyed yourself immensely, it didn't mean a damn thing."

He could see her fighting tears. Once they began to flow, they would extinguish any fiery missiles she might want to let fly. That would probably be a good thing.

And then he realized they weren't alone. Mitch Houdini stood near the shed, and by the looks of it, he'd heard more than he bargained for.

Sophie followed Will's line of sight, the shock registering in her gasp. "Mitch."

But he disappeared so fast, Harry Houdini would have been proud.

"Damn you, Will. Why couldn't you leave things alone? You're ruining everything."

"Just doing my part as the shitty husband. Correction. Shitty *ex*-husband. Now you can ride off into the sunset with Hoodoody. Or not."

Her face swelled. He'd seen it before. She wouldn't speak for fear of blubbering. "What?" he pressed, the flames of revenge flickering.

"Never." She started to seethe her old warning.

"Not even if you begged," he said, finishing the sentiment for her.

Her gaze bore into him, and again he fought to be the last one to blink.

"I hate you," she said.

She stalked off, leaving him rooted in a puddle of guilt and an ache in his gut that said she meant it.

"Loved it, Sophie!" Allison called as she leaned out the window of Mitch's Lamborghini. "We need to do this again."

Mitch had practically sprinted to his car with Allison on his heels. In the time it took for the Lambo's scissor doors to rise and fall, he was out of there, and Sophie arrived just in time to smell the burned rubber he left in her cul-de sac.

Her guests filed out, thanking her for a lovely party and the entertainment they didn't even have to pay for. Sophie bore it, unable to hide the humiliation. Tess and Ruta wanted to stay, but Sophie shooed them away. Then she watched out the back windows as Will and his tough-as-designer-nails crew finished clearing out the shed.

As the sun waned and the truck drove away, she walked to the shed and found the floor bare except for her garden tools and a bag of potting soil in the corner. He'd even swept and wiped down the plywood counter where they'd made love.

A warm evening breeze whistled through the transom he'd broken to let in fresh air, lending an eerie emptiness that echoed in the expanse. Everything stored in there was gone, their history wiped clean. She stared at a lone item on the counter, at the dirt-smudged manila seams and the worn metal clasp. She picked up the envelope and dumped its contents on the plywood. Will had signed every page of their divorce decree. So it was done but for the county recorder's stamp.

Under the envelope was a dusty Kodak photo pack. One by one, she pored over snapshots bowing and faded from exposure. Photos of Will and Sophie mugging for the camera before one of his gigs, and backstage afterward, entwined in each other's arms, eyes alight with a zest for each other she was loath to relive. Back when they'd had that groovy kind of love, no act of God could have torn them apart.

A cascade of tears burned her cheeks, and a deepening ache squeezed her chest and made her knees weak. It felt like somebody died, right then and there, and she didn't know whether it was Will who died, or the Sophie who loved him.

Chapter 30

Monday morning, Will spent an hour in the escrow office signing paperwork that allowed him to walk out with a fat proceeds check. After that, he wanted to get far, far away. He rented a Jeep, since the Jag couldn't handle rough back roads, and headed straight for Sophie's. Grampy waited curbside, dressed in a short-sleeved plaid shirt, khaki Bermudas held up by red suspenders, and a canvas hat poked through with dangling metal jigs and feathery lures.

On leaving the cul-de-sac, Will's cell rang. Sophie's name came up, but he let the call go to voicemail and turned off the power.

He made a third stop to pick up Jake, who stood in the open doorway of his condo holding a duffel bag and a fishing pole. He bobbed his head toward the guitar case propped against the doorjamb beside a tackle box.

"Well? What's the word?" Jake said. "Is it finished? You get all five dates in?"

"Screw that," Will said. "I'm done."

"Are you saying you don't want Ursula?"

"I'm saying the last thing on my mind is the damn dating debacle. It's a game—a goddamn game, and I have serious shit on my mind."

Jake turned and locked his door. "Whatever you say, man. It's just that, much as I want to keep Ursula, I know winning her and selling her is your ticket out of neo-poverty."

Will picked up the guitar case that housed his old Stratocaster and took a deep breath as he examined the pocked and weathered surface. His shoulders were tight as guy wire. "I've been so pissed at Sophie, I can't see straight."

Jake patted him on the back. "I get it, man. Chicks."

"You got that right."

"But, dude. Twins? That can't have been so bad. How about some dirty details?"

"No dirty details." Will glanced sideways. "I know. Pathetic. They got me wasted. I have zero memory of anything but humiliating myself on a dance floor. Just as well. Fact is I'm not sure I have another date in me. This little game those girls are playing could not have come at a worse time. And by girls, I mean Sophie and Tess."

"Does that mean you're going to sell the house?"

"The house? Dammit, can't anybody keep a secret?" That was his last-ditch effort to get some fast money in their accounts so they wouldn't lose everything. Will grabbed Jake's tackle box in his other hand and headed for the Jeep.

"Sorry, buddy," he heard Jake say to his back. "Tess was trying to help. She didn't want you to sell the house, so she concocted a way you might not have to. Of course, it would have been nice if she'd told me that before I wagered Ursula."

"I'm not sure who's sneakier," Will said over his shoulder, "my ex or yours."

"Definitely mine. But man, I really thought—"

"You thought giving up Ursula was the ultimate gesture and would convince Tess to give you another shot."

"Can I help it? I dream about the woman and obsess about her while I'm awake. Half the time, she doesn't take my calls. No woman has ever made me work so hard."

Will stopped on the sidewalk and turned. "You're pitiful, man."

"Dude, I've seen the way you look at Sophie."

Will thought how obvious he must have seemed to the whole world, including his wife, who clearly didn't want him. Why had it taken him so long to see it, too? It had all been about him and what he wanted—until it wasn't.

"Looks like we've both lost our man cards. And for what? In the end, not a damn thing. You don't have Tess, and I sure as shit don't have Sophie."

Will tossed Jake's stuff into the back of the Jeep. "Listen, Grampy knows I'm hard up, but he doesn't know about the Ponzi scheme."

"Yeah, I got it. I won't breathe a word."

"I mean it, man. Knowing I took his advice on an investment that leached me clean would kill him."

Hours later, Jake, Grampy, and Will sat in metal-framed lawn chairs on the granite shoreline of Lake Buchanan in the shade of mature oaks and mesquites. Grampy was in fine spirits, having finished his Egg McMuffin, OJ, and a decaf. With shaky determination, he baited his hook and cast his line into the middle of the cove. Will watched him slump back in his chair in time to see a bald eagle soar overhead and disappear behind the granite cliffs.

Grampy adjusted his hat. "I'll be damned. Now that's something to wake up for."

"You have a little more than that to keep you going, I think." Will jerked his line to see if the bait was still on the hook.

"If you mean Eunice, then you got that right. Got to have things that bring you joy to counterbalance the horse manure—and we all know there's plenty of that. It's the dang'dest small things I remember most, though, and I don't want to forget them."

"I hear ya." Will opened his tackle box for a new lure and saw the faded old photo still duct-taped to the inside of the lid. He pulled it free, staring at Sophie's smile as she posed with her catch, a largemouth bass dangling by iridescent gills from her fingers. The memory of that camping trip remained as vivid as if it had happened yesterday. He stared until his fingers curled around the dusty paper. If he crushed it, would he be crushing her?

"I ever tell you about the time Sophie caught that 12-pound bass, Grampy? She lost it, and then it circled back and hit her line again. She actually reeled that sucker in."

Jake sat forward in his chair, his fishing pole propped between his knees. "I remember that. You had the pontoon boat then. And Tess still wanted to jump me."

"Yup, that was the night we made the bet for my Stratocaster." He slid a glance toward Jake. "I lost Ursula, and you lost Tess."

Jake's face twisted into a snarl. "Thanks, buddy, for that little reminder."

"Sure thing." Will refocused on the photo and wagged it at Grampy. "For years after this, she told everybody how she caught the one that got away." Made Will doubly sad now to think that she was the one that got away.

Grampy toyed with the line, giving it a few jerks. "Yep. You fell for our girl hook, line, and sinker, didn't you."

It wasn't a question; the old man knew as well as anybody. Back in the day, Sophie and Will were the "it" couple, and he would have done anything for her. When had he changed?

"Unlike the fish," Grampy continued. "Where you s'pose the bass are today?"

"Sorry, Gramps. I was hoping we'd have better luck."

Grampy watched his rod for movement. "Have to be patient, son."

"Patience is not part of my repertoire. Besides, I'm not sure it pays off."

"After ninety years, I can promise you, it does."

Will peeked at the pale blues and off-whites of the old man's eyes as they scanned the water. "I'll bet I could still learn lots from you, Gramps."

"S'pose so, if it's true we never stop learning."

Mid-morning breezes rippled across the lake and through the cedars overhead, when Will succumbed to asking the question that had plagued him for days. He knew he'd hate himself for it, but what the hell. "So, how is Sophie?"

Grampy shrugged. "A little stressed out, I think. Comes with the territory, though, working single mother and all. But she's a trooper."

"It's what she wanted."

"Yup. Sometimes we get exactly what we ask for." Grampy played with the slack. "And sometimes we just have to take what we've learned the hard way and try to not make the same mistake again."

Will followed Grampy's lead on the fishing wire, letting the bobber drift. Water undulated from the wake of a passing boat outside their cove, and he smelled traces of outboard exhaust and fish that bubbled up from the depths.

"I don't think I learned anything."

Grampy flicked his pole. "Sure you did."

"Well, maybe one thing. Making a living is not the same as making a life." The words out loud sounded like a no-brainer. "I don't know, guess it's cliché, but the idea never hit me before the way it does now."

Grampy pushed out his lower lip. "No, you're right, that's a good lesson."

"How good is it if I learn it too late?"

Grampy's hovering dentures made ticking noises as he worked his tongue around them. "Well, you learned it, and that's the important thing. That's not a judgment, just a point of fact."

"So, what's your advice to the man who learns too little too late? How does that man know what to do? Where does he go next?"

"Hell if I know. Eunice does all my thinking for me." Grampy's smile traveled from his droopy cheeks to his sallow eyes. "But if I were to have an idea of my own, this is what I'd tell that man..."

He adjusted himself in the chair and gazed at the scenery for so long, Will figured he'd lost his train of thought. "What? What would you tell that man?"

"Pardon? Oh, yes. Confucius once said, 'Life is simple, but we insist on making it complicated.'"

Will mulled this over. "I'm not feeling it. Got anything better after ninety years?"

"I don't guess you need a bunch of trite nonsense, do you, son? You know, when I was, oh, twenty-four I guess, I was about to be married—planning to elope, you see, while I was on leave from WWII. I'd been corresponding with my sweetheart for months about it while nearly getting my keister shot off in France. So I was glad to come home and get my bride.

"Well, for something supposed to be top secret, you never saw so many women there to greet me when I walked onto her front porch about sundown. Figured it was a welcoming committee. Soldier home from the battlefield, you know, with news of what it was like over there in Frogtown. But I couldn't have been more wrong. My big sister Hattie pulled me aside after I arrived and said five of my girl's pals were assembled to look me over, and if I passed inspection, they'd give my girl their blessing to marry me. Hattie warned me to be on the lookout for a wild country girl—the coquette type—because she was what you call a tester."

"A tester?"

Grampy tipped his head and cracked a half-smile. "Double agent. Her mission was to flaunt herself and present temptations while the others watched to see how well I behaved. If I caved, then my girl would know I'd be the adulterous sort. If I resisted, then she'd know I'd make a good husband."

"Whoa, that's brutal."

"You're telling me. Those girls were *all* vivacious farm girls. I couldn't tell which one was out to do me in. You'd have thought I was the sultan, much as they doted on me with home cooking and lemonade, and my favorite sweet potato pie."

"So, what happened?"

"Well, I thought it interesting that my girl was nowhere around, but Hattie said that was just part of the deal, that she'd be back around ten to see how I'd fared. Meanwhile, the girls put me through my paces. They played records—Glenn Miller, Bing Crosby, the Andrews Sisters. Boy, I loved that stuff. Nothing like it today."

"And what, you had to fight them off all night?"

"Son, I'd been out in the trenches so long, I thought I'd died and gone to heaven. Danced with every one of them. But as the evening wore on, one did sort of flirt more than the others. Once I realized she must be the ringer, I figured she was gonna get me in trouble because she was a doll. So I stayed away from her, but she kept butting her way in, trying to get in the middle of things, you know." He began to laugh, so much that he coughed.

"She was hard to resist, I'll tell you that. By ten o'clock, I got to thinking it was too bad I was getting married, because she really was the most interesting woman I'd ever met. Gorgeous eyes, long wavy hair—curvy in all the right places, if you get my meaning. She was the kind o' dame a man'd go into the poor house for; the kind who, if you weren't careful, would have you going AWOL or shooting some drunk in her defense. Still, I figured the girl I was already betrothed to was the wiser choice. I'd known her since high school, and she had a reputation for being reliable and levelheaded. Sweet and adorable—you know the type. Girl like her would be with me for the long haul, give me children and a good life."

"Do you regret it? You're coming up on your sixty-sixth anniversary now, right?"

He grinned broadly. "No regrets. I said to hell with Marilyn; that was her name, my high school sweetheart. I chose the wild country girl—that very night in fact, and I never regretted my choice for a second. Life with Eunice has never been dull."

Leave it to the old man. "So you took a chance, and it turned out to be the right move."

"I followed my heart. That's all you can do. Turns out, I was the last one to know that Marilyn had run off with another man and didn't have the nerve to tell me. Hattie knew it all along. In her crazy way, she was helping a homesick soldier choose a suitable replacement. Kind of easing me into thinking I might could find a better deal with one of her other friends. Maybe you can identify? Hear you got one date left. Oughta be a good'n."

Will played it close to the vest, stared at the rocky shoreline beneath his sneakered feet. "It's not quite the same thing, Grampy."

Grampy patted Will's arm. "I could have pined and cried over the girl who jilted me for another guy; but instead, I took the opportunity right in front of me and never looked back. I say, life is too short, misery is optional, and what's meant to be *always* finds a way." And then he chuckled, his bony shoulders shaking. "Always room for a good cliché. But truth is a man has to find the courage to follow his heart toward something new and different. Something better. For sure, in time, a better place awaits us all. Now hand me some more worms."

Sophie sat in a window booth at Magnolia Café staring at the tennis bracelet on her wrist. In the ambient light, it sparkled and clashed with the kitschy plastic table coverings. The waiter placed bowls of warm chips and cold salsa in the center of the table, along with a large glass of hibiscus tea so fragrant she could smell it before the icy liquid hit her parched taste buds.

The waiter with tattoos snaking up both arms, all the way to his ears, pulled a pad from his back pocket. "You ready to order?"

Magnolia always felt like a different world, with its cast of mega-inked, over-pierced, and dread-locked help. So wrong, yet so right. So Austin. Any other day, Sophie would have ordered the Cabo San Lucas, with chicken breast, chipotle, spinach, mushrooms, and lemon cream sauce. But she was too nervous to eat.

As the waiter left, Mitch slid onto the red vinyl bench across from her. She had hoped he would show, since she left messages that she'd be waiting if he wanted to talk; yet his sudden appearance was unnerving. She'd needed more time to mentally prepare.

"I guess you got my messages," she said.

Mitch leaned on his forearms, looking across the table at her, then down at his hands. A little fidgety. A lot uncomfortable. "Yes. I'm sorry I didn't call back, but I had to think things through. Your situation is complicated, and my life is, well, simpler than it might appear."

He shook his head and sighed. His whole demeanor seemed clenched, and Sophie got the sinking feeling that she'd ruined everything. She braced herself.

"I almost didn't come," he said. "No matter how I look at it, I jumped the gun. I suspected you weren't quite finished with Will, but I let my feelings get ahead of me. So, that's my fault. No excuses. I think we may have rushed into it. I hope you know, I never meant to push you."

"No, I'm finished with Will. I just... our one night was a mistake, and it isn't going to happen again." She measured the words as she said them. "So, I was hoping that you and I could pick up where we left off."

His eyes locked onto hers, but he didn't speak.

"Thing is, Will is my kids' father, so he will be in my life. Somehow. I don't even know how anymore. But we've both accepted that we're done. So, maybe you and I could, you know, date some more, and—and see where it goes. Take it slow."

He squeezed her hands. "People only say they want to take it slow when they doubt they can make it work. I should know. I've been a runner my whole life. But, I haven't wanted to run too far from you."

"Maybe it doesn't mean anything, these stops and starts, just a few bumps getting off the ground. I'd like to see us move forward. If you still want to. See how far it goes."

And now his gaze bore deeply into her, as if second-guessing what he wanted to say. He flashed a tentative smile, seemed to struggle, and then shrugged. "Hey, all the great love stories have a little tragedy in them, don't they?"

Sophie gulped. She felt a deep and abiding *like* for him. She hoped theirs would be a love story, but she was too raw to think that far ahead.

Mitch bridged the weighty gap in conversation. "You're special to me. You know that, right? I actually don't think I've ever been so attracted to a woman."

He rose and moved to her side of the booth and held her face in his hands. "I'm sorry if I was an ass about your ex. I got jealous and wasn't sure what to do with all that green stuff bouncing around inside me. So, if you'll forgive me, and if what you say is true, then what do you say we leave the past behind and start fresh? No more looking back."

Sophie's chest swelled, and she smiled into his hopeful eyes. And then they sealed their venture with a deep kiss.

And in that moment, it felt right.

Wednesday evening, Will stumbled through the front door lugging his duffel bag and equipment. He'd spent three days with Grampy and Jake on the banks of Lake Buchanan, cooling off and getting his head on straight. Now on returning to his musty motel room, the measure of his success was up for debate.

He turned on his phone to find a slew of messages, the first one from Sophie.

"I don't know why you didn't come in the house to pick up Grampy. I thought we declared a truce last week. I mean, if we could get past... our little mistake in the shed... The kids want to see you. Take good care of Grampy."

The second message was from Sophie too.

"Why aren't you answering your phone?" He heard her breathing and then, "I've been thinking." A few more beats. "Look, I'm sorry about what happened. Call me back about Friday's party on the lake."

She was determined; he'd give her that. He pounded the delete button and listened to the next message.

"Hey, Will. It's Edwina."

"And Jessica."

"We need to talk to you. Call us back."

"Yeah, call us back, sexy man. We don't like waiting."

Laughter. "We have a surprise, Will, but I can't tell you about it over the phone."

"Yeah, we have to show you in person. You're gonna like it."

The Marshall Twins could immobilize his fight-or-flight response faster than a stun gun. He stared at the paisley drapes of his motel room, trying to imagine what sort of surprise the Marshall twins might have in store. It could only mean trouble.

He thought of Grampy's story and wondered if getting into trouble would be such a bad thing after all. Maybe Sophie was right. He'd been playing it safe for too long.

The next message was from the dean at UT. They'd had a long conversation about Will putting his PhD to use, though the last thing he wanted to do was teach. He just didn't feel the fire for it that he once did. But as it turned out, they didn't have a place for him anyway.

The most surprising message came from his old boss at Waterloo, offering him a job. New division, different team of workers. And his whole body shuddered with relief in the knowledge that he could be earning steady income again. He could afford all the things he'd had on hold—particularly his new toy at the marina awaiting one sloppy John Hancock on the dotted line and a fat down payment. He'd put it off long enough.

Why then did his gut coil like a rusty spring at the idea of returning to the old grind?

Another message from Sophie added a new dimension to his exasperation.

"You still owe me, Will. And Tess, if she loses this bet. You have to follow through to the last date. She can't win Ursula if you don't go on all five, and that means you can't win Ursula either. You're not selling my house. We expect your payback in full. Friday. Date Number Five. Ten o'clock. Party barge at Hurst Harbor. Call me."

She abso-frickin-lutely had to be kidding.

Chapter 31

With the start of summer, most of Sophie's clients were focused on vacations, so she took advantage of the breathing room to immerse herself in marketing and activities for the kids (including team mom for the Austin Jaguars), Grammy's tutoring stint at the school, her renewed relationship with Mitch, and trying to wrangle some sort of response from Will, who hadn't even returned her call.

Okay, maybe it was eight texts, five calls, and three messages. But who's counting?

Two nights in a row, Grammy had grilled fresh fish for dinner—catch of the day, courtesy of Grampy by virtue of some unnamed fishin' hole. Like a blood brother under sworn oath, Grampy kept their expedition hush-hush, and not even Grammy's practiced needling had loosened his lips: "Come on, wanksta, you know you wanna tell your mama what's crackalackin, if you know what's good for you."

Meanwhile, Sophie and Mitch enjoyed long lunches getting reacquainted and an after-hours drink at the Oasis, overlooking the lake while the sun went down. He dropped the jealousy business and made every attempt to woo her at the more languid pace she wanted, which helped her reconnect with the Mitch she'd crushed on from the beginning. And that gave her the courage and fortitude to take the one step she'd put off—dropping off the signed divorce papers at her attorney's office.

She needed the closure. Desperately. Divorce meant a true end with Will, a true beginning with Mitch, and a more adventurous life that deserved her full attention. She was so ready for it.

Sophie and Tess were the first to arrive at the two-story barge on Friday morning for Mitch's annual company party, which this year he would not be attending. He'd gone to New York on business with Allison, who was no doubt out of her mind with glee. Sophie dressed in a one-piece and cover-up, buoyed by not having to compete with his protégé.

She and Tess introduced themselves to the boat captain and his first mate and found a spot on the upper deck where they could gaze beyond the marina at the lush greenery and low-rising mountains. The sun promised to be a scorcher in a clear blue sky, with occasional gusty winds ripping through the Highland Lakes chain.

Tess leaned against the rails. "Honey, can I be honest? Your Fresh Factor is teetering between five and six. You have stuffed pitas for eyes. Have you been sleeping on your face?"

"Sleeping? What's that?"

"It's that thing you do with your pillow every night. What's up with you?"

Sophie hesitated to say. The story was too long, too tragic, too epically frustrating.

"Remember what I went through when I divorced Jake?" Tess said. "What a blithering moron I became? And I didn't even put him through the dating-another-woman thing. But you'll bounce back. Will can go on Date Number Five, and I'll win the Strat from Jake—after which we'll do some major celebrating—and then Will can win the Strat from me and sell the damned thing instead of your house, and everybody will live happily ever after." Tess patted Sophie's shoulder. "Right?"

In the next breath, Tess had shifted her attention to the new guy walking down the pier. "That is one hot and spicy Paco, with just the right touch of tang."

Sophie admired him too. Armand Andrade, whom everybody called Paco, was in his twenties, underwear-model handsome, and with no shirt and quite the display of eight-pack abs, no woman breathing could take her eyes off him.

"I'm going down to mingle," Tess said. "Don't go jumping into the lake without me."

More people arrived on the barge. Real estate agents, managers, and assistants. And Ruta. She navigated the steep-pitched steps to the top deck with ease, accompanied by Jimmy, her wagging tail in designer swim trunks and a T-shirt that showcased his rock-hard physique.

Sophie thought, if nothing else, the eye candy was pretty sweet today. She greeted Ruta with air kisses. "How was Belize?"

"How else? Fantastico." Ruta took a seat in a cushy lounger and stretched out her pencil legs. She wore a gold-and-aqua print maillot, matching pareo from her signature collection, and a wide-brimmed hat. From a new Kayfuyu bag, she pulled a bottle of cocoa butter. "Tell me, darlingk, my date eez showing up?"

Sophie took the lounger beside Ruta and pulled her hair into a ponytail. "I left him messages, but in case you forgot about our disastrous run-in at my house last Sunday, he may never speak to me again."

"I don't forget." Ruta donned rhinestone-studded sunglasses in the shape of cat eyes. "At least one good thing. Allison eez with Meetch. She can't irritate you, she's not here."

Sophie gave her a knuckle bump. "Here's to a nice, lazy day in the sun."

The boat began to move and Sophie figured they were getting underway, when a horn sounded three times and she heard a man shout, "Hold up!"

Sophie and Ruta stood and looked over the railing to see a bright yellow ski boat with a flat deck and a high tow bar on its back end drifting alongside the barge.

"This party can't leave without me," Mitch said. "I'm paying for it."

He jumped to the barge and shook hands with people as Allison Summers followed behind him. In his trademark Aloha button-down, khaki shorts, and shades, he spotted Sophie and waved up at her.

Moments later, he had scaled the steep staircase to the upper deck. "Surprised?" he said, hugging it out first with Ruta.

"Yes," Ruta said. "Pleasantly. How was trip to Beeg Apple?"

"Highly productive." He half-grinned, half-leered, an indicator that deals had been struck for obscene amounts of money. Mitch never worked on the cheap.

The moment his eyes landed on Sophie, Mitch's face lit up like the North Star with that grin he seemed to reserve especially for her. He pulled her in to a tight embrace and kissed her full on the mouth in front of everyone—a first official public display of affection.

"I couldn't wait to see you," he said. "And miss this shindig? No way."

Sophie felt good being in his arms, even if she also sometimes felt inadequate. They were so new, they had no messy history, no litany of heartbreaks, no lovers' anguished pushing and pulling, no bittersweet kissing and making up—well, maybe a little. But she thought he was right when he'd said all great love stories had an element of tragedy. This was their beginning—hers and Mitch's—and she intended to make it a good one.

"I missed you too," she said.

"And don't think I showed up empty-handed. Since I know you're always up for adventure, I brought the parasail boat."

Sophie's eyes inflated to the size of full-blown parachutes. Plunging from the sky was not the element of tragedy she had in mind. "Oh, no, no, no. Heights and me, we don't mix. You know this. I get dizzy and panic and cling to people's ankles. I don't go too near our office windows. You remember rescuing me from the tree house in my yard, right?"

He clasped her hands and turned on his calm, confident motivational speaker voice. "We're leaving the past behind, remember? Today, we're conquering your fear of falling."

She had a feeling he referred to more than her fear of heights. Much as she wanted to appear adventurous, dangling from the clouds had the potential to turn her into a stark-raving banshee. *Nobody* wanted to see that. Just the thought made her wish she'd brought extra underwear. She mentally exercised the word "no," but the only response that came out was a peep.

Mitch moved closer, his breath on her neck like the pleasurable pulses of her vibrator. So nice, so sexy, until he said, "I'll be right there with you. I promise. You're more fearless than you know."

His plan might hold lake water, but she'd have to muster a whole lot more courage to leave her fear of heights behind.

Mitch let his hands linger as he pulled from her, then turned and reignited the enthusiasm he was known for, his fist pumping the air. "This is going to be one helluva day, people."

Allison poked her head above Mitch's entourage and delivered a sneer before vanishing into the throng. Sophie glanced about to see who might have been the recipient, but she couldn't help thinking it was meant for her.

Ruta stood next to her, chortling. "Looks like quiet, lazy day just go to hell."

The hulking barge puttered through the no-wake zone, and Sophie began to get her sea legs, shifting her weight to accommodate the rocky swells. Two additional crewmen followed behind in the yellow parasail boat. Every time Sophie caught sight of the obnoxious craft, she went on alert, much like a recoiled cat with her paw raised to strike the family Roomba.

Thirty minutes later, they reached a cove nestled between steep limestone cliffs that sloped into a flat, rocky bank dotted by scrub cedar. Sophie could see a covered pavilion a hundred feet offshore with six picnic tables and a big smoker where caterers busily prepared lunch. Once the captain had guided the barge to the shoreline and dropped anchors, the on-board crew laid a wide plank to dry land and most everyone headed toward the shady pavilion.

Sophie and Ruta met Tess downstairs and decided first things first: girl float. Into the cool water they went, each carting a pastel Styrofoam noodle.

They drifted from the barge, performing various balancing acts on their flotation tubes, when Sophie saw Allison execute a perfect "ten" jackknife from the top deck. In a string bikini, she made hardly a splash and emerged from the water like a model for a Caribbean cruise commercial, water cascading in slow motion around her tawny breasts.

"If she sinks her talons into our new Paco," Tess said with the resolve of a Doberman, "I will personally pull them out with pliers."

"Better get out your toolbox then," Sophie said.

Tess scowled her agreement. "So, how's it going with Mitch?"

Sophie smiled dreamily. "Good."

"Good, as in I'm in love? Or Good, I'm horny and satisfied?"

Sophie moved to deflect a classic Tess Inquisition. "Good *good*. We're starting over, dating and taking it slow." She shrugged nonchalantly. "Seeing where it goes."

"People only say they're taking it slow to see where it goes when they have zero confidence it will work."

"Well, he likes me, and I like him. That works for me."

"How anyone sits on these things?" Ruta's frustration with finding a comfortable position on her noodle was punctuated by Russian mutterings in a tone that indicated their unfitness for polite company.

"Oh, for Pete's sake, give me *something*," Tess said, bobbing on a pink floaty.

Sophie held her breath, her teeth on edge, teetering on indecision like she teetered on her noodle. Right now, things were tenuously wonderful. Plus, there was Ruta, sloshing in the water. Did she want the Russian Princess to know her secret? The emotional dam was close to bursting.

"Well, I guess, there is... *something*."

Tess's whole demeanor glinted with curiosity. "Keep talking."

"A few days before the barbecue..."

"Go on."

"Will and I, well, we were alone in the gazebo. And we called a truce. For the kids' sakes. And we, you know, we had a couple beers together and we made jokes and..."

"And you did it."

"He told you?"

"I've known you for two-and-a-half decades. You think I can't sense this stuff? You both acted supremely weird last weekend."

Ruta finally took note. "How they were acting?"

"I can't believe you're just telling me now," Tess said.

"It gets worse. Before Mitch left the barbecue, he overheard Will and me talking about what we did."

Ruta was about to come off her noodle. "What you did?"

"Ah," Tess said. "That explains his burned rubber in your driveway."

"It gets *worser*." Sophie's chest tightened. "Will thought it meant something."

"Okay, that's it." Ruta kicked in the water to get closer. "What it means?"

Tess narrowed her eyes. "Well, didn't it? Mean something?"

"No. It was ex-sex."

"With your husband?" Ruta said. "How thees happen?"

"We got locked in the shed. By accident. We were stuck, and one thing led to another. I mean, it was purely, completely, *obviously* accidental."

"Of course it was," Tess said. "What else are two people who don't want to be together supposed to do, besides bone each other the minute they're alone—by accident?"

Ruta's face was awash in fascination. "You got the chutzpah. Thees why I like you so much. You are boning two men at same time?"

Sophie shrank at the idea. "Mitch and I haven't actually done any *boning*."

"Well, that explains a few things," Tess said. "But tell me, how many *accidents* with Will are we talking here?"

"Just one night." Sophie squeezed her eyes and held up four fingers.

"Four times? You mean four orgasms?"

Sophie shrugged by way of admission.

Tess's face filled with a cheesy grin. "Slut puppy. And where do we stand on regrets?"

Sophie shook her head, to herself as much as Tess. She didn't want to dissect it again. "It just happened. Innocent and natural and spontaneous."

"Eez worst kind," Ruta lamented.

"Thing is, my stomach's been a mess, and... I don't..." Sophie closed her eyes as she let the words trip off her tongue. "I don't... think... I do regret it."

"Pressure eez off," Ruta said. "No expectations. When I am in New York last week, I do the ex-sex with Griffin. I do the blow job, and I never like that before."

Tess's eyebrows converged over her nose. "You never gave him a BJ before?"

"Sure, sometime. Just never the swallow." Ruta's face contorted and she gagged. "See? Even thought makes me to retch, but for some reason, I let heem do eet." She shook her head and waved her bejeweled fingers. "But I admit, sex was better than ever."

Sophie contemplated the rationale that no expectations equaled better sex and decided Ruta was probably right. She rolled over on the noodle, relieved to have confessed.

"So, who's it going to be?" Tess said. "Mitch or Will? Or someone else?"

Sophie stabilized on her floaty. The wind strafed her wet skin, inciting chill bumps that stood her hairs on end. "Why would I go backward?"

"You tell me. On the one hand you have dashing and adventurous and all the things you've been dreaming of in Mitch Houdini, and on the other hand, all those things Will Camden does that make you crazy, right?"

Sophie stared into the shoreline and adjusted her sunglasses. "You know, I like Mitch so much. He's giving and exciting and, yes, adventurous. And he dances like Fred Astaire. He radiates so much energy, it's contagious. I want to be more, do more when I'm around him. Thing is, the fast lane he lives in is attractive, but it demands an exhausting game face and the sacrifice of my family time, not to mention a resilient liver. I'm just not sure I'm cut out for his lifestyle."

Tess prompted with her fingers. "And Will? How does he compare?"

Sophie watched the fluffy clouds drift overhead and squinted when the sun peeked out. Mitch was the big brass ring—emphasis on the *big*—and Will...

"Will plays beautiful music, and he sings to me. He builds tree houses for my kids, and he does dishes and tells hilarious Famous Books Never Read jokes. He makes me laugh. He makes pyramids out of salt dough and cooks migas with my grandmother and fishes with my grandfather, and he makes everyone in my family feel important and alive."

Ruta gazed dreamily in the direction Sophie did. "Don't forget the orgasms."

"And he still loves you," Tess said.

Sophie swiveled toward her. "No. He just hates losing to Mitch."

"Maybe. But I know you're holding on to all the old hurts—"

"He quit fighting for us, Tess."

Ruta had shut up, and now she bobbed on her floaty in the tense space beside them.

"And now he's changed. Don't you think?" Tess said. "You wanted to teach him a lesson, and you did. He is not the same man he was before you guys split."

Sophie thought about the last four weeks Will Camden had lived under her roof. About all his activities with the kids, *volunteering* to handle family responsibilities. The lively, challenging, sometimes confounding conversations. His irreverent sense of humor that left her shaking her head, and at the same time giggling, even hours later. Their passing encounters around the house. The extended glances she would deny happened. The small thrills she'd get when she knew he was home, especially when they occupied the same room. The stirring she felt in her core when she remembered viscerally his naked body next to hers in the shed. And the ache—oh, the ache that sat right in the middle of her chest whenever she thought about him. Was she ready for the finality of losing him? Forever? Did she have a choice?

The tweaks of emotion backed up on her. "I— I think I— Tess—" She grabbed Tess's arm and squeezed.

"What? Are you all right? What is it?"

Sophie strangled a sob, held her chest, struggled to breathe. "There's something wrong with me. I mean... dammit. *Dammit.* Omigod. Tess, I miss that son of a bitch!"

Tess busted out laughing.

Allison shouted from the barge, and all eyes shot toward her as she performed some kind of twisty flip off the upper deck. On surfacing, her audience clapped and shouted for an encore, but she swam away from them—and toward Sophie.

Sophie could only watch in dismay as Allison freestyled closer and closer, faster than a Great White. *Like Sharknado.*

Allison stole a stray noodle as she treaded water. "Having fun, ladies?"

Ruta fingered her chin. "You are really at home in the water, no?"

"I love it," Allison said. "I learned to swim when I was three months old."

"How nice for you," Tess said.

Jimmy called out from the barge, holding Ruta's cell phone in the air. "Ms. Khorkina. It's your agent. Should I take a message?"

Ruta slipped off her noodle. "I take call. Carry on, girls."

"Gosh, I need a pee break," Tess said. "Sophie, let's head in."

"You go." Sophie wanted nothing to do with the crowds. She needed to think.

Watching Ruta and Tess swim toward the barge, she corralled a vacated noodle with her feet, then closed her eyes in attempt to locate some Zen spot where she could make sense of things. And ignore Allison.

She juggled two concepts, both terrifying: epiphanies and petrification. Was she so afraid of getting hurt again that she gravitated back to the familiar?

Well, that was absurd; Will had hurt her enough for a lifetime.

She felt Allison's eyes on her, silently pressing for conversation. There would be no epiphanies with Allison around.

Just as well. This was not a day to be consumed by the man who was her past. Not when the man of her future was across the water. Her eyes found Mitch on land at the pavilion doing his life-of-the-party thing.

"So, any new listings this week?" Allison wagged her legs in the water as she balanced atop her noodle.

Here we go. "Why do you ask?"

"Figured since Mitch was out of town and you got Ruta handed to you on a platter—after you sabotaged me with your eel cream—you might want to get a listing on your own."

Sophie dug deep for her cool. "That cream was from Ruta's line. I could not have known you were allergic. Ruta decided she'd rather work with me than you, and Mitch told me he explained all that to you. So, what is your real problem, Allison?"

"You're my problem."

"You know, I'm not the rookie you met a year ago. I know where I fit and how I can make a good living, with or without Mitch throwing a client my way. I can do this." And she realized for the first time that it was true. "Not you or anybody else has the power to change that. Guess that bothers the hell out of you."

Allison looked on Sophie with mock pity. "Hardly."

"Doesn't matter. My deals are not your business. *Nothing* about my life is your business, including Mitch. Because that's what this is really about, isn't it? You don't like that I'm seeing Mitch."

Allison shoved herself in reverse, splashing water in Sophie's face. But she didn't go away. Instead, she snatched Tess's pink noodle out of the lake and bopped Sophie's shoulder with it. "I like *that.*"

What the? Sophie flinched when Allison swung again, making hard enough contact to leave red marks. "Are you kidding me?"

She reined in Ruta's abandoned noodle and returned the swipe at Allison's shoulder.

Bop! Now it's on.

Allison retaliated, and the two exchanged frenzied noodle strikes, each bop stinging more than the last. But Sophie couldn't deny, with her adrenaline pumping, how great it felt to unleash her frustration.

"I didn't know how much I wanted to hit you, Allison. I should thank you. "

Allison grunted as she batted Sophie's arm hard. "You are such an amateur."

The wet Styrofoam smarted, and Sophie almost fell off her noodle. She detested this witch, and worse, being the klutzy underdog with spotty confidence. But she didn't dare whine about it. That would be immature. So instead, she popped a hot one across Allison's ear.

Allison volleyed three back-to-back smacks so solid, Sophie's sunglasses flew off and she keeled sideways into the drink. The impact flushed lake water into one ear, and she snorted a tankful up her nose before coming to the surface.

Allison drifted in the water with a wicked smirk and red impact splotches on her bulging biceps, the noodle in her hands poised for another strike. "You can't compete with me." *Thwack!* "I give you a couple months clinging to Mitch's coattails." *Thwack!* "And then he'll get tired of you and you'll go back to your bit part on the PTA."

With the thwacking out of control, Sophie retreated underwater, but she rose in a fury, gasping for air, and seized Allison's foot. She twisted it sharply, forcing Allison off balance and prying her off the noodle. Allison hissed, plunged into the water, and quickly reemerged.

Face to face with only their heads above water, Sophie wondered how long this could go on. Allison had turned schoolyard bully, and Sophie had unwittingly gone along. But now, she just felt pity.

Sorta sad. *Sorta* being the operative word.

"I'm not trying to compete with you, Allison. I'm trying to find my way. At least I'm trying. Right? Isn't that what counts?"

Allison's glare only intensified. "Try counting your delusions. The most important one being that you could *ever* tame Mitch."

"Why, because you tried? And failed?"

"Is that what you think? That I failed? That I'm just hanging out with Mitch because we're professional *pals*?" She punctuated her invective with a wicked laugh, smacking right where Sophie lived all too often, in the heart of insecurity. "How dense are you?"

Allison swam off at an Olympic gold medal pace, and Sophie's addled brain backstroked across time, reconciling all of Mitch's business trips with his protégé's.

What. The. Hell.

She squinted in the sunlight at people on the barge. Tess flirted outrageously with Paco. Jimmy watched his chatty Russian Princess from the bulkhead. Mitch entertained like he was on stage, and people listened raptly.

At the iron clang of a chuckwagon bell, people headed for the pavilion. Aromatic smoke from the barbecue tweaked Sophie's stomach, but trying to eat and be sociable dropped to the bottom of her to-do list, far beneath the barely containable urge to scream.

She left Allison behind and swam to the barge, wandered the lower deck under ineffectual ceiling fans, and fished a soda from the ice chest. She popped the top and took a long, refreshing swig, leaning against the rail and contemplating Allison's cryptic message.

"There you are," Mitch said. He pressed himself behind her and rocked her in his arms, planting a kiss on her shoulder. "Did I mention how beautiful you look today?"

Sophie turned in his embrace, mulling the best, most tactful way to ask. "Have you been honest with me, Mitch? About us? About Allison?"

He hesitated, cocked his head. "What about Allison?"

"Your protégé implied that maybe..." She steadied her voice, reluctant to make accusations. "Am I the only woman—I mean, I know we never said we were exclusive. We haven't even been seeing each other that long, but—"

"I'm not seeing anyone else, if that's what you're asking."

Thank god, Sophie thought, followed by, *It would make things easier if you were*. Wait. Where did *that* come from?

"To be honest," he went on, pressing her hands between his. "I'd like to be exclusive. I was speaking from the heart when I said I wanted you more than any woman. It's crazy, I know, but I like the man I am when I'm around you. You make me feel grounded."

She stared in wonder. *What a gorgeous, sexy hunk*, her libido growled. *I'm not sure what I want*, lamented her heart. But her head squawked, *Man, I wish he'd be quiet!* He was only confusing her more.

"And I'll tell you something else from the heart. Allison and I had a very brief relationship long ago, but it never went anywhere—for a reason. I promise you, other than as a friend and business associate, Allison doesn't mean a thing to me."

Allison popped through the archway behind them. "I don't mean anything?"

Mitch whirled around. "Allison, this is a private conversation."

Allison was a caricature of ready-to-burst, blood-red facial features and steam shooting out her ears. "Fuck you both."

She stormed off, with Mitch calling after her. "Really, Allison?"

Ruta and Tess materialized in her place.

"Everything okay?" Tess asked.

Sophie felt stunned, it had all happened so fast. The sound of a boat motoring through the water nearly went unnoticed, until she saw people from the pavilion trekking back to the barge to check out the commotion.

"Who eez that?" Ruta asked, pointing.

A blue-and-white Ski Nautique slowed and idled into the cove. Its wake, two hundred feet out, rocked the barge. The driver seemed to search for a familiar face while two delicate creatures with dark, flowing hair and plump yellow life vests appeared beside him. Their skinny arms jutted from the vests like twigs, and their tiny hands squeezed the gunwales.

Ruta positioned herself breasts-to-shoulder with Sophie in the shade of the main deck. "You were wrong, darlingk. He eez here."

Sophie's heart stopped. *Will? And her kids?*

Mitch's voice was a growl. "What's he doing here?"

"Don't pop a vein," Tess said. "He's here because of Ruta."

"I am fifth date," Ruta said, clapping her hands. "I love the leetle ski boats. Look at heem with his shirt off. Oh my, he did the manscape."

"Holy—" Mitch knotted his fists. "Are you kidding me?"

Will motored closer to the barge.

"He's here," Sophie said. "He's got our kids, and he's... *driving a boat.*"

"Just like the old days," Tess said. "That's the big purchase he's had on hold till his escrow closed. That's why he ran into you at the marina last month. You didn't know?"

"Ahoy!" Ruta shouted, waving and nudging Sophie into Mitch. "What I tell you?"

Sophie regained her balance and nudged Ruta back. No offense to Ruta, but her ex-knight had arrived on his steed.

Her kids waved. "Hi, Mommy! Look at Daddy's new boat!"

The inboard/outboard idled thirty feet away as Will made eye contact with her. Or did he have Mitch in his sights?

Mitch glowered with his fists clenched at sides.

Then someone dove off the upper deck. Someone in a string bikini.

Allison came up for air and swam through the chop to the Nautique. She hoisted herself on the teak platform and took Will's hand as he helped her into the boat.

Sophie watched, dumbfounded. "No. Way."

"Oh my," Ruta said. "What she's up to?"

Will took a seat behind the driver's wheel and put the boat into gear. As they motored away, Allison turned and blew Sophie an exaggerated kiss.

"Omigod," Sophie said. "He thinks Allison is his date."

Ruta's face turned a bloated shade of Russian red.

"Hate to tell you," Tess said. "But your husband just fell into a penis flytrap."

Chapter 32

Mitch looked relieved. Without Will to rain on his parade, he could concentrate on making sure everyone had a good time, including Sophie. It was one of the things that made him a great catch. He cared about his people.

And Sophie, in that moment, couldn't have cared less.

"Hey, this is some party, right?" Mitch said to the gathering crowd. His transplanted Texan twang coincided with the level of his hospitality. "We have plenty of beer and soda in the coolers, and the caterers have key lime pie, so y'all be sure and get you a slice. First mate has the ski boat ready for anybody who wants to try parasailing." Then he yelled to the boat's captain. "Turn up the tunes, and let's get this party on its feet. Bada-bing!"

A bunch of the guys echoed Mitch's battle cry.

"That's what I like to hear. Bada-bing!" Then louder, "BADA-BING!"

People shuffled back inland to the pavilion while Prince's "Let's Go Crazy" blared over the speakers, and Mitch pulled Sophie aside. "You ready to parasail?"

Sophie stiffened. "I don't think today's the day to conquer anything but a few beers and a fajita. But don't let that stop you."

"Nonsense," he said, rubbing her shoulder. Deliberately lightening the mood, she suspected. He beamed like a boy with a crush, as if he couldn't help himself. "Come with me, have a bite to eat. Let me hold your hand."

"You go ahead. I'll join you in a few."

She saw the indecision in his face, heard the disappointment in his voice.

"Okay. After lunch then. You and me." He pointed to the sky and waggled his eyebrows. "Parasail time."

"Oh, yippee," she said, like Eeyore.

With his buddies calling from shore, he kissed her mouth, left her with a reassuring smile, and headed across the plank. She watched him go, giving oxygen to the short months she'd dated him and the nine months of flirtation before that. He'd romanced his way right into her heart; and by the looks of it, she had captured his. And still she felt sick inside.

Allison had just taken off with her husband—and her children—and Sophie was stuck on the barge, dead in the water.

"Well?" Tess said, standing at Sophie's side. "Whatchya gonna do about that?"

"I know what *I* do," Ruta said under her breath. "I break her legs. I know people."

"That's a little harsh," Tess scolded. "Unless you're Sophie."

Sophie paid little attention to their chatter. Her chest was cramping. "This is disastrous."

"Hoochie gonna get someting from the orgasm guy," Ruta said, her face sour. "I tink we know what."

Sophie stared at Ruta blankly, her heart flip-flopping. "That's not helping."

"You have that can of hairspray look," Tess said. "Under pressure and ready to spurt if pressed. You've got a decision to make, don't you?"

"Do I, Tess? Today?" Her best friend's face had that piteous How-could-you-not? stare that lingered long enough for Sophie to get out of her own way. "This is so... unexpected."

She looked back toward Mitch, hanging out on shore, catching her eye and nodding an I'm-thinking-about-you hello, tweaking her emotions anew.

She turned toward Will's boat as it motored off. Her daughters sat in the front playpen in bulky life vests that dwarfed their little faces. Sophie wanted to be there to protect them. They were in good hands with Will, but a certified viper lurked in their midst.

As the boat shrank in the distance, Sophie could see Allison standing with one knee in the passenger seat, her long, tan back facing the cove, her lithe frame barely covered by the string bikini. Then she moved right next to Will and spoke into his ear, and as the boat picked up speed, so did the drumbeat of Sophie's resolve.

"Oh, *hell* no." *What to do, what to do.*

She had zero choices. Zero.

Save one.

She turned to the driver of the parasail boat, a rail-thin, lake-rat of guy with hairy feet and wing-like ears, a scruffy gray beard, and beige teeth that spiked in all directions.

"You," she barked. "I need your boat."

The lake rat curled his upper lip. "Say what?"

"Your boat. I need you to follow that other boat that just left." He gaped at her as if she'd spoken gibberish. "*Now* would be good."

"No, ma'am, it wouldn't. My boss'll fire me if he sees me cruisin' the lake without a paying customer in the saddle."

"Saddle? You mean that... that parachute thingy?"

"Yes."

"But I don't like heights."

Lake Rat screwed up one side of his face so he could hardly see out of one eye. "Well now, I don't like my boat being hijacked."

"You're crazy if you think I'm going up in that thing."

"Then no can do, sister."

The thought of Allison pawing her husband and breathing on her children had Sophie's need to fight clashing with her need for flight. She gave one last look as Will floored his new boat and the prow rose above the water.

Her panic escalated when Lake Rat adjusted his baseball cap and scooped the air with one arm, inviting Sophie aboard. Five minutes later, the parasail boat idled somewhere outside the party cove. Lake Rat strapped Sophie into a helmet, life vest, and harness on the launch deck of the big yellow boat.

"Hurry up," she said, the engine grumbling below her feet.

"Don't get your panties in a wad."

"But they're getting away."

Lake Rat's co-pilot had a shirtless barrel belly, a red bandana around his neck, and dark spots between his teeth at the gum line. He finished his pre-flight inspection and stuck a pen in Sophie's hand, along with a clipboard holding a document that said *Waiver*.

"Sign here. Just a precaution so we're not held liable for stuff."

Sophie's tunnel-visioned mission came into question as she blinked a numbing understanding of "not held liable for stuff."

She didn't think she could tremble any harder, until she tried to write her name. The co-pilot helped by moving the clipboard under the ballpoint.

Lake Rat then explained the procedure and use of hand signals. "You got it? You wanna go right, pull the right riser back here. You wanna go left, pull the left riser. Easy. Now, hand signals. Remember what I said? Thumbs up for higher, thumbs down for lower, and a slash across your neck to stop."

Sophie mimicked the signals mechanically. "You won't have

trouble seeing me signal, right?"

As the boat turned into the wind, the rope unfurled and she began to ascend beyond the tow bar. The canopy above her filled with air.

"I'll have my binoculars," Lake Rat said.

"Binoculars? How high does this thing go?"

He made a megaphone with his hands. "Four hundred feet."

Sophie's heart pounded as Lake Rat gassed it and she floated higher, faster. Her exhilaration was tempered by the fear of falling to an early death towed behind a boat that had shrunk to the size of a rubber ducky. Only when the rope stopped unfurling and she could see the entire Lake Travis panorama from a real duck's point of view did she realize she'd been screaming. Her mouth had been blown dry, yet her eyes dripped.

Then she saw the blue-and-white Ski Nautique as the yellow boat came upon it. She pointed to it. "Stop! Stop! Bring me down!"

The co-pilot looked through his binoculars and made hand motions to Lake Rat. The boat made a wide, painfully slow arc that took her faster and farther away from her target.

Sophie blared alternately at both boats as she passed overhead. "Hoochie! Stop this boat! Home wrecker! Let me down! Keep your skanky hands off him! Stop! Those are *my* children!"

In her frenzy, she pulled on the left riser and the canopy tilted, causing her to veer sharply. She yelped and pulled on the other riser to balance out, which made for a continuous seesaw effect. Her heart pounded as she hurtled through the sky, her legs dangling and flopping in the wind.

When he left a mile of water between himself and the party barge, Will brought the boat to a stop, far from any shoreline. In his plush white captain's chair, craft rocking, he swiveled toward his fifth date while the kids stretched over the front gunwales in search of fish below the surface. Allison sat on the adjacent L-shaped bench and stretched her legs toward him, crossed at the ankles. An obnoxious yellow boat zoomed by towing a parasail high overhead with its passenger whooping in delight.

"Look, Daddy," Keely said, pointing. "That looks like fun."

"It looks like Mommy," Annabelle said.

Will squinted up. "No way would your mother be caught dead parasailing, sweetie. She's not that brave. Remember how she froze up on the tree house ladder?"

Allison shaded her eyes, staring up at the parasailer. "I'm sure Sophie is cozying up with Mitch on the barge right now."

Will stared at her curiously. His wife must really be bent on payback to fix him up with her own nemesis. "You're quite the thorn in Sophie's side, and while I know it's her mission to fix me up with the most challenging women she can find, you're a more intriguing choice than most. Why do you think Sophie picked you as my last date?"

"I assume she thought we'd hit it off."

He remembered her muscular body from their first meeting on Mitch's boat, how athletic she was on the wakeboard. With her windblown, sun-kissed blonde hair falling across her shoulders and a uniquely pretty face, she was the picture of temptation. Still, after his first four dates, he had to wonder what Allison had in store for him.

He glanced toward his daughters in the playpen, their twiglet legs folded beneath them as they held the rails, entranced by the parasailer.

"I'm happy to take you around the lake with us on our maiden voyage," he said, "but I'm not sure if what you have in mind matches with what I have in mind. Have no doubt, my kids are priority one."

Allison leaned back and crossed her arms. "Okay, what do you have in mind?"

"To be honest, all I want to do is see how well my brand-spankin' new inboard/outboard with a 330-horsepower V-8 engine, strapped inside twenty-three feet of floating, boating joy will run for me. That day I met you, Ruta, and Houdini at the marina? That's the day I put this baby on hold, but as of this morning, she's all mine."

Allison sat back on the plush bench. "I'm just happy to be off that party barge, away from the office politics and backstabbing, if you know what I mean."

"Unfortunately, I do." He opened the ice chest behind his seat. "Can I buy you a beer?"

The wind blew her hair everywhere, and she wiped it from her face. "Absolutely."

He popped the top and handed it to her, then fetched the girls two juice cartons. They pounced into the main compartment with their hands out.

"I want to get in the water," Annabelle said, hopping in place.

Keely twirled the strap on her life jacket. "You said we could learn to ski."

Will settled them down and told Allison, "I wanted to make this a fun event for the kids, so I bought a few things. Two wakeboards—one for me and one for the kids—and a water sled to tow behind the boat, but I need another adult to help."

"This is your lucky day then," Allison said. "I happen to be an adult."

He pulled a wakeboard and an orange towrope from a

compartment under the bench. Allison examined it, then stood it on end and rested an elbow on it.

"Look. You seem like a nice guy. I'm not your date. Obviously, right? I just had to get off that barge. But if you want me to teach your kids how to wakeboard or drive the boat while you ride with them on the sled, I'm happy to do that. If you want to take me back to the barge, I'm okay with that too."

Well, whaddaya know. "If I take you back, Sophie will consider it a non-date and I'll still be four for five. In the interest of repaying my debt in a hurry, I think I'll keep you around."

Her hair kept blowing in her face, and she constantly fended it off.

"Want my Rangers cap?"

Allison took the cap, bent over, and piled her mass of blonde hair into it.

"I'm curious," she said, tucking in the loose ends. "Why would you bring your kids on a blind date?"

"Self-preservation. Nothing more frightening to single people than kids. Figured they would protect me if you sprouted fangs and an appetite for blood. Left to the devices of children, you'd throw yourself overboard eventually."

"Look, Daddy," Keely said. "Here comes the crazy lady."

The big yellow boat motored past as the parasailer waved her arms and shouted.

"Daddy," Annabelle cried. "It *is* Mommy. It is."

Will shielded his eyes against the sun. "No way."

"She's kicking and screaming, Daddy," Keely said. "Is she having fun?"

"I think so, sweetie. She's kicked and screamed so much lately, she *must* like it."

Allison took aim down the barrel of an imaginary rifle, one finger on the trigger. "If only," she mumbled. "I'd put us all out of our misery."

Sophie could not believe it. What in hell was wrong with them? Couldn't the kids see their mother? Didn't Will recognize his own wife? And Allison? Clearly, she had a bead on exactly who buzzed overhead. And wearing Will's baseball cap? Oh, priceless.

Getting Lake Rat to turn the boat around was hopeless. At least they were headed toward the marina—er, hopefully. She thought things could not get worse, until the boat slowed. Her chest tightened and her hands death-gripped the wires as the canopy descended. She dreaded smacking hard into the water and breaking her neck.

But instead of plummeting, she floated. The lake zoomed closer and closer at a placid pace until her toes dipped in the water.

Aahh, sweet relief. Agua firma.

Then the boat took off again, and she could see her captains of the sea sniggling at her expense. They had returned her to the blustering currents at four hundred feet where she screamed new and improved obscenities that only disintegrated into the wind. She imagined the accumulation of her curse words—now numbering in the hundreds—congesting the atmosphere with squalling cumulonimbus formations that might rain Sophie's Revenge onto Will's boat. If she was going to die, it seemed only fair.

But then she stopped screaming. She wasn't dying. She pulled in a lungful of air and let it out. Again and again she inhaled deeply, exhaled slowly, until her breathing steadied and the gentle rocking became soothing. Her hands, stiff from white-knuckling the harness, began to relax, and in place of the terror, a new energy bloomed.

For the first time, she saw the panorama. Four stories up, she heard nothing but the wind and allowed herself to notice the fertile green hills and copses of scrubby cedars that speckled the sheer, rocky cliffs; the choppy, sunlit water buoying tilted catamarans; hurtling cigarette boats and shallow-carving jet skis that left undulating trails and white caps in their wake. Majestic was the word that came to mind. And Zen.

You wanted adventure, Sophie, and adventure has invited you in.

She sat back in the harness, absorbing the world in a way she never had before. She was in it alone; nobody else with her but the birds and the clouds. No Mitch, no Tess. Not even Will to lean on. And she was okay. She would survive this.

Was Mitch right? Dare she imagine herself to be fearless? She wished he could see her. He'd be gushing with pride—or rolling his eyes. But it didn't matter. She was filled with happiness anyway. So happy, tears streamed down her cheeks.

How cliché that she had only to look inside herself for the life she longed for: the adventure, the exhilaration, the contentment. Why had it taken so long?

After a few hours on the lake, Will maneuvered his new baby into its slip at the marina. While the kids folded wet towels, gathered swimming paraphernalia, and tossed trash, Allison wiped down the seats and the hull. She seemed bent on arching, showing her voluptuous cleavage, and flexing her muscular posterior. Will found himself thinking of Grampy's story, wondering if Allison might be his Eunice, his wild country coquette. When the kids weren't looking, she brushed unapologetically against his sweaty, shirtless body, and Will imagined what she would be like if they spent some time alone.

They all went for a late lunch at a lakeside bar and grill where the dockside dining was relaxed enough that Allison could wear only her swimsuit. It was the least he could do after she'd taught the kids to ride the water sled. If his kids liked her, that was saying something. He began to think Allison might be good dating material after all.

And with any luck, his family stones would escape another crushing blow.

Afterward, at Sophie's house, Will was thankful to find nobody home. Grammy and Grampy had gone on the Duck Tour, but they were due home soon. He put the kids into the shower and stowed Allison in Annabelle's room. Then he hurried into Sophie's closet, hunting for something Allison could use to cover up.

He was having trouble finding anything Sophie wouldn't freak about, when he heard the muted warbling of his cell phone from Annabelle's room. He hurried toward it, pausing for a quick peek into the bathroom to check on the girls. *All systems go.* When he entered Annabelle's room, he found Allison perched on the bed with his phone to her ear.

"Hi, Sophie. Oh, now that's not a very nice thing to say."

Will braced himself as he took the phone. Sophie blared incoherently, her voice three-pack-a-day hoarse.

"Excuse me?" he said.

"What is Allison Summers doing answering your phone?"

"Well, let me see. Fifth date?"

"Allison is not your fifth date. She's a ho."

He rummaged through Annabelle's closet and pulled one of his own dress shirts off the hanger. "Can I call you tomorrow? My ho needs a shirt."

Sophie's voice skipped a whole octave. "She's naked? Where are the kids?"

He handed Allison the shirt, and she slinked out of her bikini with no trace of modesty. Before she slipped her arms in the shirt, he saw her round, firm breasts and a fuzzy strip of pubic hair that looked more like a welcome mat.

"Relax. We're at the house. Kids are in the shower, and Allison is not naked anymore."

Sophie gasped. "Will."

"There," he said, watching Allison fasten the buttons. "My shirt looks good on you."

Sophie's response came, he suspected, through gritted teeth. "Gross."

He moved into the hallway near the kids' bathroom, able to see Allison and the kids at the same time. Allison leaned back on Annabelle's bed, flipping through *Skippyjon Jones*, unconcerned with trivial matters like propriety.

"I take it my grandparents are not there?" Sophie said. "Grammy would have ripped out Allison's eyes and fried them up by now."

"I talked to Gram already, and they're on their way home. I have to leave the kids with her because I'm meeting with my old boss at Waterloo. They have an opening for me."

"Will, that's so great." Her shrillness evaporated. "Are you going to take it?"

His anger with her was unfinished, and he would not be swayed by dulcet-toned encouragements. "Depends. It'll be good money. All the bennies." He stepped into the foggy bathroom. "Girls, say hi to Mommy."

Annabelle and Keely squealed hellos from behind the shower curtain.

"Hi, babies," Sophie said, then darkly, "What is Allison doing now?"

"So, how'd you like soaring with the eagles today?"

"Do not change the subject."

"I don't even know what the subject is."

She was quiet, and he knew the gears were shifting. He could almost hear them when she said, "The subject is a fifth date. You still owe me."

"But I like this one. Why do I need another? I mean, isn't that what you wanted? Me tied up so you can date Houdini freely? There's nothing stopping you now, and I win the Strat."

"You owe me one more date, Will, and I'm going to insist you make good on it. Tess will too. Jake won't give her Ursula if you don't go on all five dates. And you need Ursula so you can sell *her* instead of my damn house."

There it was. Sophie was still scared he'd sell the house out from under her—terrified, by the sounds of it. All her faith in him was truly gone. The only way for her to feel at ease was if he went on that last *real* fifth date and he could show a bona fide offer of sale for that guitar.

"One more, Will."

"Nah."

"One more, Will!"

He huffed back and forth, knowing she would not let it go. God help him, he would have a one-word epitaph and it would say, *Pussy*.

"When?"

"Next Tuesday. The real estate gala. It's a black-tie benefit. I have a ticket for you."

"No can do. Already have a date. Allison is taking me." He waited for her response. "What, no pithy comeback?"

"You've known Allison for ten seconds. You have no idea who she really is."

"I've known you for twenty-four years, and I still don't have any idea who *you* are." Again with the silence. He waited another beat. His good day on the boat with the kids had left him feeling generous. "All right. What do you say to a counteroffer?"

"I'm listening."

"I take Allison to the gala, and I meet your friend for drinks at, say, eleven o'clock, and we'll call *one drink* a date."

Sophie hesitated, then. "Eleven o'clock in the bar. Come alone."

"I don't suppose you're going to tell me who she is."

"Someone I owe. You better not stand her up. I'll know it if you do."

"She better be worth it," he said.

But Sophie had already hung up.

Chapter 33

Sophie stood in the tree house with the kids as the waning sun sifted through the branches. She felt as high emotionally as her free-float above Lake Travis. Crossing a personal threshold so enormous left her almost giddy. She had the Roberts' Pecos property in escrow, and if all went according to plan, Ruta would be next. Her fingers itched to scratch out a few checks for the mortgage arrears and pay off some burgeoning credit card balances. Everything had changed. When she looked back, it seemed like a slow evolution had happened without her realizing it, and then BAM! It had hit her.

She glanced at the sunset through the trees and the yard far below, and then at the time on her cell phone.

Show time.

Sophie had picked her evening gown from Ruta's Princess Collection, a backless blue sheath with a plunging neckline, connected at her cleavage by a diamond-shaped brooch of blue tanzanite stones. With her hair swirled atop her head and held in place by a tanzanite-studded clip, curly tendrils around her face, she *felt* like a princess. She slipped into glamorous gemmed sandals that she otherwise would never wear, and twirled out of her bathroom to model for the family.

The girls clapped and hooted. Grampy put two fingers in his mouth and whistled.

Grammy propped her hands on her hips and wagged her head. "Girlfriend, you are some sweet boo-tay."

"Grammy!" Sophie said.

Tess peeked out from behind the bathroom door. "My turn?" She emerged in a pale green satin number with lacy accents around the bodice and spun slowly. A high neckline gave her an angular look, and the back plunged to a deep U shape that skimmed her posterior. Upswept auburn hair gave even more length to her bare back.

Grampy pointed with a shaky, knotted finger. "Is it supposed to be that revealing? Another quarter inch and the mystery's over."

Tess walked over and kissed his baldpate. "Exactly the review I was looking for."

"It's supposed to be suggestive, Grampy," Sophie said. "That's the whole point."

"Well, if you can't find any men tonight, don't be surprised to turn around and find them sniffing at your tookises."

Annabelle and Keely rolled on Sophie's bed, giggling the word *tookis*.

Grammy held her arms out. "Bring your tookis over here, Sophie, so I can hug you."

"What for?"

"Because I'm proud of you. You've come into your own. We don't have to worry about her anymore, Hal. She's a thriving businesswoman who's not afraid to go after what she wants. If your mom and dad were alive today, they would be so proud."

In a snug-fitting black tuxedo and blinding white dress shirt that made his skin itch, Will drove his Jag toward downtown. Allison Summers occupied his passenger seat in a silky green-and-purple number with a neckline that was more of a bellybutton-line it dipped so low. He figured the only way the dress stayed in place over her massive boobage was with super glue, since there was no connecting fabric across her cleavage. The whole outfit seemed designed to encourage ogling.

Of the positives he could list for Allison, unlike the dates Sophie had cooked up for him, Allison had been a pleasant, if gusty, breeze. Since Sophie *had* apparently picked his final date, he could only imagine he should have worn an athletic cup.

From the backseat, the envelope containing his final divorce decree cast a grim shadow over his mood. The lawyers had delivered it that afternoon, so he'd had six hours to get used to his bona fide bachelorhood. He only hoped his mission tonight would prove a good distraction.

Built in 1886, the Driskill Hotel was the embodiment of old Texas money. It was one of the most recognized and distinguished hotels in Texas, an opulent and imposing facility with soaring ceilings, three-story columns framing a marble floor, and a stained glass dome ceiling. High-end art abounded, as did heavy leather furniture, dark woodwork, and elegant appointments from floors to windows.

Will found a sign that read: *The 23rd Annual Real Estate Gala, Benefit for Habitat for Humanity*, and followed the arrow up the grand staircase. Halfway up, the staircase split. Up the short left staircase was a western-themed bar where he would meet his fifth date. Yippee. Up the longer right staircase were the mezzanine and ballrooms where women strolled gingerly in revealing formals, accompanied by men in penguin suits just like him. For the most part, this group ranged from upper-crust real estate professionals and developers to local celebrities and city leaders—anybody who had influence.

Allison hooked her arm around Will's as they walked into the ballroom under the bright amber glow of massive crystal chandeliers. She nodded and smiled to everyone, and he got the feeling she was proud to be at his side. He adjusted his collar and bowtie, wondering if this was how James Bond felt popping into a Monte Carlo casino.

Camden, Will Camden. Shaken, not stirred—especially with the beautiful woman on his arm.

Table Five's proximity to the stage meant they had front-row seats. Like the other tables, it seated eight and was precisely set with cloth napkins, plates of fresh salads that looked like works of art, and gleaming silverware and glassware. A miniature two-story house took centerpiece honors, serving as table lighting instead of candles, every tiny window lit up to signify the warmth of home and hearth.

"Shall we get something from the bar?" Will asked as they found their seating assignments.

"Actually, I'm going to see if I can find my nephew," Allison said. "If he's free, I'll bring him over to meet you. I can't wait for you to hear him play."

Will appreciated the breathing room. He liked Allison more than he'd anticipated, but she had a certain air about her that took some getting used to.

He'd agreed to come to the gala with her to see her nephew play guitar. "He's a phenom," she'd said when they were out on the boat. Will was skeptical; phenom was a word reserved for the most uniquely talented, but anything was possible. Since he'd struck on some new ideas for himself concerning music, he figured it couldn't hurt.

At the bar, he ran into old pals talking boats, hunting, and fishing, along with his years leading the Wild Boys Band; and he began looking forward to getting the Strat after his big win tonight.

In the meantime, he took his beer and headed to the stage where he could salivate in private. The band had set up on a three-foot-high stage. Will knew well how it all worked. The musicians had already done sound checks and waited in the wings. He gazed at their instruments longingly. The drum kit gleamed. Though percussion wasn't his forte, he could bang out a tune.

Guitars, on the other hand, were in his blood. Worn black-and-gold amps were strategically placed out of the way and connected by endless cords to inert four-strings and six-strings, perched upright on thin, aluminum stands. Nostalgic for people rocking and cheering, clapping and flicking lighters in the dark to summon his encores, Will had a powerful urge to pick up an unsupervised Fender and shred the stage with sound.

As he turned to survey the ballroom's several hundred guests, he noticed Tess in the distance, decked out and looking incredible. Her need to surgically enhance her Fresh Factor—in Africa, of all places—perplexed him. He noticed her best friend a few cliques over, surrounded by black ties and glittery dresses.

To get a better glimpse without being seen, he skirted the ballroom. When she turned around, he saw the whole package.

Wow. On Tess Baker's Fresh Factor Scale, his ex was off the charts. Her icy blue sheath suited her, yet *cold* was not how she came off. In fact, Sophie oozed warmth and carried herself with confidence. That hadn't always been the case, regardless of how beautiful she looked to him. Maybe it was the sexy getup.

Houdini was nowhere to be seen but certain to be lurking, especially with so many admiring his *girlfriend.* Rankled Will's bones to think of Sophie that way.

A blinding flash went off in his eyes, and he couldn't see anything but blue and yellow spots. Another flash, and he thought he was seeing double.

"Check you out," a voice said.

Will squinted as his eyes readjusted on a tight pink-and-black tuxedo. The woman wearing it had long brown hair that flounced in unbridled, wavy cascades over her shoulders. "Edwina?"

She laughed, revealing a space between her teeth. "How soon they forget."

"Jessica. I didn't know you'd be here."

"Hired hand." She indicated the camera and gigantic zoom lens hanging from around her neck. She leaned back to eyeball him properly. "You're an Oreo cookie. Good enough to dip and suck out the creamy center."

"Jessica, you are the ultimate fast-forward vixen."

"Smile." She arched back and took his photo. "Have you seen Edwina yet?"

"Not yet. Should I be on my guard?"

She pretended to zip her lips. "You'll get nothing out of me." She moved in closer and fiddled with his bow tie. "Sure hope you like your surprise."

"Why do you two keep taunting me with a surprise?"

"We Marshalls have a flair for the dramatic. Grandfather's here somewhere. He's been looking forward to seeing you."

That news piqued a note of anxiety. "I hope you told him that my date with you and your sister was just two girls and a guy having dinner and drinks, and that's all. That's what you told him, right? I mean, *I* don't even know what we did, so I sure hope he doesn't."

Jessica's toothy grin left much unsaid. "I'll let him know I saw you."

A man waving from across the room caught Will's attention. A kindred spirit from the old days—not Gerald Marshall, fortunately. He kissed Jessica's cheek and hurried off with a quickly uttered, "Happy flashing."

Sophie's impatience got the best of her, and she marched to the check-in table to confirm Will's arrival. He and his user-schmoozer date had been checked off the guest list for Table Five, but she had yet to see him.

"Relax," Tess said as Sophie rejoined her.

Sophie shook out her hands and nodded. "Okay, I am. I am. I'm relaxed. Totally."

"And I'm Michelle Obama."

"Oh. There he is!"

Sophie's skin felt hot. Milling near the bar was the man of the hour. The eleven o'clock hour. She navigated the throng, nervous to speak to him, and imagined the impact his fifth date would make. She had made a promise, and she was going to keep it.

"There you are," she said. "I've been looking for you."

Will's eyes were unwelcoming. "You remember my ex-wife Sophie, don't you, Ray?"

"Sure," Ray said. "You used to wear your hair kind of pink back in those days, didn't you? Some spiky thing that was all the rage."

"Ray?" Sophie said. "With the Hairy Young Hoodlums? How are you?"

"Can't complain. Same gig, different band. And we shave now."

"Ray's band is the entertainment," Will said. "Cover tunes, right?"

"Oh yeah. Older crowd likes oldies. We give 'em what they want and that way we get paid. But our new prodigy, little Sage, will knock out some solos to wow the place."

"Is he that good? His aunt tells me he's a phenom."

"Even better than you used to be. You'll see." Ray checked his cell phone. "We're having a pow-wow over the set list backstage. Gotta run. Nice to see you, Sophie."

Sophie anxiously fingered the brooch between her breasts as Will stood silently beside her. Amazing how awkward she could feel with a man she'd known since college.

"You look so handsome," she said.

"You too," he said tightly, fidgeting and shifting. "Beautiful, I mean." He cleared his throat. "So, where's my blind date? Slithering under a table? Testing out her fire-breathing tactics? Sharpening her rapier?"

"It was your idea to meet her at eleven, remember?"

He nodded, looking everywhere but at her. "I guess you're here with that egotistical, rat bastard, jerk-off, slime ball, asswipe, fart-breath Houdini. Not that I care."

She couldn't help laughing. "He's president of the Real Estate Council, so I'm sure he's getting ready somewhere back stage to emcee this shindig. Look, Will, I—"

"Excuse me," he said, already moving off. "I see someone who interests me."

Of course. Allison Summers. Sophie watched him kiss her cheek, and she responded by wrapping her arms around his waist as they walked to their table.

Ugh. Sophie had to force herself to look away. She wondered where Mitch was and discovered him strutting across the stage to the lectern.

"Good evening," he said into the mic, followed by finger taps to test the sound. The murmurs faded and people took their seats. "Welcome to the Twenty-third Annual Real Estate Gala. We're here to raise money for a very special cause, Habitat for Humanity."

Applause erupted, and Mitch raised his hands to quell the clatter. "What better reason to come together than to dig deep in our pockets and give to those less fortunate than ourselves?" He went on to thank a long list of business and government leaders and flashed his trademark grin, the one that guaranteed ladies throughout the ballroom would be swooning. "After dessert, the Ray Collins' Band will take center stage and play some old favorites. Then we'll begin the auction. Get your checkbooks ready. And now I'd like to introduce tonight's keynote speaker. Our own mayor of Austin."

Sophie sat next to Tess at a table in the middle of the ballroom where she watched Will and Allison in the distance picking at their salads and laughing.

"I hate her."

"You said that three times already."

"I mean it more now."

"Honey, stop worrying about them. You should be enjoying this evening and feeling fine that you are *looking* so fine. Your Fresh Factor is off the charts in that Khorkina gown."

"I'm going to Africa with you, Tess. I need youthanizing too."

Everyone's attention was diverted then toward Ruta Khorkina making her grand entrance with an entourage. Jimmy marched at her side, along with two other well-dressed broad-shouldered men who, all together, presented an imposing blockade.

"Hello, my darlingks," she said when she reached Sophie's table.

They all shared air kisses, and Ruta introduced her friends, who, it turned out were Jimmy's friends. Before Ruta could sit down, the event managers hurried to accommodate her, while the wait staff ferried ice buckets with bottles of champagne.

Sophie marveled at the deference. "It's good to be the Russian Princess."

Tess nodded toward the hovering help. "I think they're on high alert in case she farts crossways and requires help to wave the air clean."

Ruta shooed them away and took her seat next to Sophie. "I must say, you two look fabulous in my couture."

"Thank you very much," Sophie said. "I know people in high places."

"Yes, you do." Ruta grinned. "So? You have my good news?"

Sophie tried to be cool and collected, but inside she was happy dancing. "I do."

"Oh, tell me! My leetle property?"

"Your offer has been accepted. You are the proud owner of a Mediterranean villa overlooking a very secluded cove on Lake Travis. Far from the maddening party crowd."

Ruta squealed and squeezed Sophie's arm. "And Will? What eez verdict? He's here?"

Sophie gulped her drink and pointed to a corner table in front of the stage where Allison was whispering into Will's ear.

Ruta's red-rimmed upper lip squiggled in disgust. "Oh, my lord. How thees happen? She's not sticking her claws into heem tonight. The plan eez set?"

"It's set," Sophie said. "The *real* Date Five, in the bar, eleven o'clock."

"Good girl. I can't wait. Let me know when eez my cue."

In the distance, Ray Collins jumped off the stage and squatted to chat with Will. Will said something in return, and Allison threw her head back in laughter.

Sophie could only scowl. "Will was never that funny at home."

Not long after, while the wait staff cleared plates, the Ray Collins Band took the stage and played a couple do-whop numbers from the sixties featuring a young guitar player that Sophie assumed was the phenom. Yet, with all that great music, the dance floor remained empty. Until Ray made an announcement.

"I have a special treat for you tonight. The king of Austin's live music scene back in the eighties and nineties—who gave it all up for a real job—is here tonight. He was the DJ for many years at KFUN, where he became as well known for his music trivia as his guitar shredding. And you all know him best from his hit single, 'Sophie's Kiss.' Let's have a hand, ladies and gentlemen, for Will 'The Tunemeister' Camden."

Sophie heard the introduction and choked on her drink.

"Did you know about this?" Tess put her fingers in her mouth and whistled.

Will stood beside Ray under the lights. "It's been a real long time," he said into the mic. "So bear with me. I'd like to play a number that my old fans used to request nightly."

He turned to the band and started off with the peppy solo riffs of "Brown-Eyed Girl," and the young phenom joined him.

Sophie couldn't take her eyes off her ex-husband, and her feet moved of their own volition between the tables. To get to the stage, she had to squeeze between a swaying and gyrating crowd, and she realized she was one of the few people *not* dancing to the sound of Will's guitar licks and his singular voice.

As the song ended, Mitch took the stage again. "Let's give the band a hand, shall we? It's time now to talk about our silent auction. We have a hundred items for sale in the gallery, but we're showcasing a dozen on stage. Let's bring them in, shall we?"

A security detail wheeled in eleven sheet-covered items on individual carts and positioned them on both sides of the band. Sophie recognized Officer Spike Chingaso in a security uniform, apparently moonlighting. With her cohorts standing by, Will's Date Number Two uncovered the first item. The spotlight hit it and Mitch read from cards.

"First item is an antique Scottish Tall Case grandfather clock made in 1846 donated by Mr. and Mrs. Henry Rosenburg. Bidding starts at $7,000."

The sheet dropped from the second item and the spotlight panned to it. He went through the next items, one after the other, while Spike uncloaked them on cue. For the twelfth and final item, four men carefully steadied and guided to center stage a cart with a massive tarp.

"Our last entry is donated by Miss Edwina Marshall, granddaughter of the celebrated international artist and Austin's own son, Gerald Marshall. Looks like artistry runs in the family, Gerry. Careful now," he said to Spike. "You break it, you own it. Let's have a look, shall we?"

The white tarp dropped on cue, revealing a ten-by-ten canvas.

"Miss Marshall has called this masterpiece, *Willpower*."

Edwina stood beside her artwork, her famous grandfather shadowing her. They both gazed proudly at an oil painting of a man larger than life, completely naked except for a silky red loincloth.

The subject faced the audience at an angle, half sitting, half lying against a backdrop of pillows and an ornate brass headboard, his legs spread and knees bent. His arms were outstretched like a gymnast in an Iron Cross, chiseled muscles bulging and contracting against leather restraints that held him captive. Edwina's strokes, reminiscent of classic Michelangelo, had captured her subject's chest, ribs, and stomach, all tensed in sinewy muscle. His head tilted back, face grimaced in anguish. Or was it ecstasy?

Sophie felt like she was dreaming. Her ex-husband had been painted on a canvas the size of a drive-in movie screen for the whole world to see, wearing nothing but a filmy red codpiece.

Chapter 34

"Hey, man," Ray said. "Looks like you."

"What?" Will walked to the edge of the stage and looked at the canvas.

"I want to thank my very cooperative subject," Edwina said into the mic. Her grin could not have been wider and she waved her arm at Will like Vanna White showcasing a new Buick. "The incredible Mr. Will Camden."

Will was flummoxed, flabbergasted, and flooded with white-hot mortification. He felt naked, exposed, violated.

And he wondered, *Is that what I really look like? Not bad.*

Mitch cleared his throat in the microphone. "Well, I guess we know what everybody's favorite guitar geek does in his spare time. Bidding starts at..." he hesitated before eking out: "Twenty thousand dollars."

Gerald Marshall shouted to be heard as he took the hand mic. "Good people, this is my granddaughter's signature piece from her new collection, which will be on exhibit at the Austin Museum of Art from September 15 through November 1, and after that—we found out today—in New York. So, it will be a few months before the buyers can hang it in their home. Edwina and I, and Habitat for Humanity, thank you for your generous support."

Will scarcely recognized the old man. Gerald Marshall was once his flinty steel guitarist and a card-carrying redneck. He had not aged well in twenty years, but his fame and fortune had sweetened considerably with his career change, along with his evolved fashion sense. The guy looked every bit the internationally recognized artist he'd become. And now it appeared his granddaughter, the not-so-schoolmarmy Edwina, was heading down the same path—and taking Will Camden with her.

Marshall returned the mic to Mitch and saluted the crowd, then patted Will's back and shook his hand vigorously. "If you ever lay another hand on my granddaughter, old friend, I'll kill you myself." And then he grinned cheerily for the crowd.

People pushed forward at the foot of the stage, closing in on the canvas. They perused it curiously, making comparisons to the real man, and Will wondered if his expression looked like the one in the painting: tortured.

He felt dazed, as if he'd swallowed some of his dad's leftover Percocets. This was some crazy shit.

On stage, Officer Spike tilted her chin flirtatiously and flogged him with her thick black eyelashes. Edwina grinned smugly, a proud mother releasing her baby to the universe. Jessica eyed him like he was a juicy steak while snapping photos with zealous abandon. Allison stared at the painting and at Will, beaming as if she'd won the Lotto. Only Coach Casey was missing from this menagerie. The great umpire in the sky had her sitting this game out. He wasn't about to balk.

Across the stage, Sophie's eyes narrowed on him. Will assumed she was contrasting the bold, broad strokes of Edwina's paintbrush with the average Joe she knew so intimately. Her lips clamped together in a straight hard line, and he knew he might as well have walked naked down Congress Avenue with Christmas ornaments dangling from his nipples.

Tess and Ruta gathered around her, clutching her arms supportively as they, too, seemed to judge the painting against the man.

All around, people looked at him differently. Somehow his persona had morphed from "Rusty Musical Geek" to "Stud on the Cover of a Torrid Romance Novel." Boring old Will, single father of two—who was fond of lamp Clappers and prided himself on music trivia, who grunted through Hulk poses in his bathroom mirror and contemplated the holes in his underwear—had been, at the drop of a sheet, transformed.

Ray pulled Will front and center. "Can we get some applause for the man who served as inspiration for that mind-blowing painting?"

Mitch came from behind and stuck his head between them, placing a chummy hand on each man's shoulder. "See you finally got a job, Camden. How much do porn stars make these days?"

And all of that was broadcasted through the speakers.

Will's ego ignited like the Hindenburg. Anybody else could have said that, and hardy-har-har. But not Houdini, not Sophie's boyfriend, not the guy who'd sucker-punched him in her backyard. Will watched the guy walk off and debated the wisdom of resuming their slugfest in front of seven hundred people.

The spotlight encircled Ray Collins in a white glow and, by

extension, Will. "I don't know how we follow an act like that, ladies and gentlemen, but we'll give it a go."

He gave Will a friendly shove, nodded to his band, and launched into a bouncy version of Right Said Fred's "I'm Too Sexy."

Will trudged off the stage contemplating a permanent vacation on some tropical island, when Ruta and Tess met him at the foot of the steps.

"I hope you're here for a mercy killing," he said. "I won't resist."

Tess took his arm. "We want to be the first to dance with the Greek god."

"Remember me?" Ruta said, grabbing his other arm.

Will floated between them, his eyes searching for Sophie, his go-to person to blame. "This is a nightmare, Tess."

"If you don't shake it off, Mitch Houdini will have won."

"He's got my wife and the whole world thinks I'm a porn star. I think he's won."

"Blow him off, sweetie. The more you're surrounded by people who love you, the more you'll prove what a jackass he is."

"He doesn't need me for that."

"That is best attitude," Ruta said. She sang the lyrics and danced to the bouncy beat, smiling all the while and inviting him to join her. "You know thees song? You are too sexy for your shirt, so sexy you hurt me."

Will looked to Tess for a rescue, but she just laughed.

"Loosen up, William. Time to have some fun."

She pulled on his neck so that she could reach his cheek with her lips. The kiss lingered, and when one hand caressed his face as she stared into his eyes, his friendship meter redlined into the danger zone. What the hell? He was so confounded by Tess's unusual affection that when Ruta pulled him away, he gladly followed.

"Come, come, Willpower. Show me your moves."

Like he had any of those. He had the music in him, but not the rhythm. "I'm afraid my dancing skills are limited to the Big Bird Shuffle."

"Eez okay. This perfect song for us. I lead, you follow. Come, come."

Ruta spent a lot of time spinning him while women all around ogled, crowded in, and winked—even if they were dancing with other men. By the time the song ended, he felt like the booby prize everybody had to get their hands on.

After Ruta and Tess, Will's dance card filled up fast. Developing a quick exit strategy seemed imperative, but he'd seen enough of Ray's new guitarist—Sage the phenom—to know he wanted to see more.

Allison's nephew excited him. With stringy, sand-colored hair hanging across his forehead and his short, lanky body, the nineteen-year-old could have passed for just another musician, but once the kid started playing, divinity flowed out. Will's head was spiraling with the possibilities. Just like it had for weeks. Ever since Coach Casey had told him her husband was trying to sell his music studio. Ever since he'd heard the Latin version of his own song, "Sophie's Kiss," while Spike had him blindfolded and tied to a chair. And now, with this phenom tearing up the stage with extraordinary talent—and a decent voice that could be developed—Will's brain was in overdrive.

Another forty minutes passed when Ray's band unleashed The Village People's "Macho Man." The whole place was singing and dancing and pointing.

And Mitch Houdini's blatant glares did not go unnoticed. The guy knew everyone and, to Will, that meant a whole lot of Camden trashing was going on.

When the spotlight found Will later in the evening, Allison sidled in for a slow dance. She squeezed together more cleavage, if that were possible, and tilted her head back to expose a long, enticing neck that smelled like spiced soap mixed with a tinge of perspiration.

He wasn't sure if that move was designed to coax his lips to action or not, but he complied. Beneath his lips, he felt the rumble of a moan.

And he had an audience. Mitch Houdini was eyeing him again, and it occurred that he hadn't seen Houdini with Sophie for more than a few minutes. She'd been quite the social butterfly, flitting from person to person with her buddy Tess. He'd expected to see Mitch hanging all over her, possessing her.

"You know," Allison said, "the only reason Mitch picks on you is because he envies you. You have things he'll never have."

Will narrowed his gaze on his sexy date. "Such as?"

"Kids. A family."

"That's not it."

"No?"

He shook his head. "Houdini doesn't want kids. Far as I can tell, he just wants my wife."

"You mean your *ex*-wife?"

The new term would take some getting used to. "That's right."

"And?"

"And, he can have her."

"Good."

She stuck her knee between his legs as they danced in place, and Will maneuvered around her provocative gestures. She had that look about her. That hiding-secrets look with a smile that's only a half smile, as if the other half is conspiring to do him in.

"You know, Will, I reserved a room here tonight. I could make you

307

forget all about Stratocasters and blind dates." Her focus shifted from him to, of all people, Houdini as he danced with Ruta.

"Oh yeah? You're not using me to make Houdini jealous, are you?"

She turned up her nose but cut her eyes toward her mentor. "I have no time for someone who has no time for me."

"Guess the fact that he chose Sophie over you put a real kink in your ego."

"You know better than anybody what a mistake that is. She'll do to him what she did to you. I can't imagine how Miss Amateur Realtor could cast such spells over you guys."

The spurned woman strikes again. Just in time for Sophie to be heading straight for him with a look that warned of hell-fire missiles.

"Uh-oh. Incoming."

Sophie tapped Allison on the shoulder. "I'm cutting in."

"Hardly." Allison pulled herself against Will's chest, clinging to his lapels.

Sophie shifted, her shoulders squared and head angled like a gangsta. With her chin jutting and eyes threatening, all she lacked were tattoos and a switchblade.

Will moved Allison aside. "It's okay. We'll consider this one for old time's sake."

Allison's whole face twitched, but after a few moments of mysterious posturing, she released her hold and stormed off. Girl fight averted, Will placed his hand in the small of Sophie's back while leaving a foot of space between them.

"You must really hate her," he said, leading like Big Bird.

"I don't hate her. Okay, I hate her. But she has to live with herself, and I wouldn't wish that on anybody."

"Well, you got one wish today." He stepped on her toes, refused to apologize. "I got the decree. Our marriage has been officially severed, and you are free."

She made a face he couldn't decipher, and by then he noticed Houdini on the move in their direction. Will only wondered what had taken him so long. Hell, maybe Houdini wanted to dance with him too.

A man in black and white, one of the servers, interrupted with a hand on Will's arm. "I'm supposed to tell you it's almost eleven o'clock, and you're supposed to be—"

"I know where I'm supposed to be." Will glanced at Sophie. "And it's not here."

He walked away then, feeling gratified to have spurned her face-to-face after what she'd put him through; but his guilty conscience got the better of him. He turned back with the intention of at least apologizing for his rudeness, only to see Mitch Houdini fill up the empty space, wrapping an arm around Sophie's shoulder as she leaned into him.

What-the-fuck-ever.

He stopped in the men's room to splash water on his face. Allison had a room for them. Maybe he ought to just go find her and give her what she wanted. Maybe she wasn't so difficult, and maybe she didn't want anything but a one-nighter. Tonight, he could deal with that. Tonight, he was ending this fixation on his past.

His reflection in the mirror told him he ought to just fixate on hitting the sack, but he sucked it up. One more date and the Strat was his again. One and done.

He wandered down the long staircase to the landing, then across to the shorter staircase that led to an open lounge area with thick paisley carpet, deep cushy sofas and chairs, and sturdy rustic coffee tables. On the walls, longhorns with thick horns the width of duallies were mounted, along with the heads of other game. And then came the bar, where everything was big and leathery and tooled.

The lights were low and apparently his date would recognize him, so Will found a barstool where he could see people coming and going. Bar-backs swooped between tables, stacking empty glasses on large trays and pocketing their tips. Some people stared, probably associating him with the *Willpower* painting, but nobody threw herself at his feet.

Eleven-o-five. If his date didn't show soon, he was history.

When again he looked across the lounge, the petite Tess Baker and a towering Ruta Khorkina walked toward him, side by side in their glamorous evening gowns. They wore expressions that reminded him of cats that fought over a canary, tore it in half, and spit out its balls to be used as baubles in Ruta's fall line of haughty couture.

Tess took his hands. "You are the most lusted-after man in the house tonight. You know that, right?"

"I think you mean the most laughed-at man in the house."

"Nonsense," Ruta said, with a flourish. "Every man in thees place eez jealous. You are a living god, darlingk."

There would be no arguing with these two. "I'm confused. Is one of you supposed to be my fifth date?"

"Yes," Ruta said. "One of us is."

Tess smiled up at him.

Tess? Had that weird kiss earlier meant something? His stomach twisted. Not his best friend's girl. Please, not that complication.

"Will Camden," Tess said, "I'd like to introduce you to your fifth date."

Tess and Ruta parted like double doors, revealing a woman who stood a few feet behind them. When he got a look at her, his heart played a train beat for five seconds, and crashed.

Chapter 35

Sophie hesitated for long moments, staring across the expanse at the man who had once adored her, confounded and infuriated her, then given up and left her. And though only weeks ago she thought she had let go, she now knew her heart would never suffer that loss without exhausting all the improbabilities too.

The cool hotel air wafted across her bare skin, and she pulled her arms in protectively, waiting for the recognition in his eyes that would tell her he was happy she'd changed her mind. Until that moment, she hadn't allowed herself any ugly second thoughts.

The bar was busy, Tess and Ruta had slunk into the shadows, and random faces watched her curiously. Or maybe that was just her. If she didn't already feel silly, like Cinderella at the stroke of midnight, she might take off running—because *that* wouldn't look more cliché. But no, she had to see this through. This was the moment that would change everything. This was her last chance to make things right.

The brown eyes she had loved so long seemed to embrace her while dimples played at the corners of his mouth. Dimples that always held her in suspense, that hid a thoughtful tease or the chance to be a smartass just to keep things real. Which was it now?

"Tell the truth," Will said. "Am I being punked? Where are the cameras?"

Ah. Smartass.

"Surprise, I'm your fifth date." She held out her trembling hand to shake his, but he left it untouched for so long, she let her arm fall away.

He paced warily around her, keeping his distance. "I don't know what you're up to, but I'm not playing games."

"It's no game, Will. I thought—"

"What? That I'd fall at your feet? That I wouldn't be able to say no to you?"

She shrugged into a soft-sell of her truth so as not to appear too cocky, but then thought better of it. "Well, are you? Able to say no?"

"We can't go back, Sophie. You told me that."

"Yes, I said that. We have our history, but we can write a new history—a better one."

She held both hands out this time, hoping he would claim them. But he acted like she was radioactive.

"Okay, okay. Yes, we screwed up our marriage, but since you've been back home—not really being married—it's actually been kind of wonderful, like the old days. I mean, we don't take each other for granted anymore, and I've found myself missing you since you left; and if I'm honest, I missed you even when you were sleeping across the hall. And I thought, maybe there's something to this 'not married' thing."

She paused to breathe and gather her wits—and her courage. He was just staring through her, like he didn't even know her.

But she was all the way in it now.

"It's just that I don't, I don't want to lose you. Again. And I was thinking we could go forward, you and me, but maybe stay unmarried. It works for us. What do you say? Do you want to not be married to me?"

"Sophie, you've been trying to get rid of me since I walked back in the door. That's how this ludicrous bet came about in the first place. You wanted me dating other women so you didn't have to feel guilty about dating Houdini. Then after the shed, when you *could* have had me, you didn't want me. I can't keep up with you."

"I know it seems like—"

"What about Houdini anyway? Where's he in all this? Can't the biggest dick in town satisfy you? You gotta come running back to boring old Will to get the *big* thrills?"

So much for the happy falling-into-his-arms reunion. She felt overheated, her whole body glistening with sweat. If there's one moment you don't want to look foolish, it's this one—smack in the middle of a crowd, attempting to convince your ex to take you back. She could feel the achy build-up in her jaws.

"It's not the sex, Will. It never was. I thought so at first, but that was just me making sure I wasn't lining myself up for another big fall with you. I mean, if it's just sex, we can't hurt each other, right? Only, well, you know me. I don't do sex without emotion. Sex with you was..."

The pressure of their audience was getting the better of her. People were leaning forward on their barstools.

"Sex with you was..."

Will raised an eyebrow, and she suspected this might be the stupidest move she'd ever made in the history of all the stupid things she'd ever done—which was saying something. But, dammit, nobody was ruining this, not even Will.

"Actually," she said louder, with a dopey smile, "sex with this guy was phenomenal. Hey?"

She pointed at Will who, of course, only looked mortified, and she knew she was blowing it. But when the tears threatened again, she knew he had to know everything—*everything*—before this night got by them.

"Look, I promised myself I would tell you the truth, and I don't care who else hears. So here goes. I think I made myself believe it was the sex that made me feel so incredible for days afterward, but it wasn't the sex."

Will's eyes roamed their audience self-consciously.

"It was you, Will. The *possibility* of you and me again. It was your apologies, your revelations before we even got to the sex. I felt like you finally *got* me, that you *got* where we went wrong. You changed when you moved home. I don't feel like I'm walking on eggshells or that you expect me to be perfect. You've been so much more present, for all of us."

Keep it together, keep it together. The tears were right at the gate.

"And I realized that you may have ignored me and taken me for granted once upon a time, but I've been reliving it a thousand times ever since and resenting you, and staying mad as hell at you."

The pent-up regret for all the hopes and dreams they'd foolishly let go of—all they had together, all the love, all the promise—liquefied in her eyes. "I don't want to do that anymore, Will. I'm no longer mad as hell."

"Well, I guess you rubbed off on me then, because I *am*. I am mad as hell."

His expression was so hard, Sophie could only blink to stave off a crying jag.

"I'm going to pretend I met my fifth date," he said, "and now I'm getting on with my life. My debt to you is hereby paid in full. Tess wins her bet; I win mine."

As if on cue, Jake Baker appeared at Sophie's side. He had dressed like he was out for a romp on the beach, in a T-shirt, plaid Bermuda shorts, and a clueless grin. He held a guitar case in one hand and extended his other hand to Will.

Tess hurried behind him and tugged his arm. "Not a good time, Jakie."

Jake indicated the Stratocaster. "I got this, Tessie. Congrats, buddy. I didn't think you had five dates in you, but I'm happy you proved me wrong. Let's make it official, shall we?" He held up the case and offered it to Tess. "You know how much Ursula means to me, Tessie."

Tess nodded and placed her hand on his arm. "I do."

Sophie thought Jake might change his mind, he was staring at it for so long. Then he took a deep breath and glanced back and forth with glassy eyes.

That's true love, Sophie thought. He was giving up something priceless for the woman he loved, not knowing if she would take him back. The whole scene bolstered Sophie's resolve.

"I hereby acknowledge that Tessie wins the bet," Jake said. "Will went on five blind dates, like she knew he would. But I still think she ought to give me a second chance."

Tess took his face in both hands and kissed him full on the mouth. Then she accepted the bulky guitar case and laid it across a sofa table, flipped the latches and opened the lid. Everyone stretched their necks for a closer view. Ursula gleamed in the low lights as if Jake had polished her up one last time.

Tess braced the smooth curved instrument in her hands and presented it to her old friend. "I could not be happier to deliver Ursula back to you."

Will took the Strat and gave it a cursory examination, then ran his hands up the neck with care. He gave somber thanks to his friends and put her back in the case, flipping the latches into place with sharp clicks.

"That's it?" Jake said. "I thought you'd be on Cloud Nine having Ursula back."

Will patted Jake's shoulder. "I am, buddy. You're the best."

"He's not going to keep it," Tess said, entwining her arm around Jake's. "Right, Will?"

He turned to Sophie, squeezed her hand and kissed her palm. "That's right. Everything has worked out the way it was supposed to. I'm giving her up. Just like you and me, I've changed too much to go back. And you... you have Houdini."

"But I don't. I told him I couldn't see him anymore. He understands—sort of. We're... just friends now."

As if he hadn't heard a word, he walked away, lugging his guitar in one hand and weaving through the crowd.

"Will Camden, don't you dare walk away."

Will descended the stairs and stopped on the landing where the staircase split, as if debating whether to go up to the ballrooms or dogleg toward the lobby and escape.

"Wait!" Sophie hurried down the stairs. "Don't you even want to know why?"

Without looking back, he started up toward the ballrooms.

Damn him! If she could be shameless for anyone, it was Will, but realizing she still wanted him would not preclude her from strangling him. By the time she caught up, he had reached the top step.

She grasped his arm. "Will. Please. Are you really not going to give us a chance?" Her voice quaked, and despite the pitiful, ugly sounds escaping her, she didn't care. "Have I ruined it?"

He rubbed his brow, and she didn't know if he was furious with her or out of patience; but as her tears exited, so did the last vestiges of her pride.

"I'm not with Mitch for so many reasons, but mostly because I'm not in love with him. He doesn't know me intimately the way you do. He and I have no sacred memories, no glory days before kids, no struggles to bond us after kids. He would never give up his passion for me. He would never put the kids and me first, like you have these past few months. He can't hurt me the way you can, and he can't love me—" she stopped, afraid to add, *the way you do—or once did*. Because even though in the shed he'd justified it and said he'd been wrong, she still heard him saying, *I'm not in love with you anymore*.

He shook his head, and she could see him struggling. "It's too late for us, Sophie."

And still she searched for some sparkle of love, until it finally began to sink in that he truly didn't love her anymore. Maybe five dates was all it took to get her out of his system once and for all. And maybe she was just, still, and always in love with him, and she would only ever be in that space by herself.

It was then that the bar-back hoofing downstairs with a loaded platter of used glasses stepped on the hem of her dress. His deep-treaded rubber sole tugged the fabric and pulled her off balance. The tray flew into the air and people shrieked, jumping aside while glasses crashed around them. Sophie's terror reverberated with every bump and bounce as they tumbled over each other to the bottom of the staircase.

Long moments passed before the movement behind Sophie's eyelids came to a standstill. She focused dazedly on the paisley carpet and people gathering around.

Will crouched beside her and steadied her shoulders. "You okay?"

Sophie smeared the wetness across her face, hardly noticing that her dress was bunching up at her waistline. "Will, when I was up in that parasail, I realized I'd been a scared little titty baby all these years. I don't *need* you anymore. I really am free."

He pulled her to her feet. "That's nice, Sophie. That really helps. You should go freshen up and get back to the gala."

"Maybe it's hard for a man to understand this. But when I realized I didn't need your self-worth to prop up my own, I also realized that as much as I don't need you, I really, to the depths of my soul, want you in my life." She smiled awkwardly through tears that seemed endless, and she knew she'd hit rock bottom. "Look at me. I said I'd never beg you to come back."

He wiped his own gathering tears and held her hands. "And I said I wouldn't take you back, even if you begged me."

His sad gaze lingered, and when it seemed he could no longer look at her, he kissed her forehead hard, as if he were pressing into her brain the one thing he could not bear to tell her. As if he was saying, once and for all, good-bye.

In another moment, he'd picked up his Strat, descended into the lobby, and disappeared onto Sixth Street.

Chapter 36

Sophie sat at her desk, staring out her office window at the gray day. The sky had drizzled tirelessly since the early morning commute and only now in the late afternoon showed signs of giving the city a break.

"I could use a cocktail. How about you?" Tess stood in the doorway. "Let's call it a day, shall we?"

Sophie looked down at a half-finished check awaiting her signature. She scrawled her name with a hand that felt heavy, and tore it from the book.

"My first-ever mortgage payment. Actually, five payments in one to get caught up. I made it online already, but this is symbolic."

"You should frame it."

Sophie imagined the check on her wall when a line of people trickled down the hallway outside her office. Mitch was sure to pass with the rest of the happy hour exodus.

"You must feel pretty good about not needing Will's help anymore," Tess said, plopping into a chair. "Wasn't that the goal?"

Sophie exhaled a deep sigh. "I do, and it was."

"And Jake said Will has a buyer for the Stratocaster."

"I heard. But he's not talking to me, so I assume the rumor is true. Grammy says he'll get enough to restructure his investments and replenish the kids' college fund. We're still a little behind, but—"

"But at least you don't have to worry about living under a bridge and washing your hoo-ha in a bird bath. Think of your Fresh Factor. And Will still has a settlement in his future for that Ponzi scheme."

"We'll see. Sometimes what's lost is lost for good." As soon as she said it, she wished she hadn't. Why did everything link back to Will?

"It's been three weeks. Time to rejoin the human race, don't you think?"

"Of course. It's just..." Sophie grappled for the right words, her stomach clenching at the cold hard truth, that he was gone for good; but she couldn't vocalize her feelings any more than she could understand the confounding depth of them, and she finally gave up with a shrug.

"I don't blame you. But some good came out of it, right?"

"Like?"

"Well, if you hadn't sent Will on those dates, he never would have changed. You made him get out of his comfort zone; he needed that. You did the same thing. I don't want to sound uncaring, because I'm not, but you're both different in some ways now and, well, life goes on."

It was hard to shake herself out of her funk, but Tess was right. "You knew, didn't you? I know I put the idea in your head—I wanted to teach him a lesson—but, you knew it would change us."

"I knew you still loved each other. You guys once had this romance we all envied. You gave us hope. I thought the Sophie and Will of yesteryear were still in there, waiting to be let out. Jake knew you still had unresolved matters of the heart, too, or he never would have risked Ursula."

"He's a softie, deep down. Only for his best friend would he have given up that guitar."

Tess shuttered her eyes and bit her lip. "And for me. He was willing to trade Ursula for another chance with me."

"That's the one good thing that came out of this. You and Jake."

"Don't rush me," Tess said, beaming. "He's been trying extra hard to prove he's worth another go."

"And?"

"And, don't rush me."

"I think he's found cracks in your armor. Nice to be in the driver's seat, isn't it?"

"That it is." She gave Sophie a piteous stare. "You know, and I say this with all my heart, you're an up-and-coming mover and shaker, a woman with huge—*huge*—deals in escrow, and you've got such a bright future ahead of you, with or without Will."

Sophie swallowed the lump that had taken up residence in her throat. "I'm fine."

"You will be. Now let's go have a drink and talk about our new business venture. I liked that office in Westlake, didn't you? It's the perfect space for a baby real estate firm."

Sophie sat up straighter and inhaled afresh. "I do like that it's not far from my house. Makes it easier to get to Keely and Annabelle's school functions. Keely's Jaguar softball team is in the playoffs. You knew I was the team mom, right?"

Mitch leaned halfway into Sophie's office, announcing himself by clearing his throat. "Sorry to interrupt, I thought Ruta might be in here."

He looked tired after a long day, and just as disheartened as he had after the company lake party when Sophie had confessed to still being in love with Will. Now she wanted to hide but instead smiled another apology. "Ruta's in New York."

"She's back today, I heard."

"That's right," Tess said. "She's coming to have a drink with us. Be here any minute."

"She is?" Sophie would rather go home and sink into a nice, hot bath. Drink some wine, eat ice cream. Mope around in private.

"She is," Tess said. "And you *are* going with us."

Neither of them looked at Mitch, because if they did, they'd feel obligated to ask him along. Sophie had been so disconcerted and embarrassed, she hardly knew how to behave. Seemed every interaction was an unpleasant souvenir of what she'd done to him. "Here's Ruta's offer on the Lake Travis house," with undertones of *Sorry the lake is where I laid that horrible break-up thing on you*. Or "Hey, I have to miss this week's sales meeting because of Keely's softball," *and because everyone on the sales force knows my ex-husband stomped on your game*. Or "Hey, Gertie's got our commission check," *which, by the way, we're splitting*.

"Come in, Mitch," she said finally, with a vague sense of self-loathing. "You can wait for Ruta with us, if you like."

"That's okay. I wanted to tell her about the auction results and when she could expect to hang your ex-husband's painting in her new place."

"*Willpower*," Sophie mused. "I hope she's happy with her purchase. Seventy-five thou is a helluva lot to pay to see Will Camden naked over your mantel."

Mitch's shoulders dropped and he shifted uncomfortably.

Sorry I said his name and that I chose him over you, Mitch—if only Will had wanted me too. Which he didn't. Yet, even after that... I'm sorry, I still don't want you.

She wished she did.

"That was the high-dollar amount of the night," he said, very businesslike. "The silent auction brought in almost $865,000. So, Habitat will put that money to great use."

"I'm glad, Mitch. I know Habitat means a lot to you."

"Yes." A hush settled between them, grim as a funeral dirge. "So, once you and Tess move out, I have a new guy who wants this office."

Sophie exchanged smiles with Tess. It seemed his sign of acceptance that they were going off on their own to start a new firm.

Ruta appeared in the doorway then, announcing herself with her usual two-armed flourish. "I am here."

Sophie rose to give her friend some welcome-back air kisses, relieved to have the distraction. "I thought you were in New York for another week."

"I was. But, now I am here." Ruta looked at Tess. "You have arranged with Hip-Hop Grammy?"

"All arranged," Tess said. "Sophie, the kids are hanging with their great grandparents tonight because Ruta and I are taking you out."

"That's fine." Mitch looked down at his hands. "We'll talk later. You guys have fun."

They all watched him go, and Sophie could find no words to assuage her guilt.

"The guy still holds a torch for you," Tess said. "I never saw him like that about anybody."

"Stop, please," Sophie said. "I know I was awful."

"Mitch eez fast healer," Ruta said. "Come, darlingk. Let's have a glass of that nasty beer you like."

Jimmy drove the limo into the parking lot of a bar and grill called Hank's.

"What is this place?" Sophie said.

"Hank's," Tess said.

"Thank you, Captain Obvious."

"Eez my new fave for happy hour," Ruta said. "Lot of locals. You will like."

Inside ten minutes, Sophie was perched on a barstool, embedded between her friends with the smell of cheeseburgers tweaking her stomach. The icy gulps of lime-tinged Corona made for a surprisingly pleasant wind-down to her long day.

Even Jimmy sat with them at the bar-high table instead of posting guard. Seemed Ruta was changing too. They all chatted as the band set up on a small stage in the distance, and for a few minutes, Sophie felt the old pangs of being Will's groupie.

"There he is," Ruta said.

Sophie sensed someone's presence at her shoulder. She turned, and a man leaned in to give Ruta a squeeze. He smelled like fresh, musky spices with the faint tang of alcohol.

"Great to see you again," he said, flashing a smile that Sophie imagined came easily and often. "I see you brought friends. We encourage that around here. Perfect timing too."

He stood far enough away that Sophie could see the cut figure of an athlete in denim and a Henley with a "Hank's" emblem machine-stitched over his left pocket. His blue eyes were set in a handsome, rectangular face framed by curly black hair and the trace of beard.

"Hank owns thees place."

Sophie felt Tess's elbow in her side, and with their long history as each other's wing-women, she knew immediately what that meant. She elbowed her right back. "Hi, Hank. Nice place. Is it always this busy?"

Tess shoved her arm across Sophie's chest to shake Hank's hand. "Ruta's told me all about you." Then with a flirty scrunch of her nose, "We came to see if you lived up to the hype."

"Uh-oh," Hank said. "The pressure is on."

Their waitress sidled next to him, and Hank told her whatever Ruta and her friends wanted, they got. "Pronto, on the house." He informed them he'd check back, but his eyes lingered on Sophie.

Those eyes could melt meteors, she thought. She watched him leave, admiring the way his faded blue jeans fit his narrow hips and musing that no Hank she ever knew looked like that.

"Mm-hmm," Tess said, looking self-satisfied.

"What?" Sophie said.

"He's cute, right?"

"Don't tell me you planned this. I don't want to be set up."

"No set-up," Ruta assured her with a wave of her bejeweled hand. "We are just three ladies out for the cocktails. And cute guys make the cocktails taste better, no?"

Tess clinked her beer against Sophie and Ruta's.

"Hello, ladies."

Irritation thrummed inside Sophie's chest like agitated honeybees. She knew that voice without seeing the pretty face that belonged to it. Allison Summers flanked Ruta's opposite side, looking quite friendly for someone who'd fallen out of favor with every woman at their table.

"I see you're all here for the big reveal." When no one responded, Allison directed herself to Sophie. "My nephew Sage is making his debut as the star recording act for Will's new record label. Will didn't tell you?" One side of her mouth curled up, and she raised an eyebrow for effect. "Huh, how about that."

She sauntered off then, leaving Sophie to simmer. "What's she talking about?"

"Oh my," Ruta said. "Did we forget to mention? I join partners weet your husband and that artist guy, Gerry Marshall. We are starting our own label. We signed papers today, so it seems only natural to celebrate. Don't you tink?"

Sophie's eyes narrowed to slits as she shifted on her barstool and drilled a hard stare into Tess. "Did you know that?"

"Oh, um, yeah. Heh, I knew I was forgetting something. Guess what, that artist guy and Ruta are the funding sources, and they bought a music studio from Will's first date. Remember? Coach Casey and her husband were selling their studio in the divorce, so Will snatched it up. Sage is the guitar phenom who played at the gala—"

"I know who Sage is," Sophie said. And now it made sense, Ruta's early return and this impromptu happy hour—although not much good sense.

A crowd gathered at the front of the restaurant. Musicians. One looked familiar. Ray Collins from the Hairy Young Hoodlums. And then the thought struck her like a dull ax in her back. "Is Will here?"

"Not yet, darlingk," Ruta said.

Sophie's glare tick-tocked between her friends. "What's going on?"

"Now, Sophie," Ruta said. "Eez because of you that Will and me, we get together for thees ting. You een-troduce us. I want my good friends to celebrate with me. I know eet's awkward as asscrack, but you have to admit, this eez good venture for everyone."

"And you didn't think to tell me?" Sophie still hadn't recovered from Will's very public rejection. This was Sophie's Kiss-off backfiring big time.

Tess tapped Sophie's shoulder with the back of her hand. "Hey, don't you want to congratulate Ruta?"

"Congratulations. Now why am I here?"

"Oh, look," Tess said. "There's Jake. Jake! *Jake!*"

At the entrance, Jake Baker scanned for the face that had called his name. When he found her waving, he hurried over, gave Tess a big hug and kiss, and then pulled an empty barstool from an adjacent table.

"Hi, Sophie," he said, clasping her arm. "Isn't it incredible how things work out?"

Sophie was devoid of incredible but brimming with panic. Why did they put her in this awkward position? Were they in cahoots with Will? Didn't they realize how humiliating this would be?

"I'd rather pull out my fingernails, Jake."

She snarled through her teeth and decided to ask Hank to call her a cab. As she slid off her barstool, Will came through the front door with Gerald Marshall and his granddaughter twins, Edwina and Jessica—all happy-happy family-like. Coach Casey and Spike followed them inside, and the late-afternoon sun washed them in a rectangular glow before the door closed again.

Will was there with all of his blind dates? *What the?*

Sophie's first instinct was to run for cover because, after all, this was not her party. But she couldn't move, couldn't turn her eyes from the massive pile-up taking place before her. And then, the *coup de grace*. Shuffling in last were Grammy and Grampy with Annabelle and Keely in tow, headed toward the stage.

Sophie felt someone tugging her arm. Tess.

"Come sit down, Sophie. We're here to support Ruta and Will and Gerry. Supporting Will is supporting your kids, too, right?"

"I'm sure you can make a case for that, but I don't know why I have to be here to *not* be part of it, tucked in the back here. If Will wanted me here, he certainly would have invited me."

"Or, he would have asked your best friend to bring you."

"So now we're supporting him being a coward? He doesn't want me to be part of his life, but he wants to make sure I see him doing... *wonderfully*? How selfish is that?"

"Do you hear yourself?"

"No. Yes." She wanted to cry.

Tess threw off to Jake. "I think she deserves to be pissed, Jake, don't you?"

"I do. Maybe you should march right up there and tell him."

Sophie could only stare at them lamely. How did she become the butt of this joke?

"Come, come," Ruta cajoled. "You are not going to leave your kids in a bar, are you?"

Sophie wilted at the idea. "I know. Why did they bring my kids *to a bar*?"

"They are with Hip-Hop Grammy," Ruta said. "They're gonna be fine."

The lights dimmed, but a spotlight targeted the stage and, moments later, Will stood at the microphone. Sophie's legs felt unsteady; she needed to sit, but what was the point if she was just going to blow this fiasco?

"Welcome to Hanks," he said, into a squawking mic. "And welcome to the celebration of our new label, Willpower Records. Tonight is sort of an impromptu gig; we just signed the papers for our new venture today, so we appreciate you allowing us to share in our good fortune with you here at Hank's. I know you'll all be psyched when you hear our premier recording act, Sage Summers, accompanied by Austin's own Ray Collins Band. You're getting a free taste of the next rock-and-roll phenomenon, but it may be the last time you'll see him as a freebie, because we think Sage is going to skyrocket in this business."

The audience applauded, and Will introduced his new business partners. The spotlight swiveled first to Gerald Marshall near the stage, while Edwina and Jessica cheered loudly; then back to Ruta Khorkina at the table with Jake and Tess. Will shielded his eyes to see them across the room, as Sophie ducked into the shadows.

He next introduced the loves of his life, Annabelle and Keely, and the two people who were like his own grandparents, Grammy and Grampy. The little girls stood at the foot of the stage, staring up at their father with larger-than-life admiration, while the sound engineer ran on stage and traded out his hand mic for a headset that Will attached to his ear. With the band playing quietly behind him, he wrapped an acoustic guitar across his shoulders and talked over the chords he picked.

"Because this is a special day for me personally, and before Sage and the band kick off the evening's entertainment, I'm asking for your indulgence. I'd like to play a little something I wrote for someone special, who I think is here somewhere." He shielded his eyes again, peering over the crowds as he spoke into the mic at his chin. "Sophie? Where are you?"

Sophie backed farther into the shadows as the spotlight scanned the room. Tess, Jake, and Ruta all pointed to her, and the spotlight quickly found her.

"There she is," Will said. "Sophie and I, as many of you know, just got divorced."

A collective groan of sympathy circulated the room, along with congratulations.

"Yeah, after twenty-four years together, twenty-two married. But if I'm honest, Sophie is the reason I'm here today. If not for her, I would still be some poor schmuck playing cover tunes for tips in a Podunk bar in small-town Texas, watching the gray hairs grow out of my ears. Sophie taught me to be more. Sophie taught me to be better."

Sophie crossed her arms tight as a Spandex across her chest. *This ought to be good.*

"Everything I am I owe to Sophie. So you can understand why I divorced her."

Amid hoots and whistles, Sophie gave a tight-lipped sneer, cursing him for cutting her out of his life and then laughing about it.

"So, little story. My dad died close to six months ago. Naturally, that hit me pretty hard; and I started taking stock of my life and the decisions I'd made. As you might imagine, I had second thoughts about the divorce. But Sophie had other plans. She was moving on. Next thing I know, she's hitting up strange women, practically begging them to 'Take my husband, *please.*' I thought, wow, who does that? Fixes her husband up with blind dates to get him out of her hair?" He shook his head and frowned melodramatically. "You think you know a person."

People were laughing at the story of his life—*her* life—and eyeing her for reaction. She felt their scrutiny and twitched in anticipation of the right moment to dash out the door, yet her feet felt cemented to the floor.

"Thing is, all five of my dates did teach me something. So, I brought them here tonight to take part in our celebration. They all helped me to become a better man."

Sophie glanced back at Tess and rolled her eyes. *Gag me.*

Will picked a few chords from his anthem to her, the song that had hung in the number one position on the pop charts for twenty weeks running, and the place erupted once again in applause. He nodded his thanks, but he was talking past them.

"I'll tell you something else. Even though I said awful things and broke my promise to be the best husband I could, Sophie never stopped loving me. I thought, wow, what kind of person does *that?* Puts up with all my bullshit?" He laughed and shook his head. "And then I realized, no one. *No one* has ever loved me like that. Not like that."

"You are kidding me." Sophie felt like stomping her foot. What was the point of this? To give her a real Sophie's Kiss-off?

"And I wanted to tell all my blind dates publicly that as much as you all are beautiful and fun and way out of my league, I enjoyed our brief time together. You taught me just how great I had it with my wife and what I gave up. So with your permission, I'd like to play this song in honor of its true inspiration, the person who taught me—the hard way—to never give up. Sophie? Can you come up here?"

"Oh, no, no, no, no." Sophie dug in her heels. She would not let him use her as a publicity stunt. "You're on your own, *Willpower.*"

But Tess and Ruta had other ideas. They appeared at her side and escorted her arm-in-arm to the stage. At first Sophie put up a fight, but when she saw her kids bouncing up and down in excitement that their mother had become part of Daddy's show, she had to acquiesce.

Meanwhile, Will began singing that damn song.

I admit that I am shameless,
Without you in my life, I'm aimless.
Save that sweet mouth for me, baby please,
I'll beg you, beg you, down on my knees,
Please, please, don't tease.

Of course. That was all she needed. Another reminder of their pissing match over the last three months and her own last-ditch attempt to get him back.

Cuz I can't take just one sip,
You're the honey I crave on my lips.

Grammy and Grampy sat forward in their seats, energized like Sophie hadn't seen them in years. Their beamish grins and vigorous applause spoke of their tremendous pride. And for what? What had she earned?

Yippee, the Most Surprised Ex-wife award.

The band quietly accompanied Will's lyrics and the audience began singing the chorus, words they'd all warbled in their cars or sang in the shower or mumbled while crying in their beers over someone they loved.

If you left me now, to the end I would miss
The thrill in my soul from the taste
of Sophie's Kiss.

Will crooned like the old days, when begging for her love would have been considered romantic, as if since then they hadn't both ruined everything. And she stood there dumbly, paralyzed in the spotlight and the surreal beam of Will's face. She was so unsure what to make of him standing at the edge of the stage, smiling down at her, coaxing her forward with the flick of his fingers—silently asking her to trust him.

When he crouched and extended his hand like he did when they first met, she felt halfway sick, halfway elated. Was he for real? How far was he going to push this charade? Was he about to reveal the punch line? Was *she* the punch line?

Before you, I was an empty shell,
But one look at you and I fell.

Annabelle and Keely gazed googly-eyed, aglow in their father's magnanimous gesture and charmed by the idea of romance. Hope-dashing, promise-breaking, spirit-crushing, heart-slaying romance.

Sophie felt trapped. And terrified. Her better judgment warned against it, but her instincts said this was the dare of all dares. Shaking with ungovernable nerves, she reached out and took Will's hand, and he pulled her onto the stage.

"What are you doing?" she said, steadying herself, her eyes darting anxiously across a hundred strangers, five blind dates, her grandparents, and her children.

Now she knew how Will had felt at the gala after Edwina's painting was unveiled—Edwina, who was looking up at her now, grinning as if she were an integral part of this. All of Will's dates fixed sappy smiles on her. All of them nodded knowingly. She looked back at Will, searching for something to hold onto, for the truth.

You filled me up and I knew,
That this heart,
This heart, this heart,
Beats for you.

The band played the instrumental bridge, and Will set the guitar on the stage. He took Sophie in his arms and pulled her so close, they were hipbone to hipbone. She leaned back, her palms flat on his chest, resisting, when the whole place shushed.

"I was wrong, and you were right." His voice carried through the speakers. "I let my pride get in the way. Every night since the gala, I've thought of nothing but you, and I finally realized that I just don't work without you in my life."

Sophie's eyes pooled and her heart pounded. She shook so hard, she thought the whole world must see it. "Is this really happening, Will?"

The warmth in his eyes reassured her. "Can you ever forgive me?"

And then she knew. This was no charade. No publicity stunt. This was real.

She couldn't take her eyes off him, and the tenuous sense of happiness finally found its way to her smile. And then Will laid her back and kissed her the way he did when they first met at the Punk Palace all those years ago. A perfect kiss, filled with all the love she had ached for.

"This heart," he said in a whisper, the last lines of his song. "This heart, this heart... beats for you."

And then the mounting clamor of the audience, giving them an embarrassing standing ovation, disintegrated into background noise, and he removed the microphone so she alone could hear. "I am more in love with you now than I ever thought I could be—than I ever knew *how* to be." The wetness in his eyes held her completely rapt, and she knew he meant it when he said, "You're my girl, and I will always love you, Sophie."

Annabelle and Keely climbed onto the stage and tugged on their legs.

"You saved her, Daddy," Keely said.

With Sophie snug against him, Will rubbed their heads. "Nope. This time, Mommy saved Daddy."

Sophie wanted to believe he was never going to give her up again.

He felt true. Being with him felt right. And she thought, after all this time, after all the craziness, all the heartache, she had finally found her fun, excitement, and adventure right here with this man who truly loved her.

"It's a rule," she said, repeating Will's first words to her. "If you save a person, that person must marry you."

"Now that is a good rule," he said. "But first, I owe you a date."

Thank you!

It is my great hope that you enjoyed this book. If you did, please tell your friends and consider it for your book club.

Word of mouth is an author's best friend. People can't read this story if they don't know about it. Your review on Amazon, Goodreads, and elsewhere will help them find it. Thank you!

For more about Kimberly Jayne, visit readkimberly.com.

Other Books by Kimberly Jayne
Take My Husband, Please
Gillian Parker is Dead (Coming in 2016)
Demonesse (October 2015)
All the Innuendo, Half the Fact: Reflections of a Fragrant Liar

21212019R00190

Made in the USA
San Bernardino, CA
12 May 2015